Dead Man's Touch

Also by the author
At Risk

Dead Man's Touch

Kit Ehrman

Poisoned Pen Press

Poisoned
Pen
Press

Copyright © 2003 by Kit Ehrman

First Edition 2003

10 9 8 7 6 5 4 3 2 1

Library of Congress Catalog Card Number: 2003110853

ISBN: 1-59058-089-3

Poisoned Pen Press
6962 E. First Ave., Ste. 103
Scottsdale, AZ 85251
www.poisonedpenpress.com
info@poisonedpenpress.com

Printed in the United States of America

Acknowledgments

First off, I would like to extend a heartfelt thank you to Lt. Richard McLaughlin, Commander, Investigative Services Division, of the Laurel Police Department for kindly and thoroughly answering my numerous procedural questions. Any and all mistakes are mine. A special thanks goes to Kelly Hutton and her husband, jockey Greg Hutton, for their invaluable assistance in answering my numerous and oftentimes unusual questions about life on the backside. Any mistakes that exist do so because I didn't know to ask the question. Thanks also to my parents, Bill and Kathy Graber, and to Vicky Graber, Kenn Davis and Kitsey Cannan for their encouragement, to Donna Marsh, Connie Kiviniemi-Baylor, Almo Smith, and Teddy Saddoris for their invaluable input, and to Susan Francoeur for her unbiased feedback. As always, I am grateful to all the hardworking folks at Poisoned Pen Press, especially Barbara Peters and Robert Rosenwald, for their continued support.

And finally, this book would not exist without my family, who good-naturedly put up with the writing process, especially my two wonderful sons, Phil and Ray.

Chapter 1

There is a gash in the earth where his casket will rest. The sharp dirt edges are draped with green matting. Softened. The stark finality of this place hidden from view. Above our heads, a hot breeze rustles the canvas as a stray beam of light glints off the rounded end of the casket's support. I focus my gaze on the metallic sheen, and even as my vision blurs, I convince myself that all I feel is regret.

Maybe if I'd had some kind of premonition he wouldn't live to see sixty, maybe then I would have made an effort to make it work...to be his son.

The priest concluded his eulogy with words I half listened to. Words extolling the virtues of a man he did not know. When he signaled for us to stand for the closing prayer, I glanced at Rachel and squeezed her hand. She looked more sorrowful, more distressed than I was capable of feeling, and a twinge of guilt nudged my conscience. Her sorrow was for me, I knew, yet she needn't have bothered.

Father had been a strict, controlling authoritarian and little else. And yet, I'd still been surprised when he'd kicked me out of his house for leaving college, and in the past two years, I hadn't gone back.

When the prayer was concluded, Mother stepped across the carpet and placed a dozen white roses on the casket. My brother, Robert, had his arm importantly around her waist, as if she needed his support, but when she turned to leave, I saw she was in full command of her emotions. As usual, she was dressed to perfection. Her elegant black dress shouted money, and if the designer threads didn't get your attention, her four-carat diamond ring was likely to do the job. The woman could make a statement without opening her mouth.

She paused in front of me. "Stephen, you are coming back to the house, aren't you?"

I glanced at Robert and almost said no, but my sister moved into view behind him, and I changed my mind. Sherri clung to her husband's arm with her long slender fingers bunching the sleeve of his suit coat as she looked at me beseechingly. Her eyes were red-rimmed, and a faint sheen of moisture glistened above her upper lip.

I turned back to my mother and mumbled, "Yes, ma'am."

The corner of her mouth twitched, then she nodded, and the four of them joined the crowd heading toward the row of cars that shimmered in the hot June sunshine.

I put my arm around Rachel's waist. "Guess I changed plans on you, huh?"

"That's okay," Rachel said as she slid her hand along the small of my back, beneath the Armani jacket Mother had had delivered to the loft along with a silk shirt and tie. The getup felt alien after slogging around a horse farm in jeans and work boots. "To be honest, I was surprised when you told me you weren't going."

"Yeah, well…I guess I better. I'll take you home first, if you prefer."

She shook her head. "I'll go with you."

I squeezed her tighter, then we stepped from beneath the canopy into a flood of sunlight. I paused and squinted against the glare. A group of people I hadn't expected stood farther down the slope in the shade of an old oak. Marty and Mrs. Hill, my boss, and behind them, at what I took to be a symbolic distance, Detective Ralston.

"Stephen, my dear boy." Mrs. Hill came forward and clasped my hand. "I'm so sorry, dear. What a shame." She patted my arm. "Losing your father at such a young age. So tragic, dear. So tragic. Is there anything I can do for you? Any way I can help?"

"No, ma'am." I cleared my throat. "I appreciate your coming."

"I wouldn't have it any other way, dear. You know that." She released my arm. "Let me know if there's anything I can do."

"Thank you."

She nodded, then made her slow way across the grass. She looked dignified in her generous black skirt and blouse, but to my mind, motherly described her best.

"Marty, thanks for coming," I said.

"Shit, Steve." He glanced over his shoulder. "She would of canned my ass if I didn't come pay my respects."

I smiled at him. "Thanks anyway."

"Yeah, well. Just kidding. For you, I'd come." He looked me up and down, then fingered my sleeve. "Man, you clean up good. Almost didn't recognize you." His grin faded. "You gonna move back home, now?"

I shook my head.

"Which reminds me," Marty said, and I knew what he was going to say before he opened his mouth. "Got any idea when you're coming back to work? It's been what, eight weeks since you got out of the hospital?"

I glanced over his shoulder at Detective Ralston. "Nine weeks and a day," I said, thinking about how my life had changed since I'd interrupted a horse theft back in January.

Marty snorted.

"I don't know, Marty. Soon."

"Christ. I hope so." He reached over and awkwardly hugged me. "We miss ya, bud." Marty grinned at Rachel. "Don't we, Rache?"

"We sure do."

"Rache? You're calling her Rache, now?"

Marty shrugged, and I decided I had better get my butt in gear and get back to work. He filled me in on what was and wasn't happening at Foxdale, and when he said good-bye, I watched him stride down the hill with his familiar, carefree gait.

"Steve, sorry about your father." Detective Ralston shook my hand, and as usual, he'd been quietly observing everyone with intense hazel eyes. "How're you doing, otherwise?"

I shrugged. "Okay, I guess."

I watched his attention zero in on the lack of conviction in my voice. He simply said, "Mind if I stop by one afternoon?"

"Sure."

He shook my hand, and after he left, Rachel said, "It was nice of them to come, wasn't it?"

"Hmm."

"They're worried about you."

"They'll get over it."

She shook her head, then entwined her fingers in mine. "You need help, Steve, and if you can't see that, you're worse off than I thought."

I cleared my throat. "Let's not talk about that, now."

She blew her bangs off her forehead and hugged me, then she rested her head against my chest. "I'm just worried about you."

"I know. It's just that I can't deal with it right now."

"You've got to, sooner than later, or you'll never be happy."

I put my arm around her shoulders. Beyond the rows of tombstones, the Baltimore skyline lay shrouded beneath a shimmering cloud of heat and exhaust.

"Come on," I said. "Let's get out of here."

I kept the windows down until the pickup's pathetic air-conditioner kicked out a few stray molecules of cool, and we drove to my parents' house in silence.

"My God," Rachel exclaimed as I turned into the hedge-lined drive. "It's a mansion."

"That, it is." Three stories of cold, gray stone. Impersonal. The home of my childhood.

"I had no idea."

"Yeah. Home-sweet-home."

Rachel glanced uncertainly at my face, and even I could hear the bitterness in my voice. I idled the truck and listened as the muffler rumbled obscenely in the quiet, opulent neighborhood. The service hired to park the cars was still on duty, but I wanted a quick exit when the time came to leave. I dropped the Chevy into reverse, backed down the driveway, and parked alongside the gate house. I switched off the engine and rolled down my window.

When I didn't move, Rachel slid across the seat and rested her head on my shoulder. "You really need to go in, you know?"

"I don't belong here," I said as I leaned against the backrest, "and I haven't for a long time."

Rachel lifted her head. "Your parents...they make me so angry. You deserved more from them."

I grunted. "Maybe that's been my problem all along. Thinking I deserved more. Why should I have had it any better?"

"Because you're a good, decent person, that's why. You deserved parents who cared more about their kids than their social status."

"Most people would think I had it damned good, Rachel."

"Money isn't everything."

I kissed her forehead. "Let's get it over with."

I walked around the front bumper and opened her door.

Behind me, someone said, "What a gentleman," and I would have known my brother's sour voice anywhere.

I turned slowly around. Robert squinted at me through a haze of cigarette smoke with a sneer twisting his mouth.

"Nice to see you, too, Bobby."

He scowled, and the muscles in his face settled into a pattern they were well accustomed to, deepening the wrinkles around his eyes and bunching his eyebrows together over the bridge of his nose. He'd always hated being called Bobby. Not dignified enough, I supposed. And if I wasn't mistaken, he was already half-soused.

He looked from me to my truck with loathing. "What a piece of junk. Doing well for yourself, I see."

"What's the matter, Robert? Mother doesn't need your support anymore?"

"You stupid little shit." He flicked his cigarette into the grass, glanced at Rachel, then turned abruptly and headed for the house.

I walked over and ground out the butt.

"Nice welcome," Rachel said as she slid off the seat.

"Yep. Pure Robert. He's always like that." I rubbed my forehead. "Well, not always."

I looked toward the house. "Robert idolized the old man. Ever since I can remember, he's wanted to be like him. Dressed like him. Styled his hair the same way. Shit, I'm surprised he didn't become a doctor." I wrapped my arms around Rachel. "I'm glad you came, you know that?" I whispered as her hair brushed against my lips. "You give me strength."

She leaned back and gazed into my face. "You're the strongest person I know."

I grunted.

"Trouble is, you don't see it."

"That's because it isn't there to see."

She tilted her head to one side. "You don't go through hell and back and come out of it in one piece, unless you're strong."

I brushed her bangs off her forehead. "If I'm not mistaken, you were just telling me I needed help."

"You do, but that's what guys just don't get. Just because you need help doesn't mean you're weak. Everyone needs help now and then."

I wished to hell I felt strong. All I felt was uncertainty and self-doubt, as if the fibers that made up who I was were disintegrating before my eyes, and there wasn't a damn thing I could do about it.

Rachel looped her arm through mine, and we walked down the drive. When she paused inside the entrance, I glanced at her face. Her lips had formed into a silent "oh." I followed her gaze to the wide double staircase that flanked both sides of the massive foyer. They curved upward and joined two stories above in a long open hallway, drawing the eye upward to a magnificent chandelier of sparkling crystal.

The temptation of those broad mahogany banisters had gotten me into trouble more times than I cared to remember. When I was six, and no longer satisfied with simply sending an assortment of toys down the highly polished wood, I had slid down myself and broken my arm. Looking at them, now, I realized I'd been lucky I hadn't broken my neck.

"Something else, isn't it?" I said, and Rachel nodded.

It was spectacular, even to my jaded eyes. My mother's grandfather had commissioned Ephraim Francis Baldwin to design the mansion back in the early nineteen-hundreds, after he'd made a fortune importing and distributing spices to a global market, and neither one of them had been inclined to spare any expense. The marble tile I was standing on had come from Italy, and the intricately carved doors at my back were chiseled from teak that had been hand selected and shipped from the island of Java.

A heavy hand rested on my shoulder, and someone whispered in my ear. "Brings back memories, doesn't it?"

I grinned, and as I turned toward my mother's personal assistant, he clamped his massive arms around me in a bear hug that almost lifted me off my feet.

"My God, boy, it's good to see you." Parker released his hold and gripped my shoulders, instead. "You comin' home, now?"

"Uh, I don't know," I said.

He let go, and the crow's feet etched into his dark skin softened as his smile faded. "No, then."

I shrugged. "You know how it is."

He tousled my hair like he'd done a thousand times before, and a sad weariness filled his eyes. "Don't let 'em get to you, Steve," he said softly.

"I won't," I said as the front doors flew open, and two of my cousins and their girlfriends swept noisily into the foyer. They shook my hand and slapped my back and said all the proper things, then they drifted into the drawing room in search of something to eat.

I nodded to Parker, then I squeezed Rachel's hand, and as we stepped across the threshold, the dense carpet underfoot swallowed the sharp click of our footsteps.

Two long tables divided the length of the room. They were draped in fine linen and overloaded with delicacies only my mother's chef could conjure up. Waiters busied themselves offering drinks. I scanned the room but only recognized a couple of faces, which was no surprise as most of the crowd were from the hospital or the numerous benefits Mother committeed. A new Monet hung above the fireplace mantel, offset by crystal vases brimming with calla lilies. As always, the overall impression was one of unselfconscious wealth.

I led Rachel over to an arrangement of high-backed chairs alongside one of the tall, narrow windows that lined the west-facing wall. Beyond the glass, early afternoon sunlight sparkled on a reflecting pool in a formal garden that had been off limits when I was growing up.

"Would you like something to drink?"

Rachel nodded absentmindedly. Guess the place wasn't what she'd expected from someone who spent his days mucking stalls.

I intercepted one of the tuxedoed waiters and snagged two tall iced teas complete with lemon wedges and mint sprigs.

"Oh, Steve."

I smiled softly and turned to find Sherri at my side.

She wrapped her arms tightly around my waist. "I've missed you so much." Her voice was muffled against my chest.

"I've missed you, too, Sher," I whispered. "How's California treating you?"

She straightened. "Good. Alex is wonderful, business is booming, the weather can't be beat. I love it."

"I'm glad."

Alex drifted over as Sherri disentangled herself. She narrowed her eyes and studied me. "You've lost weight."

"A little."

"I'm sorry I didn't make it out when you were in the hospital."

"Believe me," I said, "you didn't miss anything."

She swallowed and shook her head. "I almost lose my baby brother because of some maniac, and Mother doesn't even bother to call me. Five days, Steve. It took her five whole days after you were shot before she picked up the phone." She frowned. "I don't know what her problem is."

"Mother's problem is what it's always been…Father."

"Steve, that's unfair."

But true, I thought and decided I had better keep my opinions to myself. Sherri had always been Father's little girl, even when she'd chosen to marry beneath her social position. And it wasn't as if she'd scraped the bottom of the barrel when she fell for Alex Carter. Californian by birth and appearance, with windblown blond hair and a year-round tan, Alex was sole owner of a profitable landscape firm. It was his habit of working with his crews and getting just as dirty as they did that had really irked Father. Alex stood beside Sherri now, looking at her with such obvious love, I felt overwhelmingly happy for them and even managed to ignore a selfish twinge of brotherly jealousy.

"I can't believe he's gone," Sherri mumbled.

"Me, either."

Alex moved closer and embraced her. As she leaned into him, he nodded. "Steve," he said, "my condolences."

"Thanks, Alex." I looked to where I'd left Rachel and almost dropped our drinks.

Robert had Rachel backed up against the wall. He towered over her with his broad hand braced on the gold-flecked wallpaper. She shook her head in response to something he'd said and glanced in my direction. I took a step toward them as Rachel ducked under his arm and threaded her way through the crowd. She smiled when she reached me. It didn't quite work.

"Boy, I'm thirsty." She removed a glass from my hand and took a sip.

"Stay here." I sidestepped her, and she grabbed my arm.

"No, Steve. Don't." Rachel tightened her grip. "Please."

I unclenched my teeth. "What did he say?"

"Nothing," Rachel said as Sherri edged around her. "Nothing important."

"Oh, hi. I'm Sherri, Steve's sister." She nudged me in the ribs.

Robert was staring across the room with such open hostility, I was only vaguely aware of Rachel introducing herself.

Sherri followed my gaze and sighed. "Oh, Robert. He's a mess."

"What else is new?"

"He shouldn't be drinking," Sherri said. "Not today."

She turned back to Rachel, and I formally introduced them.

Sherri hugged her as if they were long-lost sisters. "Steve's told me so much about you." She glanced at me, and I caught a mischievous glint in her eyes. "I'm so happy the two of you are together."

I grinned at my sister. With her living a continent away, we talked very little.

"Rachel, while you two are getting acquainted, mind if I go upstairs for a minute?"

"No. Go ahead."

I climbed the stairs, and midway down the hall, I paused outside the second door on the left and slowly turned the knob.

Except for a stale odor of disuse, the room hadn't changed. When I closed the door, my lacrosse stick rattled against the wood like old times. I unhooked my helmet and dropped it on the desk, then I lifted the stick off its hook. The feel of the smooth varnished wood in my hands, the weight, the balance, even the faint smell of the net were surprisingly familiar. Welcomed. Triggering memories of long afternoons and wide grass fields, of sweat and pain, of burning lungs and muscles cramped with fatigue. Of victories and disappointments. Friendships and rivalries.

I flicked my wrist, catching and throwing an imaginary ball, then I tossed the stick on my bed. I turned slowly around and surveyed the room, a room that was at once comforting, yet strange. Part of another life. A freeze frame of the past. My past.

I fingered the backpack that hung from the desk chair where I'd left it. A program from one of Sherri's concerts lay open on the blotter, and my high school graduation cap was still draped from one of the dozen or so lacrosse trophies on the shelf above the desk. I looked across the room at the poster of a fire-engine red Ferrari and another one over the bed of a hot lookin' babe in a string bikini. I grinned at that one.

Melissa, my former girlfriend, had always hated that poster. I kicked my old rugby ball across the floor, sat on the edge of the bed, and picked up the gold-framed photograph of Melissa and me, smiling into the camera a week before she dumped me, a week before I was thrust headlong toward independence. I'd learned more about myself in the past two years than in the twenty preceding it, not all of it welcomed.

I laid the picture face down, slid my hand under the mattress, and felt the cool smoothness of glass. I wrapped my fingers around the narrow-necked bottle and pulled it out. Cheap, smooth, American blended whiskey, eighty proof. I unscrewed the cap and inhaled the heady vapors. I lifted the bottle to my lips and paused.

Alcohol was the last thing I needed. I rested the bottle on my thigh.

Behind me, someone tapped tentatively, and the door creaked open.

"Hey." Rachel stepped into the room, and her smile faded when she saw the bottle in my hand. "What are you doing?"

I screwed on the cap. "Resisting the urge to have a drink."

She sat next to me. "That's not what it looked like." Her voice was low.

"I know, but that's what it was. I only deluded myself once, thinking this crap would solve my problems." And the combination of pain medication and a steady diet of alcohol had nearly landed me back in the hospital. The threat of going back had been enough to stop me cold. I stood and slid the bottle back where I'd found it.

Rachel shook her head. "What am I going to do with you, Stephen Matthew Cline?"

I bent over and placed my hands on either side of her hips, and she leaned back to keep from being knocked over. "I'm sure you'll think of something, Rachel...Anne Miller."

She overbalanced and flopped down on the bedspread. "Ouch." She shifted the lacrosse stick out of the way and frowned at it. "And you forgot my middle name."

"Did not." I grinned down at her, and if truth were told, I'd only had a moderate chance at getting it right.

She giggled. "And we should both be—"

I put my lips on hers and felt her grin fade into a mildly responsive kiss. I moved from her lips to her throat and marveled at the familiarity of her scent. Her skin was smooth, like...

"You played lacrosse, I see."

"Uh-huh."

"Look at all those trophies."

"Um-hum." I bit her neck.

"You graduated high school with honors?" Rachel said as I slid my hand along her thigh.

"Um."

"No wonder your father had a fit when you quit college."

"A break." I moved to kiss her, and she turned her head at the last second.

"What did you say?"

I slid onto my side and rested my head on my hand. Rachel grinned up at me mischievously, and I couldn't help but smile at her. I smoothed her bangs off her forehead. "It was a break, Rachel. I was only taking a break. At least that's what I thought at the time."

Her grin faded, and I let my gaze travel down the length of her body, across her breasts, her flat stomach, her dress hiked halfway up her thigh, and with regret watched as she stood and walked over to the window.

I stood also. "What did Robert say?"

She turned around. The late afternoon sun streamed through the window behind her and shimmered off her black hair like a halo. I couldn't read her expression, but when she spoke, her voice was somber. "He's so," she waved her hand, searching for the right word, "bitter. What he said doesn't bear repeating."

"You're a pretty smart girl, aren't you?"

She crossed her arms under her breasts. "Uh-huh."

I glanced at my watch. "All I need to do is check in with my mother, then we can leave, unless you want to hang around longer. Get something to eat."

She shook her head. "No, I've seen enough of the high life for one day. I am glad I got to see your room, though." She frowned at the poster girl. "Except for her."

"Awh, Rachel. She means nothing to me."

"Uh-huh." She headed for the door, and I could see her grin. "Except on how many countless nights?"

"Rachel." I feigned astonishment as I closed the door behind us, and she totally ignored me.

Downstairs, Mother, Sherri, and Alex were seated by a garden window. Robert stood at attention beside Mother, looking more and more like an unwanted escort. One more duty completed, and we were on our way. I introduced Rachel, then formally expressed my condolences, and it seemed enough.

"Are you leaving, then?" she said coolly.

"Yes, Mother."

She nodded, said goodbye to Rachel, then headed off to join a group of Father's coworkers. I watched her for a moment, then turned back to Sherri, intending to ask if she'd have time to visit me before she headed back to California, when Robert clamped his hand on my shoulder and spun me around. His drink sloshed in its crystal tumbler.

"Nice little bit of play acting, Lover-boy."

I felt as if I'd been smacked in the face. The last person to call me that had done his level best to make sure I preceded Father to the grave, and he'd damn near pulled it off.

Robert poked my chest. "Did you hear me, Steve? I'm sick of you pretending you care about his dying. You're—"

"Of course I care. He's—"

"—nothing but a hypocrite."

"—my father, too," I said.

"That's what you think." Robert pointed his finger at my face.

"What do you mean, 'that's what you think'?" I said, but in true Robert fashion, he ignored the question and kept on going.

"You never cared about him, or listened to him. You're a spoiled little brat, and you always have been. Hell, your running out early today proves it. Everything that went wrong in this family, went wrong because of you," his voice cracked, "and I hate you for it."

"Robert, what are you talking about?" Sherri said.

Robert spun around, and half of his drink splashed onto the carpet. He didn't notice. "He ruined everything."

"If you mean Steve not staying in school, then you're—"

"That's not what I'm talking about." Robert turned back to me and focused his gaze on my face, although he had to work at it. "He stopped caring for all of us because of you. All their arguing and week-long fights and him sending us away every damn summer." He waved his hand. "It's all your fault. You're a bastard, Steve, and that sordid little fact tore this family apart."

Chapter 2

"Wha—" Sherri began.

I licked my lips. "What are you talking about, Robert?"

"Like I said. You're a bastard."

I stared blankly at him.

"Not blood…illegitimate…a bastard."

It felt as if the walls were closing in on me. I couldn't move, couldn't speak.

He smirked. "You're the result of some putrid little fling, Steve."

"Robert," Sherri said, and she sounded out of breath. "You're crazy. Mother would never do that."

"Shows how much you know. Always off in some fantasy world, playing your precious violin."

She looked uncertainly from Robert to me, then she squared her shoulders and looked into his face. "It can't be true. And if it is, how come you're the only one who knows about it?"

"'Cause I'm older, that's why. Remember during Easter break, when you were thirteen, and Steve," Robert glanced at me, "he must've been nine or ten, and he ruptured his spleen when he flipped my four-wheeler? Well, the blood work came back all wrong, and Father knew right away that Steve wasn't his son. I heard them arguing about it, and the following summer, they sent us away. They sent all of us away, Sherri. All because of him." He pointed his finger shakily in my direction, then slowly dropped his hand. "He sent *me* away."

I stood with my arms held stiffly at my sides, my hands clenched into fists, and I couldn't feel my feet on the carpet. "It's not true. You're lying."

"Oh, no I'm not." A glimmer of amusement flashed in his eyes. "You're the progeny of some two-bit racehorse trainer."

I twisted around and went after Mother.

Behind me, Robert choked, he was laughing so hard. He gulped, then yelled at my back, "Guess slingin' horse shit's in your blood, huh Steve?"

Mother had turned toward our raised voices with an irritated expression on her pretty face. As she watched me stride across the carpet, I imagined she instinctively realized that her proper little social gathering was about to come unhinged.

"Stephen, I'm warn—"

"Robert says I'm…that Father's…that he really isn't," I shook my head, "wasn't my father."

"Not here," she said sharply. "This isn't the time or—"

"Oh, yes it is. And you're not going to put me off."

Mother spun away from me just as Robert and the others joined us and unintentionally blocked her way. She hesitated, then asked the couple she'd been talking with to excuse us. They drifted off but remained discreetly within earshot. I didn't care.

Rachel slipped past them and stood by my side, and I was conscious of the strength she gave me.

"Well?" I swallowed. "A racehorse trainer. That's what he said."

"I will not discuss this here, Stephen."

So, it was true. As she turned to leave, I clutched her arm.

"Tell me." I relaxed my grip and let my hand drop to my side. "Please. I need to know."

"In the study," she said, then she left the room.

We followed her across the marbled hall and filed into the dimly lit study. With its floor-to-ceiling bookcases, heavy velvet drapes, and thick carpet, I had always found the room oppressively quiet. The air smelled faintly of dust and old books. Robert clicked the door shut, leaned against the wood grain, and crossed his arms over his chest.

"Well?" I said.

"Yes, Stephen," she said flatly. "It's true."

"Mother!" Sherri raised a trembling hand to her lips.

Alex put his arm around her shoulders, and when I turned back to Mother, she looked me straight in the eye. She was poised and controlled, her back rigidly straight, and there was an air of defiance to the tilt of her chin.

"Did Father know?" I said, asking the one question that would explain so much.

"Eventually." Her voice was calm.

Robert edged between Sherri and Mother.

My heart was pounding in my chest so hard, it hurt. I exhaled slowly through my mouth and said to Mother, "Why didn't you tell me? If I'd known, I might have understood why he was such a cold-hearted bastard."

Robert hooted. "Now, that's a good choice of words, Steve." His mouth twisted in a malevolent grin. "You oughta be careful who you call a bastard. Don't you think?"

I slammed my fist solidly into his nose, and he yelped and went down on one knee. In my peripheral vision, I saw that Mother had clasped a hand over her mouth as blood ran between Robert's fingers and splattered on the thick Prussian rug, and I wondered which she found more distressing, her ruined carpet or Robert's busted nose.

"You're the real bastard, Robert." I shakily grabbed Rachel's hand, skirted around them, and headed for the door.

"Steve?" Sherri said to my back.

I didn't stop. Couldn't. More than anything, I had to get out of that house. We climbed into the Chevy, and when I backed onto the drive, I paused and looked at the house for what was quite possibly the last time.

I awoke sometime after midnight. The air was still and heavy with moisture and unbearably warm. Lacing my fingers behind my head, I thought how, if a semi loaded with twenty-seven tons of sheet metal hadn't plowed into my father's car, he'd still be alive. I'd still be oblivious, secure and content in the knowledge of my identity, even if I didn't feel loved. Yet, I was sure I had been when I was quite young.

I closed my eyes, and a long-forgotten memory of a hot, sunny day, much like today had been, flooded my mind. We were in the park by the river. He was pitching to me, taking the time to explain position and technique, telling me to keep my eye on the ball. My father had been a muscular, powerfully built man, and even then, his black hair was sprinkled with gray. He carefully lined up his pitch and let go. The ball floated across the space between us, stark white against the green grass. Full of confidence, I had swung without hesitation, and as I lay there some thirteen years later, I could still feel the memory of that swing. I could still feel the impact as the bat connected solidly, the sound of it echoing in my mind. The ball had sailed high over his outstretched glove, and he had whooped and yelled to me that that was it.

I could still hear his voice.

A tear seeped from the corner of my eye and trickled into my hair. I rubbed my face and wiped the moisture from my skin. After I'd made that hit, he had scooped me up and spun me around, his bright blue eyes sparkling with pride as he told me what a great job I'd done.

I opened my eyes, and the image faded the way a dream does with the return of consciousness. I could no longer see his face, hear his voice, feel his touch. And I never would again. I swallowed and tasted salty tears at the back of my throat. Gone forever was the chance, the hope, that he'd be proud of me.

Willing myself not to cry, I stared at the high-peaked ceiling and watched as distant lightning flashed across the paneling. Outside, the night was eerily still. The mockingbird that had been talking incessantly all evening was silent, now, so were the tree frogs and crickets, all of nature holding its breath, waiting for the storm.

Beside me, Rachel stirred.

I hadn't bothered with a sheet, but Rachel always liked to be covered. She'd been restless tonight, and the sheet was twisted around her legs. Her dark hair was fanned across the pillow, and in the dim light, her skin looked pale. I watched as she opened her eyes and focused on my face. She kicked her legs free and rolled onto her side.

Rachel touched my cheek. "Have you been awake long?" Her voice was husky with sleep.

I cleared my throat. "Not long."

"Hmm." She leaned across my pillow and kissed the side of my face. Her lips were cool and dry on my skin. After a moment, she lifted her hand and traced her finger down my face and across my lips, then she kissed me lightly on the mouth.

I pulled her on top of me and wrapped my arms tightly around her.

Even though I now understood the reason for his coldness, I couldn't forgive him. Yet, as irrational as it was, I still longed for another chance.

I pressed my forehead against Rachel's shoulder and closed my eyes. My throat burned with the effort of not crying. She slipped her arm beneath my neck and stroked her fingers through my hair, and I felt unbelievably comforted. After a moment, I rested my head on the pillow. She propped herself on straightened arms, her knees sunk into the mattress alongside my hips, and looked down at me with an expression I couldn't read. Behind her, lightning illuminated the loft, and the first ominous rumble of thunder rattled the windowpanes.

One of my oversized Foxdale shirts hung loosely from her shoulders. I slid my hands up her thighs, across her silky panties, and along her smooth skin, feeling an impression of ribs. I cupped my hands over her breasts. She kissed me with lips and tongue and teeth, with passion and heat, and when the storm finally hit, bringing with it the smell of rain carried on a sudden wind, I hardly noticed.

By the time she slid off me and collapsed on the damp, crumpled sheets, the storm had rolled through the valley and was fading in the distance. I lay still, breathing hard, and listened to the rain pelting the tin roof while a cooling breeze drifted across our skin.

Rachel pulled the sheet up to her chin, then moved her arms up and down, billowing the sheet and letting it drop back down, doing it over and over again.

"What'n the hell are you doing?" I asked with a grin in my voice.

"Cooling off."

"Hey." I sat up. "I have an idea."

"What?"

"Let's go outside and stand in the rain." I jumped to my feet, reached across the bed, and grabbed her hand. "That'll cool us off."

"What? Are you crazy? Somebody might see. Plus, it'll be freezing."

"No, it won't." I pulled her off the mattress. "And nobody'll see. Not out on the deck. Not this time of night."

"What about Greg and…?"

"They're asleep." I frog-marched her into the kitchen.

She giggled. "And how do you know that?"

"I just do."

"Greg might be on a call or something," she said over her shoulder.

"Well then, if he's an incredibly lucky man, he'll be coming home just about now and catch a glimpse of your gorgeous, naked body."

"Steve." She stood still while I flicked the dead bolt and opened the door. When I slid my arm around her waist and propelled her forward, she planted a hand on either side of the doorframe and braced her arms. "Steve, this is silly."

"No, it's not. It'll be fun and different, and maybe a little crazy, but I've always wanted to stand in the rain without any clothes on."

She giggled. "Go by yourself, then."

"Things like this should be shared." I slid my hand up her side and tickled her armpit. She shrieked and jumped through the doorway.

The rain was colder than I'd expected. We hugged ourselves and hopped from foot to foot, giggling like idiots. But in a few seconds, the rain didn't seem so cold. Rachel stood still then and felt the uniqueness of it. The rain and the breeze and the dark. She closed her eyes and tilted her head back. There was something stirringly primitive, almost forbidden, about standing in the rain and the wind, feeling it against your skin. When she opened her eyes and looked at my face, a subtle change moved in her eyes.

"I've never made love in the rain," she said.

"Me, neither." I stepped over to her and smoothed my hands along her shoulders, slick with sweat and rain. "And I think we ought to correct this deficit, don't you?"

"Hmm."

◇◇◇

Sunday evening, after I drove Rachel home, I hesitantly picked up the phone and called Mother.

"What's his name?" I asked.

"What?"

"The racehorse trainer. What's his name?"

She sighed. "Why don't you leave it alone?"

"Because I can't. What's his name?" A pause, and I knew she wasn't going to answer. I also knew that appearances were more important to my mother than anything else, and God help the person who marred that picture. I said, "If you don't tell me," I said, "I'll be forced to ask around until I find out."

"You can't be serious."

"What's your girlfriend's name? The judge's wife? Miles, isn't it? Sharon Miles? I could start with her."

I listened to her disembodied voice, thick with anger, as she told me his name.

"Wait," I said before she could hang up. "Does he know? Does he know I'm his son?"

"No, Stephen. He doesn't have a clue."

The following morning, as light seeped into the eastern horizon, I nosed the pickup off Greg's farm and headed south on Interstate 95 on my way to Washington Park, home of Thoroughbred racing at its finest or so the commercial said. I wasn't sure I was doing the right thing, wasn't even sure I wanted to meet him. But I was certain of one fact. If I didn't, I would always wonder.

I let the truck roll to a stop at the bottom of the off ramp, flicked on the dome light, and glanced at the map lying open on the seat beside me. I turned left and drove through the center of town. After a mile or so, I made another left. A ten-foot-high chain-link fence bordered the road, and beyond, barely visible in the early morning light, stood row after row of identical-looking barns. The backside.

When I reached the guard post, I breathed a sigh of relief. It was busy. Two cars and a pickup waited in line for the guard to wave them through. When the truck in front of me, older and rustier than my own, drove off, I pulled up to the guard's window.

"The name's Cline. I have an appointment with Mr. Kessler."

The guard, an elderly black man with wiry arms and enlarged, arthritic knuckles, scanned his clipboard. "You're not on my list."

"He probably forgot to phone it in. Could you give him a call? Remind him?"

He eyed the growing line behind me, snatched up the phone, and punched in a number. After a second or two, he hung up. "It's busy. Here." He checked off a line on a thick, yellow pad and thrust the clipboard across the space between us. "Sign here, and I need to see your driver's license."

I scribbled my name, slipped my license under the clip, and handed it over.

"Which barn's he in?" I said when he held out my license. "I forget."

"Sixteen."

"Thanks." I let my foot off the brake and drove down the access road, thankful I'd been able to fake my way in.

Except for different color-coordinated stall guards and feed tubs hanging outside every stall, each building was a duplicate of its neighbor. I found barn sixteen and pulled into an empty space by the perimeter fence. As I walked down the alley between barns, I breathed in the heady, welcomed aromas and felt like I'd come home. I missed my job. Somehow, I'd have to find the courage to go back.

I asked a skinny, black kid where I could find Kessler, and he pointed me toward the far end of the shedrow. I hesitated in the wide doorway. A young woman led a big chestnut mare down the covered aisle that circled the long central row of back-to-back stalls. The horse's loppy ears flopped with each stride as they rounded the far corner.

I was dressed in a tee shirt, dirty jeans, and work boots, and no one gave me a second glance as I stood there, working up the courage to go inside. I wiped my hands down the front of my jeans, walked over to the office, and paused in the doorway. Kessler was standing behind a battered wooden desk with his back to the door. He was on the phone, and there was an edge to his voice that caught my attention.

"No," he said. "If it doesn't stop, soon, Everrod's going to find another trainer."

The office was far from neat. Sheaves of paperwork covered the desk, and stacks of binders were piled haphazardly on top of a row of filing cabinets.

"Shit, you don't think I did? I hired a firm out of Baltimore almost immediately. They were useless." He rolled his shoulders as if he were trying to work a kink out of his neck. "No. Are you kidding? Look, Charles, if I don't find out who's behind this, I'm going to lose—"

Whoever he was talking to cut him off. He rubbed a hand through his hair and listened without comment.

Framed photographs covered the walls. Horses stretched full out, muscles straining as they crossed the finish line. Horses standing in the winner's circle, their coats glistening with sweat. Conformation shots and bloodline charts. Horses gazing from their stalls with alert ears and intelligent eyes.

"Yeah, yeah," he said. "I know."

The huge desk, what I could see of it, was old and scratched, the varnish nearly worn off, and the chair behind it was missing a chunk of stuffing. No attempt at pretense in this room.

"All right. Don't forget." He switched off the cordless phone and stared at the wall in front of him.

When he turned around, I felt like I'd been socked in the gut. Except for an additional thirty pounds or so and an extra inch or two, I was looking into a mirror some thirty years into my future. The same sandy brown hair. The same dark eyes and straight eyebrows. The same nose. The same everything.

Kessler frowned as he set the phone on his desk, and I imagined he wasn't too thrilled that I'd overheard his end of the conversation.

"Can I help you?" His voice was mildly unfriendly.

Chapter 3

I cleared my throat. "Did you know that…" I couldn't do it. What if Mother had lied? What if he already knew he had a son and didn't care? "I…"

He hooked his thumbs in his pockets. "Yes?"

"I've got the wrong barn," I mumbled as I backed through the doorway and hurried outside.

The sky had lightened considerably, and the level of activity had picked up. I headed down the alley between barns, past horses being bathed, their grooms cursing at a raised hind leg, at a horse that refused to stand still. Voices called back and forth. Buckets rattled. Horseshoes scraped the hard-packed ground.

I walked toward my truck, silently despising myself. I had chickened out. Hadn't had the nerve to tell him who I was. Maybe it was for the best. Maybe I should forget it. Let it go.

I had parked on the grassy verge alongside the perimeter fence ten feet from a portable round pen constructed of tubular steel. The gate that had stood open earlier was now latched. Inside, a colt rolled in the sand. His chestnut legs sliced through the air as he wriggled from side to side. As I approached, he jumped to his feet. He splayed his legs, lowered his head, and shook the sand from his coat. I paused by the Chevy's front fender, and he trotted over to the fence.

The colt studied me with liquid blue-brown eyes and pricked ears. Something about his expression, a look of raw intelligence and confidence, announced to the world that he was special.

I turned away from him, climbed into the truck, and backed onto the access road. As I shifted into drive, I glanced toward barn sixteen. Kessler was standing outside the doorway at the far end of the shedrow, and he was looking my way. I quickly averted my eyes and drove toward the exit.

By lunch time, I had changed into a polo shirt and a reasonably clean pair of jeans. I grabbed my binoculars off the kitchen counter and headed back to the track. This time, however, I parked in General Parking and strolled toward the grandstand along with a steady stream of racegoers. Like everyone else, I bought a program and a copy of the *Daily Racing Form*. I walked past the administration offices and an empty gift shop and rode the escalator to the second level.

Bettors already waited in line at the pari-mutuel windows along the back wall. On every pillar, television monitors displayed the runners' statistics for the first race while a lunch time crowd patronized the Paddock Grill. The Trackside Bar and Lounge was doing a brisk business, as well. Apparently, alcohol and gambling went hand in hand.

I walked down a sloped floor covered with indoor/outdoor carpet that had seen better days and sat in an aisle seat that reminded me of grade school. Cheap plastic seats with collapsible tables. I left my table down and scanned the day's program.

As I had hoped, Kessler had a runner. No, two runners. One in the second race and another in the ninth. I studied the statistics, slowly learning my way around the abbreviations and unfamiliar jargon, until the horses for the first race came onto the track.

I slipped on a pair of sunglasses and tucked the *Daily Racing Form* under my arm. Pushing through a pair of heavy double doors, I walked into the heat and glare of the last day of June. The stained concrete floor sloped down to the dirt track, and rows of uncomfortable-looking benches fanned outward from either side of the central aisle. A four-foot-high chain-link fence separated the public from the actual racing surface where a procession of high-strung Thoroughbreds paraded by. Following them, I turned right and walked down a narrow walkway that paralleled the track.

The concrete was cracked and grimy and pockmarked with flattened wads of chewing gum. Somehow, I hadn't expected that the place would be so sordid, but it made sense if the majority of patrons were concerned only with their handicapping skills.

I turned right at a barricade that kept the public from walking onto the horse path connecting the track to the parade ring and joined a group of die-hard race fans who had abandoned the air-conditioning to view the horses up close. After the horses stalked around the parade ring a couple of times, their grooms guided them into open-ended stalls where they were saddled.

I flipped through my program and matched names to faces. None of the trainers looked younger than forty. Most were much older. One was a woman, and all of them were white. The grooms were easy enough to spot, wearing numbered pennies over tee shirts and jeans. They were a mixed group. Black, white, Hispanic. Old, young. Male, female.

The horses themselves were not what I was accustomed to. Nothing like the fat, glossy horses, essentially expensive pets, that resided at Foxdale. These animals were lean and hard. As I watched the bettors along the rail study the *Form*, I realized that the horses were viewed simply as a commodity. If they couldn't earn their keep, they were out.

A signal must have been given, because the trainers legged the jockeys up onto the horses' backs, then the grooms took them out onto the track.

The grooms peeled off their pennies and dropped them into a plastic bin as they slipped through the barricade. They walked back on the path I'd taken while the trainers went into the grandstand through a side entrance. A guard stood at a podium just inside the doorway, checking passes or ID's of some sort. I retraced my steps. As I drew level with the barricade, I turned and looked back at the grandstand. A wall of sheer glass reflected a single line of cumulus clouds drifting across the horizon.

I walked back and leaned against the fence next to four of the grooms, three guys and one girl with halters and lead ropes draped over their shoulders.

A distant bell rang. The horses broke from the starting gate and surged forward in a rainbow of color. As they sorted themselves out along the rail, the announcer's voice clamored over the PA system, nearly unintelligible to my ears.

When the horses swept around the turn and entered the stretch, the crowd screamed their encouragement. Two of the grooms next to me jumped up and down in a frenzied effort to get their horses across the finish line first.

"Come on, Blue. Put it in gear!" the guy next to me yelled as if his horse could hear him. He was leaning across the fence, his fisted hand beating the air. "Smoke it, baby!"

The girl, whose face was flushed with excitement, screamed at her horse. Next to her, a stocky guy with short-cropped, black hair and bushy eyebrows watched the action without a trace of emotion.

The horses' hooves pounded the ground as they neared the wire, stretched full out, muscles straining, breath coming fast and hard. Sheer guts and determination. Their physical nearness, as they flew past us in a blur, was intoxicating, and I couldn't imagine watching the race from anywhere else.

A gray filly crossed the finish line two lengths in front of her nearest competitor, and I smiled to myself as the opposition's encouragement turned to disparaging remarks and downright profanity. It appeared that the winner belonged, so to speak, to the girl. She smiled with proprietary pride while the groom with the buzz cut looked pleased with the result. His reaction surprised me since his horse had lost.

The group walked through an opening in the fence and stood on the section of track just in front of the grandstand. As I scanned the program, a few of the trainers followed them onto the dirt, and the runners straggled back from the race one by one.

The guy with the buzz cut snapped his lead onto horse number six, a bay filly. She skittered around and looked energetic enough to go another mile. No trainer had joined them, and I frowned as he led the filly down the track toward the barns. I checked the program. Horse number six, Mary's Gilded Girl, owned by Benjamin Campbell, trained by Larry McCormick.

As I folded the *Form* and shoved it into my back pocket, I considered the groom's reaction. It could have been significant, or it might have meant nothing at all. Although his horse had been odds-on favorite at the start of the race, he simply may have placed a bet on another horse. Nothing illegal in that. Then again, maybe he knew his horse wasn't going to win.

I pushed through the double doors into a wash of cool air and walked past the rows of plastic seats. I purchased a Coke and a ham and Swiss hoagie from a cute blonde working behind the counter at the Paddock Grill. She was too thin, but she had a great smile and intense blue eyes, which she used to advantage. Pretending I didn't notice her come-on, I found an empty seat, laid my food on the table, and spread the *Form* across my lap. Larry McCormick, number six's trainer, had one other runner, another filly, this one entered in the ninth. Seven horses were competing for the biggest purse of the day, Kessler's among them.

I had just finished the last of my sandwich when the horses for the second race came onto the track and made their way past the stands. Unlike the jeans Kessler had worn earlier in the day, he looked professional, dressed in a cream-colored blazer, striped oxford shirt, tie, and brown trousers. Kessler's runner, number seven, was a dark bay gelding named Devil's Ace.

The gelding chewed nervously on his bit, keen to get on with the job. I lowered the brim of my ball cap, slipped the sunglasses back on, and followed at a distance, but in the end, I walked right up to the parade ring railing and stood among a group of bettors.

Kessler leaned against a post, crossed his arms over his chest, and talked casually to a young woman without looking at her. Both were watching Devil's Ace as he stepped sideways down the length of the ring with his neck arched and tense. The woman, who was almost as tall as Kessler, and thin, gathered her sandy brown hair that fell to the middle of her back and lifted it off her neck. She fanned her face with a program.

Kessler's groom, a huge, black man with a shaved head and bulging biceps, looked like he didn't take crap from anyone, especially his charge. He wore a royal blue polo shirt beneath an orange pennie with the number seven printed across the front and back, and that's where any attempt at neatness came to an abrupt halt. His jeans were worn through at the knees, and his work boots weren't much better.

Devil's Ace did not care for the saddling process. His groom held a rein and lead rope in one hand and flattened his palm on the horse's shoulder in an effort to keep the horse from swinging around in the saddling stall. The woman stepped to the horse's off side and did the same thing, and the jockey wisely stayed out of the way. Kessler quickly adjusted the saddle. As he tightened the girths, the bay lashed out, first with one hind leg, then the other.

When Kessler was satisfied, he moved out of the way, and his groom led the horse back into the ring. Kessler spoke to his jockey. J. Garcia, according to the program. After the jockeys mounted and guided the horses onto the track, Kessler and the woman entered the grandstand through the side entrance.

I watched the race from the fence. Number seven took the lead early but faded in the straight and finished an undistinguished fifth.

"Fucking Garcia," Kessler's groom said to his neighbor. "My grandma can ride betta'n dat asshole. Motherfucker got run away with. He suppose ta lay back, make his move after the turn."

The guy next to him shrugged. "Least your horse can run. Mine couldn't if his life depended on it, the useless pig."

As they grumbled their way onto the track, I turned, planning to go back into the air-conditioning, and nearly walked straight into Christopher J. Kessler.

"Excuse me," he said as he skirted around me.

I exhaled breath I didn't realize I'd been holding and walked quickly up the sloped floor that was now littered with torn betting slips, paper cups, and cigarette butts. Halfway up, I glanced over my shoulder and was startled to see Kessler looking in my direction.

By the time the ninth race rolled around, I had convinced myself that I was just another face in the crowd, that Kessler looking my way had simply been a coincidence. I watched the preparations for the race among a swelling crowd that lined the parade ring. An air of excitement moved through the paddock, unseen yet tangible.

This time around, Kessler was joined by the owners, a petite female groom, and the mystery woman. I flipped through my program and read the statistics for the ninth race for the second time that day. Kessler's horse, Icedancer, was a well put together bay with a blaze down her elegant head and a pedigree even I recognized. If she won, and it seemed the majority of bettors thought she had an excellent chance, she would earn thirty-two grand for her owners. Unlike Kessler's gelding in the second race, she walked around the ring with her head low to the ground and little apparent enthusiasm.

When the horses cantered down the track to warm up, the crowd by the fence shifted, and I squeezed into a space next to Icedancer's groom. The guy on my left gave me an annoyed glance, then shifted his weight. Icedancer's groom stood quietly with a lead rope clenched in tense, slender hands. She didn't look strong enough to handle a pony, much less a thousand-pound Thoroughbred.

"Is your horse always so subdued?" I said.

"What?" She frowned, and oddly enough, she looked scared or nervous. Or both.

"Your horse, Icedancer. Is she always so quiet before she runs?"

She glanced around and seemed unsure whether she should be talking to me. Her face was fine-boned with high cheekbones beneath huge, brown eyes.

"She's a nice, sweet, quiet filly. Real laid back. But not like today." She glanced down at her hands and mumbled, "I don't think she feels too good."

"Hmm."

As the horses circled by the starting gate, I said, "What's your name?"

She glanced shyly at me, then stared at the ground. "Trudy."

"Well, Trudy, I hope your horse wins."

"Thank you." A brief smile crossed her lips.

As the last horse was loaded into the gate, a hush fell over the crowd. The bell rang, the gates sprung open, and seven half-ton Thoroughbreds surged forward, heads lowered, hooves digging into the soft loam, heavily muscled hindquarters propelling them forward as a roar rose from the grandstand. I glanced at Trudy. With her petite build and smooth, almost translucent skin, she looked oddly childlike as she watched Icedancer's progress with motherly concern.

The beautiful bay filly with an irregular blaze down her noble face never made a bid. She hung in the middle of the field and faded as the leaders entered the stretch. When the horses crossed the finish line, I turned toward Trudy, but she was already walking through the opening in the fence with her shoulders hunched forward.

I had no intention of running into Kessler again, so I hurried up the central aisle and sat on one of the narrow, aluminum benches midway up the sloped concrete.

Almost as soon as I'd sat down, Kessler strode down the walkway and joined Trudy on the track. His face was dark, and even from a distance, I could see the tension in the set of his jaw. Several yards behind him, Mystery Woman ran to keep up. She looked as distressed as Kessler.

I focused my binoculars and watched them, an isolated, dispirited group. As the horses returned, someone down on the track walked past and blocked my view. When my field of vision cleared, I saw that Kessler had spun around. From his expression, I realized that the man must have said something disparaging. Kessler turned back around, and I tracked the man. Wrinkled gray two-piece suit, ugly paisley tie, white hair cut so short, his pink scalp glistened under the hot sun. His face was puffy, and his fleshy cheeks drooped on either side of his chin like a bloodhound's jowls. I watched as he strolled into the winner's circle.

I'd seen him earlier in the afternoon. I scanned my program and found his name. Larry McCormick, trainer of a chestnut filly by the name of Chessere, winner of the biggest race of the day. Larry McCormick, whose groom had been smugly satisfied when his horse, looking full of herself, had lost the first race.

I refocused on Kessler. He listened to his jockey's comments with his head bowed and thumbs hooked in his pockets. Behind them, Trudy smoothed her hand down Icedancer's face. When she led the filly toward the barns, Mystery Woman followed.

The jockey shrugged in response to a remark from Kessler, turned on his heel, and walked toward the opening in the fence. With obvious disappointment, Kessler idly watched his jockey ignore a rude comment from a patron who had made one too many trips to the Trackside Bar and Lounge.

Kessler started to turn, pivoting on his right leg, when he paused abruptly and seemed to stare directly into the binoculars' lenses.

I froze. My fingers tightened around the housing as I lowered the binoculars, and sure enough, he was looking straight at me.

Damn. I edged my way down the length of the bench, stepping over congealing puddles of soft drink where losing tickets lay scattered like confetti, soaking up the syrupy liquid. As I strode up the slope, I resisted the urge to look back. I was almost to the door, when I got caught behind a slow-moving stream of patrons.

Someone grabbed my arm. I spun around and found myself face to face with Kessler.

Chapter 4

Kessler was slightly out of breath, and his skin was flushed and damp with perspiration. He looked furious, and I didn't know why.

He tightened his grip. "Who the hell are you working for?"

I yanked free, and he shifted his weight onto the balls of his feet, ready to give chase if I made a break for it.

"I don't know what you're talking about," I said.

"The hell you don't. First thing this morning, you're snooping round my barn, and then this afternoon, I see you everywhere I go. Who are you working for?"

As I opened my mouth to respond, someone knocked into my back, hard.

"Move outta the alleyway, asshole," he grumbled.

The man was adding to the air pollution index with breath and body odor foul enough to drop an elephant in its tracks. He glared at both of us before he hobbled down the aisle with an unsteady gait.

"What are you doing to my horses?" Kessler said.

I looked back at him. "What? I'm not doing anything to your damn horses, and I don't work for anybody. No one you'd be interested in, anyway."

"Then who the hell are you?" His voice was hostile, his gaze intense, determined. "You sure as hell aren't a racegoer."

Lines of stress etched his forehead, and the tension in his jaw and puffiness under his eyes marred an otherwise pleasant face.

"No," I said. "You're right. I'm not." I inhaled deeply. "Do you remember Patricia Cline?"

"What?"

"Patricia Cline." I watched as he ran the name through his memory and came up empty. "Twenty-three years ago. *That* Patricia Cline." Still no connection. "Married to Robert J. Cline, M.D."

Interestingly enough, that name clicked. Although, once I thought about it, I supposed it made sense. Father's death had been well publicized. You didn't go through all your adult life as one of the most innovative, top-ranked cardiovascular surgeons in the country without being interviewed and criticized, sometimes hounded, and oftentimes recognized.

"Oh...her."

"Yeah, her." I unclenched my teeth. "Patricia Cline. Twenty-plus years ago. Married." He wasn't getting it. "She's my mother."

He looked at me dumbly. "So?"

"The two of you—" I shook my head. "Never mind. What's the point? You didn't even remember her."

As I turned to leave, Kessler cut in front of me.

"Wait a minute. That was a long time ago." He quickly sized me up. "How old are you?" A trace of hesitation in his voice.

"Twenty-two."

"Christ. You don't mean?"

I watched his eyes as he worked it out and felt an immense rush of relief. Unless he had missed his calling and should have been, at that very moment, starring in some Academy Award winning movie, he hadn't known.

I sat down as he studied my face and build, noticing the obvious similarities between us, coming to the realization that he had a son he hadn't even known existed.

"Yeah, that's what I mean," I said. "I happen to be the result of your...encounter with my mother. I'm your son."

"Jesus." Kessler looked skyward, perhaps for divine intervention. He ran his fingers through his hair, then stepped into the next row of benches, looked down at me, and frowned.

I felt so weak, it was an effort not to hang my head. And it was so damn hot. The slow breeze that had moved the air earlier in the day had fizzled out altogether. I wiped my forehead with the sleeve of my shirt, then braced my hands on my knees.

Kessler planted his foot on the bench across from me, rested his arm against his thigh, and leaned forward. "What's your name?"

"Steve."

"What do you want, Steve?"

I looked up at him. "Nothing." I stood up. "I don't want a damned thing." I turned and headed for the exit.

"I didn't mean it that way," he said, and I heard his hurried footsteps behind me. "You're taking it the wrong way."

I kept walking. I pulled open the heavy glass door and walked out of the glare and into the dark coolness of the grandstand. The place was emptying fast. Only die-hard fans and the desperate, hoping for one more chance to score big, ignored the rush to beat the traffic.

"Steve."

I walked past the turnstiles. As I neared the exit, I caught a glimpse of Kessler's reflection in the glass. He was watching after me, his expression unreadable as a steady stream of people walked past him.

Outside, the sun hung low in the sky, shining into my eyes like an obscene spotlight. "What did I want?" he had asked. Trouble was, I had no idea.

I crossed the wide expanse of asphalt that still radiated heat from the long day and opened the Chevy's door. A furnace blast of air hit my face. I rolled down the windows and waited a few minutes before sliding onto the hot vinyl seat. I tossed my ball cap on the dash and ran my fingers through my hair.

Just what did I want?

I pulled the binoculars over my head and jammed them into the crease between the backrest and seat so they wouldn't slide around. Easing the truck into the line of vehicles pointing toward the gates, I headed home with an emptiness in my gut that had nothing to do with hunger.

Detective James Ralston stood just outside my door, and when he caught sight of my face through the screen, his eyes narrowed. "What's happened?"

"Oh, nothing much." I opened the door wider and waved him inside. "Except I met my real father yesterday."

"What do you mean?"

"Oh, I guess the correct term is biological father, or maybe sperm donor would be more accurate. More descriptive, less sanitary, but accurate. He wanted to know what I wanted." I snorted. "Like I know."

I picked my jeans off the floor, pulled them on, and started pacing. I couldn't shake an underlying feeling of urgency, an overwhelming need to escape, to run. But run to where? Or, more pointedly, from what?

A weak breeze trickled through the screen.

"So, after a terrific day at Washington Park—Oh, he's a racehorse trainer of all things." I shook my head at the irony. "I spent an absolutely wonderful, soul-searching hour or two last night sitting by the lake. Didn't accomplish anything. No enlightenment, no earth-shattering revelations. But, shit. No big deal. So what if my life so far's been a scam. You know what's worse?" I turned to face him and caught my balance.

Ralston waited, his face expressionless, his pale eyes unreadable.

"I went to Foxdale last night...or tried to. Couldn't get past the office without thinking I was gonna barf. I was stone cold sober at the time, mind you." I braced my hands on the counter and stared at the floor.

"Damn it. I haven't been there for two months, and I don't know if I'll ever be able to go back. All I could think about was…" I pushed myself upright and walked aimlessly around the kitchen. "Then I came on home and got juiced, plastered to the eyeballs. Can't remember most of the night after that." I glanced at the whiskey bottle sitting on the kitchen counter.

Ralston was standing at the far end of the island counter. His face was blank, giving nothing away. A tactic I imagined he used frequently on the job. Letting the suspect, witness, or whoever ramble on while he kept all emotion from his face, quiet and controlled. Yet I had glimpsed the other side.

I slid onto one of the barstools and rested my elbows on the counter. "No wonder the old man hated my guts. We, Kessler and I, look so much alike, it's uncanny. Every time he looked at me…he must have been reminded."

"I'm sorry, Steve."

I shrugged. "I'd often wondered why I looked so different from them." I stood up, walked into the living room that also served as my bedroom, and looked down at the pile of tack lying on the carpet.

I picked up the bridle and fingered the smooth, supple leather. Listened to the creaking of leather against leather, the metallic jingle of the bit. "So, here it is, a Tuesday afternoon, and I've got nothing to do, no place to go, and the rest of the days, weeks, and months to come look about the same, unless…." I dropped the bridle back onto the crumpled, dirty saddle pad that was still flecked with hair, still smelling of horse, and turned around. "Unless I get up the nerve to go back."

"Have you thought about getting a job somewhere else? Another horse farm?"

"Yeah. I could do that." I walked back into the kitchen and looked out the bank of windows that ran along the length of countertop. One of my landlord's crew was taking the John Deere 6310 through its paces, mowing tracts around the lake. "I'd feel like I wimped if I did. Foxdale's my job. If I don't go back, he's won even that."

There was no need for me to explain who I meant. After I'd been shot, *he* was all Ralston and I had talked about in the weeks

THE PARADOX SYNDROME

KEN HODGSON

ibooks

DISTRIBUTED BY PUBLISHERS GROUP WEST

DEDICATION

This book is for Preston Darby, M.D.
And
Pamela W. Darby, RN, MSN, CNS

A Publication of ibooks, inc.

Distributed by:
Publishers Group West
1700 Fourth Street, Berkeley, CA 94710
www.pgw.com

ibooks, inc.
24 West 25th Street
New York, NY 10010

The ibooks World Wide Web Site Address is:
www.ibooks.net

ISBN 1-59687-299-3
First ibooks, inc. printing January 2006
10 9 8 7 6 5 4 3 2 1

Printed in the U.S.A.

"Silently we went round and round,
　　And through each hollow mind
The Memory of dreadful things
　　Rushed like a dreadful wind,
And Horror stalked before each man,
　　And Terror crept behind."

The Ballad of Reading Gaol
Oscar Wilde

"Do not disturb the sleeping dog."

Alessandro Allegri

"I had a little bird,
　　It's name was Enza.
I opened the window,
　　And in-flu-enza."

Children's jump rope song, 1918

PROLOGUE

Paradox, New Mexico
November, 1918

When Dr. Robert Wheeler came to the gate in the courtyard that surrounded the two-story adobe hospital, he was met by two *brujas*—Mexican witches—one on each side of the peeling wooden posts that marked the entranceway.

In the cold crimson light of early morning the witches looked up from their low fires and regarded him as they did everyone, with a look of stoic indifference.

Dr. Wheeler gave them a nod of acceptance and continued on his way. He sincerely wished them well. Like him, they were doing their best to battle the common enemy: death. So far, the witches' chants, medicines, and ceremonial fires were working as well as anything conventional science had to offer.

A light dusting of snow had fallen sometime last night during the brief time he had returned home to catch a few hours of much-needed sleep. The doctor noted glumly the many footprints and wobbly outlines of tracks left by gurneys that were either wheeling in those too sick to walk, or removing those who had died to the single hearse that serviced the remote coal mining town of Paradox. No matter. He would find out the details soon enough.

The doctor stomped his feet clean, then thumbed the iron latch on the massive wooden door that had once been the entrance to a Mexican mission. The door opened before he pushed it.

"Thank God you are here," the rotund head nurse, Maria Santos, greeted him with a concerned voice. The physician often wondered

1

how she could sense his unseen presence. It certainly counted as one of her many talents. "There has been an accident in the mine."

"Not the flu?" Dr. Wheeler asked shutting the door. "That would be different." He motioned with a flick of his hand to where rows of corpses lay wrapped in white sheets, stacked like cordwood to the height of the windowsills. "I thought I ordered those buried. The sooner a source of the disease is put in the ground, the better."

The nurse lowered her gaze. "Yes sir, I know you did, but the men you appointed to dig the graves have died." She gave a slight nod to the many corpses. "Both were brought in while you were home."

"Damn it!" Dr. Wheeler said. "This flu is like nothing I've ever experienced. Normally influenza only takes the very young and the very old. This form of the disease seems to seek out the healthiest people in their prime and strikes them down in mere hours."

He lit a cigarette, the smoke almost certainly offered some protection against the unknown germs. Many people had begun wearing useless masks to keep from catching the flu. Wheeler knew better. Smoking a few cigarettes and washing your hands with soap and water, along with staying warm and away from other people, were the only defenses he knew. He looked down the narrow wainscoted gray hallway to the ward. *Well, so much for avoiding crowds.*

"There are eighteen, doctor." Maria once again anticipated his next move. "All but one are miners. Most have already sent their wives and children to relatives, or rented rooms for them in Tucumcari. They all think everyone in Paradox is doomed."

"It's just the flu, Maria," Wheeler said with far more confidence than he felt. "I know it's a bad strain, but the disease will run its course."

"When?"

Dr. Robert Wheeler grimaced. "You said there was an accident in the mine. How bad is it?"

"Only one man is being brought in by the ambulance. The superintendent said over the phone that the man's name is Juan Arroyo. He was crushed bad when a slab of rock fell from the roof and hit him."

The doctor sighed. This type of accident was all too common, but at least it was one he understood. Wheeler's employer, the Bessemer Fuel and Iron Corporation, operated huge steel mills in Colorado. This was a source of steel that the country needed to win the Great War, the war to end all wars. In such desperate times, safety was often sacrificed, at least that was what he was told when he had accepted the position of company doctor straight out of medical school.

Now he was developing doubts—serious doubts that possibly the company had hired him simply to patch up those who could return to work and bury those who were killed while being a shining example of how much the Bessemer Company cared for their valued workers. The doctor noted there was a line in front of the employment office every morning. Hiring replacements for dead coal miners presented no problems. It was staying alive after they were hired that was the difficulty. Lack of timbers caused gruesome cave-ins, bad air wrecked lungs, unguarded machinery caused accidents. Then came the Spanish Flu.

Nothing in his medical training nor his brief career had prepared him for such a deadly onslaught from an invisible enemy. He reassured himself that massive scientific research efforts were being focused on a cure. Unfortunately, for now, all he could do was practice palliative medicine and hope.

"Doctor," the nurse said, shaking him from his reverie. "I hear the ambulance coming."

"Let's get the surgery prepared," Wheeler said as the distant wailing siren of the Model T truck the company had converted to act as both ambulance and hearse became louder.

The door swung open with a white cloud of powder snow. Men with worried dusky faces carried a wire stretcher with blood dripping through the thick screen.

Dr. Wheeler knew none of the miners understood English. He motioned to the operating table and Maria told the men in their native Spanish to place the injured man upon it.

It did not take a medical school diploma to diagnose a man whose chest had been crushed. After cutting open the victim's shirt with a pair of scissors the doctor marveled at how tenuously a person could cling to life. Shattered ribs moved like scurrying insects beneath abraded skin with each shallow breath. He hesitated to apply even enough pressure to use his stethoscope.

"Ask them if he has any relatives," Dr. Wheeler said to Maria.

After a moment of talk the nurse turned to him. "Arroyo was hired only yesterday. No one knows where he is from. They think possibly somewhere in Mexico, but the company hiring records should tell us."

"There's no rush," Wheeler sighed at the now-stilled chest as he pulled a sheet over the dead miner's face.

"*Madre de Dios*," Maria said. All present except the physician crossed themselves.

As the men wheeled their dead companion to the door Maria said, "They mentioned that Juan Arroyo had a cough and was running a fever before the rock fell on him. They said he had the flu and would die anyway. God was determined to have his soul."

When the door opened wide, the chants of the witches blended eerily with the moaning of a cold north wind.

Maria Santos busied herself with removing the blood-soaked sheets and preparing the surgery for another patient. It would not be long before the table would be needed again.

Dr. Wheeler stood silently staring at the now-closed door. After a while he lit a fresh cigarette and walked past the row of corpses to the ward. It was time to see how many would live and how many would die this day.

CHAPTER ONE

Houston, Texas
Present day

Dr. Laura Masterson brushed back an unruly lock of short brunette hair and surveyed the luncheon gathering from behind the podium. Her audience was restless, bored, or both. It wasn't always easy to tell. The time had come to do her best to garner the attention of Noon Lions Club members who had paid her the grand sum of one hundred dollars to give a thirty-minute talk on the history of the 1918 flu epidemic, a subject on which she had authored many articles.

"The Spanish Flu killed more people in twenty-four hours than AIDS has killed in twenty-four years." She paused to allow the figures to sink in. "Before the pandemic, which is what we call an epidemic that bolts out of control and covers wide geographic areas of the world, ran its course, possibly one hundred million lay dead. The true figure will never be known as many of the fatalities were in India and other undeveloped countries that kept no records."

A sweating fat man seated at a table nearest the buffet line scooted back from an empty plate and raised his hand.

"Yes," Dr. Masterson said, anticipating the question she knew was coming.

"Uh, ma'am, excuse me, I mean *doctor*, but isn't this all ancient history. I mean it's too bad all of those folks died, but we have antibiotics today, flu shots and stuff like that. Don't you think it should be made clear people don't have to worry about something like the Spanish Flu ever happening again. We wouldn't want to go around scaring people needlessly now, do we?"

Dr. Masterson suppressed a sigh, then continued. "Any infectious disease is something we should all be afraid of. The flu shots you mention are effective only against a specific strain of the virus. To make a vaccine effective you must have a sample of the virus to target the immunization shots. But flu viruses are notorious for shifting or mutating very rapidly. In effect, this makes the job of developing a vaccine akin to shooting at a moving target. If the virus mutates or shifts even slightly, that particular drug will be as ineffective as distilled water."

The man snorted. "Well what about antibiotics? That should take care of those pesky little bugs."

Dr. Masterson waited until the few muted chuckles had died out. "No antibiotic is effective against a virus, that's a common misconception. When, not if, another shifting antigen virus such at the one that caused the 1918 pandemic reappears, given the increased population and the rapidity with which people can travel, many scenarios suggest a possibility of over two hundred million to five hundred million deaths will occur worldwide. The only defense we will have against this happening is preparation. And that will require a sample of the virus to use to focus the vaccine."

Another man seated at the rear of the room commented. "I'm sure the government has had a vaccine against that Spanish Flu for years now."

"No," Dr. Masterson said simply. "They don't. No one does. All viruses are living organisms that can exist only within specific parameters and only for a limited length of time. The Spanish Flu virus is long gone. To add to the problem, the 1918 flu was almost certainly a very rapidly shifting antigen. No one knows where it came from, or why it went away. I suspect it mutated itself out of existence. The best we can hope for is to catch another pandemic at its outset and rapidly develop a vaccine. The 1918 pandemic was only an example of the terrible nature of a shifting antigen virus. The next one could be far worse. Remember, all viruses are a product of evolution, not logic. And it is a fact that all life forms adapt to what exists."

Laura glanced at the wall clock. Her time was up. She began folding her notes. "Thank you folks, for asking me to speak. For some odd reason I seldom get invited back. But for those of you who are sincerely concerned for their safety, I recommend getting a pneumonia shot. It is good for five to eight years and flu-related pneumonia accounts for a great many fatalities."

She was going to add another thank-you but the crowd was already foiling out. Dr. Masterson began tucking her notes into her briefcase when the man from the bach of the room, who had asked about the government having developed a vaccine, walked over to her.

"My name is Delvaney, Dr. Masterson." The man's voice had the ring of authority. He was neatly and expensively dressed, with chestnut hair. He held out a card, not offering to shake hands. "Michael Delvaney of the firm of Delvaney, Morse, and Goldman. I would ask that you take my card and give me a call. I have a client who wishes me to propose a business matter to you. I believe you will find it extremely interesting."

"I already have a full-time job," Laura answered, taking the card and placing it into her briefcase. "And in any case, I don't have any interest in being an expert witness in a lawsuit."

Delvaney's deadpan expression didn't change, the trademark of an experienced trial lawyer. "The proposal has nothing to do with any litigation in progress or pending. This is not the appropriate time nor place to discuss the matter. I am aware that you are presently assistant director of research for Roth Pharmaceuticals here in their Houston cosmetics facility. I also know you enjoy fine Italian food. How about allowing me and one of my associates to take you to dinner at your earliest convenience? We keep a table reserved at the Tuscan Villa every night for the purpose of entertaining clients."

Laura Masterson tilted her head with a slight smile. Obviously the lawyer represented some rival firm who had checked her out rather thoroughly. She decided it might be interesting to play along even through she had no plans to change employers. The Tuscan Villa was one of the most expensive restaurants in Houston. It would be an excellent opportunity to see if the cuisine there warranted the constant rave reviews along with the exorbitant prices they charged.

"You have piqued my curiosity, Mr. Delvaney. I believe I can safely assume your client isn't going to want to hire me to do a series of luncheon speeches on the Spanish Flu. You have seen firsthand how well they go over."

The lawyer's face could have been chiseled from granite. "I assure you, my client's offer will be much more lucrative and interesting. I assume you agree to the meeting?"

"I do. Why not this evening? I can meet you and your associate there at the restaurant say, eight o'clock?"

Delvaney replied, "That will be most acceptable. My client will be pleased. If you prefer not to drive I can have our limousine pick you up at your condominium at seven-thirty."

"I would like that," Laura said. "The address is—"

"I know where you live, doctor." Her eyes widened but soon realized that her address was listed right along with her name in the phone book. "The driver will pick you up at your front door precisely at seven-thirty. Lin is from Taiwan and speaks no English, but I assure you that he is a very competent chauffeur."

"I'm sure he is." Dr. Laura Masterson finished clasping her briefcase closed. When she looked up, the chestnut-haired lawyer was gone.

CHAPTER TWO

The sleek, imposing Mercedes Benz limousine drew attention even in the affluent Pearl Meadows area of Houston where Laura leased a two-bedroom condominium. More than a few faces appeared behind windows to watch as the gleaming black luxury coach pulled to a stop. A thin Asian man dressed in a navy blue suit and wearing a matching chauffeur's cap sprang smartly from the driver's seat to escort her from her doorway to the limousine. He bowed as he opened the passenger entryway, then wordlessly shut the door that closed with the heavy sound of a bank vault.

This car has been armor plated, She thought. *I didn't realize lawyers were that much of a target even here in Texas.*

Michael Delvaney had informed her the driver spoke no English. It wouldn't have mattered; a thick shield of glass like those found at drive-up teller windows kept any conversation with the chauffeur out of the question. Laura noticed an iced bucket of wine on the bar that was unfolded from the opposite seat. The bottle was uncorked. A note was attached which read:

Please enjoy your ride. I believe you will find the wine to be acceptable.

Laura Masterson was no connoisseur of fine wines, but quickly decided a 1979, bottle of Mouton Rothschild, was worth a try. She poured a small amount into a chilled glass and took a sip. With a smile she filled the glass with what was the best wine she had ever tasted. The she eased back into the soft leather seat and enjoyed her drink while the limousine knifed through the traffic beneath a twinkling canopy of stars and city lights.

The Tuscan Villa was near the Southwyck Golf Course, off of the Nolan Ryan Expressway. Not a long drive from her condominium. The traffic thinned in the affluent area and Laura barely had time to

9

finish her wine before the driver pulled the limousine to a stop in the covered valet parking space at the front entrance. It was an impressive building constructed of white and red marble.

A white-shirted young man wearing a red bowtie scurried to open the door for her.

"Good evening. You must be Dr. Masterson," the fawning lad said, standing aside while offering her a hand. "I was told to expect your arrival. Mr. Delvaney and his secretary are waiting for you inside. Please do not hesitate to ask if there is anything we here at the Tuscan Villa can do to make your visit a more pleasant one."

"Thank you," Laura said, then followed the man past throngs of occupied tables to a back room where a closed door swung open to allow her to enter. Her escort motioned her inside, then stepped away to melt into the shadows of a row of fake palm trees.

"I wish to thank you again Dr. Masterson for agreeing to join us for dinner," Michael Delvaney's silvery voice chimed from behind the sole large table in the room. "I trust the wine was acceptable."

"It was quite excellent, thank you. I can't say I've ever had better."

"Then I will have the wine steward bring us another bottle," He smiled. "They keep a few cases in reserve for us."

Laura Masterson's eyes began to adjust to the shadowy private room. Paintings of what were presumably Italian landscapes graced the marble walls amongst a gathering of either flowering or vining plants. Then she made out the form of a thin, pinched-faced, gray-haired woman sitting at the far end of the table, in front of what, surprisingly enough, appeared to be a stenotype machine.

"Please take the seat across the table from me," Delvaney's voice chimed. "It will make our conversations easier if we face each other."

Dr. Masterson did as the lawyer asked, sinking into the plush leather chair. Immediately a waiter placed a glass of water with a slice of lemon and a finger bowl in front of her. Delvany ordered the wine, then the man slipped silently away. Laura could not help but take another furtive look toward the lady at the end of the table. There was no doubt from Laura's few court appearances as an expert witness that the hatchet-faced woman who had yet to move a muscle *did* sit in front of a stenotype.

Delvaney noticed Laura's interest and spoke. "I asked Candace Eaton, my private secretary, to join us this evening. Miss Eaton will transcribe our conversations along with any agreements we may hopefully make to permanent record. I have found that keeping a precise written account of all verbal proposals, accepted or rejected, can be most useful at a later date should either party have, let's say, *difficulty* remembering what was said."

The lawyer's conversation was accompanied by the clacking of stenotype keys.

Laura began to grow increasingly uncomfortable. "I simply agreed to join you for dinner to hear what it is some client of yours wants from me. I really don't understand the necessity of having a legal secretary present."

More metallic clicks further unnerved her.

"Tut-tut my dear, and please relax. I assure you that your sole obligation is to enjoy a delicious meal along with a limousine ride back to your lovely condominium. Should you not wish to take advantage of the lucrative offer my client has authorized me to make you on his behalf, I promise that I will cease to have any contact with you, nor bother you in any manner in the future."

"What do you mean, 'lucrative offer?'" Laura had decided the rhythmic metallic clicking was akin to rain splattering on a window and made up her mind to ignore it. As long as she remembered to measure her words like a dangerous chemical there would be no harm in listening to what some headhunter attorney had to say. "I have an excellent job."

"Ah, yes you do my dear," Delvaney's voice blended with the stenotope clicks. "Two hundred twelve thousand per annum, with not inconsiderable benefits. But as the old saying goes, 'There's no hope for the satisfied person.' I believe the quote used to have a definitely more masculine slant, but these days a more equitable approach is warranted."

"You know exactly what my salary is." Laura Masterson was aghast and growing increasingly irritated. "What did you do, hire a detective to check me out?"

"Privacy is a fiction, my dear. The Internet has seen to that. And yes, a very reputable detective firm *did* check you out. Once again I assure you that every bit of this information will remain private and confidential. My client is simply doing due diligence to check out a potential highly placed employee, nothing more. Their methods are no different than Roth Pharmaceuticals used before they hired you straight out of Princeton, where you received your doctorate in molecular biology, which so nicely complements your Doctor of Medicine Degree from Johns Hopkins. Also, if I recall correctly, your degree from Princeton was Magma Cum Laude. Very nice. These are quite wonderful accomplishments for a young lady of a mere thirty-eight years of age."

Dr. Laura Masterson fixed the lawyer in a steely gaze. "Should I fax you copies of my bank accounts along with any old love letters I keep in my safe?"

"Why, the steward has arrived with our wine," Delvaney's gray eyes sparkled liked flint in the lights from a candelabra that had been brought in and placed in the center of the table along with the wine and glasses. "Let us enjoy our repast. We should delay any more discussion of business for later, possibly over a scoop of vanilla ice cream with a sampling of Frangelico. I can honestly recommend anything on our private menu. Please order whatever your heart desires."

Laura Masterson acknowledged him with a nod. While the obsequious waiter and Michael Delvaney went through the ritual of tasting, she glanced at the short menu, which had no prices. The rack of lamb or the lobster: there was no good reason not to order as the lawyer had suggested before telling him she was actually content with her boring job. Certainly whoever the mysterious, unnamed client Delvaney represented would simply offer a somewhat better salary in an equally boring job. Having already avoided to decline any change in employers, she actually began looking forward to dinner.

CHAPTER THREE

"Five hundred thousand dollars a year!" Laura nearly spilled her small glass of hazelnut liqueur. She was shocked and amazed at the unexpected and unbelievable figure.

"Yes, my dear," Michael Delvaney's almost musical voice chimed in concert with metallic clicks from the stenotype. "The Hammond Foundation, who asked that I not disclose their identity until this time, is quite generous with those favored to be in their employment. I am also empowered to offer a five-year contract at that figure, along with all benefits you now receive with the addition of four weeks vacation time and complimentary use of the company jet to visit any of their numerous resort facilities worldwide."

"I must say, I've never heard of the Hammond Foundation."

"Few have, doctor." Delvaney paused to finish his dish of ice cream before it melted. "They are a group that prefers to remain anonymous, yet many branches of the arts and sciences reap tremendous benefits from the Foundation. Often without disclosure. The organization's mission, which was established by Sir Wilfred Hammond, who made a fortune in African diamonds, is one of pure research and discovery. It is also a totally altruistic organization. Even I have no estimate of their resources, but the Hammond Foundation's wealth exceeds that of many countries, including some of the more affluent ones."

Laura took a moment to consider her words. The lawyer's unexpected offer had shaken her. "I've worked for the cosmetics division of Roth Pharmaceuticals since I finished school. I can't imagine being hired for such a huge salary to make wrinkles disappear or diminish body odor."

Michael Delvaney gave the first hint of a chuckle she had heard from him. "No my dear. Cosmetics has nothing to do with this generous offer. What first attracted their interest was an excellent article you had published in the *New England Journal of Medicine* on the Spanish Flu Epidemic of 1918. That sparked a perusal of all of your writings. The culmination of their interests in your research is why we're having this meeting."

Laura studied her empty liqueur glass. "I'm surprised. I thought only my parents or critics ever read any of those articles."

The deadpan expression that met her gaze when she glanced up confirmed her opinion that the lawyer had been born without a sense of humor.

"The research doctors at the Hammond Foundation believe you would be a perfect addition to their staff, based on your paper on the possibility of cloning long dead viruses from remnants of genetic material to be extremely interesting and quite valid." He signaled a waiter to refill Laura liqueur glass. "I am afraid I've exhausted my medical vocabulary. My studies have been limited to the law."

"Then the Hammond Foundation must believe, as I do, Mr. Delvaney, that's its only a matter of time that another flu pandemic may occur. If we are successful in obtaining a sample of genetic material from a shifting antigen virus such as the 1918 flu, then are able to clone a living sample, we would stand an excellent chance to engineer a vaccine and have it in reserve before the disease ever appears."

"Yes, those are basically the same comments they made to me. Our scientists believe the lives that could potentially be saved are in the hundreds of millions of souls. This makes the hiring of someone as capable as you, my dear, an urgent mission. Hence the lucrative offer. I am told that time is of the essence if we are to prevent a worldwide tragedy."

"Unfortunately, Mr. Delvaney, that is the cold fact of the matter. Considering the speed with which people move about, the disease could envelope the globe in a day or two. And the average time to develop a vaccine, once the disease is identified, is approximately six months."

"That was why I was so gratified when you agreed to such a quick meeting. Should you decline the tender—excuse me, I mean not accept the offer—the Hammond Foundation must immediately proceed to look for another research person to spearhead their projects."

Laura Masterson watched as the waiter refilled her glass then she began turning it slowly on the table. "The Foundation has a research project on the Spanish Flu in progress?"

"I know little of the details. But I should add that the Foundation has been studying the disease for some time. This much I do know. There is a small town in northeastern New Mexico with the odd name of Paradox. It is basically a ghost town that flourished only because of some coal mines that have been long since closed. The population there had one of the largest mortality rates during the 1918 pandemic; nearly one out of every four succumbed to the flu, I believe." The lawyer took a long drink of water and continued. "Six years ago, I acted as the agent when the Hammond Foundation surreptitiously purchased the town, along with all buildings and the surrounding ten thousand acres. All of the homes and businesses built there are on ground leased from the owning company. Now the leases have expired and the remaining residents are on a grace period to remove themselves and their belongings. The Foundation has deeded all of the land over to the federal government, which is going to build a dam for irrigation and recreation that will place the entire town"–he hesitated–"along with the cemetery under water."

Dr. Masterson's face lit up with understanding. "The bodies will have to be moved."

"Yes, and with no messy legal problems. The project can begin just as soon as we have a research doctor to oversee the matter."

"There *must* be some satisfactory genetic samples available for recovery. There have even been samples obtained from Egyptian mummies. This would be an exciting, but dangerous, undertaking." Laura Masterson hesitated. "We'll need a complete laboratory along with the most modern containment and isolation facilities. Actual cloning of such a potentially deadly virus must be performed under the most careful and stringent laboratory conditions. We cannot risk causing an outbreak while trying to prevent one."

"I believe everything you will require is now in Albuquerque. I am assured it is all state-of-the-art equipment. Since I acted as the purchasing agent I *do* know the cost was nearly twenty million dollars. Should you require anything else, all you need do is phone my office. I am fully authorized to act on behalf of the Hammond Foundation in all aspects of this matter."

"I really don't know what to say," Laura gave a sigh. "I will need to give notice to Roth Pharmaceuticals and settle my condo lease."

"Ah my dear," the lawyer's monotone now seemed to be in perfect harmony with the clicking of keys. "Such details are trivial in view of the vast number of human lives at stake. I shall be all too happy to have one of my staff handle such mundane matters. The Hammond Foundation and I have an excellent relationship with the management of Roth Pharmaceuticals. I assure you they will be most happy to release you from your position there accompanied by a glowing letter of recommendation, or give a leave of absence. A competent moving company shall see to your belongings, should you agree to accept the offer."

"I really am in awe of how all this came to be, but in view of what you have presented me this evening, I cannot refuse. Yes, I accept the position with the Hammond Foundation."

"Now, my dear, I hope you understand the importance of making a record of our conversations. Your new title, by the way, is director of research. I am certain you are aware that all of your activities in Paradox, New Mexico, must remain secret. We can't go causing any undue panic, can we? The word has already been put out that certain, ah, *precautions* will be taken during the exhumation of the corpses to prevent any possibility, no matter how remote, of chancing the release of any germs."

"I agree fully, Mr. Delvaney. We'll do our job quietly and quickly. I only hope we are successful in obtaining a genetic sample of the Spanish Flu."

Delvaney held up his glass in a toast. "Here's to success, Dr. Masterson, and all of the delightful trappings that come with it."

After Dr. Masterson left and the secretary had gone home, Michael Delvaney opened his cell phone. He punched in an international number that was routed through enough firewalls and countries to be untraceable.

When the party answered the phone, all the gravelly voice said was, "Ten."

The lawyer responded, "Ten times ten."

"That makes one hundred," the voice on the cell phone said. The lawyer then hit the end button.

Immensely satisfied with himself, Michael Delvaney ordered a double Crown Royal to sip while he awaited for Lin to return with the limousine. Clients like the one he represented were the type he had always dreamed of having. It was sweet when one's dreams came true.

The lawyer allowed an honest smile to cross his face as he sat alone, drinking expensive whiskey, and dreaming of a lot more money yet to come his way.

CHAPTER FOUR

Rio de Janeiro, Brazil

Philip Quinton Roth, III was awakened by the reflection of a newborn sun off the huge mirror on the ceiling above his circular bed. He blinked sleep from his pale blue eyes and studied the naked forms of the identical Chinese twins that lay on each side of him.

They were exquisite, lovely as dolls at the tender age of seventeen. He had named the twins Yin and Yin Again, which he thought clever. He owned them. He could call them any damn thing he pleased. Once he tired of having them in his bed, which would happen soon, he maintained a contact in Bangkok, Thailand, who would retrieve the young ladies and bring in whatever replacements he desired.

Being able to trade luscious young girls with the same impunity as a person leases a car or airplane was but one of the many benefits of being chief executive officer for life of an international firm as wealthy as Roth Pharmaceuticals.

Philip Roth's father had had the same passions as his son. This was one of the reasons he had moved the corporate headquarters from Europe to Rio de Janeiro, Brazil. He built the Roth mansion in the same compound high on top of a mountain overlooking Guanabara Bay, with a stunning view of the crystal blue waters of the South Atlantic Ocean.

It was both smart and delightful being headquartered in such an open-minded country as Brazil, where the officials were easily bribed to turn a deaf ear or blind eye to nearly all of the firm's activities. Not having an extradition treaty with any other country was another wonderful attribute.

Roth slid the back of his hand across a firm breast, which elicited a giggle. He smiled, then scooted his lean fifty-nine-year-old frame over the edge of the bed and headed for the bathroom. He showered, shaved, then dressed in an expensive white silk suit and made the short walk to his expansive office in the headquarters building.

Every hundred feet or so, a stern-faced young man cradling a submachine gun stood in the shadows of trees or buildings. It was quite expensive to have to pay for such precautions, but totally necessary. Things often went awry. The anti-allergy medication Roth had provided an African country unfortunately had an unforeseen side effect of causing heart failure. This oversight had killed a dictator's young daughter, which had peeved him enough to send a squad of soldiers to Brazil to exact revenge. The plot of course, failed. But the list of enemies went on and on. Having an army of his own was simply the cost of doing business in this day and age.

"Good morning, sir," his attractive and efficient private secretary, Pilar Zamora, greeted him with customary cheerfulness. "*Señor* Buno is in your office awaiting your arrival." She checked a notepad. "And your wife left a message that she will remain in New York City for another week. She is having little Philip's teeth straightened and whitened."

"Very good," the CEO said as he headed for his massive office. Having Jane extend her trip was good news, and would give him an opportunity to stay gone all night without the bother of making excuses. A wife was necessary only to produce a lineage. The rest of the time they were nothing but a bother. At least he had a strong and healthy son who had just turned twelve. Soon the lad would be old enough to begin grooming in the art of running an international business with an annual gross income of nearly a trillion dollars. As he opened the door, Roth mused that if things went as planned, the gross figure would be many times higher than that very shortly.

The CEO brushed past the somber Buno Eberhard to take his seat behind the Italian marble desk he was so proud of. His chief of secret operations could wait until he had sipped some of the steaming coffee that awaited his arrival. Eberhard had no feelings anyway, which was one of his biggest attributes—aside from being loyal as a pet dog.

Buno's father had been a Nazi SS officer in charge of a concentration camp in Germany. As the war drew to a close, the Nazi was so anxious to immigrate to Brazil that he had not taken the time to put an "R" in his son's name. No matter, Buno had learned well from his efficient father who had managed security for Roth Pharmaceuticals for twenty years—before stupidly trusting an opponent, and taking a bullet to the head as his reward.

Philip Roth studied the sixty-two-year-old Buno through white tendrils of steam rising from his china cup. The blonde man looked overweight, but what appeared to be bulk was in actuality iron muscle covered with thick body armor, which he wore everywhere. It was rumored Buno carried an even dozen weapons on his person—knives and firearms, not including the hypodermic syringes built into the heel of each boot that extended to inject lethal cobra venom with a swift kick backwards. Buno Eberhard was determined not to wind up like his father.

"Tell me, Buno," Philip Roth said after some time. "Is there any word from the United States?"

"There is," Buno's voice came as a low growl.

"Then tell me what our man there said, please." Sometimes Eberhard could be downright exasperating.

"We have a ten times ten, sir."

Roth's expression brightened. "Excellent news. I will have Pilar wire the necessary funds to Houston immediately. I want this project to proceed without delay."

Buno dug in his left ear with a pencil. "The cost of that project is now up to thirty-five million dollars, sir."

Roth suppressed a snort. Small minds never were able to grasp the fact that in business, money was like seed to a farmer; it must be broadcast on fertile ground then carefully cultivated to reap a harvest. This particular crop could very easily, if handled correctly, reap the largest profits in corporate history. *Any* corporation's history.

The CEO noticed Buno had replaced the pencil with a little finger, which he had inserted into his ear all the way to the knuckle. He shot his security officer a scowl.

"Got a bug in my ear."

Roth decided to avoid the issue. "The United States project is now the first priority you have. I plan to authorize the expenditure of unlimited funds for its execution."

Buno grinned on hearing the word "execution." He removed the finger from his ear. "Then this is now a code-one operation?"

Roth nodded approval to the now-beaming Buno. A code-one operation meant he could use any means to kill anyone who stood in their way.

"I guess you'll want me to go there immediately?" Buno asked.

"Yes, but we first have to make proper arrangements. You will need to take the small company jet to Mexico. From there we'll arrange for you to enter the United States across the Mexican border at Del Rio, Texas. There are quite a number of items I want you to have that will need to be brought into America most surreptitiously." The CEO noticed Buno's blank stare. "We'll have to sneak all of your guns and such across the Mexican border."

"Yeah, boss. We can do that."

"I am personally heading up this project. You will report directly to me by secure cell phone only." Roth gave Buno a cold glare. "Is that understood?"

"Yeah, boss."

"Another thing: You will be in United States of America. They frown on killing people there and they have an efficient police force. If, and *only* if, I order someone removed will you do so and then I expect the utmost care be used to avoid detection."

"You mean for me to hide the bodies good."

"Yes, Buno, I'm certain you'll take care of the matter at the time in a satisfactory manner," Roth said cheerfully, knowing that a code punched into Buno's cellular phone from Rio would cause it to explode with enough of a blast to eliminate the security guard and anyone within fifty feet of him. Good planning kept even faithful employees from becoming a bother.

"Where is it you want me to go again?"

"We've been over this before, Buno. I expect you to go where directed, observe, and check in with me often, but *do nothing*, I repeat, do nothing without a direct order from me personally."

"Yeah boss, you can always count on me."

Roth eyed Buno with the coldness of a snake. "Oh, I *do* count on you. Now remember what I say this time. You will be going to the very small town of Paradox, New Mexico. Get packed. I have other matters to attend to."

THE PARADOX SYNDROME

The CEO watched as his operative left his office picking at his ear. When the door closed, he opened a desk drawer that was never left unlocked and extracted a telephone. The most potentially profitable operation in the history of pharmaceuticals was now underway.

CHAPTER FIVE

The next morning Dr. Laura Masterson was backing her candy apple red BMW convertible out of the garage when a moving van pulled up behind her, blocking her exit. A pair of muscular, smiling African American men jumped out. One held a clipboard, which both studied.

Laura climbed out to see what the problem was. Most likely the movers had gotten a wrong address.

The man holding the clipboard spoke first, "Mornin' ma'am," he said politely. "But is this the home of Doc," he checked the paperwork once again, "Masterson, a Dr. Laura Masterson?"

"That would be me," she replied, with a glimmer of understanding. "Might I ask if you're working for a lawyer by the name of Michael Delvaney by chance?"

"Yes, ma'am. That's the fellow who hired us to box up everything except what you tell us not to and put it into climate-controlled storage," the clipboard man said. "There's a note here that he'd not only paid a hefty deposit, but that we were to wait right here until you showed up no matter how long it takes."

"I'm not ready for *anything* to be moved," Laura said, her ire rising. *This is getting downright presumptuous of Michael Delvaney, even if he is paying me five hundred thousand dollars a year.* Thinking of her new salary had a calming effect. "There are matters to be taken care of first."

"That's mighty fine with us ma'am," the man with the clipboard said with a glance at his watch. "We're on the clock for two hundred dollars an hour. Billy and I got a cooler with sandwiches and lots of bottled water and sodas. It's a lot more comfortable to sit in the shade an' relax than move stuff anyhow. I'll pull the van outta your way so you can get on with your day." He grinned. "And you have a good day, doctor. We have no hurries on our part. Been working union too long to get into a dither over much of anything."

Laura went to get into her car when the cell phone in her purse rang. She fished it out to notice the caller ID showed only "private call." The way the morning was starting off, telling a telemarketer to move to a hotter climate didn't seem out of line.

"Good morning, Dr. Masterson," Delvaney's voice was unmistakable. "I hate to bother you at this hour, but there is a situation I need to talk over with you. Are you alone and at a place where we can safely visit?"

"I'm in my driveway with some movers. Give me a moment to go back inside."

"Of course. my dear, I am certain it will be much more comfortable in your home. Even though it's only early in the month of April, the heat and sultry humidity becomes oppressive quite early in the day, doesn't it? I'll hold."

Laura ducked under a low palm frond to head straight for her front door. She definitely wanted to know what the lawyer had in mind this time. The lock clicked open after she punched in the security code. A keyless lock was reassuring for anyone living in a large city. Michael Delvaney was correct about the air conditioning feeling good. After a breath to clear her mind she held the cell phone to her ear.

"We can talk now, sir," Laura said.

"I will make this as brief as possible. First off, I wish to apologize for scheduling the movers without your knowledge, but I hope you will understand shortly.

"The headquarters of the Hammond Foundation are in another time zone that is several hours earlier than ours. I am fortunate enough to require very little sleep. Knowing this is not the case for most people, I sometimes take the liberty of speeding things up at an early hour without disturbing important people such as yourself."

"I don't know about the important part, but I'm wide awake. I was really expecting at least a couple of weeks of transition time here."

"I know. The Hammond people want me to tell you just how glad they are that you have accepted their offer. Also our timing may be, if anything, now much more crucial than anyone expected."

Laura felt a twang of anxiety. "What do you mean?"

The lawyer's voice grew tight with tension, "Last night we discussed how a strain of flu similar to the 1918 pandemic might appear?"

"Yes."

"In one of your articles you wrote that the Spanish Flu possibly had its etiology in swine, and the first outbreak occurred in Haskell County, Kansas. From there it spread worldwide with the movement of Army troops being deployed in World War I."

Dr. Masterson swallowed hard. "There's been an outbreak."

"So far it has been limited to a pig farm south of Ciudad Acuna, Mexico, not too far from Del Rio, Texas. There are six dead, all young men in their twenties. The outbreak is being kept quiet. The Mexican government has a containment in progress. Even the Centers for Disease Control in Atlanta are being kept out of the loop to stop a panic."

Laura took a seat at her dining room table, her knees weak. "I have postulated that the etiology of new viruses will come from similar climates and areas as previous outbreaks. I don't need a map to know that the longitude of Del Rio and Sublette, Kansas, are very close to the same. The fact that the 1918 strain might have been swine-caused is too scary to ignore."

"The Hammond people believe the same thing."

"What I can't understand is the CDC being left out of the loop. Their technology is cutting edge, their people are the best."

"And every reporter in the country knows this, too. Whenever the CDC is called out to investigate anything, the news media often beat them to the scene. Besides, it may turn out to be a localized, contained event. What we need to focus on is developing a vaccine for a shifting antigen virus. If this outbreak actually is the Spanish Flu, or a similar strain, the Paradox research you will be doing takes on a very urgent tone."

Laura wondered how much the lawyer really new about viruses and how much he was parroting. No matter, the scenario of another outbreak like the one that had struck in 1918 was chilling. She now understood the lawyer's actions.

"How do we proceed?" Dr. Masterson asked.

"Pack two suitcases with only what you will need for a couple of days. I'll have Lin drive you to Hobby Airport where a jet will be waiting. Then you'll fly to Amarillo, Texas, which is closer to Paradox than Albuquerque. When you arrive in Amarillo you'll be met with ground transportation. I'm afraid you may have to stay in a nearby motel until the facilities are in place in Paradox."

"Of course. Time is of the essence if there actually is an outbreak. What about my job at Roth Pharmaceuticals? And I have obligations."

"My office has already spoken with Dr. Colson, your supervisor. Roth Pharmaceuticals has placed you on indefinite leave. We will handle all of the mundane matters. Dr. Masterson, what we need, no, what *the world* needs, is for you to do what must be done. Go to Paradox, find a sample of genetic material, clone it, then we can engineer a vaccine."

"I'll do my best."

"Godspeed," the lawyer said then the connection clicked off.

Laura composed her thoughts. After taking a moment to pour a cup of coffee from the cooling pot she went outside to where the two moving men were resting in the shade.

"Let's get to it," she said firmly.

CHAPTER SIX

Laura Masterson sipped a cup of tepid coffee while in her living room the movers began packing boxes and wrapping furniture in thick padded quilts. Things were progressing too fast, much too fast for comfort. Her long years of training as a researcher had taught her to be questioning, methodical, to check and recheck everything.

She went to her computer and logged on the Internet. The Hammond Foundation was new to her. The fact that such a wealthy, influential group could exist without her ever having heard of it before caused a pinprick of concern.

A few minutes of websurfing put that worry aside. Just as Michael Delvaney had said, it was a very wealthy and very seclusive philanthropic organization that had been around for decades. There were rumors that the Hammond Foundation was covertly responsible for easing the famine in Ethiopia, the plight of the Aborigines in the Australian outback. The list went on endlessly. All speculation.

A glance to the back cover of any Houston phone book showed Michael Delvaney's granite face advertising the law firm he headed.

You're being too careful here girl, she thought. *For years, you've wanted to do pure medical research on viruses. The bus carrying your dream has pulled into the station and you hold a ticket. Climb on board and get with it.*

Feeling better now, Laura set about sorting what to pack in her suitcases and what to leave for the movers. From the bathroom she selected a few personal items; from the closet Laura packed only the clothes she thought appropriate to her destination. Blue jeans and blouses, along with a pair of hiking boots seemed suited for how she envisioned New Mexico would be. Should any occasion arise requiring a dress, she would have to go shopping for one. Having modest expense account was something she needed to bring to the lawyer's attention. Private jets, expensive restaurants, and moving companies seemed to present no difficulties. A modest amount of money for clothes shouldn't raise an eyebrow.

She added her new laptop, which had an extensive virology and medical reference library installed that would almost certainly not be available in Paradox.

The lawyer's call about the six pig farm workers dying in Mexico flashed into her mind. The computer was still connected to the Internet and a quick search of news from the area of Ciudad Acuna seemed in order. A story with that many fatalities would be nearly impossible to suppress. At least Spanish was a language she had a grasp of. Anyone living in Texas most of their life garnered at least a working knowledge. Laura was more skilled at reading Spanish than speaking it; the "Rs" never rolling off her tongue in the right direction to be understood.

Again, a few clicks did the trick. A small article read: *Lightning strike kills six workers at hog farm near San Carlos, a farming community fifteen miles south of the border town of Ciudad Acuna.*

Dr. Masterson felt reassured that the Hammond Foundation had actually managed to cover up a potentially catastrophic outbreak of what could have been a deadly flu strain. It may not have been a wildly mutating one such as the 1918 variation but only sophisticated laboratory tests could determine that. The story of a lightning strike almost certainly meant the bodies had been burned, a crude but effective method of sterilizing an area. She hoped the infected hogs had also been slaughtered and burned. Dealing with a potentially emerging shifting antigen flu was not handled with kid gloves.

She turned off the desktop computer to once more focus on the task of packing. A quick phone call to her mother who had retired to an oceanside condo in Port Aransas, Texas, would take care of most of her personal matters. Her sole romantic relationship over the past few years had been an on-again, off-again tryst with Andrew Burns, a microbiologist at the Roth Pharmaceuticals laboratory. This relationship now resided permanently in the off mode.

Every time Laura thought of her lovely mother, a burning lump formed in her throat. Her father, Frank Masterson, had been more than ten years, killed when he went to a local convenience store to pick up some raisins for a cake her mother was baking and interrupted a robbery in progress. He hadn't lived to see her graduate from medical school, let alone receive a Ph.D. in molecular biology. This saddened her beyond measure as her father had taken out a second mortgage on their home to pay the tuition.

Laura had regarded her beloved father's senseless and tragic death at the hands of hoodlums as a message to be learned. There were beasts out there, mindless, vicious predators who responded to and respected only brute force.

She thumbed the butt of her Glock 9mm and dropped the clip. Carefully, she placed the pistol and a box of hollow point shells in a leather case along with its holster, and stowed both in the bottom of her suitcase.

Laura Masterson had been one of the first to obtain a concealed firearm permit after they were legalized in the state of Texas back in 1995 when then Governor George W. Bush had made it legal to carry a loaded firearm. If it ever became necessary, she knew she could use the efficient Glock to eradicate beasts with as little emotion or hesitation as she used to sterilize a container of germs.

She forced the bitter memories of her father's senseless murder into a far corner of her mind to focus on the present. Events were unfolding far too fast not to check and recheck every move. Laura mused that none of this would be happening if she hadn't written her Ph.D. dissertation on shifting antigen viruses, using the Spanish Flu pandemic as a model.

But all of that was now history. Here in the present day she was being called upon to use all of her many years of scientific training and research to defeat a very real and very frightening foe. One that could easily kill millions of people.

Laura glanced at the open suitcase containing her pistol. *That damn flu virus is a beast just like the ones who shot my dad. It'll take a special bullet to kill it. But I'm just the little lady who's up to kicking some microscopic ass.* She smiled at the thought.

The sound of a horn brought Dr. Masterson outside. Lin, the chauffeur from last night, had arrived driving the Mercedes Benz limousine. A young man casually dressed in a sport shirt exited the passenger compartment and stepped to face her.

"Dr. Masterson?" the man asked.

"Yes."

"Mr. Delvaney asked me to drive your car to a secure storage garage."

Laura nodded and fished the keys from her purse. "I have two suitcases in the house...." Before she had finished speaking Lin was already heading inside the condo, causing her to wonder both how the cat-like man had managed to get out of the limo without her noticing, and just how much English he really did understand.

She removed the ignition key from the ring and handed it to the young man. Past experiences with valets caused her to add. "I'm making note of the mileage and the fuel tank is full."

"Don't worry, Doctor," he replied grasping the key. "I drive a Porsche myself. I bought it new when I passed the bar two years ago."

Laura nodded meekly then quickly scurried inside, feeling chagrined. The kid looked barely old enough to own a razor, let alone be an attorney. This was one of the reasons she had chosen laboratory research over being a practicing physician—her people skills were not always the best.

Lin stood straight and stoic in the living room awaiting her entrance. When Laura gave a motion to the open bedroom door, the chauffeur instantly went inside, retrieved the suitcases, and carried them to the limousine. The little man's actions made no more sound than a passing cloud.

Laura waited until she heard the distinct exhaust tone of her departing BMW before grabbing up her purse. She was too embarrassed to want to see the young lawyer again any time soon. A quick look around showed that the moving men were being careful with her belongings.

There was no reason to tarry. She headed outside to the waiting limousine. A long overdue High Noon for a deadly virus was coming to Paradox, New Mexico. The Terminator couldn't afford to be late.

CHAPTER SEVEN

The ever-silent Lin drove slowly through a security gate at Houston Hobby airport and nodded to a hulking guard who obviously hadn't missed a meal or calorie since Bill Clinton was president. The chauffer drove onto the tarmac and pulled alongside a small, sleek two-engine jet that sat with the door open, engines whining.

A smiling uniformed man wearing sunglasses hopped down the steps of the jet and came over to the limousine at the same instant Lin swung open the passenger door.

"I'm Captain Adam Nelson, Dr. Masterson. I'll be flying you to Amarillo this fine morning." The pilot wore the permanent grin of a car salesman. "The weather's good so we shouldn't experience any turbulence."

Laura simply nodded and watched the chauffeur hand her suitcases to someone inside the dark interior of the airplane. Then she followed the captain to the set of steps that led to the open door of the idling jet.

"Take care, Doctor," the pilot said as he offered her a hand. "The most dangerous part of flying these days is twisting an ankle getting on or off of the craft."

"I'm fine, thank you," she said. Laura avoided his grasp as she bent low to enter the airplane. All of her adult life she had disliked men who were too ready with their hands.

"Welcome aboard, Doctor," a very pretty blonde woman dressed in a trim gray suit said cheerfully. "Please stay low so you don't bump your head and take whichever seat you prefer. Captain Nelson, Copilot Boggs, and myself will be the only others on board for this flight. My name is Candace, but please call me Candy—everyone does. I will be your private stewardess."

The captain came inside, turned, and after assuring himself the steps had been retracted, closed the door and secured it. He then beamed at Laura Masterson. "The craft is a Hawker 700, Dr. Masterson. There's a headwind we'll have to face that will hold our cruising speed down to approximately four hundred miles per hour. Once we get clearance, I'll have you on the ground in Amarillo in about an hour and a half. In flight we have a Magnastar Flitephone at your disposal, along with sandwiches, video games and, or course, a fully stocked bar. If there is anything you desire, all you need to do is ask Candy. She'll take good care of you."

"Thanks," Laura said rather sharply, hoping to put an end to the conversation.

With a final big-toothed grin the pilot went to the cockpit and closed the door. Mere moments later the engines roared to life. The aircraft made a turn, then began its takeoff roll. Laura guessed that private jets either had priority or possibly access to another runway other than the one used by commercial airliners. In any event, the slim Hawker roared skyward within brief minutes after Laura fastened her seatbelt. This set a record time in her experience with flying.

After a steep and rapid climb into the blue Texas sky, the small jet leveled off to a surprisingly smooth and quiet cruising speed. Laura stared out the square window by her seat, amazed at how much distance had been traveled in such a short time. Already the sprawl of Houston was giving way to green rolling hills and small farms.

"Excuse me, Doctor," Candy said, shaking Laura from her reverie. "But there is a phone call for you. Perhaps you might wish to unfasten your seat belt and take the call on the sofa. I'll be happy to bring you a cup of coffee to cool while you are busy."

"Thank you," Laura unsnapped the belt. "I could use another cup. This morning is turning out to be a long one."

"The Flitephone is in the cubbyhole at the end of the sofa. Just pick up the receiver and speak." Candy started for the galley then turned. "How would you like your coffee?"

"Black and strong will be fine."

"Just like the captain prefers his."

Laura stood, amazed at how much headroom the jet had. She slid into the tan leather sofa and grabbed the telephone.

"Dr. Masterson," she answered.

"I trust your flight is comfortable?" Michael Delvaney's chiming voice needed no introduction.

"It is. The pilot informs me we'll be in Amarillo in about an hour."

"That is why I called. The selection of vehicles available there is simply appalling. Since the roads in the vicinity of Paradox can be rough and unpredictable in bad weather, I wanted you to have a substantial four-wheel drive. The best I could find on such short notice is a Chevrolet Suburban, bright red in color. The rental company shuttle will meet the jet at the terminal."

"No problem, Mr. Delvaney. And Suburbans are nice vehicles, I've driven them many times."

"Thank you for being flexible. What I disliked most about the vehicle was its lack of leather seats. However, we are working under a fast timetable and must make concessions. There is a room reserved for you in Tucumcari at the Broken Arrow Motor Inn. Once the facilities in Paradox are in place, I'll let you know."

"Wouldn't it be better if I stayed in a motel there?"

Michael Delvaney's voice gave a rare chuckle. "My dear, there *is* no motel or much of anything in the way of facilities in Paradox. My understanding is there is a combination bar and restaurant, a general store, a small RV park, and possibly a couple of other small business still open. As I mentioned, the entire town is slated to become inundated. Everyone there has orders to be out within ninety days. After that I believe every building left standing is to be bulldozed out of existence."

"Tucumcari sounds quaint. I'll need to do some shopping there. I wasn't able to fit a lot into two suitcases. I believe you mentioned Paradox isn't too far from there."

"No, only about forty miles. But the last eight of those are over gravel roads that can become quite muddy and slick during and after a storm. The facilities you will need are on their way. I would not expect it to be more than two days at most." Michael Delvaney gave a low cough. "Do not expect to be welcomed. A lot of the people still in Paradox have lived there all of their lives. The Cougar Canyon Development Corporation is the name under which title to the land was taken. It will likely be best if you tell people that you are simply contracting with the company to assist in moving the cemetery."

"I'll take your advice. I assume some of the residents *are* rather upset over being displaced."

The lawyer was slow to reply, obviously carefully measuring his words. "That is stating the facts rather mildly, Doctor. The attitude of the locals in Paradox is bitter. This is why I am asking you to stay in Tucumcari until, uh, arrangements are in place to secure your complete safety."

Laura moved her arm to allow Candy room to place a silver tray containing her coffee on the sofa beside her. "I'm only a physician assuring their safety, Mr. Delvaney. I expect no problems, especially violent ones."

"Of course not. But it always pays to be prepared."

"I hate to bring something like this up, Mr. Delvaney," Laura said. "But I didn't bring a lot of money with me. A modest expense account will be helpful."

"The matter has already been attended to. Ask the stewardess to bring you the envelope that was delivered by courier. I believe there are sufficient funds enclosed to tide you over for a few days."

"Thank you," Laura remembered the lawyer might not know her private cell phone number and mentioned the fact to him.

"Do not use that phone for any reason, Doctor!" Michael Delvaney's voice nearly spat. "I demand that you destroy it. The work you will be doing is both vital and secret. All conversations must utilize a secure line such as the one I am speaking to you over. *Any* cellular phone not properly equipped and protected is open to monitoring by anyone. There will be another phone provided to you."

Laura was taken aback by the lawyer's gruffness, but realized the importance of what he had said. Hackers and spies were everywhere. The Hammond Foundation likely was the target of a fair number of them. "I'll back the Suburban over my cell."

"I am glad you are understanding, Doctor. The work you will be doing is vital. Tell no one anything. We must be cautious not to cause undue panic."

"You can count on me."

"I will. And so will millions of people. Godspeed." The phone clicked off.

Laura returned the Flitephone to its niche then picked up her coffee cup, savoring the chocolate aroma. The blend had certainly not come from any grocery store. A testing sip confirmed her supposition; the coffee was simply delicious.

"The captain reminded me to give you this," Candy said with a voice that sounded more like a purr. She handed Laura a large manila envelope. "A courier brought it only moments before you arrived."

Laura gave a nod and waited until the stewardess had gone aft to the galley before opening the thick envelope. When she did, her eyes widened. A quick count disclosed ten bound stacks, each containing two thousand dollars in twenty-dollar bills.

I think I can grow to like this job. Laura tucked the envelope into her briefcase, leaned back in the comfortable sofa, sipped the delightful coffee, and watched clouds float past the windows as the rugged red rock landscape of the Palo Duro Canyon below signaled that her mission in New Mexico was drawing nearer.

CHAPTER EIGHT

Picking up the Suburban from the rental agency at the airport, Dr. Masterson encountered treatment like she was accustomed to from such businesses. It seemed neither Michael Delvaney's or the Hammond Foundation influence extended to car rental agencies. At least not in Amarillo, Texas, it didn't.

The clerk, who sported red, spiked hair, along with an assortment of hardware in his ears, nose, tongue, and one eyebrow, seemed to be going through the paperwork for the first time. He studied every entry as if he had never seen the form before. And his supervisor seemed to be out to lunch.

Cash would not serve as a deposit, so Laura gave her credit card. Then this byproduct of faulty DNA was unable to push the correct button to make a copy of her driver's license. Thankfully, after many unsuccessful tries, another clerk who appeared relatively normal emerged out from a back room to assist in the stupefying task of completing a car rental agreement.

After spending nearly as much time checking out the four-by-four as it had taken to fly up from Houston, Dr. Masterson pulled the red Suburban onto the approach ramp to Interstate 40, mashed on the accelerator to blend in with what she considered sparse traffic, and headed west for the New Mexico state line, which lay only about eighty miles distant.

Dr. Laura Masterson had been born in Houston, Texas, and educated in the east. Her entire life had been spent in big cities with all of the accompanying hustle and bustle. She had heard and read about the wide-open spaces still left in the west, but had not seen it firsthand, until now.

Only scant miles out of Amarillo, which for some inexplicable reason meant "yellow" in Spanish, the countryside turned into barren flatlands. There were a few fenced fields with cattle that appeared healthy and an occasional ranch house that looked prosperous, but they were all miles apart. The windmills jutting from flat prairie lands, pumping water for livestock, were more plentiful than people.

The few sparse, gnarly trees that spiked the landscape had a similar distinct list to the east from constant winds blowing in that direction. Laura mused that the trees might simply be trying to escape their fate and move to a lush area. She couldn't blame them. The Piney Woods of East Texas, with the accompanying humidity and masses of people, were already beginning to be missed.

A sign proudly announcing she had entered New Mexico, "The Land of Enchantment," was the only way Laura could tell she had left Texas. Certainly the countryside showed no improvement. The Diet Coke she had bought before leaving Amarillo prompted her to make a much-needed stop at the Welcome Center. While there, she picked up and studied a few of the free brochures advertising various tourist attractions. There was the gravesite of Billy the Kid, a ghost town by the unlikely name of Shakespeare, even a brochure touting car parade along old Route 66, which apparently runs straight through the main part of the town of Tucumcari. The excitements that went along with being in New Mexico seemed boundless.

Dr. Masterson stepped from the Welcome Center into what was, to her, a dry breeze. She took a moment to watch a circling of vultures against the brightest blue sky she had ever seen. Most likely whatever had died had chosen to do so after taking one final look around. Then she climbed back into the Suburban to drive the rest of the forty-odd miles to Tucumcari.

"Maybe I'll feel enchanted there," Laura mumbled, shipping the key into the ignition. "One should never lose hope."

To Dr. Masterson's utter surprise, the countryside took on an amazing change for the better after only a few miles of driving. Flat-topped mesas rimmed with red rocks were stunningly gorgeous against the cloud-studded azure sky lining both sides of the interstate, as if they were castles in a fairy tale.

Then the highway turned and began to drop into a canyon. Beautiful green trees she knew to be juniper and piñon jutted from the red rocks like ornaments on a Christmas tree.

"All right," Laura said to herself after turning off the radio, "*now* I'm becoming enchanted."

The town of Tucumcari didn't disappoint her. Colorful hills surrounded the small city on all sides. Laura was in no hurry to get to the motel so she took the first exit, which enabled her to drive along historic old highway Route 66 for a few miles. There were a few new motels and gas stations close to the interstate, then it was like driving back in time. With the sole exception of the smallest K-Mart store she had ever seen, Tucumcari appeared to consist solely of renovated mom-and-pop businesses from a bygone era. She found it utterly charming.

All too soon the sign for the Broken Arrow Motor Inn appeared. Keeping with tradition, a huge arrow (most surely a power pole) lay broken over the entryway. The older bald-headed man who waited on her was cheerful and competent, a delightful contrast to the spike-haired punk at the car rental agency. The clerk was also expecting her arrival.

"We've been holding our best room for you, Doc," he said. "A courier came by with a package for you. We don't get a lot of them here. Must be important." The clerk lowered an eyebrow. "You a real doc?"

Laura couldn't help but give a smile. "I'm a physician and a molecular biologist."

The clerk nodded, then began fishing around under the counter. He eventually came up with a small box. "Here's what the courier brought you." He slid it onto the glass countertop along with a pen and piece of paper. "The manager will want a receipt that you picked it up."

"Of course." Laura signed then grabbed the package wondering what it contained. She noticed it was from the Cougar Canyon Development Corp.

Apparently the clerk had also taken note of it. "That's the outfit that's going to clean out the town of Paradox so the government can build that lake, isn't it? You working for them?"

Laura had expected people in a small town would want to know everything about her, she just hadn't expected it to happen this fast. "Yes," she acknowledged, remembering to not volunteer information. "I do."

"Be good to have another lake. Drought's been a real bad problem in these parts lately."

"I'm sure it will be nice." She was relieved the clerk hadn't gone into a tirade.

"Got a question, ma'am," the clerk said handing her the key to her room.

Laura felt her skin tighten. "Yes?"

"What's a mole doc gonna do up there? Can't say I've ever heard of one before. Must be a specialty."

"It's a government requirement," she said.

"That figures," the motel clerk grumbled. "You enjoy your stay here in Tucumcari, y'hear."

Dr. Laura Masterson smiled at being able to appeased the clerk and walked to the motel room to see what was inside of the small box that was important enough to have been delivered by special courier.

CHAPTER NINE

Laura was pleasantly surprised with the spacious, neatly appointed, and spotlessly clean room. The rustic name of the Broken Arrow Motor Inn had fostered visions of having to build a fire to boil coffee. Even the clerk had given her a much-needed chuckle. But this was close to luxury. She kicked off her shoes, extracted her laptop from a suitcase, and ran a cord to the data port behind a small desk.

After a few agonizingly slow minutes she was connected with her e-mail. Laura had heard that New Mexico was called "the Land of *Mañana*," tomorrow. Apparently the same sentiment also applied to the Internet providers.

While the little laptop ground away trying to pull all of her messages through what she considered the slowest and most out-of-date dial-up service in the country, she unpacked a few clothes, hanging up a couple of blouses in the closet in hopes of removing at least some of the wrinkles.

There was little reason to hurry. She made a quick scan of the Tucumcari telephone directory, which, surprisingly, had a cowgirl on the cover and an advertisement for a towing service on the back. Perhaps the plague of lawyers advertising to sue almost anyone had spared New Mexico, but Laura doubted that was the case.

The lack of shopping was appalling. It seemed that every store she had ever heard of aside from the diminutive K-Mart was in Clovis, New Mexico, a town about eighty miles southeast near the Texas border. If she had known this would be the case she could have bought some badly needed clothes before leaving Amarillo.

No matter. Whatever she really needed could be found locally. It was unlikely the governor, or even the mayor, would invite her to a formal ball. No, the town of Paradox would keep her working in a laboratory most of her waking hours. All she needed was a supply of comfortable, durable clothes, along with a goodly stock of personal items. The lawyer had mentioned there was a general store in Paradox. A place with such a quaint name might be the shopping experience of a lifetime. Anyway, it would be a nice gesture on her part to patronize the locals. Laura could understand their ire at being forced to move away, but doubted there would be even a hint of violence directed toward her. Michael Delvaney was simply being overly cautious.

The high-powered, state-of-the-art laptop signaled that it had finally managed to wrestle her messages from the Internet. After a few dozen clicks to delete the inevitable spam, something no program or filters seemed to be able to eliminate, she read a short note from Andrew Burns asking about her unexpected leave, hoping all was well, and offering to take her out for dinner this coming Saturday evening.

"What's the matter, jerk," Laura said aloud. "Are Linda and her breast implants out of town for the weekend?"

Andrew had moved the buxom salesclerk from a health club into his apartment several months ago, not bothering to tell Laura or quit dating her. The microbiologist might have been smart in school, but he knew nothing of women or their feelings. He had been taken totally aback when Laura got upset with him the second she learned about what he called his "newly adjusted living arrangements."

Laura marked Andrew's e-mail as spam, hit the delete key with relish, and continued going through the messages. There was a long letter from her mother and a few notes from friends at work wondering what had prompted her to take an unexpected leave of absence. Laura decided to call her mother later to spare the poor little laptop another strain on the Tucumcari dial-up. The others could wait until she got to Paradox and hopefully find a much faster computer service installed in the lab.

Then she remembered the package the clerk had given her, causing a smile to cross her face. It felt good to smile after thinking of Andrew, a man whose general demeanor could put a circus clown into a funk.

Laura shook the small box as she rolled it around trying to figure out how to open the thing. Layers of shipping tape enveloped the package like a cocoon. After a moment she took a small medical kit from an open suitcase, slipped out a scalpel, and sliced the box open. A doctor was always prepared for such emergencies.

Inside was only a cell phone and its leather holder along with a charger. Laura noticed the phone was somewhat thicker and bulkier than any she had had experience with.

It's probably the security screening that Delvaney was talking about, she thought. *I suppose such things are necessary. I might as well get used to playing James Bond.*

A closer examination of the solid black phone disclosed no name plate or even a model number. There were none of the extras she was used to. Laura flicked a simple switch and turned it on. The screen lit dimly. That was when she realized the keyboard did not even have the standard pound and star buttons. One single "phone" button completed the arrangement.

She remembered the lawyer's firm orders to destroy her private cell phone. Reflecting back on the matter, the less reasonable and more rash that action seemed. Michael Delvaney wouldn't know any differently if she simply kept it shut off and inside of her purse. Having a backup in such a remote area seemed prudent. Laura was reaching for her personal cell phone when the black one she still held in her other hand rang, startling her so badly she nearly dropped it.

She took a deep breath to compose herself and keyed the "phone" button. "This is Dr. Masterson."

"I am glad the courier was efficient," Michael Delvaney's silver voice chimed. "This phone is the only one you will use for our future conversations, Doctor. It contains the very latest anti-bugging technology. We can talk freely over it without fear of being overheard or recorded."

"I understand. What I don't understand is how you knew I was here and had turned the phone on."

"*Any* time you key that phone it automatically dials me, a feature you will find useful as *all* contact with the Foundation—excuse me, the Cougar Canyon Development Corporation—shall be through my office."

Laura eyebrows lowered. There certainly was every reason to be cautious, but the whole scenario was growing increasingly chilling.

As if he understood her trepidation, Michael Delvaney said, "I don't wish to frighten you, Doctor, but there are possible efforts by a Middle East group to steal the virus if and when your efforts to clone a live strain are successful. I am certain you are all too aware of the ramifications. Terrible ramifications. A single vial of the Spanish Flu virus in the same hands as those who engineered the nine-eleven tragedy could be devastating."

Suddenly, the room felt cold. "I had not thought of that happening."

"And *I* couldn't have mentioned it before because of the fact we had no secure connection."

"I think I'm beginning to realize the need for total silence on the Paradox Project."

"As you should, Doctor." Michael Delvaney's commanding voice came across as if he was instructing a dull client before their trial. "You very well may hold in your hands the power to save millions of innocent lives. The hard fact of the world we live in today, is that there are others who are anxious *and* able to use scientific discoveries to destroy untold numbers of human beings. I'll be in touch when your security in Paradox is assured. No one knows where you are. Enjoy Tucumcari."

She heard a click as the phone connection closed and the screen went blank.

Dr. Laura Masterson had been looking forward to trying an authentic Mexican restaurant for dinner this evening. Now she had no desire for food. Her stomach churned and her mind raced.

What are you into girl, and more importantly what are you going to do? The thought had not left her head before it was replaced by an answer. *Save lives, save them at any cost. That is what a physician does.*

Dr. Masterson turned off the laptop, stuffed the clutter on the bed away in various drawers, then began undressing to take a long hot shower. Perhaps she could feel, at least for a brief while, that she was washing away the stain of beasts that lurked in dark places, waiting to pounce on the unwary. And the innocent.

CHAPTER TEN

Rio de Janeiro, Brazil

Philip Quinton Roth, III used a silver cutter to nip off the end of a Havana cigar. He carefully and methodically used two wooden matches to fire it properly. Only barbarians resorted to gas lighters to light a fine cigar. He was in no hurry anyway.

The head of the worldwide drug manufacturer sat behind his massive marble desk across from Andre Bettencourt, his chief of acquisitions, and the only man he really trusted. Andre worshiped only one god: money. That one simple, laudable goal made him both easy to appease and predict. The fact he was a graduate of a French medical school and spoke seventeen languages fluently enabled the slender forty-four-year-old white-haired man to head up sales and acquisitions throughout the world without need of a translator. His lack of being burdened by any trace of conscience was simply a bonus.

"Lucas is late," Roth said, turning his gaze to the telephone.

"Patience Mr. Roth. He has never failed us before."

Roth rolled the Havana in his mouth. "And no one gets a second chance."

Across the shining bay from the Roth Pharmaceuticals compound, about two miles away and on approximately the same elevation, stood the once-resplendent Tres Palmas Hotel, which had once been a playground for the rich and famous.

Many years ago, a series of bad investments from its owners had caused the Tres Palmas to lose its luster along with its reputation. The hotel had deteriorated into a seedy hangout for those down on their luck, prostitutes, hoodlums, or people wishing to keep a low profile. The latter was the reason Colton Maxwell had rented a room there several weeks ago. Having a room with an unobstructed view of the distant sprawling mansion and headquarters of Roth Pharmaceuticals made it ideal.

Colton Maxwell sat on a wobbly wooden straight chair facing the open window. Various types of long-distance surveillance and listening devices, all state of the art, were pointed across the azure sea toward the Roth's compound. Colton was in the process of moving a long listening rod from pointing toward the mansion to the headquarters when he heard a knock. He cursed under his breath, then pulled a curtain to hide the spyware and went to see who had come to bother him.

"Who's there?" Colton asked through the bolted wooden door.

"Room service, *señor*," a pleasant voice said. "There is a telephone call for you."

Colton Maxwell gave a shrug. This sorry hotel had no room phones, only a few portable ones a person could barely hear over. He had no idea who might be calling but it would not be wise to cause a scene by refusing to be courteous.

With an effort, Colton slid back the warped and rusty bolt. He swung open the door to a smiling middle-aged Spanish man dressed in a hotel uniform. A name tag pinned on a tattered white shirt announced his name was Lucas. The beaming attendant held a tarnished silver tray upon which there was a somewhat large black cellular phone.

"This is for you, *Señor* Maxwell," the servant said, picking up the phone and handing it over. "You may return it to the lobby later."

Colton Maxwell was taken aback by being offered a cell phone. All of the others he had used in the hotel were simply portables. "When did the Tres Palmas switch to cellular?"

"Ah, *Señor*," Lucas said with a toothy grin, "we have but a few as they are expensive. But I thought you would *appreciate* my help and thoughtfulness."

Colton fished some change out of his pocket and tossed it onto the tray. "Thank you," he said, then closed the door and slid home the bolt.

Before answering the call, he took a moment to pull back the curtain and check that the video and sound recorders were functioning properly.

The phone was larger than any cellular he had ever held. *South American technology has a long ways to go*, he thought. Then he pushed the "phone" button.

After a brief moment a happy voice came on. "Hello, my friend. I do hope you have enjoyed attempting to invade my privacy."

"Who the hell is this?" Colton Maxwell growled.

"I am the one you have been trying to eavesdrop on. But since hired spies are notoriously dense, I will answer your absurd question. My name is Philip Quinton Roth, the third."

Colton Maxwell felt his blood run cold. "What do you want?" His voice was as weak as his knees.

"Tell me Mr. Maxwell," Roth said cheerfully, "do you *really* enjoy your work?"

"Uh, yeah I do."

"Then I expect you'll get a big bang out of this."

"Huh," was the last word Colton Maxwell would ever utter. A blinding flash of white light blotted out his world for all eternity.

From their vantage point across the serene blue waters of the bay, Philip Quinton Roth and Andre Bettencourt watched through the massive picture windows of the comfortable air-conditioned office as a narrow tongue of flame and smoke erupted from a room on the top floor of the Tres Palmas Hotel.

"I did not think Lucas would fail us," Andre said.

"And now we have one less spy to deal with. Do we have any idea yet as to who hired that bastard? A rival—some damn government?"

"No, sir, but we are giving the matter high priority. At least as much as we can considering the code-one operation we have going on in the United States."

"At least he's out of the picture...permanently."

"Yes sir," Andre Bettencourt twirled a cell phone with his long, dainty surgeon's fingers. "Plastic explosives are *so* handy these days. Only recently have we been able to harden them into usable shapes such as cellular phones, or even toothbrushes. Such developments makes disposal of those who have outlived their usefulness much easier than in the past."

"It's generally cheaper to kill them than to pay them."

"And the bottom line is all that matters in the long run. Our stockholders demand results. We give them their returns, no matter what it takes," Andre set the phone on the marble desk. "Is Buno in place?"

"Soon," Philip Roth said. "The operation is going as expected."

"Not quite, sir," Andre Bettencourt's fine features took on a dour cast. "The expense is overrunning our projections."

"Damn your projections," Roth spat. "That's *my* name on the wall. I'm attempting to make this company the single richest one on this earth. An undertaking of this scope requires money, tons of money. I'll take personal responsibility for all expenditures."

"Of course sir, there is no problem. I merely am pointing out that as an international corporation we must account for all large expenditures. This code-one project cannot be kept under wraps for long."

Roth calmed. "I predict that within a few weeks, no company and no government in the whole damn world will be meddling in our affairs. They'll have too damn many *other* things to worry about."

"I'm certain you are correct sir." Andre stared across the bay to a distant pillar of black smoke that was growing larger by the moment. From all appearances, the entire hotel could burn to the ground.

"I hope we can extract Buno from the United States after the project. He can often be *so* useful."

"We'll do what we can. Success is all that really matters, but yes, I agree Buno's return will be given priority. If not..." Roth's expression was that of a cat looking at a caged bird. "I'll give him a phone call and bid him a fond farewell."

The two executives gave a cold chuckle then wordlessly sat watching as the fire in the distant Tres Palmas Hotel spread hopelessly out of control.

CHAPTER ELEVEN

Tucumcari, New Mexico

For three days Dr. Laura Masterson idled about in the small town of Tucumcari. While she explored quaint shops and tried out various restaurants, she felt a cold trepidation of the task ahead, worrying that time was wasting away. Indeed, if a new form of shifting antigen flu virus had appeared in Old Mexico, developing a vaccine as quickly as possible would be paramount to saving millions of lives. She was getting antsy.

Late the previous night, Laura had bolted awake from the embracing arms of a nightmare, bathed in sweat. In her dream she had cloned a living specimen of the Spanish Flu. Then, to her horror, the deadly virus had mutating wildly—so wildly that any possibility of a vaccine was impossible. Anyone exposed was doomed, possibly the entire world. Then, for some reason that can only be explained in the chimeric shadow world of a nightmare, she dropped a glass vial containing the live virus, breaking it in a laboratory sink, above which was an open window overlooking a playground full of laughing little children....

In the light of a bright and cheerful New Mexico sunrise, Laura looked back on the dream for what it was, a vivid nightmare. It was preposterous; there were no windows in a biohazard laboratory. Yet she was unable to completely shake the feeling of dread that lingered like a foul odor that refused to go away.

She showered, relishing the undulating waves of hot water. After dressing in blue jeans and a tight-fitting red blouse that she had found, in of all places, a hardware store, it was time to begin another day of waiting on a phone call from Michael Delvaney.

Briefly, Laura thought of keying the cell phone to check in, just to see how things were progressing in Paradox. A little more thought on the subject caused her to forget calling the lawyer. First he knew exactly where she was staying; he'd made the reservations. A simple call to leave a message with the Broken Arrow Motor Inn would take care of a non-working telephone. Secondly, Michael Delvaney had made it perfectly clear in their last conversation that he would call her when all was in order and had given her instructions "to enjoy Tucumcari."

The lawyer's admonition was becoming increasingly difficult. When it came to entertainment and diversions, Tucumcari's options were definitely limited. She had taken in a couple of movies that were somewhat new and visited an interesting museum. The problem was, the same movies were still playing and museums didn't change their exhibits daily.

This morning, Laura had decided to try her luck on a little hole-in-the-wall Mexican restaurant in the old part of town near the abandoned depot. A few questions she had asked when she was out shopping assured her the dubious-looking adobe building held a very good restaurant. Then the people inevitably took several minutes to explain how prosperous the town had been before the trains quit stopping in Tucumcari.

It seemed the railroad used to maintain a repair station here and the town had been a major stopover for tourists. Nowadays, due to progress, not even Amtrak stopped here. Grass and weeds grew thick between the sets of iron rails that fronted the once-proud and faded depot, which sported broken windows and now housed only multitudes of pigeons.

Laura parked the Suburban on a lonely street then took a walk past dozens of closed businesses. The sprawling Spanish-style depot that once had been bright and alive with people stood in the distance, stark and dreary as an old tombstone. The rows and rows of vacant business buildings reminded her of graves in a cemetery.

Snap out of it girl, Laura thought. *You're still in a funk over that nightmare. Have a good breakfast and get some rest because you've got some microscopic butts to kick real soon.*

Feeling better, she entered and took a seat in the El Lobo restaurant, choosing a booth near the front window. The wood top and seats of the booth were deeply etched with carved initials and hearts that had been scratched there over decades. Briefly Laura wondered how many of those whose initials which were surrounded by hearts were still together.

"Morning, ma'am." A smiling older Mexican woman came with a menu and steaming cup of aromatic coffee. Unbidden, the lady sat the coffee in front of her. "You looked like you could use a cup."

"Thank you," Laura said. "I had a rough night, a nightmare actually."

"You need a dream catcher, miss."

"A what?" Laura asked, intrigued.

"They're from the Indians, Navajo I believe, or possibly the Apache. Anyway, they're round, knitted like a spiderweb with feathers to funnel dreams. You hang them on the wall over the head of your bed. Any bad dreams coming in get snagged up in the web. Give one a try. They don't cost much and they look nice. Most any store sells them."

"After last night I'll try anything," Laura said sincerely. Being a trained scientist she knew such things were only legend, but then all legends are based on fact."

"You'll be glad you did." The waitress smiled and brushed back a strand of gray hair from her bifocal glasses. "And a good breakfast also helps."

"What do you recommend?"

"Missy, we make the best plate of *huevos rancheros* you ever put on a fork. They come in two varieties. One's red chili—that's mainly for easterners. Then we have a homemade green chili sauce that'll burn the lint out of your bellybutton, but it's mighty tasty."

"I'll have the green. Until I get a dream catcher I suspect the chili might keep my mind off any old nightmare," Laura said feeling adventurous. Besides, she not only liked the waitress, but from living in Texas she had worked up both a taste and tolerance for fiery Mexican dishes.

"You got it, dearie," the waitress scribbled some notes on a pad. As she turned to depart she said over her shoulder. "Warn your taste buds to take cover."

Waiting for her breakfast, Laura thumbed through a day-old local newspaper, and sipped the strong coffee. A front-page article said some scofflaw from California had been ticketed for going twenty miles per hour over the speed limit. Another column predicted a bumper crop of watermelons this summer. Yet another held hopes for higher school enrollment for the coming fall. All in all, Tucumcari reminded her of the old *Andy Griffith Show* set in mythical Mayberry, a town where the law had little to do. She thought how pleasant it would be to live in a place where no beasts lurked in shadowy places.

A huge plate of *huevos rancheros* being set in front of her shook Laura back to reality. She took a testing forkful and smiled. In certain parts of Houston, the green chili served here would seem mild as milk.

Laura was able to finish only half of the heaping plate of food. The waitress noticed this and came over to the booth.

"Too hot for you, dearie?" she said. "I'm sorry, but I did warn you."

"No, they were actually quite good. Just more than I can eat."

"Folks around here want big portions of everything...."

A ringing from the cell phone in Laura's purse stopped the conversation. She extracted the black phone and held it to her ear. After a few minutes of listening silently, she keyed the cell off and returned it to her purse.

"Bad news, dearie?" the waitress asked. "You look like you've seen a ghost."

"No, it was just my boss who's still very much alive. I've got to go to work."

Laura Masterson paid the modest bill, left a five-dollar tip, then quickly walked to the Suburban. Once she had gathered her clothes and belongings out of the Broken Arrow Motor Inn all she needed to do was make one quick stop then head for Paradox.

Michael Delvaney had told her not to say a word if she wasn't alone, just listen. All was in place. Her instructions were to drive through Paradox on what he said was the only well-traveled road for a half mile past the old two-story hospital building, which she could see on her left. There, at a fork in the road, would be the laboratory and living quarters.

The man who would meet her was to act as a bodyguard. He had the odd name of Buno Eberhard.

CHAPTER TWELVE

Dr. Laura Masterson drove north from Tucumcari on Highway 101. It was a smooth, two-lane strip of pavement that ran through a valley lined with lush irrigated fields along with an occasional well-kept home. Then the road began climbing up into the red mesa country of rimrocks and steep cliffs. It was as if a few scant miles marked a line where anyone lived.

Aside from scrubby cedar and junipers, there were no trees. Here the bush-like cholla cactus grew several feet high to rival the sparse gnarly trees in size. An occasional windmill creaking in the morning breeze, pumping water into concrete tanks to slake the thirst of a few cattle that appeared happy to stay in one spot, along with miles and miles of barbed-wire fences in poor repair, became the only visible trappings of civilization.

Laura kept an eye on the odometer that she had set to zero when she drove out of Tucumcari. Exactly when it registered thirty-two miles, there was an intersection where a gravel road turned off to her right. She slowed to read the faded signs. There was one likely placed there by the state highway department that announced: *Paradox, eight miles. Road may be impassable in wet or snowy weather.*

Wonderful, simply wonderful, she thought. Then she scanned a few of the other signs: *The Black Rock Bar and Grill, open seven days a week; Deep Canyon General Store, fishing tackle, bait, guns, and groceries, Vernon Bright, Guided Mountain Lion Hunts.*

The list went on, but many of the signs were so riddled with bullet holes, they were illegible.

"You're not in Kansas any more, girl," Laura said with a sigh as she wheeled the Suburban onto the gravel road that had probably been graded not too long ago. It was wide, smooth, and didn't look the least bit threatening.

Laura's luck and attitude held for about six miles as the unimproved road ran straight and true across the top of a cactus-studded red rock mesa. Then, ahead, she saw the opening of a wide canyon that looked immeasurably deep. A yellow road sign warned: Sharp Curve, 15 MPH.

When she saw the cliff dropping into the murky depths, Laura slowed to a crawl thinking that whoever had posted that sign must have either been a daredevil or had a really black sense of humor. Where the road made a ninety-degree turn to drop down into the canyon, Laura braked to a stop. From her vantage point on the very rim of the red rock mesa, she could look down on the backs of flying black birds. Most likely they were buzzards, dining on the remains of the last person to ignore the small sign.

In the very bottom of the steep gorge, a creek could be seen winding tortuously through green fields. On the opposite side were numerous buildings, trailer houses, and seas of assorted detritus. A short distance down the canyon, also on the opposite side of the creek, were three huge blackish piles of rock along with gray wooden skeletons of what had once been coal tipples. Those were the mines that caused the town to be built.

"So this is Paradox," Laura said, chewing worriedly on her lower lip. "It looks like a lot of people have traveled this road and lived to talk about it." She took her foot from the brake and tapped gently on the accelerator pedal. "Let's see how well my luck holds."

The lack of guard rails was daunting, but as she quickly noted, there simply was not enough flat ground available to put any; the road itself needed every foot that could be blasted and bulldozed out of the cliff.

About a half mile further, the road did a switchback only to repeat another, and yet another, as it made its way down to the creek and town below.

Laura's knuckles were white and her hands sweaty when she drove onto the level strip of ground that lined the bottom of the steep canyon. The bridge spanning the creek was wooden, old, and rickety. After what she had just been through, crossing it did not cause her to raise so much as an eyebrow.

The rushing water below was a definite thick red color, causing her to wonder if the "fishing tackle and bait for sale" sign was simply a bad joke. She would find out soon enough. The town of Paradox,

New Mexico, or at least what remained of it, loomed only a few hundred feet ahead, basking in the shadows of a cliff whose escarpment reached hundreds of feet heavenward toward a clear blue sky, and stretched as far as the eye could see in both directions.

Her first impression was that the sad train depot and closed business buildings in Tucumcari were downright cheerful in comparison to the utter desolation that made up what remained of Paradox. The few business buildings still standing were of pallid wood, unpainted for generations. Decrepit trailer houses were scattered about willy-nilly, interspersed with rusted-out old cars and trucks of all descriptions.

The Black Rock Bar and Grill, a rambling one-story affair on the main street, had a few vehicles parked in front. The aptly named Deep Canyon General Store had an "open" sign in the lone front window, but no one seemed to want to buy bait or groceries at this time of morning as there was no indication of activity.

Laura realized that hers was the only car on the road, and had been ever since she had turned off the pavement for Paradox, a drive of a supposed eight miles that took a half-hour to navigate safely.

This might not be the end of the earth, girl, but it can't be too far from here.

A few late-model travel trailers that looked fiercely out of place amongst the aged remains were lined up in a RV park on her right. Some of the trailers were so large Laura doubted the sanity of anyone who had towed them down here over that steep and narrow road. A few vehicles parked alongside the shiny RVs had U.S. Government license plates. This was not surprising considering the Bureau of Reclamation was overseeing the removal of the town preparatory to them building a dam.

A can of gasoline and a book of matches would save the taxpayers a fortune, Laura thought. Then she was through the town.

The road fork that Michael Delvaney had said led to the cemetery was unmistakable. Beyond a huge sign with red letters declaring this to be private property of the Cougar Canyon Development Corporation with smaller print threatening various fines and imprisonment to those foolish enough to continue on without authorization, she saw her destination. It would be her home for an unknown length of time.

The mobile laboratory was out in the open, adjacent to the dilapidated gate to a cemetery containing rows of wooden and marble grave markers. A ray of sunlight glistened from the glass windows of the truck lab. The laboratory unit itself was painted white. A glance at the ventilation openings told Laura it was a biohazard level-four unit, equipped to handle the most deadly viruses known to man including Ebola or even a shifting antigen Spanish Flu. Perfect.

Three very large motor homes were lined up on a section of flat ground to her right, opposite the mobile laboratory. A yellow backhoe was parked behind the farthest one. Everything was obviously very new and very expensive. The pair of jet-black Hummers blocking the road ahead was an indication that money was no object to achieving the Hammond Foundation's goals.

No, girl, make that the Cougar Canyon Development Corporation. Learn to keep your stories straight and your mouth closed. This is the most important thing you've ever attempted in your whole life, don't screw it up.

Laura braked to a dusty stop at the orders of a tall older man with a blonde crew cut who came to her with his palm raised, the other hand hidden behind a khaki shirt.

"Hold it right there, lady," the man barked through the open window. "This is private property. There's no trespassing past this point."

"Are you Buno Eberhard?" Laura said.

The big man's bushy eyebrows lowered over pale blue eyes. "Yes, that is me."

"I'm Dr. Laura Masterson. I believe I'm expected."

Buno gave a snort. "Sorry, I was not told when you would arrive. Damn cell phones don't work in this hole. Have to drive to the top of the mountain to make a call on one or go to the bar and use a public phone." He clucked his tongue. "The boss does not like me to use them."

"I understand," Laura said. "I have the same instructions."

"The motorhome next to the laboratory's yours, Doctor. Mine is alongside it. The other is for your helper, if the son of a bitch ever shows up. Can't figure what's keeping him."

"I'll get unpacked and set up, then we can go over the plan of operations. Is that all right with you, Mr. Eberhard?"

"You're the boss here, Doctor. I've been told to keep you safe, that is all. The digging up of those dead bodies is your job." He glared at her, the sun glinting off the silver automatic pistol that was now visible in his other hand. Buno stuck the gun under his belt. "I was also told to tell you, 'Welcome to Paradox.'"

"I consider myself welcomed." Laura drove past the lone human being she had seen since entering the town, then parked alongside her new home and mentally prepared to make the best of whatever lay ahead.

CHAPTER THIRTEEN

Dr. Masterson forced herself to mask her stern disapproval of Buno Eberhard. The very name of the man had caused consternation for some reason. The fact that he met anybody coming to a cemetery with a gun gave her more than a little reason for concern. Then she remembered Michael Delvaney's warnings of people possibly out to steal her research for sinister purposes.

There isn't anything to steal, she thought as she parked the Suburban,*there may never be. Everything I proposed in my papers is nothing but scientific theory.*

Laura climbed out and stood, her boots causing small clouds of red dust to rise from the powder-dry ground, such soil being one of the criteria she had laid out to recover genetic material suitable for cloning. A desert environment would mummify flesh causing an encapsulating effect, which would serve to protect pockets of virus rather than dissipate them into the earth as a wet climate tended to do. A quick look around showed the cemetery was on a bluff many dozens of feet above the muddy creek. Perfect.

She noticed no people about other than the sinister Buno. Laura turned to go into the long motorhome that was likely to be her home for sometime. She gasped at the distant two-story adobe building that stood stark against a bleached strip of sandstone cliff. It was surprising that she had not seen it before. The lawyer had told her she could not miss the old hospital, yet for some reason she hadn't seen it until this moment.

The long-abandoned hospital had, she remembered reading, been a company affair run by the Bessemer Fuel and Iron Corporation. What had stuck in her mind were the statistics. Two hundred and forty-seven men, women, and children had been admitted with flu symptoms in that terrible fall of 1918. Of that number, nearly sixty percent, or one hundred and forty-five, had died. The average across the nation was a less than ten percent mortality rate, even in the hardest hit areas. Laura wondered anew if the Paradox influenza outbreak could have been a different strain altogether, or if the virus here had for some unknown reason mutated differently to become even more deadly.

You're here to find the answers, girl. That's why you're getting paid the big bucks. Get to it.

Laura decided to check out the impressive brown and silver motorhome before unloading her belongings from the Suburban. She had seen a few coaches this big on the road, but never up close. Mostly, to her knowledge, expensive Prevost bus conversions were reserved mainly for touring rock musicians or the extremely wealthy. In any event, it was time to get acquainted with the luxury coach.

Laura's first impression when she went inside was one of wonderment. Attending medical conventions and such, she had had an opportunity to stay in many expensive hotels, but none of the rooms she had experienced before came anywhere close to exuding the opulence and splendor she beheld.

A few moment's perusal of the appointments was cause for awe. There were not one, but two plasma TVs, including a 46-inch screen in the living area that folded up into the roof via remote control. The lavatory sink was made of clear crystal. The plush mauve carpet was so thick and deep she felt as if she were wading through it instead of walking. The refrigerator and pantry were stocked with assorted foodstuffs, most of which she liked, causing Laura to wonder again just how much her employers really did know about her. The bar even held bottles of her favorite wines along with a stock of Miller Lite beer, something for which she had acquired a taste when she was a struggling college student, and something she still enjoyed.

How did they know about my liking beer? The question was only one of many flashing about in her mind like lightning bugs. *Why spend so much money on a field project?*

On a hunch, Laura went to the driver's section and began thumbing through paperwork she found in the console. She found the registration and accompanying bill of sale. Cougar Canyon Development Corporation had paid over 1.6 million dollars cash for the Prevost conversion bus. And the other two parked alongside appeared to be identical.

Leases and rentals leave paper trails. That's the reason only your name and address is on the Chevrolet Suburban you drove here. Girl, if this wasn't the Hammond Foundation you were working for, there would be good reason to be concerned.

Laura clucked her tongue and returned the paperwork to the console. She needed to quit worrying over every little thing and focus on what she was being paid to do. And it was something she had wanted to do all of her professional career: save lives.

After a few trips to the Suburban and back she began hanging clothes in the closet and filling drawers with personal items, while luxuriating with bare feet on the super-plush carpet. There was a data port behind the desk so she decided to try her luck getting on the Internet with her laptop.

The connection was made in the blink of an eye. Where the Tucumcari connection was slow enough to paint a house while her e-mail downloaded, the service inside the coach was awesome, faster than anything she had ever experienced. There was no doubt the black dome on top of the bus housed a state-of-the-art dish along with technology that was unbelievably cutting edge, perhaps reserved for the government. Anyway, her e-mails appeared the second she touched the keys. Laura realized with a start that there was no spam, only a few messages from friends and her mother.

Whatever Internet service provider the Hammond Foundation has, a few million people would sure love to subscribe to it. Why the cellular phones don't work I can't fathom.

Laura took a few minutes to send replies to everyone, assuring them she was fine but very busy on her new job and would get back to them when time allowed. She carefully omitted any clue to her location.

Buno Eberhard had said that the cell phones did not work down in this steep canyon, which was certainly not surprising. The fact that the Internet and televison did was absolutely unbelievable. When she thought of having to drive all the way back up that narrow, dangerous road to make a call, she shivered. Then it struck her that whoever had driven the huge Prevost buses into Paradox had managed to do so without a problem.

Just don't look down when you're driving. And remember, it isn't the fall that kills you, it's that sudden stop at the bottom. You can do it, girl. You have to if you're going to get the job done. There are a lot of people counting on you.

She filled a thick glass with crystal clear ice cubes from a built-in ice maker, then took a Diet Coke from the refrigerator and popped the tab. The cold drink relaxed her as she wondered about the motorhome. From the front windows Laura had a grand view of the Paradox cemetery. From all indications it had been a long time since anyone had been buried there. This was an auspicious event. After a body had been in the ground for many years the worst odor was usually an unpleasant musky smell when the coffin was opened. That was certainly not the case with the recently interred. Excavating and exhuming fairly fresh bodies was definitely not a pleasant task. Back in school, more than a few of her colleagues had run from the autopsy room when the instructor had unzipped a black body bag with a flourish to disclose a bloated or rotting corpse.

No matter. She was a doctor now, twice over. The bodies buried here would be treated with respect, but they were also scientific material. It was no different than if they lay on a coroner's stainless steel autopsy table being dissected to determine cause of death. Detached, unemotional professionalism was how research was conducted.

If only I could ever look at a dead body without realizing it once was a living, breathing human being, my job would be a lot easier.

Dr. Masterson gave a deep sigh, finished her drink, and had just placed the empty glass in the sink when she heard a knock. She swung open the door to the stern face of Buno Eberhard.

"Yes?" Laura said.

"I was told to give you time to get settled in before telling you that Michael Delvaney wants to talk with you over the secure phone."

"Then that means I have to drive up to the top of the mesa."

"Ja," Buno shrugged. "Like I said there is no service here in this hole. The boss is unhappy about that."

Laura looked up at the cliff where the road made a white scar across it as it rose to the high rimrock. "I can't say I like the idea of driving that road to make a call either. It'll take a lot of time."

"Nah, I'll run you up in the Hummer if you want, no problem."

Even though Buno made her uneasy, Laura had no difficulty accepting the offer. "Let me get my purse, the phone's inside." She went to the bedroom and grabbed the bag, nearly running before Buno changed his mind.

The Hummer she climbed into (Buno made no attempt to open the door for her) was as plush and expensive as everything she was coming to expect from the Hammond Foundation. The seats were tan leather with power adjustments. Overhead, a sunroof gave a splendid view of the cliff they were preparing to navigate.

Buno Eberhard turned on the ignition and swung the huge vehicle around with a flourish. The blonde bodyguard obviously enjoyed driving the four-by-four. He mashed on the gas, sending up a cloud of red powder dust in their wake. Suddenly he braked to a quick stop.

"Oh shit, it's him again," Buno said with disgust.

CHAPTER FOURTEEN

"I just knew that son of a bitch would show up," Buno growled as he sat glaring through the windshield. A white Dodge pickup with government license plates was slowly pulling over to the side of the road.

"The government *is* here to oversee the moving of the town and cemetery," Laura said. "I believe it's in our best interest to cooperate with them as fully as we can."

Buno gave a deep snort. "*Other* places I would deal with a guy like him my own way, but here you're in charge."

Laura did not understand Buno's irritation with the pleasant-looking man who climbed out of his pickup to great them. She decided the bodyguard was simply a grouch, a common symptom in all too many of those who were forced to deal with beasts on a regular basis. She put a smile on her face and opened the Hummer door.

"Jack Stoner," the government man wearing a short-sleeve khaki shirt said, extending a hand. "I'm with the Federal Bureau of Reclamation. If I was a betting man, I'd lay odds that you're Dr. Masterson."

"Give the man a prize," Laura said grasping his hand. "He's a winner."

"I'm glad to meet you at last, I've heard a lot about you." Jack Stoner's grin showed a set of the whitest, most perfect teeth she had ever seen. They almost sparkled in the bright New Mexico sunlight.

"We look forward to working with you people on this project," Laura said, sizing him up. She guessed Stoner was in his mid-to early forties. He had short brown hair with a slash of gray at the temples, and was maybe six feet tall and average weight. Glancing, she at his left hand, noticed he wore no wedding ring. Except for his teeth, Jack Stoner could meld anonymously into most any group of people.

"The sooner we get started the better." Jack Stoner waved the back of his hand toward the cemetery. "Those folks are all dying to get out of here."

Laura raised an eyebrow; humor of any kind was not common among federal employees. She decided it would be best to play the part of a professional, however, as, Stoner might have worked on that line for days. "We have to make preparations first."

"Of course, Doctor, I understand." His teeth flashed in the sun again. "Just trying to brighten up a dead subject."

"The possibility of disease being spread when any grave is opened is very real," Laura snipped. "Tuberculosis, smallpox, all forms of bacteria could be released unless we take the utmost care."

Jack Stoner's expression grew serious. "And the Spanish Flu, we can't forget that. I was told that's what killed most of these folks. Well, that and mine accidents." He nodded at the mobile laboratory. "From the looks of things you'll be able to take care of all the nasty little bugs we might dig up. The boys and I will mark the tombstones and body bags to make sure they get matched and reburied properly at the new cemetery down in Tucumcari."

"Careful is the watchword, Mr. Stoner," Laura said. "And all of that takes time. If you will kindly give me your card so that I can contact you when we're ready to actually begin disinterment, I'll be happy to do so. Now, however, we must be on our way."

Jack Stoner fished a card out of his shirt pocket and handed it over. "You'll need to use the phone at the bar, cells don't work here in this canyon." He grinned. "Or you can just yell loud when you drive by. We're all going to be stuck here until the project is completed."

"We all want things to go both quickly and safely, Mr. Stoner."

"Call me Jack, please. I believe out here a little less formality will make things more pleasant."

Dr. Masterson smiled as she turned to rejoin Buno in the Hummer. "And you can call me Dr. Laura."

"Yes ma'am." Jack Stoner took a pair of sunglasses from a case on his belt and put them on. With a fairly good John Wayne voice he added, "Out here in the Wild, Wild West we aim to please the little ladies." Then he jumped into his pickup started up the engine, and was gone in a swirl of red dust.

Laura Masterson fastened her seatbelt, then turned to Buno. "That was a surprise. I didn't expect the man in charge of the Federal Bureau of Reclamation team to do anything but growl at us because we were taking too long. This Jack Stoner is shaping up to be a character."

Buno sighed. "Nothing but trouble's what that guy will be."

"We'll see. For now let's try and get on the rimrock without any incident and check in."

"Yeah," Buno grumbled. "They'll want to talk with me, too." He hit the gas and started the big vehicle on its way through the dying town of Paradox.

Laura paid no notice to anything except the imposing two-story hospital at the base of the cliff. She was still amazed that she had missed seeing it before.

When Buno Eberhard pulled the black Hummer to a stop well off the road on a flat expanse of cactus-studded rimrock, Laura breathed easy. The drive into and out of Paradox was going to take a lot of getting used to. A brown UPS truck had met them on a switchback half way up the cliff. Neither the young truck driver nor Buno had appeared to think anything of the encounter even though they had missed each other by scant inches. Laura thought her heart had stopped for a time and just resumed beating.

"I'll go outside and walk around for a bit," Buno said as he opened the door. "That will give you some privacy for your call."

Laura acknowledged the courtesy with a nod. She fished the large black cell phone from her purse, and keyed it on.

"Thank you for phoning so promptly, Dr. Masterson," Michael Delvaney's silvery voice greeted her instantly, causing her to wonder if he had the phone in his hand awaiting her call. "I trust your living quarters are acceptable."

"Yes, they are actually much more luxurious than I'd expected."

"Only the very best for our valued employees. Have you inspected the laboratory?"

"No, I haven't had time. From the appearance, it's a new biohazard level-four unit, which is precisely what we need. If the motorhome is any indication, I expect the lab will be appointed with the best equipment available."

The lawyer chuckled. "About sixteen million dollars worth. The cloning of viruses does not come easy, or cheap."

Laura hesitated, then answered, "Whether or not it is even possible to clone the Spanish Flu virus is only scientific theory. I know that some of the best laboratories in the world are doing experiments along these lines. I do believe, however, we'll be the first to move directly into attempting to clone a dead virus."

"That is what we are counting on. I must tell you there has been a setback. Dr. Singh, the assistant we had planned on having in Paradox before you got there has been killed in a tragic automobile crash in Africa. He had been doing AIDS research. Dr. Singh will be sorely missed. The Foundation is, as we speak, attempting to recruit at least an M.D. to help you with your work."

Laura Masterson was taken aback. There had been no earlier discussion of an assistant, yet another competent molecular biologist would certainly speed up the research process.

"I can manage, Mr. Delvaney," Laura said. "All I will need to do is open the chests of the bodies and take samples of lung tissue. I can do that in the cemetery. From all appearances the government has more than enough men here to move the corpses."

"Ah, Doctor, you are *so* agreeable. I only wish I had more loyal and enthusiastic people like you to work with. Proceed with the project as soon as possible."

"Have you any more information on the Mexico outbreak?"

"There have been no more cases, thank God. We're hoping the quick sterilization procedures implemented were effective."

"So do I." Laura looked to Buno, who was standing at the very edge of a rimrock, staring down into the canyon's depth idly picking his nose. "I believe you wanted to talk to Mr. Eberhard?"

"Yes, briefly, please put him on."

"Right away." Laura climbed from the passenger seat and walked to Buno, stopping well before reaching the edge of the cliff. "Mr. Delvaney for you."

Buno strode toward her with a glowering look. He grabbed the phone, then walked out to the very edge of a finger of red sandstone that overhung the rim of the mesa by at least a dozen feet. Laura got the message that he wanted to be alone and returned to the Hummer to allow the man his privacy.

After several minutes the ominous bodyguard returned. Laura thought she could detect the trace of a smile on his normally stone face.

"You must have gotten some good news," she said to Buno as he climbed into the driver's seat.

"I have a task to perform that will take me away for tonight and possibly all day tomorrow." He returned the cell phone to her. "Do you think you'll be all right? Mr. Delvaney doesn't believe you will be in any danger until you have...uh...the product others may want to steal."

Laura found herself looking forward to having Buno gone. "You go ahead and take care of your business." She chuckled, "As long as I don't have to drive on the side of a cliff, I'll be just fine."

Laura Masterson's attempt at levity failed again. The stoic bodyguard's expression returned to granite. "Good" was all he said before sending the black Hummer shooting back into the depths of the canyon, while she held her breath and mouthed a silent prayer that the UPS truck wasn't on its way back up the narrow, dangerous road.

CHAPTER FIFTEEN

Rio de Janeiro, Brazil

Philip Quinton Roth, III was fighting down a red rage as he stomped through the marble hallways of his mansion in his black silk bathrobe. He intensely hated being interrupted during playtime. And his wife would be home in a few days. There never was enough time for his well-deserved pleasures due to incompetent help. To aggravate him even further, the lovely Chinese twins, Yin and Yin Again, were scheduled to leave the following morning.

And the trouble was all due to a greedy lawyer.

Andre Bettencourt had been right to call him out to listen to the recorded phone call between Buno Eberhard and that Houston lawyer, Michael Delvaney. The slimy lawyer's continual grasping for more of anything he could get his greedy hands on was becoming annoying. Most annoying.

When the attorney began skimming kickbacks for the purchase of items the company needed, that was understandable. At least it had been for as long as the bastard had kept his thievery to a reasonable figure.

Then had come the mobile laboratory and motorhomes for the United States project. A little digging had disclosed that Michael Delvaney had pocketed almost a million dollars on the laboratory alone. The figures on the three bus conversions were not yet known, but a little digging in the right places, a little *persuasion,* would certainly show a substantial amount had been skimmed.

The phone call that had taken Philip Roth from the pleasures of his bedroom was the final straw. Michael Delvaney had ordered Buno to drive to Amarillo, intercept Dr. Luu Kwan in his hotel do away with and him—make it look like an accident or at least a robbery gone bad.

The bastard! Dr. Kwan was one of the most skilled molecular biologists on the planet. And a good backup should Dr. Masterson fail. The lawyer was doing this solely to avoid paying Dr. Kwan. Michael Delvaney would put the cash that he had given the doctor in Houston, a considerable quarter of a million dollars, in his own pocket and tell everyone it had been stolen. Then the money in the various bank accounts that had been set up to pay the biologist's salary could be depleted at Delvaney's leisure. The project was too far along to do other than see how thing played out. Damn it!

It was infuriating to wait for retribution, but it *would* come. The project had to proceed as rapidly as possible. Perhaps Dr. Laura Masterson might accomplish the goal rather quickly. That would be gratifying. *Most* gratifying.

Roth Pharmaceuticals maintained a clinic on Grenada, a pleasant little out-of-the-way tropical island in the Carribean that had drawn little notice in recent years. The place was perfect for their use as an organ transplant center for needy patients; rich desperate patients who needed transplants and were not about to wait on any government bureaucracy to give permission or work their way down some arbitrary donor list.

Roth began to grin. Here was a place he could recoup at least some of his losses on Michael Delvaney. The attorney could easily be lured to the tropical paradise without kidnapping him, and he'd come with a smile on his face. Perfect. The man was still young enough to be valuable.

It was amazing to Roth how much body parts fetched on the open market these days. And utterly fascinating how long a person could be kept alive until the needy patients arrived. One kidney, the eyes, bone marrow—none of those losses were fatal. Michael Delvaney could be maintained on life support for weeks. Months if necessary.

Roth decided to make a tape recording of his CPA's recounting of the money the lawyer had stolen and send it to the clinic. Delvaney wouldn't even need his eyes to set the message. Then the pharmaceutical magnate planned on adding to the tape just how much Michael Delvaney's heart and liver would bring. He thought he might be witty and include a gibe or two about just how little a lawyer's heart is worth, being so small and hard.

When he came to the doorway of his bedroom, Philip Roth decided that it did a man good to vent his feelings. There were handcuffs and whips along with some very interesting leather toys in the closet. Yin and Yin Again needed to be taught a lesson in humility. He was just the man to teach them. At the very worst he might have to pay for damaged or lost merchandise. It had happened before.

He felt a pleasant sensation building in his loins. The sex potency drug his company had ripped off a major U.S. pharmaceutical company and made a generic copy of to sell in third-world countries was functioning just the way it should. His erection was becoming rock hard.

With his passions and his fury growing, Roth opened the ornate mahogany door, went inside, and bolted it closed.

It was *playtime*.

CHAPTER SIXTEEN

Laura Masterson briefly wondered why she felt more comfortable after her bodyguard had tossed a pair of suitcases into the black Hummer and sped off, leaving her alone in the camp outside the Paradox cemetery.

Having Buno Eberhard around was enough to put a lottery winner into a funk. There was something about the muscular blonde man that exuded a reptilian coldness, like a rattlesnake or water moccasin.

Alone now, Laura felt like doing some exploring. The other Hummer, a twin to the one Buno was presently leaving a trail of dust across a cliff with, was parked at the entranceway. She was not surprised to find it locked. The vehicle was probably meant for the unfortunate Dr. Singh, who was to be her assistant. The third Prevost coach most likely was to have been the good doctor's home. For some reason she decided to walk over and try the door. Laura was taken aback when she found out it was unlocked.

The interior of the luxury coach was identical to hers, right down to the clear crystal lavatory sink. What was different, however, was the total lack of anything in the pantry, not even dishes or silverware. A quick check disclosed that the refrigerator was not only empty, it had not been turned on.

Perhaps Dr. Singh had followed some strange diet. Yet even if that were the case, the lack of even the basic utensils and staples such as salt, pepper, and sugar was odd. It was as if they never expected him to show up.

Then the answer came with the power of an epiphany. Michael Delvaney had said the Foundation was already looking for a replacement assistant. Dr. Singh had been killed after the motorhome had been delivered. That explained everything.

Quit being so paranoid, girl. The Hammond Foundation is a philan-thropic organization that's been around for decades. All of the secrecy along with the importance of the project has you on edge is all. Lighten up.

Feeling much more relaxed, Laura bounded from the luxurious motorhome, running square into Jack Stoner. He was grinning, a small piece of straw dangling from the corner of his mouth. The fact that the government man had appeared from out of nowhere making no noise caused her to gasp with surprise.

"I didn't mean to frighten you, Dr. Laura," Jack Stoner said. "But I noticed Puno go breezing off about the time I realized that I really hadn't been very cordial earlier."

"His name is Buno," Laura said.

"Yeah," Jack Stoner spat out the straw. "Whatever. I'm not very good with names."

"How'd you manage to get here so quietly? I didn't hear your truck."

"Shanks mare, Dr. Laura." He noticed her brow furrowed question-ingly. "I walked. It's only about a half mile at the most."

"Of course, I should have realized. You'll have to forgive me for being distracted but I just found out that my assistant, Dr. Singh, was killed in a car wreck."

Jack Stoner's expression remarked neutral. "I'm sorry to hear that. Did you know him well?"

"No, we never met. The Cougar Creek Development Corporation had arranged for his services." She went on to stifle any worries the government man might have. "I told the company that I could handle the project alone. There won't be any delay with moving the cemetery."

There was a soft gentleness in Stoner's voice, "I meant what I said about being sorry about the sad news. I've been working for the government too long to get my tights in a bunch over things taking a lot of time to get done. We'll be here for however long it takes. If there's anything I can do to help, just ask."

Laura Masterson took comfort as the sun setting masked her in shadow, helping hide her look of humiliation at her misjudgment. Jack Stoner was obviously trying his best to be friendly. Maybe she had been living in big cities too long. Here in the remoteness of Paradox, working on the most important—and secret—project of her life, she needed allies, not confrontation. It was a source of chagrin that she had started off on the wrong foot.

"Thank you...Jack," Laura said, her tone apologetic. "I appreciate the offer, but I'm certain we'll get by just fine. It's just upsetting to lose a team member, even if it is someone you've never met."

Jack Stoner stared into the shadows of the escarpment, his voice tinged with sorrow. "I know about loss, believe me, I know."

Laura realized it was time to change the subject. It was obvious she had inadvertently struck a nerve. "You came to visit about something?"

Jack Stoner whipped his head back and forth a couple of times, attempting to toss off bad memories like a wet dog shaking water from itself.

"Uh, yeah," he said. "The finest restaurant in town—actually the *only* restaurant in town—is serving gourmet mystery meat barbeque sandwiches with not-too-out-of-date potato chips for the special tonight. It'll be my treat, Doctor."

Laura couldn't help but smile. "I'd like that, and if you're a drinking man, I'll buy the beer."

"Make that Miller Lite and we'll be friends for life."

"I'll make up my mind in that department if I don't have to get my stomach pumped from the dinner you're paying for." She laughed, it felt good. "And please, just call me Laura."

Jack Stoner smiled. "Just Laura it is. Actually the Black Rock serves very good food, it's just more fun to tease them. You'll see what I mean soon. There's not a heck of a lot to do in Paradox but raise a little ruckus whenever you get the chance."

"The shadow's over the yardarm and it's been a long day. What do you say we walk to town? The exercise will do me good."

"Coming back at night walking could be hazardous, so I'll drive you."

"What do you mean 'hazardous?' This isn't Houston with muggers lurking in the shadows."

Jack Stoner clucked his tongue with a concerned look. "Rattlesnakes crawl out at night to hunt, lots of 'em around here. There's been a pair of mountain lions working the canyon lately. So far they've only eaten a few dogs and cats, but lions *are* unpredictable creatures. Not too long ago, one ate an investment banker in California."

"Hop in the Suburban," Lara said without hesitation. "I'll be glad to drive."

"Thank you, ma'am," he grinned, using the John Wayne allactation again. Jack Stoner was in a fine mood now. The corn on his left little toe was hurting from the walk; getting a ride into town was exactly what he wanted. He wondered briefly if there might actually be rattlesnakes or mountain lions about, he hadn't seen anything but rabbits and birds the two weeks he had been in Paradox. Anyway, he had the company of a lovely lady who was buying the beer. Life was good.

CHAPTER SEVENTEEN

The Black Rock Bar and Grill was not at all what Laura Masterson had expected, especially considering the general clutter of the old mining town. While the outside of the wooden building needed paint, the inside was immaculate and orderly.

In the middle of the one long room that housed both the bar and restaurant stood a huge black potbelly stove with a shiny chrome door and fittings. Across the rear, an ornate walnut bar with a mirrored backboard stretched from wall to wall. Along both sides were booths sporting white tablecloths. Doorways to the right from both the dining room and behind the bar led to the kitchen and owner's quarters. "*Private! Stay Out. Survivors will be sternly dealt with*" signs were prominently lettered over each. The agreeable smell of grilling food hung heavy in the air, a surprise from the haze of cigarette smoke she had expected. A quick scan showed three men seated on stools at the bar, an older couple with coffee cups in front of them occupied one booth. Another held two men wearing Bureau of Reclamation shirts.

"I see Frank and Rodney are already here," Jack Stoner said. "Happy hour doesn't start for..." he checked his watch, a Timex "...another four minutes. I'll put a letter in their personnel file to the effect they have difficulty structuring their time to best advantage."

Laura was still trying to figure out Jack Stoner. For a brief moment back at the camp she had glimpsed a depth to him he seemed to mask using humor. The man's pale blue eyes had disclosed a pain he lived with, an unspoken tragedy. Perhaps, she thought, someday he'll open up and talk about it. Until then, it's his business.

"I'd go easy on them if it's their first offense," Laura grinned as the two men in the booth stood to greet them. "But I bet they're chronic offenders."

"Yep, the worst," Jack Stoner nodded to a chubby, silver-haired man wearing bifocals. He appeared to be well into his forties. "This is Frank Lowry. Take care never to let him get in front of you in a buffet line." He then turned to the young, slender fellow who might not yet be thirty. He was skinny, nervous, and sported a crop of long black hair. "The kid's Rodney Simms. I keep telling him he needs to cut back on his coffee, but he never listens."

Laura made her introductions, then the four of them took their seats. Jack scooted a proper distance from the lady doctor.

"Rodney will run the backhoe when we dig up the graves," Jack said. "He's never done anything like that before, sort of has him on edge."

Laura looked at the young man. "You have to remember that you're not going to hurt them any."

"Oh geez," Frank said with a sigh. "The lady's only been in town for a few hours and already she's been around Jack too long."

Jack gave Frank a devilish glare. His John Wayne affect came back. "Listen up, Pilgrim. The lil' lady here's in charge of this operation. It's a mighty agreeable situation if'n she wants to lighten up a dead subject. And we'd all take it as a good gesture on your part if you'd buy the first round now that happy hour's officially started."

"Happy to do that for the nice doctor," Lowry said just as a thin older woman with reddish-purple hair came over carrying a note pad.

"Dr. Laura Masterson," Jack said to the waitress, "meet Thelma Ross. She owns the place and does most of the cooking."

"Glad to meet you, Doc," Thelma said, her voice was deep and gravelly. "We've been expecting you." The old woman sighed. "I reckon once you're done moving the cemetery we'll all be leaving Paradox about the same time."

Laura felt she needed to say something apologetic. "I'm sorry about the dam forcing all of you folks out of your homes."

Thelma gave a snort and grinned. "Biggest damned favor anyone could've done for the place, pun intended. This town is the end of the road, has been for years. We only catch a few occasional lost tourists and those on the run from the law. The mines are played out. My husband, Hurley, died back in '86 from black lung disease he got working in them. A nice clear blue lake filling this canyon will be an improvement, no matter how you look at it."

Laura was taken aback. This was not the attitude she had been led to expect. "I thought most people here would be very upset over being forced to move."

"There were a few grumps," Thelma said. "But everyone knew they were living on leased land. Hell, we have to make payments to the company every year, can't be any plainer than that. Beside, the Cougar Canyon bunch is paying me and Vernon who owns the general store a hefty bonus to stay open until the cemetery's moved and everybody's moved away. It isn't nice to fuss at people who pay you money."

"Where are you going to go?" Laura asked out of genuine curiosity. She had not pondered the fate of the people who were being forced to vacate the town. "You must have lived here most of your life."

Thelma gave a scouring look. "You could say I've *stuck* around here for a lot of years, but the living will start in a few weeks." She motioned with the ticket book to the kitchen door. "Sadie Helms, who helps me out with cooking, has a motorhome out back. Sadie lost her husband a few years ago, so there's just the three of us. We plan to do nothing but follow the seasons for as long as we can. The warm desert in wintertime, cool mountains in the summer. Why not, hell we get social security."

Laura asked, "You said there were *three* of you."

Jack Stoner answered for her, "They have a big black-and-white tomcat named Ulysses that's generally dragging something it killed through the restaurant. Last night it was a small raccoon, the day before he'd done in a packrat. As much as that cat likes to kill things, we think Thelma ought to change his name to 'Serial Kitty.'"

"Anyway, boys, the cat goes with us," Thelma took a pen from a pocket on her print apron. "What's your poison. I've got to get with it."

"Four Miller Lite long-necks," Lowry said, tossing a ten-dollar bill on the table. "And since we have a real lady present, a cold mug for her would be nice."

"You got it," Thelma scooped up the bill with a practiced hand. "I reckon you will all want the special, so I'll put you down for a plate. Tonight we're serving fried chicken, mashed potatoes with cream gravy, and sweet peas. There's going to be cherry cobbler for dessert."

Laura eyed Jack and said, "Barbequed mystery meat sandwiches and potato chips?"

Thelma chuckled. "That's for lunch tomorrow. Government men could mess up changing a lightbulb." She turned and went into the kitchen.

"That lady has been here working in this same place since Eisenhower was president," Lowry said. "You'd think she'd be heartbroken about having to leave."

Jack replied, "Thelma Ross is a realist, and smart enough to make the most of whatever life throws her way. I admire that trait in a person." He gave the silent Rodney Simms a knowing look. "And her husband was buried in Tucumcari, so you don't need to worry about that."

"I'll just be glad to get this whole task over and done with," Rodney said with a shudder. "The whole idea of moving dead bodies is downright spooky."

Laura Masterson remembered medical school and her trepidation at dissecting her first human corpse. She could empathize with the young man. "I had an anatomy professor who helped me through dealing with the dead. He said all any person really consists of is their spirit; the body is simply a method of moving it about. When a mortal dies, it's like a car that finally wears out. The soul moves on, leaving the worthless husk behind. That's all we're dealing with in the Paradox cemetery; empty husks. Everything that made those people human has moved on."

"I'll try to keep that in mind, Doc," Rodney said, staring at the tabletop.

Setting out the frosty bottles of beer, Thelma brought everyone out of their funk. The macabre task that had placed them together was forgotten. The four people who would soon begin moving corpses worked at enjoying the present.

CHAPTER EIGHTEEN

Buno Eberhard was always amazed and gratified at just how trusting most people were. It made his job so much easier.

The clerk at the front desk of the hotel kept yackking on the phone while keeping his gaze on a computer screen. He never noticed Buno palm a master room key card from a maid's cart that had been conveniently left in the lobby.

Earlier on, Buno had called the hotel using the premise of being a pizza delivery company driver who wanted to verify Dr. Kwan's room number as 212. The helpful clerk corrected him that the correct room number occupied by Luu Kwan was 618. People could be *so* useful at times.

Buno took care to dress in a baggy gray suit, which kept most anyone who saw him from coming anywhere near to guessing his true weight. A dapper tweed hat along with a pair of designer sunglasses and a false red goatee guaranteed that any witness to his presence would not be able to give even a close description of what he truly looked like.

But for this particular job here in Amarillo, Texas, Buno Eberhard seriously doubted it would come to that. Not if he was both careful and lucky. And he was *always* careful.

As Buno made his way down the empty corridor on the sixth floor of the hotel, he wondered again why he had been sent on this mission. Mr. Roth had made it plain to him in Rio de Janeiro that his job here was to keep an eye on Dr. Masterson and report on her progress. But his employer had also told him to follow Michael Delvaney's orders while he was here in the United States.

And following the lawyer's instructions was exactly what he was doing. Tasks like this were always so...*stimulating*. The rush that came with carrying out a successful hit, where nearly anything could go awry at any time, was a bigger high than cocaine ever had been. His senses always became so acute, he felt he could actually feel the presence of people long before he saw them.

Room 618 was a corner room, one with a balcony overlooking the town of Amarillo. Perfect. Any noise made would only be heard in the adjoining room. He knocked on the door. No one answered. Things were going smashingly well.

Buno slid the plastic card through slot next to the metal handle. The second the little light flashed green, he pushed the lever with his thumb while simultaneously holding a metal folding wand with his other hand, shaking it open to its full two-foot length.

The television was on and louder than he had expected. Buno suppressed a chortle when he realized the doctor was watching a rerun of the popular reality show called *Survivor*. The irony was simply delicious.

Then he saw the round lump of Kwan's head above the back of the sofa. The thin, silver-haired Chinese man had dozed off. A rhythmic snoring allowed Buno to relax and close the door behind him without being heard.

The metal wand made a dull thump when Buno slammed it squarely on top of the man's head. Dr. Kwan gave a low grunt and slumped forward. Buno grabbed him before he could fall on the coffee table. He did not want the police to find any unexplainable marks.

Buno scooped up the frail Dr. Kwan, marveling at how little the man was. He carried him into the bathroom, started a tubful of hot soapy water running, then began carefully undressing the unconscious man. The shoes were untied and placed in the closet. Pants and shirt were laid out on the bed along with a pair of white cotton pajamas Buno had found in a chest of drawers. From all appearances the good doctor had simply been preparing to take a nice relaxing bath.

Eberhard picked up the now-nude unconscious man and placed him in the tub, taking care not to get any water on his own clothes. Buno unwrapped a bar of hotel soap and rubbed it around in a wet washcloth to make it look well used. Then he placed the washcloth on its hanger and the soap in the proper dish. All was proceeding as he had hoped.

From his jacket pocket Buno extracted a small, silver-handled ice pick, a gift from his father. The sharp needle-like extension was precisely the proper length. It had been manufactured from good German steel for exactly this use many years ago, when the now-scarce items were often employed in state mental hospitals.

Buno propped up Kwan in one end of the tub and held him firm. With a towel draped carefully over his arm to keep his jacket dry, he carefully raised open the right eyelid, then he deftly inserted the pick at an upward angle in the corner of the little man's eye all the way to the hilt. A few circular motions destroyed the frontal lobe of Dr. Kwan's brain. He moved his attention to the left eye and repeated the maneuver.

A perfect lobotomy had just been performed on the brilliant doctor. From this time forward, Luu Kwan would require a nurse to change his diapers, let alone speak to anyone about much of anything. A slurred mewing sound was the best any of the others he had "operated" on seemed to be able to manage.

There were many pleasing aspects to a hit such as this one. With any good luck the police might be so anxious to get back to the doughnut shop that they would declare the whole thing an accident. The poor man had simply slipped in the tub and struck his head hard on the side when he fell. Too bad about the brain damage.

Any medical investigation that could actually disclose the needle damage might never be carried out. The cause was obvious, the prognosis certain. Should some neurologist become a snoop, it probably wouldn't happen until Buno was already long gone.

And the police were always far less anxious to investigate an assault rather than a glamorous, career-building murder case. The entire incident likely would be buried on page ten of the local newspaper, if it ever got reported at all.

Smiling from the adrenalin rush and satisfaction of a job well done, Buno Eberhard took his time tidying up. The rubber gloves he always wore on a job precluded him leaving any fingerprints. The thick manila envelope he had been told to bring back was easily found. He assured himself all was in order. As he turned to leave the bathroom, he wrinkled his nose. The once-brilliant doctor had just evacuated his bowels.

The hallway was still empty. A few minutes later, after taking the stairs to greatly lessen a chance of running into anyone, Buno Eberhard stepped outside the hotel into the rather cool night air of Amarillo,

Texas. A couple of blocks away, he retrieved the Hummer from a self-parking lot.

Just past the New Mexico state line, he stopped at a rest area where he tossed the pair of latex gloves into a trash can. Later, when he was in Tucumcari, the garish red goatee would also be properly disposed of in a public trash container.

In the rearview mirror, a red glow announced a new day was being born. With any luck he would be back in Paradox soon. The job had gone "smashingly well" as his father used to say, and he was famished. Buno decided to reward himself by having a hearty breakfast when he stopped in Tucumcari. Perhaps he might be lucky enough to find some decent German sausages and eggs on the menu. He certainly deserved a good meal for all of his skilled handiwork.

CHAPTER NINETEEN

It came as a surprise to Laura when she awoke from spending her first night in Paradox and discovered it was after eight A.M. The last time she had slept this late had been a couple of years ago when she was sick with the flu.

She yawned, wiped the sleep from her eyes with the back of her hands, and climbed from the bed. She did the usual stretching exercises she had done every morning since college, then put on a comfortable robe that had been thoughtfully placed in the closet.

When Laura walked to the kitchen she knew why she had slept so late. The high cliffs to the east had kept the sun's appearance at bay. Only now were a few yellow rays beginning to emerge over the high rimrocks to illuminate the canyon depths.

Laura filled the coffee maker and punched it on. The fact was obvious that she would have to set an alarm when the work began on moving the cemetery. It wouldn't do to be late for a battle against a terrible enemy.

Reflecting back on the night before, she found herself actually looking forward to working with Jack Stoner and his two helpers. Even the townspeople had been a welcome surprise. Thelma Ross not only put out a plate of fried chicken better than any Laura had eaten in years, but the gravelly voiced restaurant owner seemed to be genuinely anxious to leave the dying town.

Jack Stoner had even acquainted her with the town drunk, a muscular, tattooed fellow of about thirty-five who had long blonde hair worn in two braids that draped almost to his belt line. His name was Willie Ames.

While obviously well over the legal limit of intoxication when she met him, willie seemed pleasant enough. He bought a round of drinks for the table then returned to his stool at the end of the bar that faced a flickering television set turned to a baseball game.

"Willie's a buyer for an antiques dealer in Dallas," Jack had explained. "The man does like his liquor a tad too much, but he's helping these folks out a lot. He's been buying most anything anyone wants to sell—old cars, tractors, clothes, clocks, guns, you name it, Willie'll pay cash. I'd venture he's sent out over a dozen trucks loaded with stuff since I've been here."

"I would have thought that Willie and other antique buyers would've been trying to get everything at rock bottom prices," Laura ventured. "Mostly the people who still live here are too old to move things on their own, and they likely don't have any idea what many of their antiques are worth these days."

"There were lots of dealers who hit here about the time Willie did, when the news of the dam going in came out," Jack explained. "Willie's just either the most honest or the dumbest of the lot. When someone offers fifty dollars for a rusted-out old wreck of a car, Willie offers five hundred, and so on. These days he's the only buyer left and I'm figuring he'll be gone soon. There's not much left in Paradox worth hauling off."

"Except two hundred and eighty-nine bodies from the cemetery," Laura had spoken without thinking, which pretty much put a damper on dessert and the rest of the evening.

Buno Eberhard pulling in with the big Hummer brought Laura Masterson's thoughts back to the present. Surveying the ominous bodyguard's appearance through the window sent a shiver down her spine. Buno totally ignored her. He grabbed a couple of suitcases from the Hummer, tucked a fat manila envelope under his arm, and disappeared into his motorhome without so much as a glance toward her. She thought he looked very tired, which caused her to wonder briefly where he had been and if he had driven all night. No matter, there was too much to do today to concern herself with petty matters.

The coffee pot gurgled its last gasp, signifying the much-needed eye-opener ready at last. She poured a cup and took a testing sip. It was strong and black, just the way she liked it. The bag of ground coffee beans had a label stating it was hand-picked Columbian gourmet. Whoever had stocked the motorhome certainly knew good coffee, the brew was absolutely wonderful.

Laura went back into the bedroom and took a long, hot shower. She finished the coffee while dressing in blue jeans, work shirt, and hiking boots. Today she would have to start earning her paycheck.

There was fresh milk in the refrigerator, her favorite cereal in the pantry, and fresh bananas on the counter top. Once she finished her breakfast, she headed out to thoroughly check out the single most important item necessary to the success of the Paradox Project: the mobile laboratory.

Once inside the motorhome, Buno Eberhard pulled the drapes closed over the front windows, then, to be doubly assured of his privacy, he closed a second set that entered into the living area. He fished the remote from a pocket in the leather recliner he favored and pushed the button to lower the big flat-screen plasma television set.

It took several minutes before he found the channel he was looking for; a European station that featured classic German Opera sung in the language of the Fatherland, the way it was meant to be heard. Mozart's classic *Singspiel*, *The Magic Flute* was being played, one of his favorites. He turned up the volume, then he took off his uncomfortable, weapon-laden clothes and placed his trusty Walther 9mm PPK, which had been his SS officer father's, within easy reach. Buno often held the small, easily concealed weapon against his naked skin at night. He believed it helped him dream back upon the wonderful days of the Fatherland's glory and relive his father's, honor of killing Hitler's enemies with this pleasureful weapon.

Someday in the shining future, Buno reflected, the Third Reich would be strong and rule the entire world, as was destined to be its divine and deserved fate. Adolf Hitler had assumed the status of a god among a few true believers, a god as real as any worshiped by religious fanatics. And Buno Eberhard was counted among the center core of the true believers. He would do whatever he possibly could for the cause.

Alone now, Buno grabbed up the fat manila envelope that the Jew-loving Michael Delvaney seemed so concerned about. The Houston lawyer had become so base as to place his name alongside Jews in advertising what was, in reality, *his* law firm. This was another fine example of how far-reaching and intertwined the filthy tentacles of Semitism actually were.

He sighed. The Final Solution had come *so* close to succeeding. The next time, the eradication of inferior races would be complete. In the meanwhile Buno would kowtow as much as necessary to further the return of the Third Reich.

At least Philip Roth was of fine Aryan stock. Like Buno, Philip did what he had to do. Working for that man was not distasteful in the least.

Buno Eberhard knew what he would find inside the manila envelope before he ripped it open. Michael Delvaney had become quite upset when Buno had told him that no such envelope was to be found inside Dr. Kwan's hotel room. The lawyer had ranted, insinuated, and threatened. When Buno had reminded the seedy lawyer that Houston was not that far away and he would be *most* happy to meet with him face to face to discuss any problems they might have between them, with Mr. Philip Roth being brought into the conversation by telephone, the shyster had immediately grown apologetic and meek.

There was no doubt in Buno's mind that Philip Roth knew nothing of the envelope or its contents. He probably did not even know of the hit on Dr. Luu Kwan. Buno obviously and fervently wanted to keep it that way. The Jew-loving lawyer had been caught putting his hand in the cookie jar. This was a wonderful opportunity.

The bound stacks of American currency were in smaller denominations—twenties and fifties, mostly. All were well circulated, none of the serial numbers were consecutive. It was perfectly laundered cash. And, best of all, the rectangular green stacks added up to exactly a quarter of a million dollars. Perfect. And much needed.

The Third Reich had a budding headquarters in the cool mountains of Paraguay where both the terrain and climate mimicked their beloved Fatherland. A quarter of a million dollars would go far in helping the cause.

A sweet calm coursed through Buno Eberhard's veins as he caressed the mountain of money with one hand and his beloved Walther PPK with the other. The only thing that could make his visit to the United States even better would be to make another hit or two. He had no idea at all why he had been ordered to Paradox. It didn't matter as long as he could do what he loved best.

Perhaps he might be ordered to remove the woman doctor or the smart-mouthed Jack Stoner. Removing *both* would be even more delightful. Time and Philip Roth would tell. The direct line to the pharmaceutical magnate worked perfectly well, once he was out of this depressing canyon. And he was to check in every day. Keeping a balancing act between Mr. Roth and the lawyer Delvaney certainly presented no problems to the son of an SS officer.

Buno Eberhard placed the money back in the envelope and taped it shut. Wolfgang Amadeus Mozart's splendid creation had become overpowering; the wonderful composer's birthplace was the same as Adolf Hitler's. Buno felt such a yearning for bygone glories that a burning sensation seared his throat.

He wiped tears from his eyes, leaned back, and bathed in the sweet sounds of German Opera.

CHAPTER TWENTY

Dr. Laura Masterson spent some time studying the outside of the mobile laboratory before entering it. She had found a key ring hanging prominently on a hook in the bathroom of her motorhome labeled "laboratory," with each key labeled for the lock it fit. After finding one motorhome open, she could not help but wonder if the lab door was even locked. There would be time to check that out very shortly. Due diligence must come first when a person is preparing to do battle with a Satan bug.

The truck and built-in laboratory was, at first glance, a standard product of Safe-T Environmental products. This was a well-known company that had produced literally hundreds of mobile laboratories for field use since 9/11 and the anthrax attacks and biological panic that followed.

Further study from the outside showed that the laboratory had been greatly modified. The length of the laboratory itself, which was constructed entirely from stainless steel, was at least thirty feet, or ten feet longer than standard. The truck chassis required eight large driver wheels beneath the laboratory to support the extra weight that went along with housing electron microscopes, containment compartments, reverse air-pressure pumps, and all of the trappings of a biosafety level-four mobile laboratory.

Laura mused that not too many years ago, no one had even heard of biosafety levels. Nowadays they were as commonplace in her world as traffic lights and airplanes.

Biosafety level-one facilities were mostly for the least harmful of biological agents, those for which simple hand-washing and disinfectants such as alcohol or hydrogen peroxide could minimize the hazards.

Biosafety level-two was destined for the more pesky bugs such as salmonella, the fungi that causes ringworm, and others. Here the laboratories become more complex. There were autoclave, HEPA II air filters for breathing air, disposable lab coats, and all contaminated materials were disposed of as hazardous waste.

Biosafety level-three got a lot more complicated very quickly. Those units handled the really nasty organisms such as anthrax, hanta viruses, HIV, tuberculosis, and so on. Level-three laboratories contained almost every conceivable safety precaution: HEPA III filtered air; knee-operated or automatic disinfectant sprays at the exit; and two separate doors with an air lock similar to those used on the Space Shuttle. The entire laboratory was double sealed against leaks and negative air pressure maintained inside at all times, ensuring that if for any reason there was a breach in the seal, air would flow into the laboratory rather than out.

A mobile laboratory designed to deal with the nastiest and deadliest living organisms on earth was referred to as a Biosafety level-four unit, such as the one Dr. Masterson was now scrutinizing from the outside. The equipment and layout of the inside of the lab she would study intensely later. It was critical to learn exactly where every lever and dial was located, where every power cord was, along with the placement of every door handle. The operation of a level-four biohazard containment laboratory was akin to flying a jet airplane through a range of mountains; one tiny miscalculation and you were dead. Of course, in that case, only the jet pilot died—and died nice quick death. Viruses such as ebola, herpes B, and the Spanish Flu were not so merciful to their victims.

Laura noticed a heavy black insulated cable leading from the lab to a trailer that held a yellow generator set along with a fuel tank of considerable dimensions. Never one to take chances, she opened the filler cap to confirm the tank was indeed full of diesel fuel. The cable continued from a junction box on the trailer to a power pole which normally supplied electricity. The backup generator would only be used if the main power went out for some reason. When a person is working inside an airtight container, dependent on air pumps to stay alive, such precautions were a salve for their nerves. Because of many redundant safe-guards, no one was able to leave a level-four laboratory if the electricity went off.

Laura opened the control panel and pushed the off button for the power. After the usual ten seconds, the yellow Genset chugged to life sending a cloud of black smoke to rise against the deep blue New Mexico sky. Then the unit settled into a low steady rumble, just like it was supposed to do.

Laura shut off the generator and reset the switches for commercial power. She looked around to see if anyone else was about. The roar of the generator had silenced even the birds. Nothing moved in the eerie stillness of the canyon floor, not even a leaf fluttered on the many cottonwood trees.

The door to the laboratory entered from the rear of the unit. She walked up and climbed onto the grated steel steps. Somewhat to her surprise, the door was locked. Laura keyed open the lock, then pushed the latch button and waited a few seconds for the automatic air pressure equalizer to show a green light. Then she opened the heavy, rubber-sealed door and stepped inside the cubbyhole room. This was the airlocked decontamination area. Overhead and on the sides were spray heads where a disinfectant mist decontaminated anyone leaving. All laboratory suits were required to be sprayed before being removed.

As there were no hazardous materials to worry about at this time, Laura referred to the note on the keyring and punched in the proper sequence of numbers to open the interior door to the main laboratory. It was a simple five-digit code: 51967. The first number was the month she was born—May. The other four were the year of her birth—1967. Whoever had programmed the security codes obviously knew a great deal about her. The Hammond Foundation was thorough, that much was certain.

The negative-pressure air pump began humming softly as it was supposed to do, dropping the interior pressure by four psi. The displaced air exited through a HEPA IV filter to prevent the possibility of anything, even a single virus, being allowed to escape.

There was a familiar light gust of wind when Laura stepped through the portal of the second door and into the interior of the main laboratory. A click of the main switch on the wall by the open door bathed the interior in bright fluorescent light. Stainless steel cabinets and various glassware glistened like diamonds.

Laura took hours to inspect everything. The equipment and computer were all state of the art. There was a roomy containment cubicle with gloved entrance for full-arm use. The electron microscope was a very powerful Jeol brand. She took exceptional care to inspect the cell cloning supplies and equipment. The cloning of recombinant DNA required various plasmids, enzymes, and gels along with a host of expensive chemicals and reagents, all of which were of the highest quality. Everything seemed to be in order.

As she inventoried the supplies for the critical cloning process of genetic material from long dead viruses, Laura reflected back on the history of cloning. It began as early as 1880 when August Weissmann discovered that the genetic information of a cell diminished with each cell division. In 1953, the structure of DNA was recognized. Then with the space race, all technology exploded, including that of genetics. The word "clone" was coined in 1963 by J.B.S. Haldane. Then with more powerful computers and new techniques, the ability to clone plants and animals became not only a reality, it was commonplace.

But to revive a long-dead virus that had killed literally millions of human beings was another matter altogether. The very concept was chilling, yet necessary. One must first face a monster to be able to defeat it.

And defeating monsters was what Laura Masterson was here to do. Looking back over history, people always associated wars with death on a massive scale. But, all wars ever fought paled against the ravages disease had wrought against mankind.

As far back as historians have recorded events, there have been plagues on a massive scale. The city of Athens lost one-third of its population to an unknown disease that struck during the Peloponnesian Wars. The Black Death decimated Europe in the fourteenth century, killing an estimated quarter of the population. During the American Civil War, more soldiers died from disease than on the battlefield.

And when one looked back on the most modern, and possibly the deadliest of all diseases, Spanish Flu, the same terrifying statistics prevailed. The United States lost more soldiers to the flu than from German firepower during the Great War. Many of those soldiers died stateside during training.

Dr. Laura Masterson looked about the gleaming laboratory and steeled her resolve to do battle with a monster. The equipment that lined the walls she likened to weapons.

"Influenza," she said aloud, "I'm going to kick your microscopic butt."

She took a final look around to gather up the instruments she needed to extract the genetic samples and portable containment equipment to transport them uncontaminated to the laboratory. Laura placed the items in a canvas bag and keyed the door lock to open. After using the proper mode to assure no hazardous materials were as yet on board, the airlock took a moment to cycle the air pressure, then a small green light flashed on signaling the outside door could now be opened.

She stepped out, blinking her eyes against the bright orb of sun that was beginning to lower over the high rimrock to the west. Then Laura felt the chill of a distinct presence behind her and spun to face the stern countenance of Buno Eberhard. He was silently standing in the shadows of the mobile laboratory, twirling a silver pistol with both hands.

CHAPTER TWENTY-ONE

"I did not intend to startle you, doctor," Buno Eberhard said as he tucked the gun out of sight into a holster worn on the back of his belt. He had been raised to have good manners and to always address people by their proper, professional titles even if he planned on removing them from the world. "I'm sorry but I am simply keeping a watch on the camp. That is my job."

Laura composed herself as quickly and best as she could. The sinister tall man with a blonde crewcut and granite features was enough to unnerve a Marine Corps drill instructor. Yet she forced a show of composure. If—no, *when*—she cloned a living specimen of the Spanish Flu virus, security would be paramount. Buno could be necessary to have around then, possibly *very* necessary.

"I just didn't see you there," Laura said. "And my mind was on other matters."

"As I am sure it should be, Dr. Masterson. I trust the laboratory meets your requirements."

"Yes, it will do perfectly. We can begin the excavation of the graves tomorrow morning if the Bureau of Reclamation people are ready."

Buno lowered an eyebrow. He had not been told exactly what purpose moving dead bodies from a cemetery would serve his bosses, but it was certainly going to be unsavory work to his way of thinking. Once he put someone in the ground, he preferred to forget about them completely. There had to be good reason for all of this, a very profitable reason, but not one he wanted to get any closer to than necessary.

"I'll keep a close eye on the camp and equipment while the digging is going on," Buno said, narrowing his eyes to stare up at where a dying sun was bathing the high rocks in the crimson color of blood.

"I'm sure you will," Laura said, then she turned and walked the short distance to her motorhome.

After her brief encounter with Buno Eberhard, Laura felt unclean, like she had brushed against the essence of evil. She locked the door, closed the blinds, and took another long, steamy shower.

Her spirits were reviving now. Tomorrow would start a routine of long hard days of work. This would be her last chance to enjoy a fun, relaxing evening for the foreseeable future.

Laura chuckled at the thought of a night on the town in Paradox, New Mexico. One bar and restaurant constituted the entire spectrum of riotous fun available for many miles. Tucumcari beckoned with a siren song, but the thought of driving over what had to be the narrowest, most dangerous road in North America put a halt to that plan.

Thelma Ross served decent food, the jukebox surely held some tunes that were newer—and better—than Hank Williams, a singer whose twangy, nasal music would make a cat fight sound good. Laura definitely remembered hearing an Eagles song last night. A few dollars judiciously placed in the slot would definitely contribute to a better sounding evening.

Laura put some styling gel onto the palms of her hands and fluffed her clean, shiny brunette hair into a wispy shag. Then she dressed in a pair of tight-fitting blue jeans along with a western blouse. On a sudden wicked impulse, she daringly left the three top buttons undone. From the closet she removed and put on a simply beautiful pair of cowboy boots she had bought in Tucumcari. A few dabs of makeup, some lipstick and a splash of perfume later, Laura inspected herself in the full-length mirror on the bathroom door. A really sexy cowgirl looked back. Perfect. This was a night she wanted to relax, have some fun, and not even think about what tomorrow would bring.

Cowgirl Laura never even turned her head toward Buno's motorhome when she stepped out into the gathering darkness where a nearby covey of bobwhite quail were calling to one another, getting ready to nestle down for the night. She walked straight to the Suburban, climbed in, started the engine, and was gone.

High above the town of Paradox, on the very edge of a finger of sandstone rock, Buno Eberhard sat holding a cell phone in his lap while watching the constellations come into focus as night covered the land.

He had left the doors to the Hummer open, a CD of a German opera that he loved very much, Hugo Wolf's *The Magistrate*, played in the still desert night. Mercedes' soprano voice, as she sang to her magistrate husband, Corregidor, echoed wonderfully from the rimrocks that were now the dark color of old blood. The world desperately needed more culture. Culture only the Master Race could provide.

Buno wondered what Roth wanted to talk to him about. All he knew was that Roth's secretary had taken the call he had made at the preset time, and told him that Mr. Roth was indisposed for a while, but that he very much wanted to speak with him about a matter of importance and asked if he could stand by for a return call.

It meant nothing for Buno Eberhard to wait. Time was trivial to him, a river that flowed inexorably to a bright, glowing future world where inferior races and inferior people were either menial servants to the Aryans or snuffed out of existence.

Orion was making its appearance in the celestial equator. The bull, Taurus, and Gemini, Castor, and Pollux flickered fitfully to life.

Sitting on the edge of cliff, Buno Eberhard swayed to the sweet sounds of German opera and watched the heavens being reborn another night, and he waited for whatever instructions his boss in Rio de Janeiro had for him that were so very important.

CHAPTER TWENTY-TWO

If Laura Masterson had been betting in a poker game, she would have won this hand. The nasal sounds of Hank Williams twangy music filled the Black Rock Bar and Grill. Before looking around to see who was inside, she strode over to the jukebox and began feeding the machine dollar bills. After a few minutes of punching in some decent tunes such as the Eagles' "Hotel California" and Willie Nelson's "Red-Headed Stranger," her heart dropped when she noticed there were nineteen songs already ahead of hers. There was not the slightest doubt who she would be listening to for the next hour.

Laura sighed, then turned. There was no way she was going to let some long dead, terrible warbler ruin her evening. As she surveyed the bar, the road to Tucumcari did not seem like such a challenge. It was as if last evening had been cloned and was replaying itself for her benefit.

Jack Stoner, Frank Lowry, and the still-nervous backhoe operator, Rodney Simms, sat in the same booth in the same seats drinking the same brand of beer. Long-haired Willie Ames and the same two skinny old men in need of a shave who were in attendance last night were playing a repeat performance at the bar. Laura fervently hoped the dinner special wasn't fried chicken. Then she forced a smile on her face and went to take a seat with the Bureau of Reclamation crowd.

"You're late," Jack Stoner said seriously. "Really, really late."

"I am? For *what*?"

"Why, happy hour. Beer costs a quarter a bottle more now. Four till six is when you find the bargains here in Paradox."

"I'll never make that mistake again."

"Aw," Jack Stoner shrugged dismissively. "No problem, we've got ole Hank on the jukebox, he's worth the extra money. Never been a better singer in my book, except maybe Gene Autry."

Laura no longer needed to ask around for who had loaded money in the jukebox. *Oh well,* she thought. *After spending time listening to Hank Williams, tomorrow's task doesn't look all that distasteful at all.*

Frank Lowry said, "I noticed Buno Eberhard heading up the road again. He must have ants in his pants the way he keeps moving about so much."

"No, but I do like the analogy," Laura said eying a skinny older woman with long silver hair who was approaching the booth. "Buno keeps going up on the rimrocks to use his cell phone."

Jack Stoner grinned. "Puno must be a popular person. He could lower himself to using a calling card and land line like the rest of us do."

"That guy's creepy," Rodney Simms said. "I can't figure why he's even here let alone why he acts like he's in charge of the world."

"*Buno,*" Laura eyed Jack when she once again corrected him, "is here as my assistant is all. He keeps the camp stocked and in order while keeping away people who might be too curious for their own good, for reasons of their own safety."

The silver-haired lady sat a tray on the booth, then turned her head and coughed. From the deep wheezing sound her chest made along with her, skinny barrel-chested frame and rosy skin, Laura's medical training told her the old lady was suffering from advanced emphysema. They called patients with these symptoms "Pink Puffers."

"Laura, meet Sadie Helms," Jack said with a nod to the wheezing lady. "She helps Thelma run the place. That's her motorhome parked out back."

"We've been working on getting that old Winnebago ready to hit the road," Frank said. "Not much to do here until you're ready. Today we changed the oil and gave it a tune-up. The old bus needs new tires all around and probably brakes, but here in Paradox there's only so much a person can do."

"Glad to meet you," Sadie smiled, her cough temporarily under control. "You must be the pretty doctor folks are talking about. I'll fetch you a long neck bottle of ice cold beer. I was told that's your drink."

"Thanks," Laura said returning the smile. "I hope you get your motorhome in good order, especially the brakes. That road out of here is treacherous."

"Naw," Sadie flicked a hand dismissively as she turned to leave with the tray. "I've lived here for over thirty years. There's only been a few go over the edge. Most of those just suffered broken bones, healed up with maybe only a limp."

After Sadie had gone into the kitchen and out of earshot, Jack said, "Poor old gal's really sick. She's a great cook and a hoot to be around, especially after she's had couple of glasses of wine. Her husband passed away a long time ago, don't know for certain exactly when. I do know all he left her was a twenty-year-old motorhome." He gave a sad sigh. "The old bus is on its last legs, but I reckon it'll last as long as it needs to for Sadie's benefit."

Laura felt a twinge of sadness. "I hope they can do that—chase the seasons like Thelma mentioned."

"We *all* do," Jack said, then grew silent when Sadie came wheezing their way with a tray of sweaty brown bottles of beer.

"What's the special tonight?" Frank asked, making an obvious effort to sniff the air. "I'm famished."

Jack gently nudged Laura with an elbow. "I *told* you never to let that man get in front of you in a buffet line, he's *always* famished."

Sadie gave a gasp to fill her lungs with enough wind to speak. "How about stacked enchiladas with lots of onions and cheese with a couple of over-easy eggs on top along with plenty of refried beans and rice." She took time to gulp another breath. "I'll bring out some salsa and chips to keep you from passing out from hunger until I get things ready. Might be an hour or so."

Frank Lowry beamed at her. "If I wasn't already married, I'd drop down on my knees and propose."

"I'll feed you, but that's as far as I'd go even if you were Paul Newman or Robert Redford," Sadie snorted and said over her shoulder as she departed. "Had enough of cleaning up after men to last two lifetimes."

Laura cocked her head at Frank. "Now that's about the most firm rejection I've ever heard. Sorry."

"That's okay," Frank shrugged. "Not too long ago my third wife divorced me for the second time. I'm actually available these days...I think."

Jack shook his head sadly. "Don't go there, Doc. A recounting of Frank's love life will take hours and wipe out your appetite." Then he gently clasped her arm. "Hank Williams is playing a great Texas two-step. Let's go push each other around the dance floor."

"Be a shame to have good music go to waste," Laura said with a wry grin. "Let's hit it."

To Laura Masterson's happy amazement, Jack Stoner turned out to be an excellent dancer whether the tunes were fast or slow. After a while she really didn't care for Hank Williams's songs to end. The evening was shaping up to make not driving to Tucumcari for some nightlife a good decision. Jack made her happy and with what the morrow would bring, this was what she needed more than anything.

The sable carpet of night that draped softly over the deep canyon glistened with multitudes of twinkling stars. A wan moon was barely visible over the high rocks when Laura Masterson drove to her motorhome and shut off the engine.

When she climbed from the Suburban, the silence of night in the desert was unbelievable. Here, any small sound carried as if it was begging to be recognized. From somewhere up the shadowy canyon, coyotes wailed mournfully at the departing moon. From atop a distant power pole, an owl hooted its greeting.

The closer she got to her motorhome the more certain Laura became that she could hear opera being played. A closer inspection disclosed the sounds were coming from Buno Eberhard's coach. The fact that the sinister man loved opera, especially German opera, came as a complete surprise.

Then she could not help but gaze out over the old cemetery that held what was possibly the most deadly disease in the annals of man. The shifting antigen virus that had killed thousands was still there, buried with the poor hapless souls who were laid to rest all those many years ago.

In the starry blackness, the many marble tombstones that lay askew, victims of years of neglect, reminded her of the rows of corpses she had seen in pictures of the great flu pandemic of 1918.

Dr. Laura Masterson gave a sigh, then steeled her resolve to do battle with a monster, a nearly invisible monster that killed men, women, the old and very young with equally cold passion. Yes, the monster still lurked here. She could feel its icy presence.

Before turning in for the night, Dr. Masterson took a few moments to hang the dream catcher she had bought in Tucumcari over the head of her bed. Superstition or not, Laura needed and wanted all the help she could get.

CHAPTER TWENTY-THREE

Centers for Disease Control and Protection
Atlanta, Georgia

Ruben Hernandez pressed his right eye against the round black receptacle next to the thick steel door and awaited the retina scan to admit him. At the usual count of ten, the door clicked open. He gave a nodding smile to the overhead camera, then entered the cubicle, closed the door behind him, and waited for the elevator to drop him four stories down.

He had been through the same routine every working day for the past five years, ever since obtaining his master's degree in biology from Columbia University. Ruben still was amazed at just how much of the activities of the Federal Centers for Disease Control were underground, hidden from view, hence the nickname people who worked there gave the chambers: the Tombs.

In Ruben's particular section of the Tombs, there were thirty-six separate chambers, or rooms. There were several more but he had no idea just how many. His coworkers said the number was rumored to be as many as six hundred. They were all sectioned off, with no adjoining access, so there was no way to know. Every employee who worked in the Tombs had a specific task to perform. It was up to others to take the bits and pieces of information generated there, assimilate it, and use it for whatever purpose the government deemed necessary.

"Good evening sir," Mose Billings, the barrel-chested guard who met him at the elevator said without emotion. "Your identification badge, please."

Ruben held out the plastic card that dangled by a chain from his belt to the same guard as he had done at least two thousand times before; Mose had been working here since before Ruben had taken the job with CDC.

"Thank you sir," Billings said, then returned to sit stoically on the stool alongside the elevator door.

Ruben walked down the narrow, cold concrete passageways, all of which were dimly lit and painted a drab gray. On both sides were solid doors identified only by numbers. His access card only opened one door, A-15, his workplace.

Maria Valdez looked up and smiled when the thick door swung open to admit him. "Hi," Maria said cheerfully. "The day was routine, nothing coded to worry about. I hope your night'll be uneventful."

"So do I." He admired Maria's lithe form. If the lady wasn't married with three kids, he would push this relationship past the professional very quickly. But he merely nodded pleasantly. "You have a good night. I'll see you in twelve hours."

"*Hasta mañana.*" Then she was gone with a harsh clicking as the door locked him in for the next twelve hours.

It felt good to hear his native Spanish again. Ruben had grown up in El Paso, Texas, and was fluent in the language, a requirement for his job with the CDC.

Ruben surveyed the large television screen along the far end of the room. Dozens of smaller flickering televisions lined the sides. He took his seat behind the desk facing the big screen and keyed the computer that covered most of the desktop. Aside from the computer there were only two telephones, one black, the other red. Ruben always shuddered when he looked at the red phone.

On the large screen was the outline of the four states he was responsible for: Arizona, Utah, Colorado, and New Mexico.

Ruben Hernandez's job was to monitor televison and radio news, police and fire department transmissions, along with 911 calls for help. The high number of Hispanics in these states was the reason he had to be bilingual

The powerful computer in front of him was set to pick up watchwords such as "hazardous waste," "death," "unknown cause," "disease," and so forth. The CDC wanted to be informed of any possible problems well before they filtered their way through local bureaucracy. Monitoring all transmissions twenty-four hours a day was one method to accomplish that.

The big screen revealed the four states' boundaries, all interstate highways, and most secondary roads along with major population centers. There were numerous lights in the various states. Blue indicated biohazard level three. These were mostly permanent facilities: hospitals, power plants, military bases, chemical and gas plants, and the like. The red lights were reserved for biohazard level four. At present there were only a few lit, such as at the Los Alamos laboratories in New Mexico, and the Palo Verde Nuclear generating plant in Arizona. Strangely enough, there were red lights in Silver City, New Mexico and Kingman, Arizona. Ruben had not even a vague idea why those two were lit.

Ruben settled into the usual routine of letting the computer surf out keywords while listening to Fox national news on the nearest televison set. After a while on any job, a person soon figures out how to get the work done the most efficient way.

He jumped when the telephone rang. Thank God it wasn't the red one. That phone was only for national disasters. The last time it had rung was September 11, 2001.

"Yes sir," Ruben answered smartly. Then he began taking notes. The person on the other end did not identify him- a herself, never did. After a few minutes he hung up the phone and scratched his head. This was odd, extremely odd.

He studied his notes once again. There was no mistake. The information center for his area was directed to focus as much of their attention as they could spare on an area of 100 miles around the New Mexico town of Tucumcari.

This was very strange. If the CDC had foreknowledge of a possible biological event in that area, why simply monitor transmissions? Wasn't stopping catastrophes the mission of the CDC?

Ruben Hernandez posted the notes on the watchbook for Maria. He would also verbally tell her about the orders. He then went and turned on the police and sheriff's radios from Tucumcari and spliced the transmissions through the computer.

There was nothing really to report. There was a loose cow on the interstate, a fender bender in San Jon. All were routine happenings, yet Ruben Hernandez was familiar enough with the Centers for Disease Control not to take the order to focus on Tucumcari, New Mexico, lightly. No, it would probably be a lot healthier to avoid the area like the plague.

Literally.

CHAPTER TWENTY-FOUR

Rio de Janeiro, Brazil

Philip Quinton Roth, III wiped a tissue across his sweaty forehead, grunted, and tossed it into a wastebasket on the floor beside the satin-sheeted circular bed. He realized with a tinge of sadness that at the still-hardy age of fifty-nine, an eighteen-year-old contortionist who either had an insatiable appetite for kinky sex or deserved an Academy Award for acting like she did, could be downright exhausting to have in bed. At least the shapely olive-skinned girl with waist-length, raven-black hair had decided to take a shower, giving him time to recover.

This girl was named Vema, after the Indian goddess of sex, he was told. The description fit like a hand in a glove. Catching his breath, Roth reflected back on just how little the damages he had inflicted on the Chinese twins had cost him. The one artificial eye had been the single most expensive item. The time off to allow them to heal had been costly, but the figure did not add up to be an unreasonable one. And the delightful last experience with the twins had allowed him to vent his frustrations in such an *agreeable* manner.

Roth's wife had called to tell him that she was taking little Philip to Greece for a while, possibly as long as a month. The dental work the boy had endured in New York City had been grueling; the lad needed a nice long rest in a relaxing part of the world.

Roth had cheerfully told his wife to take all of the time she needed. There were many important projects underway that needed his personal attention. Having to walk all the way across the compound to the apartment where he normally kept his mistresses would be time wasted. Having them in his bed when he came home from work was infinitely more efficient.

He sat up and swung his nude body to a sitting position on the edge of the bed. He glanced at his gold Rolex and realized that he had had an appointment to talk on the phone with Buno Eberhard over three hours ago. He got up and put on a robe. The walk to his office and some time out of bed would be restful. Vema would be ready whenever he returned, that much he had no doubts about. Even if she wasn't in the mood, he owned the bitch. He would teach her a lesson she'd never forget if her demeanor turned sour. Handling people was what he did best, no matter what it took to get the job done. And no one ever crossed him twice.

Pilar Zamora did not raise an eyebrow when her boss came striding into his office wearing only a silk bath robe; after all, he had told her to stay and work until he said it was all right for her to go home. She had worked for Mr. Roth far too long to question anything the chief executive officer of Roth Pharmaceuticals did. And it was a healthy decision to never argue with him or mention a word of what went on here to anyone, ever.

"There was a package delivered by courier from your accountant in the United States," Pilar said as he passed. "I placed it on your desk. I believe Buno Eberhard is still waiting to hear from you."

"Yeah," Philip Roth grunted. "I'll take care of the matter."

Once in the privacy of his office and the door bolted, Roth took a key from his robe, a key that never left his reach, and opened a desk drawer. He extracted a small plate of glass, lay down two white rails of fine Colombian cocaine, and inhaled one line into each of his nostrils. The wonderful drug was the only way he could find the energy to stay awake at all hours to keep up with the pressures of business and *other* matters.

He started to close the drawer to his stash when he thought ahead to returning to his bedroom and Vema. From a jar of blue pills, he shook out one. His doctor had told him to take only a single tablet every twenty-four hours. But the good doctor obviously did not have a true appetite for sex. Philip Roth tapped out a second tablet and washed both down with a bottle of Perrier water. He checked the time. One of the drawbacks of his company's counterfeit sex drug was the half hour it took to begin working, and the effects only lasted a few hours when it gave adequate assistance. Once the Paradox Project was out of the way, he vowed to put his company's best minds on improving the total effect of the drug which he jokingly referred to as "a firm asset."

As the white powder began to take its desired effect, he felt as if his mind was expanding. He could see into every problem, every *potential* problem, and knew exactly how to handle them. Buoyed now, he dialed the number of Buno Eberhard.

Less than ten minutes later, he hung up the phone and leaned back in his comfortable leather chair. He studied the portrait of his father that hung on the wall next to the door while pondering Buno's report. The hireling obviously was unhappy with his orders, but had the good sense not to complain. Little did Buno Eberhard know that all it would take to remove Buno's head from his shoulders for Philip Roth to punch was a series of numbers into the cell phone. It always paid dividends to be prepared.

Philip Roth made a few routine notes to call people later and dictated a letter for Pilar to type and mail. Then he called his personal broker in New York City, waking up the bastard, but the man had the good sense to not complain. Any broker would kowtow for *Roth's* business. He took out warrants to buy a million shares of Roth Pharmaceuticals stock at five dollars a share over today's closing price. The option was valid for six months. No problem if things went as planned on the Paradox Project.

He found the very thought of turning a paltry million dollars into the magnificent sum of a billion with no more effort than making a simple phone call exciting and satisfying. Immensely satisfying.

Philip Roth took a moment to open the package from the accountant. He knew what it was: a tape recording detailing every dollar that the scheming attorney, Michael Delvaney, had skimmed. The tape, along with a player, would be sent to the clinic in Grenada. Thinking of the lawyer chained to a bed and being forced to listen to the tape of his misdeeds being played over and over, twenty-four hours a day, while his organs were slowly harvested, was absolutely *delicious*.

Everything was coming his way. Philip Roth felt a growing sensation of pleasure in his loins. The blue pills were working their magic. He owed it to himself to get back home and Vema. He pushed away from his desk. As he strode past his father's portrait, he smiled at the old man's stoic likeness.

"It is absolutely friggin' *good* to be the boss," he said, then opened the door and went out.

CHAPTER TWENTY-FIVE

The morning sky hung heavy over the dying town of Paradox, New Mexico. The covering was a drab gray, cheerless as old concrete.

"Maybe it'll rain," Jack Stoner said with a furrowed brow. "I could wait to start doing what we're about to do."

"This is the desert," Frank Lowry said with a shrug. "It never rains out here. Those clouds are just moving the moisture to a more deserving part of the world."

Rodney Simms took a final skeptical glance upward at the dreary overcast sky, shook his head sadly, then turned the key on the backhoe to start the glow plugs warming. A moment later, the "wait" light clicked off and he started the diesel engine. After allowing the Case tractor a few minutes to warm up, Rodney placed the backhoe into gear and led the slow procession from the camp through the rusty gate that opened onto the old cemetery.

"The weather sort of fits the occasion," Jack said to Laura Masterson as she walked beside him carrying a large canvas bag. "From the looks of those clouds it ought to be cold enough to snow, but the temperature must be in the sixties, at least."

Laura looked over her shoulder to the motorhomes. Buno Eberhard stood in front of them, drinking coffee and watching. She realized that for all of the man's apparent toughness, he was actually afraid to join them. This did not strike her as odd. A lot of people couldn't handle being around dead bodies, let alone digging them up after they'd been in the ground for many years. Not even formidable Teutonic bodyguards.

It was as if he understands the horrific remnants of a disease that killed millions of people back in 1918, Laura thought. Then she cast the notion aside. That cold fear of the disease was hers and hers alone. No one here, save herself, was aware of any attempt to clone the shifting antigen flu virus. The demon had yet to be reborn before it could be feared. But, she nearly shuddered, that *was* why she had come to Paradox.

"We'll start at the northwest corner," Jack said, brandishing a plastic-covered map of the cemetery. "From there we can work our way south, then back again down the next row of graves, kind of like plowing a field." He gave her a questioning look. "If that's all right with you, of course."

"That will be fine, Jack," Laura surprised herself with the casual use of the government man's first name, but she was beginning to feel comfortable working with him. In fact everybody on the project seemed competent and pleasant to work with. Everyone except Buno Eberhard.

Laura made up her mind to forget about the foreboding guard and concentrate on the business at hand. Her only objective, and the reason the Hammond Foundation had sought her out, was to recreate the Spanish Flu in order to find a vaccine to prevent another pandemic. But she still had to maintain a reasonably nonchalant demeanor. The men working here needed to be reassured, not frightened. And there really was not much chance of some communicable disease being found in any of the bodies. At least nothing to worry about that simple sterilization and sanitation practices could not prevent.

Rodney Simms swung the Case backhoe about with practiced ease. He extended the hydraulic leveling legs, swung the swivel seat around to face the levers, then looked to Dr. Masterson for approval. She gave a nod. The backhoe operator had noticed several lines of wooden lathes that had been set by surveyors long before any of them arrived that purported to outline all of the grave sites. Rodney had been a backhoe operator for several years and knew better. He had dug into buried telephone lines, sprinkler systems and gas and water pipes that were not supposed to be there far too often to have much of a comfort level when it came to surveyors. His trepidations would soon become horrifyingly true. He just knew they would.

"There'll be a transport crew down here in a couple of hours," Jack Stoner said to Laura, speaking loudly over the rumbling diesel engine. "Once you're done with your examination or testing or whatever, we'll tag the body bags and their tombstones. This way we can keep them matched together without a lot of chance for any mistakes." He grinned. "After all of this time I'm sure they've grown attached to each other."

Laura watched as the special grave-sized bucket on the backhoe scraped off a second pass of reddish-brown earth and dropped it to one side. "Jack, I can honestly say that you'll be the last person on earth to let them down."

Stoner was pleasantly surprised at Laura's black graveyard humor. He honestly felt some relief of this sort was absolutely necessary anytime there was a revolting or unsavory task to be performed. And, heaven only knew just how many times he had been called on to perform worse tasks than this one. *Far* worse tasks. Jack turned to Laura, the pleasant smile on his face froze, then melted into a grimace when he glanced at the pile of dirt the backhoe had just discharged. A yellow, grinning skull rolled from near the top of the heap and came to a stop against the big back rubber tire of the tractor.

A wide-eyed Rodney Simms had seen the skull. He shut off the engine and spun the seat around to face Jack. "That *wasn't* supposed to be there," Rodney said with surprising calm.

Dr. Masterson stepped close to the excavation and studied it intensely. "We're not down much over two feet." She made a moue. "I was afraid we might encounter a few of this type of thing. I just didn't expect it would happen on the very first hole we dug."

Frank Lowry came walking over. He shook his head at the weathered skull. Then glanced at the shallow hole. "Six feet under in New Mexico is not the same as it is in other places." He clucked his tongue. "Leastwise it appears that way."

Jack spoke to Laura, with a hint of harshness in his voice. "What do you mean you *expected* the graves to be shallow? Also I don't see even a splinter of wood. Weren't these poor people laid away in caskets?"

Laura kept her gaze on the skull. When she spoke her mouth felt dry, like old parchment. "I only suspected something like this could have happened. Those were hard times, terrible times. Most of the deaths occurred in the wintertime, the ground frozen solid. The gravediggers were tired and frightened. My guess is we may find more than one body in several of the grave sites." She turned to face Jack, her expression taut. "There were a lot of people dying here. They needed them buried quickly to prevent contamination. And now we know they did just that, putting more than one body in a grave."

"Yeah." Jack gave a slight sigh and stepped close to survey the skull. "I don't think anyone really should be surprised or upset over this. We weren't here when they buried these people. The job is just going to take a little longer is all."

"Whose name are we going to put on the tag for the body bag?" Frank asked. "And if we keep coming up with unexpected bodies, we'll also have to send for some more bags. There were only supposed to be two hundred and eighty-nine folks buried here."

"Just label the bones as unknown," Laura said. "And put the grave number on the tag. We'll dig this one body out by hand, then the backhoe can go on down to the coffin that's supposed to be there." She added, "We simply don't have any idea yet how many other bodies we'll find that we don't know about."

Dr. Masterson had to remember not to say too much. What had her concerned more than anything was the lack of any recoverable genetic materials available from a corpse that had decomposed to only a few intact bones. For her purposes she needed bodies that had been well encased in coffins, protected from the ravages of ground water and direct contact with acidic soils that composed the floor of the canyon and the cemetery.

"Shouldn't we be wearing masks and rubber gloves?" Lowry asked. "They do on all the television shows."

Rodney Simms gave out a low groan.

Laura reached into her big canvas bag and extracted some surgical masks along with pairs of white disposable latex gloves.

"Put these on. There's not much possibility of any germs, but it pays to be on the safe side." She knew the masks were nearly useless except to help block out any foul odors. They were meant to keep the wearer's germs from spreading, not as was popularly believed, to keep the person wearing the mask safe from disease. The gloves were always a good idea. They kept the person doing the digging from contaminating any genetic materials, along with being hygienic.

Jack Stoner went to a long covered trailer that had been parked at one end of the cemetery and carried back a black body bag which he unzipped and laid open alongside the grave. He took a pen from his pocket and noted the number of the grave as 01. Then he filled out the paperwork for the tag adding only the words "unknown remains." He placed the paperwork into the weatherproof slot and closed it. "Well boys," he said, "grab up a shovel and a rake. We need to get this person taken care of so we can get on with the program."

Laura Masterson picked up the skull and studied it. Whoever it was had died very young. From the size of the skull she guessed the person could not have been much more than eight years old. Pneumonia, flu, or accident, it could have been anything. There was nothing to do but gently lay the pitiful bones to rest at another location. Whoever it was, they would remain nameless for all time.

Frank Lowry shook Laura Masterson from her thoughts when he handed her a blackened femur bone to add to the contents of the body bag. She gently placed the skull and bone into the open rubber case and turned to help remove more old bones of a nameless child from the Paradox, Cemetery. It would be only the first of many.

CHAPTER TWENTY-SIX

That evening Laura Masterson sat with the Bureau of Reclamation people in their usual spot at the Black Rock Bar and Grill. Neither the Eagles playing on the jukebox nor the sweaty brown bottle of beer on the table was doing anything to help her out of the funk she had fallen into. Of the six graves they had unearthed today, not a single one held more than badly weathered and decayed bones.

The coffins had rotted and fallen in, and the acidic moisture of the soil had completely obliterated any of the genetic material that she desperately needed to be able to clone the Spanish Flu virus. From the sketchy records that had been kept, at least two of the people buried in those six graves had succumbed to the flu, but all that remained were weathered old bones from which all flesh had been leached away by natural processes. If all of the bodies in the cemetery had been as destroyed as the first few, her hopes, her research, would all come to naught.

"Hey, cheer up Doc," Jack Stoner said with a cheerful twang. "The only bonus body we got today was in that first hole. Maybe things will improve and we can get out of here sooner than planned."

Rodney Simms chugged beer and set the empty bottle down with a thud he hoped would be loud enough to attract Sadie Helm's attention. "This is the last cemetery I'm going to dig up. I thought the bodies would still be in nice solid coffins and all I'd do is uncover the box then it could be moved so that I wouldn't have to see what's inside. But oh no, that's not how things turned out. There's nothing but bones and pieces of rotten wood down there. Downright spooky work's what this job's turned out to be."

"Now, Rodney." Frank Lowry kept his gaze on the open doorway to the kitchen, wanting to know what the night's special was. "We're only getting started here. Why, I'm betting that as we move up the slope, the ground will be dryer and those coffins will be intact. You need to work on having a more positive attitude."

Laura felt her sense of despair lessen. "Frank is probably right about that." She seriously hoped that would be the case. "Besides, we're just getting started. And we are beginning at the lowest point in the graveyard."

"Just give me some nice solid coffins," Simms said. "And I'll scrape the dirt off of them nice and gentle like. It'd be a pleasure not to have my work look back at me."

"They're just skulls." Jack Stoner's attention was taken away by Sadie Helms coughing her way out of the kitchen. "And they're long past being able to hurt you or get hurt by you, so quit bellyaching. We're all doing the best anyone can under the circumstances."

"I didn't mean to disturb a good fuss," Sadie Helms wheezed as she began setting out another round of drinks, "but we couldn't help overhearing your conversation." She rolled her gray watery eyes to Rodney. "What did you expect for Pete's sake? You took a job to dig up a cemetery where people have been buried for over eighty years. A few bones shouldn't come as much of a shock."

"No ma'am," the backhoe operator realized that sympathy wasn't coming his way. "I'm going to see it through. It's just the idea of disturbing the dead that's bothering me, but I'll get the job done."

"Well don't hurry none on my account or Thelma's." Sadie stifled a cough. "When the last grave is moved, we're going to have to leave. Kinda hate to have that day come any sooner than it has to."

"It will be a while," Laura said.

"We're planning on that," Sadie said. "Thelma and I have a couple of freezers of food to get rod of first. We can't take much with us when we leave here. That old motorhome of mine doesn't have a very big refrigerator."

"Speaking of food," Frank Lowry said taking a sniff of air, "what's the special tonight?"

"Rib-eye steaks. Had them on the menu for fifteen dollars with no takers. Guess Paradox isn't a place for expensive food. We've thawed them out and will grill up one any way you like it and serve it up with a baked potato, sour cream, and butter along with sweet peas and a nice bowl of ice cream in any flavor you want as long as it's chocolate, for six measly bucks."

"Sounds great," Frank said with a genuine smile. "I'll take two. I'd like the steaks rare enough that a good vet might pull the cow through."

Rodney Simm's complexion took on a greenish cast. He bolted up and ran to the restroom.

"That boy definitely has a weak stomach," Jack said.

Laura felt sorry for the young man. She remembered all too well the first human cadaver she had dissected back in medical school. Having to dig up corpses from an old cemetery wasn't much better. It was, however, something that Rodney Simms would have to deal with his own way. She only hoped he might be spared the nightmares she had suffered through.

"Well, look who's here," Sadie lowered her notebook to stare out the front window at the black Hummer that had just pulled up to the bar. "It's that gun-toting guard who won't even take the effort to wave at anyone. Buno Eberhard's actually coming to visit."

The only sound in the Black Rock Bar and Grill was the Eagles haunting tune "Desperado" coming from the jukebox when Buno opened the door. His pale blue eyes scanned the room, then he strode directly to Laura Masterson.

"You need to go call Mr. Delvaney," Buno Eberhard, said ignoring everyone else as the table. "The call is important. He's waiting in his office."

Laura nodded. "My phone's back at the motorhome. I'll have to go get it. Can't see carrying the thing around since it doesn't work here in the canyon." She grimaced. "I don't like to drive that road in the daytime, let alone now that it's getting dark."

"Hop in my truck," Jack said. "We'll swing by and grab that cell phone then I'll drive you up. Been raised out here in the west. A nice wide road like that one's no problem. Now up in Colorado and parts of Utah I can show you roads steep enough that if a person drove off one they'd starve to death before they hit bottom." He grinned evilly at Frank. "Well, *most* folks would starve."

"The call's personal," Eberhard's voice came as a deep growl. The blonde bodyguard was angered to find he hadn't been able to remove that cocky smile from the government man's face. "I will drive her up myself."

"No problem, Puno." Jack stood, his eyes sparkling like flint. "I'll be happy to drive the good doctor up and I'll give her plenty of privacy. Why don't you sit down, let me buy you a beer, or maybe something stronger."

Buno Eberhard felt his muscles tense to the hardness of steel. He had just been insulted. No one insulted a true Aryan, a member of the Master Race, and lived. Yet, he had his orders. "Yeah, okay. But you keep your distance. And my name is *Buno*."

"Yep, that's what I thought I said." Jack pushed his way past the bodyguard, looked him square in the face, and smiled coldly. "Enjoy your drink." He waited for Laura to join him, then they were gone.

Buno Eberhard was so angry he ground his teeth. There was something else even more troubling that he had seen in Jack Stoner's face. It was a look he knew well: The government man was not afraid of him in the least. Jack Stoner had the icy eyes of a killer. Of that there was no doubt. No doubt at all.

Dr. Laura Masterson walked over to an open spot on the high rimrocks to be well away from Jack Stoner. The cheerful government man seemed perfectly content to stray about with his hands in his pockets while surveying the twinkling canopy of stars that now filled the sky. She was glad that Jack had driven her up instead of Buno. The air had simply been electric between the two of them, something she had not expected. While nothing had actually happened, Laura realized it would be best to keep them apart as much as possible. She liked Jack Stoner, didn't want to see him get hurt.

The buttons on the heavy black cell phone were small, hard to see in the wan light of a low half moon. Laura had remembered which single button was the lawyer's number and pushed it. Before she placed it to her ear Laura heard Michael Delvaney's voice.

"Thank you for returning my call so promptly, Dr. Masterson. I know the phone service there is trying. I understand the excavations have begun."

"Yes sir. We opened six graves today."

"And your preliminary analysis is what?"

"As you said, this is only the start of the project. I'm afraid the bodies we recovered today had been decayed to the point of not being a donor of genetic material."

"How distressing. But we must keep a buoyant attitude. The Hammond Foundation has their entire laboratory facilities at the ready to manufacture immense quantities of vaccine once we have a sample of the live virus."

"I understand the importance of my task here."

"Excellent, Doctor. I know you will succeed and do so. *Soon.*"

Laura Masterson felt her throat tighten. "Has there been another outbreak?"

"Three dead in Ciudad Acuna, Mexico. They were relatives of the earlier workers who perished. We are hopeful the containment efforts will be successful...but."

"I know, Mr. Delvaney. When I obtain a sample I'll work around the clock until a live sample is cloned."

"I'm sure you will. There are untold millions of lives hanging in the balance. And Doctor, *you* hold the scales."

Laura swallowed. "We will continue tomorrow...."

Michael Delvaney interrupted. "I have another call coming in, one that I must take. I really don't need to hear anymore of your excuses. Call me tomorrow night at *precisely* nine, *your* time." Then a click signaled the lawyer had hung up.

Laura Masterson sighed, keyed the phone off and stared upward where a small meteor was ending its life in a streak of flaming sparks on the southern horizon somewhere over Mexico, she thought.

After taking a few moments to compose herself, she returned to Jack Stoner. He gave her his usual smile, then they climbed into his pickup and started down into the black depths of the canyon. Somehow the town of Paradox seemed even more remote, bleaker than before. Of course, it was the same, Laura realized. The lawyer's phone call had only served to deepen her funk.

"Let's go put away another beer and enjoy a good steak," Jack said cheerfully. "Once we get *Puno* gone it will be reason to celebrate in my book."

"I like that book. Should be a best seller." Laura scooted a little closer to Jack as they drove deeper into the canyon.

CHAPTER TWENTY-SEVEN

When Laura Masterson and Jack Stoner walked back inside the Black Rock Bar and Grill, Buno Eberhard, who was sitting alone at a distant corner table nursing a drink, eyed them coldly before standing. The bodyguard finished the last taste of Jagermeister, which was the only liquor from the Fatherland offered by this beggarly place, then strode to meet them.

Buno Eberhard desperately wanted his knuckles to wipe away the wry smile that seemingly was permanently engraved on Jack Stoner's face. But he had orders to keep a low profile, for now at least. And one thing the dutiful son of a Nazi SS officer could be counted on was following orders.

"You made the call?" Buno asked Laura, only glancing briefly at Jack Stoner.

"Yes, I did. Thank you for the message."

"That's my job." Buno Eberhard glared now at Jack Stoner, his pale blue eyes were ice cold. "That, Dr. Masterson, and also keeping you safe from harm."

"And you're really good at it, too." Jack Stoner placed a hand on Laura's waist. "I think it's past time for that steak dinner." He gave Buno a toothy grin that he knew would irritate him more than any insult. "Mighty safe place around here, it seems."

"Take care, Mr. Stoner," Buno said as he stepped to one side to leave. "It would be a shame if you were to suffer some unfortunate accident and ruin all of this peace and quiet."

"Oh, I *always* keep my eyes open." Jack Stoner waited until the cold-eyed German bodyguard left the restaurant before escorting Laura back to the booth.

"I'd take that comment as a threat," Laura said quietly to Jack before they were close enough to the others to be overheard. "I think

I'll ask for a replacement, a guard who doesn't have a chip on his shoulder."

Jack gave a small chuckle. "Nah, ol *Puno* won't cause us any trouble." He clucked his tongue. "Leastwise none that we can't handle. He's not smart enough."

"I'm sure you're right," Laura said taking her seat. She poured the last of her beer into a glass. It would be warm, but the bracing effect was needed. Both the conversation with Michael Delvaney and the near confrontation between Jack Stoner and Buno Eberhard had been unnerving.

"They said you'd be back soon," Sadie Helms said with a wheeze. "I've got your steaks warming up by soaking them in beer. Makes 'em nice and tender—not that they are tough mind you, best cuts you can buy."

"Tenderizing and flavoring steaks with beer is a secret employed by some of the world's best chefs." Jack Stoner's good humor had returned. "We look forward to them, right after another nice cold one."

"You got it," Sadie glanced at the far table that held Buno Eberhard's empty glass. "Personally, I think that guy's face would crack if he ever tried to smile. Seemed totally pissed off we didn't have any German beer. Where the hell did he think he was, Munich for Pete's sake? This in New Mexico. At least we finally sold some of that damn Jagermeister. The bottle's been here nearly as long as the town has."

Laura Masterson smiled and relaxed. She was among friends. "I'll take my steak medium rare with a nice coating of black pepper before you grill it, if that's not too much trouble."

"Just the way I like mine." Sadie looked to Jack Stoner. "And you'd like yours the same way, or I ain't been working in a restaurant for too many years."

"You got it right, Sadie." Jack eyed the two empty plates in front of Frank Lowry. "And from the looks of it, I'm betting they'll be mighty tasty. Ol' Frank didn't leave a morsel that could be recognized." He looked at Rodney Simm's empty chair. "Did our backhoe operator call it a night?"

Sadie gave a nod. "He was still green around the gills when he left. I don't think digging up old graves agrees with his appetite."

"He'll get over it," Laura said, grabbing up her glass of tepid beer and thinking back on her own difficulties dealing with death and corpses.

"I reckon he will at that," Sadie Helms spun and was gone to fetch some cold bottles of beer. While in the kitchen she reminded herself to tell Thelma to put a coating of black pepper on the two steaks that were marinating before tossing them on the grill.

Buno Eberhard had held in so much unreleased anger he could actually feel his intestines quivering. He hated this place, hated the United States of America, hated the silver-tongued Houston lawyer, Michael Delvaney, but most of all he hated Jack Stoner.

The son of a bitch had actually faced up to him, a true son of the Fatherland, a member of the Master Race. Some day very soon, Buno would teach Jack Stoner to be afraid of him. Very much afraid. And then he would kill him, slowly and painfully. That was the way all enemies of the Chosen People should be treated. Human trash, mules that walked on two legs, that was what Semites and those who kow-towed to them were.

Buno Eberhard breathed deeply three times. Better now. He felt his insides relaxing. Atop a nearby power pole a hoot owl tooted a greeting. Desperately he wanted to pull out his beloved father's Walther PPK and turn that blasted bird into a shower of blood and feathers. But this was the damn Jew-run United States of capitalistic America, couldn't do it. Too many laws here, laws that were on the books solely to put people like him behind bars. That was how the cowardly Jews did things—pass idiotic laws designed only to collect fines and protect their sheeny rear-ends.

Calming now, Buno thought back on Jack Stoner, sizing him up like a predator does a worthy prey. And worthy prey was exactly what the arrogant government man was. The man's smile was deceptive. When Stoner walked, he kept his weight on the balls of his feet, balanced like a ballet dancer. This was the result of many years of training in the martial arts? Buno had carefully noted the dark line of callouses along the outside edges of both of the man's hands. Constant Karate practice would cause those, nothing else.

But why in the sacred name of Hitler would a simple government lackey be trained in the martial arts? Buno snorted, this *was* America.

People over here often did odd things for various reasons. But they were *all* soft, spoiled, lazy. Not at all akin to their vigorous future Teutonic masters. Jack Stoner was simply a man, and any man can be killed. That Buno knew for certain. It was always much more satisfying to kill an opponent who was dangerous enough to at least make the task interesting.

Buno Eberhard gave the irritating tooting owl one final scowl, climbed into the black Hummer, and was gone, leaving a cloud of red dust hanging in the still night air.

"This steak would create long lines in a restaurant if we were in Houston, Texas." Laura Masterson daubed a napkin to her lips then looked around the bar. Frank Lowry had gone back to his trailer. At the long back bar, even the always present Willie Ames and the other two men were missing. Laura wondered if Willie had completed his collection of Omnium-gatherum and departed Paradox for good. She could not blame him if he did; there was precious little of value to be seen here. Within a few short weeks everything that had not been carted off would have been burned and the ashes buried.

"I can honestly say I've never had a better steak dinner, anywhere, ever." Jack Stoner leaned back in his chair, a look of satisfaction on his tanned face. "We're going to miss this place."

Dr. Masterson was feeling melancholy, thinking of all the thousands of people who had called this place home through the many years, even hanging on after the last coal mine closed in 1964. It seemed sad, somehow, to destroy a legacy, even a drab little town in the bottom of a steep canyon.

Jack Stoner seemed to be picking up the same feelings. He listened to Sadie and Thelma clanking dishes about in the kitchen. Laura Masterson and he were alone, the last customers to be around at the late hour of ten-thirty. After a long moment of silence Jack said, "The worst part of the day came when we didn't have a name to put with the bones we dug up. I guess I'd never make a good Navajo."

"Why is that?" Laura asked, genuinely interested.

"I've had some jobs in northeast Arizona on the reservations. I got to know a few Navajos and spent time with a few of the clans, good people. The Navajos have a very pragmatic way of dealing with death.

They believe once the person dies, their *Chindi* or ghost leaves the body for a better place.

"The Navajo will not speak the name of the departed for a year. The reason is that the *Chindi* might hear its name called and stick around to see why it is needed."

"Maybe they are right, Jack. There are a lot of different religions, different beliefs. Who's to say what is right and what is wrong?"

"You know, Laura, the Navajo Indians do not have a word in their language for what we call religion. Yet they honor their gods and customs far better than we so-called enlightened people do. I admire them for doing that."

Laura started to say something when Sadie Helms came wheezing her way over carrying a tray burdened with two heaping bowls of chocolate ice cream. Each had a shiny red maraschino cherry on top.

"We've been listening to you two. Downright depressing it is. Here, have some ice cream and for Pete's sake cheer up. Thelma and I are trying to look forward to leaving this place." She caught her breath. "A little help in that area would be nice."

Both Jack and Laura leaned back to stare at the huge bowls of ice cream. Each one had to hold at least a pint.

"Don't sit there eyeing 'em like a cow looking at a strange calf," Sadie said in a mock scolding voice. "Ice cream, especially chocolate ice cream, and too much of it, is the world's best cure for the blues. Now dig in and act like you mean business." Then she spun and hacked her way back into the kitchen.

"We have our orders," Jack said.

"Isn't disobeying a direct order a court martial offense?"

"I'm afraid it is."

"Probably lots of jail time."

"Years and years, and that's only if the judge is in a good mood."

Laura Masterson gave an evil grin. "Beat you to the bottom." She grabbed the spoon and went for the maraschino cherry.

"You're on, lady."

The last two customers in the last restaurant in Paradox, New Mexico, began laughing their way through bowls of ice cream. Outside a lone hoot owl welcomed the rising moon that had begun to shoot wan yellow shafts dancing among the marble tombstones of the distant cemetery as if fey spirits were enjoying the night.

CHAPTER TWENTY-EIGHT

The next three days were not good ones for Dr. Laura Masterson. A total of forty-two bodies had been unearthed, zipped into black rubber body bags, and loaded into an enclosed transport trailer along with the appropriate tombstone, then taken to Tucumcari to be reburied. Not all of the sites were graced with marble stones. Many of the graves had been marked with simple wooden crosses that had suffered from the same ravages of time that had wrought total destruction of the bodies they had been placed over.

The nightly ritual of phoning Michael Delvaney was becoming harsher to deal with. The silver-tongued lawyer's voice was increasingly accusatory, as if it were her fault no usable genetic material had, as yet, been found.

The previous evening Delvaney had told her of the deaths of two more people in Ciudad Acuna, Mexico. Both were small children. The tone of his voice came across icy cold, as if the deaths were solely her fault. Laura had bristled at that, told him that they were only beginning the work here in Paradox. The genetic material she needed was there and she would find it and complete the task.

"And that, my good doctor, is what you had *better* do." With those words, Michael Delvaney had ended last night's report.

Now, under a new day beneath a stunning blue New Mexico sky, Laura Masterson had reason to be optimistic. The backhoe operator had surprised her when he mentioned that he had studied to be a geologist. Rodney Simms was working as an equipment operator only because it paid better. The pragmatic man had, when he realized just how distressed she was over the sad condition of the bodies, spent some time pointing out how the cemetery lay.

"Notice how the cliff walls of the canyon are not sheer, but stair stepped." Rodney had brought his hand down on a jagged motion to make his point. "Those are the result of faults or zones of weakness in the earth. They're common and are the result of various natural phenomenon such as earthquakes or volcanic activity. The big canyon we're in is the product of a real doozy of a fault that ran for hundreds of miles. The smaller faults are sort of like when you break a glass, a lot of little cracks come along with one or two big ones."

Then he pointed out the edges of small cliffs on each end of the flat ground that contained the Paradox cemetery. "You can see the fault on each end, just not where it runs directly through the graveyard. But it does. Half of this cemetery is ten feet higher than the other. When we cross to the other side of this fault, I'm betting we'll also be away from any source of groundwater. High and dry is where we'll be digging tomorrow."

Laura had no difficulty interpreting the science of geologic faults. She also knew that no geologist could see any deeper into the ground than anyone else. But it was plainly obvious that today's digging would put them on a higher level than before. The way her luck had gone so far, she, and the entire world, needed a break.

At least Buno Eberhard had been laying low, causing no more friction with Jack Stoner. The bodyguard spent most of his time inside his motorhome listening to what sounded like German opera. This was still a source of amazement to Dr. Masterson who had thought Buno's artistic tastes ran more in the lines of guns and ammo magazines or maybe graphic novels without a lot of big words in them.

Jack Stoner was an enigma. The muscular man who always seemed to have a smile on his face or a witty comment was increasingly pleasant to have around. But recently he had taken to almost pushing her to finish moving the cemetery. He grabbed bones they had exhumed before she had a chance to examine them and crammed them into body bags.

Yet Jack was pleasant company every evening for the now-usual dinner and drinks in the Black Rock Bar and Grill. He cheerfully drove her up that steep road every evening for what had become beratings from Michael Delvaney. But her senses told her that Jack Stoner was preoccupied, worried about something. And that for some unsaid reason, he was going out of his way to rush her through the project of moving the cemetery.

Why he was doing this, Dr. Masterson could not grasp. The job was distasteful, of course. But the handling of the bony remains of the corpses that they had unearthed so far did not bother him. She was certain on this point. No, whatever had Jack Stoner on edge, it wasn't dead bodies. What was certain, however, was the fact that under different circumstances she could take more than a professional interest in that man. But too many lives, far too many innocent people's lives, were dependent on her keeping focused. No, Jack Stoner was a nice man, but any monsters he was fighting would have to remain his alone. Laura Masterson had battles of her own to wage.

The third grave Simms dug open that morning held an intact coffin, the first one they had found in Paradox that had not rotted away to only shards of old wood.

Frank Lowry and a member of the transport crew that showed up in the late morning to haul away the bodies removed that day jumped into the open grave and tilted the coffin to wrap it with ropes. Then there was a puff of dark smoke from the exhaust pipe of the tractor when Rodney gently lifted the coffin from its resting place, swung, and set it on flat ground in front of Laura.

Dr. Masterson consulted her notes. The grave was that of a miner by the name of Roberto Rodriguez, age twenty-eight, cause of death, pneumonia, November 18, 1918.

The Spanish Flu quite often killed its victims by causing bacterial pneumonia. The cause of death given by Dr. Wheeler at the time was very likely due to the flu.

An inspection of the open grave and the coffin disclosed that Simms knew his geology. The hole was powder dry, as was the coffin. Laura felt a twinge of anxiety. Recoverable genetic material had been found in Egyptian mummies thousands of years old. The dry desert conditions had preserved it all of those millennia. The desert conditions were why she had felt certain the Paradox cemetery would contain remnants of the virus. It was time to find out.

"Bring over the portable covering," Laura said to no one in particular. The flimsy shelter was only blue plastic tarpaulin stretched over an aluminum frame. Except for the fact that the tarpaulin went all the way to the ground, it was very much like those used for outdoor parties. This covering was meant more than anything to keep unwanted eyes from observing what Dr. Masterson was going to do to the corpse once the lid was removed from the coffin. "We want to limit any contamination, if there should be any."

"Oh, jeez," Simms moaned. "I'm going to take a coffee break." He shut off the rumbling diesel engine and lost no time heading off carrying a metal thermos.

Frank Lowry and Jack Stoner set the shelter over the coffin and secured it to the ground by driving in tent stakes. There was not a hint of wind, but they had lived in the west too long to trust the weather.

A couple of minutes' work with a crowbar and the lid of the coffin had been removed and laid aside. Inside was the remarkably well-preserved corpse of a man with his hands folded peacefully on his chest, who had been buried wearing blue jeans and a red flannel shirt with a small black bow tie. The coffin had been lined with a sturdy colorful wool Mexican blanket.

"Aside from being dead he looks to be in pretty good shape," Jack Stoner said.

"The man has been mummified," Laura said keeping her eyes on the corpse. "This is what I expected all along. The dry climate should preserve bodies, not destroy them."

"I'd reckon that wasn't of much concern when they laid out the cemetery," Frank Lowry said, looking out the single open end of the shelter at the steep cliffs. "There isn't a whole lot of flat ground available in this part of the world."

Laura Masterson adjusted her surgical mask and looked at the two men. "I should be alone to do an examination. There's no reason to risk contamination for all of us."

"Doc," Frank Lowry said as he headed out followed by Jack Stoner, "you're preaching to the choir. Give us a shout when you're done with whatever it is you're planning, but don't go rushing any on our account."

Alone now, Dr. Masterson grabbed a leather bag from her supplies and bent over the mummified corpse. She unbuttoned the man's shirt, then took a long, thick needle that was much like a trocar and inserted it between the ribs over the right lung. She extracted a long round sample of tissue then ejected it into a glass vial and sealed it closed. A few more probes filled the vial. Then Laura repeated the same procedure on the left lung. With the shirt rebuttoned and the man's tie straightened, no one could tell he had been touched, let alone had genetic material removed from the chest. Perfect.

Carefully, methodically, Dr. Masterson labeled each vial and indexed them into both a small leather notebook and her laptop computer. Then she called the men to come and close the coffin. Roberto Rodriguez had done his part. Before the day would end she expected to have numerous more samples of genetic material from the lungs of victims who had died of a long-ago pandemic. The phone call she would make to Michael Delvaney this night would be of a totally different tone. She had the Satan bug's DNA. Now the work to recreate the monster could begin in earnest.

CHAPTER TWENTY-NINE

The prominent Houston attorney, Michael Delvaney, was in his office behind locked doors going over some rather private books that were always kept locked in a safe away from prying eyes. He glanced at the antique oak clock on the wall. It had been a gift from a very grateful client for whom he had won two million dollars when a restaurant chain had served the lady a dangerously hot cup of coffee that she had spilled in her lap causing the poor dear untold pain. Dr. Masterson was due to call him in precisely eight minutes.

He scanned the open books with a practiced eye. So far his tally from kickbacks on deals he had made for Roth Pharmaceuticals was l.14 million dollars. And all of this delightful cash was untraceable and untaxable. It was a peeve that Buno Eberhard had stolen a quarter of a million dollars that he should have gotten. But the stoic henchman could be trouble. Big trouble. Dr. Luu Kwan had been hired to work on the Paradox Project. Philip Roth knew nothing of Buno's paying the man a visit. And since the hired killer had taken the money, there was the added benefit of his assured silence. At least this saved him the expense of hiring another hit man to do away with Buno. The only possible loose end might occur if Buno accidently mentioned Luu Kwan's name in front of Dr. Masterson instead of using the fictional Dr. Singh. This was doubtful. The bodyguard had his orders and following them was what he did well.

Money was better than any aphrodisiac, Delvaney thought, better than sex or drugs could ever be. It was the getting of it, the collecting that mattered. The amount was only a method of keeping score. And winning was *everything*.

Michael Delvaney tucked the books away. He hoped the irritatingly slow Dr. Masterson had better news tonight. He had purposefully kept a positive attitude to Roth. All was going as planned, just normal delays. Nothing to worry about in the least.

At precisely ten o'clock the phone rang. Dr. Laura Masterson was always prompt. That trait could be used to his advantage, whenever the time came. People could be *so* helpful with only a little guidance.

A genuine smile crossed the lawyer's face as he listened to Dr. Masterson's report.

"Ah yes, I simply knew you could do it, Doctor," Delvaney's musical voice that had won over many juries was back. "The Hammond Foundation only hires the brightest and the best. That is why you were selected."

The lawyer gave her a few more accolades, then gave her leave. He had a case to prepare for trial and she needed to put that expensive laboratory to use.

Michael Delvaney chuckled after he had hung up the phone. The good doctor had asked if any more fatalities had occurred in Mexico. People could be so delightfully gullible. All it had taken was some perusing of the news. A lightning strike on a swine farm could be made to seem like a cover up. Such things are *so* easy to come up with. All it took was to get the other person to trust you. And he could be *very* convincing. So trustworthy.

The lawyer poured himself a cup of strong Columbian coffee. He needed his wits to keep all of the balls in the air without dropping a single one.

Having a secretive, very benevolent group such as the Hammond Foundation to use was so very handy. At present, he had information to the effect that the Foundation was supplying AIDS drugs and antibiotics to various poverty stricken countries in Africa. How wonderful of them to do that.

But the Hammond Foundation had nothing at all to do with the Paradox Project. They didn't even know about it. The entire scenario was a brilliant concoction of his own devising. Smoke and mirrors to motivate a skilled research physician into doing a task for him, a task that stood to earn him a tremendous fortune.

Dr. Laura Masterson, as were most people, was easily led. And she was quite disposable once she ceased to be valuable. And best of all, she didn't have a clue that she was not out to save the world. Not even a glimmer of the true reason she was in Paradox, New Mexico. Wonderful.

The lawyer sipped at his excellent coffee and began to work on a brief that would almost certainly earn him even more money.

CHAPTER THIRTY

Rio de Janeiro, Brazil

Looking through the enormous glass windows that lined the wall behind Philip Roth's massive marble desk, both he and Andre Bettencourt could take note of the distant cleanup efforts going on where the Tres Palmas Hotel once stood on the hillside across the bay.

"I do wonder who the man was spying on us from there," Andre said idly, while taking a mint from a crystal bowl and popping it into his mouth. The French medical doctor hated bad breath on anyone; he always made certain that he would never be an offender. A man of his stature could ill afford to appear gauche.

Philip Roth, III gave a dismissive shrug. "Competition, most likely. We have our spies also. Many of our best-selling products were derived from piracy."

"We are better at it than they were," Bettencourt said.

"Yes, and I intend to keep it that way. The key to successful espionage is to never let anyone know it is happening."

"The eavesdropping equipment that fool used caused an effect much like sonar. It was quite easy to detect, then pinpoint where the device was located."

"And remove the problem," Philip Roth gave a satisfied look to the distant charring on a once-verdant hillside. "And we certainly had a stroke of luck with the resultant fire and ancillary fatalities. Most likely whoever employed the spy will believe he was killed accidentally, not blame us for his demise."

"The newspaper accounts are claiming that as many as fifty-five people perished. Even better, the fire department blamed the cause on a defective propane bottle that had been condemned by them over a month ago."

"Tisk, tisk." Roth swung his plush leather chair around to face Bettencourt. "And the entire effort was for naught. Our windows are two inches thick, made of the same material as the glass on teller cages in banks. The soundproofing is absolute."

"We need not concern ourselves with those people who perished, sir. They were all too poor to afford any of our products."

"Of course you are correct, Andre, as usual. The project we have underway in the United States requires our full attention. The demise of a few impecunious people who blight the face of the earth is of no consequence."

Andre Bettencourt chewed on his mint, his cold gray eyes focused on his boss. "Have you heard from that thieving lawyer, Michael Delvaney?"

"He calls me every day. I don't trust anything he says, but I do know that Dr. Laura Masterson has recovered some intact corpses and has begun working in the mobile laboratory."

"And you know this from Buno Eberhard?"

"Yes. He also calls me often. Sometimes twice or more a day."

"I believe, Mr. Roth, that the sooner we *remove* the lawyer the better."

"That will happen, but not just yet. Michael Delvaney will, may I assure you, very shortly *pay* for his greed. Unfortunately he is our present liaison with Dr. Masterson. It is a relationship we must strive to maintain, at least until suitable arrangements have been made to keep the Paradox Project progressing with all possible speed."

"What of Dr. Luu Kwan?" Bettencourt ran a delicate hand with manicured nails through his shiny, shoulder-length silver hair. "His expertise in cloning would be most helpful. He is well respected in China for his brilliant work with recombinant DNA."

"Michael Delvaney claims he paid Dr. Kwan the requested sum of a quarter of a million dollars in untraceable cash and has heard nothing from him since."

"And the lawyer has been *so* truthful and reliable to deal with."

Philip Roth curled his upper lip to reveal perfect white teeth. "It is a fact that Dr. Kwan never showed up in Paradox as agreed. No matter if he has met with an undesirable fate due to Mr. Delvaney, an automobile accident, or simply decided to skip with our money and return to China. We do not have his needed services. That is why I have decided to send you to the United States. Far too much is riding on this project. Roth Pharmaceuticals needs their best man on the job. And that, Dr. Andre Bettencourt, is you."

Dr. Bettencourt shook his glistening hair. "Thank you for the kind words. I do have some general knowledge of cloning. It is quite necessary, however, for us to retain the services of an expert molecular biologist until the seed virus has been successfully created."

Philip Roth gave a satisfied chuckle. "And from that point on the Spanish Flu virus can be easily duplicated by anyone with even slight training in a simple laboratory set up for the purpose."

"Viruses are quite hardy and very prolific to grow," Andre Bettencourt said. "All it takes is a friendly medium. A few cc's of the living active virus could be turned into a worldwide pandemic without difficulty using the resources of even the most backward of third-world countries."

Philip Roth smiled. "The profits from selling the live virus will be tremendous. I expect we'll have an income of nearly a billion dollars from that part of the Paradox Project alone. Most of the oil countries who'll buy the product hate each other. This bodes well for us because no one will ever know who actually released the virus in the first place. But rest assured, one of them will."

Andre Bettencourt added smugly. "And then the *real* profits will start."

"An unbelievable amount of profits, my dear doctor. Once the pandemic starts decimating the world, with Roth Pharmaceuticals having a supply of and holding international patents on the only vaccine in existence against the Spanish Flu we can charge nearly any price we chose."

"But being a very altruistic company we will only charge a few dollars or so for each shot of the vaccine, nothing greedy, nothing to invoke any investigations. We were simply doing advanced research into shifting antigen viruses when the pandemic struck. So fortuitous for the billions and billions of people who will purchase our product or pay to license our patent."

Philip Roth turned to stare out the window at the distant charred remains of the Tres Palmas hotel. "And the added benefit will be quite beneficial to the entire world. The multitudes of poverty rats who infest the planet will be unable to pay even the minuscule amount of money our vaccine will cost."

"And our entire success depends on the outcome of the Paradox endeavor." Bettencourt stood. "I shall depart on the fastest commercial airline available. It is imperative this entire operation remain a deep secret. Nothing can ever connect Roth Pharmaceuticals with causing a pandemic that will kill untold millions, simply to profit over it."

"The *only* thing that matters is the profits. The making of money is what motivates the economy of the entire world."

"I will make certain there is nothing and no one left alive in the United States to link anything to us. May I also suggest that while we are scheduling flights for me to the United States, we also arrange to transport Michael Delvaney to his well-deserved vacation in Grenada? One less loose end to tie up later."

"I agree. I'll phone him once the flights have been arranged." Philip Roth glanced at his Rolex. "When you see Delvaney in Houston, I will have praised him for all of his good work, and rewarded him with a nice *vacation* to Grenada. He will be told that since Dr. Kwan has disappeared, now we're forced to send another physician, that would be you, to assist Dr. Masterson. This will pave the way for your appearance and also remove any further need for the lawyer's services."

"The sooner Michael Delvaney is out of the picture the better. We may get lucky and develop a vaccine for a shifting antigen virus much sooner than the timetable we laid out indicates."

"Our scientists assure me there will be no problem. It will only take a few months after we deliver them a sample of the live virus to not only develop the vaccine but incubate a few million doses of it for immediate inoculations."

"Then I won't tarry," Dr. Andre Bettencourt grinned. "This is *definitely* not going to be a good year to miss your flu shot."

Both men gave a chuckle then went about their respective tasks.

CHAPTER THIRTY-ONE

Dr. Laura Masterson did not like to take the time for Jack Stoner to drive her up the steep road to the high rimrocks where she could make the required phone call to Michael Delvaney that he demanded every evening. Didn't like it at all. There was an outbreak of a shifting antigen flu in Mexico that could spread like wild fire across the entire planet. The sooner it is cloned and a vaccine developed, the more lives that could be saved. And now she had some genetic material to work with.

But once some of the steps were taken, they had to be attended to on a constant basis, not left alone. The damn lawyer's requirement had made sure that she could do nothing more than store her precious genetic material in the laboratory until after driving on top of the canyon and making the phone call.

Well, I can look at it like I did back in medical school, perk up a big pot of strong black coffee and pull an all-nighter, she thought as she drove her Suburban to the Black Rock Bar and Grill after safely stowing the material and washing up from the day's work. She cheered herself by thinking that this might be the last good meal out she would be able to enjoy for a long while.

Laura would make it plain, very plain, to Michael Delvaney that she was working on cloning along with excavating the cemetery to maintain the required façade. In the future she would call *him* when time allowed. Even many of her brief moments of sleep would be spent in the laboratory, monitored by an alarm clock to awaken her when a portion of the project required her inspection.

The constant attention the cloning process called for was undoubtedly the reason the Hammond Foundation had planned on having another doctor on site to assist her. It was sad that Dr. Singh had perished in a car accident, but she was capable of making a success of the project on her own. The stakes were too high to let a little fatigue bother her.

She pulled into the parking lot and scanned the area for Buno Eberhard's big Hummer. It wasn't there, which came as a relief. The bodyguard had been gone when she returned to the camp after the day's excavations. Briefly she wondered once again as to why Buno was even here. To be much of a guard it seemed to her that his staying on the job instead of running around at all hours would be a requirement. At least Buno and Jack Stoner might be spared from locking horns on this, her last night for any type of relaxation for what would be many days, if not weeks.

Laura turned to the plaintive calling of a bobwhite quail from somewhere up the canyon. She basked in the sheer majesty of red rays from a dying sun painting a panorama on the jagged walls of the cliff behind what remained of Paradox. A few fluffy white clouds caused the shafts of light to play across the rocks as if they were living beings. Then she tore herself away from the stunning scene and walked inside the Black Rock Bar and Grill.

Frank Lowry and Rodney Simms were in the usual booth. Jack Stoner was sitting on a stool at the bar alongside Willie Ames. Jack said something to the pig-tailed antique buyer, grabbed up his bottle of beer, and went to join Laura and his friends.

"The special tonight is liver and onions," Frank Lowry said with a wrinkled nose to Laura while Jack Stoner made his way over. "I don't know about you, but a cheeseburger and french fries would beat the hell out of that dish."

"So would road kill," Rodney Simms added.

"After a day of working with dead bodies, this *is* a revolting development," Jack said as he slid into the booth beside Laura. "I don't think Thelma and Sadie came up with much of a hit for tonight's dinner. In fact, I don't think anyone's had the gumption to order the special. I'm going to see if they can cook up some pancakes or something."

"I might be forced to go back to the trailer and cook my own dinner," Frank Lowry said with a sad look. "That'd be a terrible shame."

Laura Masterson actually liked liver and onions, but to be agreeable she decided to keep silent. After all, Jack needed to drive her up that treacherous road later. It would serve no purpose to irritate the man by cutting up a piece of liver in front of him.

Sadie Helms came over, coughed, and set a cold, sweaty bottle of beer in front of Laura. "Okay, we surrender. Thelma warned me you folks weren't a liver-and-onion bunch. It was my idea, so go ahead and sue me."

Lowry said, "We'll hold off on the lawyers if you let us order off the menu."

"Already planned on that possibility. I heard you talking when I was coming over. Whenever you're ready just let me know. Cheeseburgers and fries or breakfasts are fine. The grill's hot, so it's no never mind to us. Everything's gotta go."

"The liver could have gone long before I got here," Simms said with a frown.

Jack Stoner turned to Laura, his expression serious. "You must have found something to test. I saw you carrying samples from the tent."

Laura felt her muscles tighten. She had known this time would come. The worst thing she could do would be to expose her true trepidation of what was actually going on.

"Just routine checking," Laura said, grabbing up her bottle of beer. "The Cougar Canyon Development Corporation is wanting a complete record of what condition the bodies are in, and so forth. Every time any grave is moved there are certain procedures and policies to be followed. That's why I'm here."

"There's not anything like dangerous or catching we can get from any of those coffins or bones is there?" Simms asked, his eyes wide.

Laura forced a smile then brought her bottle to her lips. "Not if certain procedures are followed there's nothing to worry about. Keep an eye on me. If I'm not worried you can relax," she said, and took a long sip.

"But if she lets out a scream and starts running," Lowry said seriously, "make it a point to beat her out of the canyon."

The group had a good laugh, then the subject was dropped, much to Laura Masterson's relief. She needed to focus on the call to Michael Delvaney then work most of the night preparing to clone what was possibly one of the most deadly viruses in all of recorded history. Some scientists even held the theory that the dinosaurs were wiped out by a virus instead of a meteor strike. Talking about anything other than the task at hand would be a welcome, needed relief.

It was a pleasant change of pace. Michael Delvaney's voice on the other end of the heavy cell phone was upbeat.

"I am *so* pleased the Paradox Project is running just as well as I had foreseen it would," the lawyer said cheerfully. "I have full faith that you will shortly have even *better* news to report."

"Mr. Delvaney, I need to remind you that the cloning will take time, possibly longer than either of us will like. The cemetery is still being moved. I must be present to examine the corpses as they are disinterred. This is totally necessary to not only maintain our actual reason for being here, but allow the harvesting of more genetic material."

"And why is that, Dr. Masterson? I was under the impression a single sample was all that was required for you to complete your task."

"No sir." Laura tried not to be abrupt, reminding herself the man was a lawyer, not a molecular biologist. "The genetic material will not only be in various states of decomposition, which can alter our results, but the cloning of a shifting antigen virus will require multiple samples to extract the various changes of the strain. This is new ground we're covering, new technology."

"And I am certain you will be very successful, Dr. Masterson. To this end I am very pleased to tell you that a replacement for Dr. Singh has been found and is on his way to Paradox by the fastest jet available to assist you. He is a French physician by the name of Andre Bettencourt."

"I would have managed on my own," She replied. Laura Masterson had every procedure already lined out. Another doctor, no matter how well trained, would take time to orient, time she did not want to spend considering the outbreak in Mexico.

"Of course you would have, Dr. Masterson. But the Hammond Foundation has already taken the bull by its horns, so to speak. The matter is settled. Buno is picking him up at the Amarillo, Texas, airport as we speak."

Laura suppressed a sigh. "Perhaps this Andre Bettencourt can oversee the moving of the corpses and collect genetic material. If he can handle that part of the project, it will free me to spend more time in the laboratory and concentrate on the cloning process."

"I am sure that is the reasoning of the Hammond Foundation, too."

"Mr. Delvaney, considering the inability of the cell phone to work in Paradox and the time it takes to drive out of the canyon to make a call, I am hoping we might hold off on these nightly check-ins, at least until there is something new to report."

"Actually, I was coming to that point. The Hammond Foundation has summoned me to a business meeting in the Caribbean. I may be out of the country for a while. I have been informed that you are to give all of your information to Dr. Bettencourt, who will relay the needed reports. I believe this will allow you to better concentrate on your work, won't it Dr. Masterson?"

Laura was taken aback at the turn of events. Now she was being asked, no *told*, to give all of her research data to someone she had yet to meet. She didn't like this, didn't like it at all. But from what the lawyer had just told her the orders had been given and nothing she could say or do would change a thing. Like it or not, Laura Masterson had an "assistant" coming who might in actuality take over the operation.

"I'll do my job, Mr. Delvaney," Laura said after a moment. "There's too much riding on the outcome."

"Excellent, Dr. Masterson, I knew you were a total professional."

"I must be getting back to work." Laura hesitated a moment then added. "Have a nice trip."

"Thank you, Doctor. I'd like to, but, alas, the journey is strictly business. I have, however, been informed that I am being given the opportunity of a lifetime."

The phone clicked off. Laura noticed Jack Stoner standing in the bright moonlight on an open grassy area. He had his hands on his hips and he was looking skyward. She stuck the cell phone in her purse and went to join him.

"From the glum expression on your face, I take it the news wasn't all good." Jack said, turning to greet her.

"Not terrible, just that there's a new doctor I don't know coming to help. I thought we were doing just fine without him."

"The Cougar Canyon Development Corporation must have modeled their way of doing business from the Bureau of Reclamation. They do dumb things all the time." He chuckled. "Most of the time, actually."

Laura felt better now, being in the company of a friend. "We'll handle things. Maybe Thelma and Sadie have some liver and onions left over. A plate of that served to the new doctor might return things to the way they were."

Jack laughed. "Liver and onions could clean out a town in my opinion, let alone some French doctor."

"Well, we'd best get back down to the camp. I have work to do."

"Hop in, my lady. Your chariot awaits."

Laura Masterson paid scant attention to the narrow dirt road as they drove into the canyon depths. She was mulling over in her mind the turn of events. But most of all she was wondering how Jack Stoner knew the doctor coming to Paradox was French. She certainly didn't remember mentioning that to him. One thing was certain: Company was coming and nothing about that boded well. Not in the least.

CHAPTER THIRTY-TWO

Laura was alone now, inside of the high-tech, mobile biological research and containment laboratory. When she had stepped into the airlock, a pack of coyotes were singing their mournful songs to a wan moon. The plaintive cries of the coyotes had fit her mood perfectly.

What is going on here, girl? A few short weeks ago you were testing cosmetics for Roth Pharmaceuticals and living in Houston. Texas. Tonight you are preparing to resurrect a monster. And the people you're been dealing with lately are becoming sinister enough to cause concern to anyone.

But Laura was too well trained, too much of a professional researcher to worry herself with what was most likely the internal politics of the Hammond Foundation. For some odd reason Jack Stoner's offhand comment about the other doctor coming to Paradox being French upset her more than anything else.

How could he have known? Did Michael Delvaney's conversation upset me enough to cause me to speak too loudly? I don't even remember mentioning the word "Frenchman." Does sound travel that much better in the desert? I must have said something. That's the only answer. You're looking for spooks where there aren't any, girl. Put it out of your mind and focus on your work. Let the politics play out the way they will. You're a medical doctor and there are millions of innocent lives in your hands. Get on with the program, girl.

Laura shook her short brunette hair as if to toss away all bad thoughts. She double-checked that the door had sealed perfectly and it was securely locked. A press of a button started the negative air-pressure pump humming softly from somewhere beneath the laboratory. After taking a moment to glance at a couple of gauges and indicator lights to assure herself that everything was working the way it should, she dressed in a white biohazard suit.

After drawing the airtight helmet and securing it, then hooking up the hose that supplied breathing air, Laura turned her attention to the thick glass window of the main biohazard containment facility. The test tubes were already inside, awaiting her return.

Dr. Masterson inserted both of her arms into the rubber apertures that were in actuality long gloves. The gloves, along with a single robotic arm that was operated from a control on the panel next to her right arm resembling a joystick the only way to access or move anything about in the maximum-containment room.

Should anything be spilled or broken in the room, a complete sterilization process would be necessary. All of the experiments underway would be lost. But that was an acceptable risk. What was of the utmost concern to anyone who worked in a biohazard level-three or level-four laboratory was a cut, no matter how tiny, in the gloves. Even worse than that would be a failure of one of the many rubber gaskets and seals around the doors and windows. Keeping the devil at bay was the single most important job. Never were any movements rushed, nothing was ever forced. Slow and methodical were the first two commandments of biohazard containment.

For some strange reason, Laura thought briefly that a single rifle shot could unleash the beast. There was no defense against a deliberate act such as that. Again she shook her head to remove the terrible thought. No one going was to shoot through the containment area.

Concentrating now on the job at hand, Dr. Masterson began the first phase of her research: to determine if some of the Spanish Flu viruses were in any of the samples she had taken today.

The work in this stage was fairly routine, not particularly dangerous. First she had to place a small amount of recovered genetic material onto a slide, stain it, then perform a scan with the powerful electron microscope. But the amount of material needed was almost infinitesimal in size and quite time-consuming to prepare. Hours flew by like a flock of silent birds.

The microscope had to be calibrated, checked, and rechecked. The virus Dr. Masterson was pursuing had a diameter of approximately $1/10,000$ of a millimeter. One of her instructors had once referred to a virus as "being a speck in the eye of a bacteria." The analogy was a good one—at least it would have been if bacteria had any eyes. The existence of bacteria had been known, documented, and written about long before the discovery of viruses. Louis Pasteur and many other pioneers in the filed of medicine were able to view the rods, spirals, ovids, or the comma-shaped vibrios with their simple microscopes.

Bacteria are not only much larger than viruses, they are also more familiar. They require nourishment, devouring dead materials and parasites that develop in the tissues of living organisms, and that are disease-producing. Bacteria multiply by the simple asexual method of fission. And not all bacteria are harmful; many, in fact, are beneficial. The digestive tract could not function without a hundred million or so friendly bacteria working away to break down food.

Viruses on the other hand are an enigma that exist on the very fringes of life itself. They live in a micro-world so minute they can only be viewed by the most powerful of electron microscopes. A single virus could best be described as a tennis ball with spiked hair. At least this is how they looked to Laura.

These little spiked balls resemble nothing else living. They do not eat. Nor do they burn oxygen for energy. Viruses do not produce waste, have sex, or manufacture any side products. In fact, they are more like a chemical than a living organism. All they require to exist is a favorable medium along with an agreeable temperature.

A virus has only one function: to replicate itself. Here it becomes unique. There is no asexual splitting or any other of the usual forms of reproduction. A virus invades cells that have energy, subverts them, and takes them over. It then forces these cells to make new viruses using the power of their genes. A genetic code is employed using a language of four letters. Each of these letters represents the molecules adenine, guanine, cytosine, and thymine. DNA and RNA represent strings or strands of these chemicals.

Dr. Laura Masterson knew all too well the nature of the beast. But to defeat any monster one first had to know both its strengths and its weaknesses. The lair must be found, a weapon developed, and a time and place to employ the weapon laid out with patience and precision. And most important of all, the monster had to be kept contained. The last time this particular beast had broken free to roam the earth, a hundred million people had died.

She shuddered at that number. Given the huge increase in world population since 1918, along with the rapidity people moved about the globe these days, a new outbreak could, if left unchecked by a newly and rapidly developed vaccine, kill hundreds of millions. The chaos and collapse of the world economy along with the resulting lawlessness would surely kill millions more.

Yes, Laura Masterson knew the beast. And as she placed the first slide into the wonderfully powerful electron microscope, the hunt was on. The monster had been lying dormant since 1918. It was time to wake it up and stomp it out of existence forever.

She clicked the microscope into focus and began searching for the enemy.

CHAPTER THIRTY-THREE

A distant rapping sound that had begun much as a tiny woodpecker testing a tree for tasty bugs kept growing in intensity until the resulting din was loud enough to rouse Dr. Masterson from a deep sleep.

She sputtered awake, blinking her matted eyes into focus. The motorhome was still new enough to cause a momentary confusion, especially in her somnolent state.

Laura sat upright in bed, glanced briefly at the colorful Indian dream catcher hanging on the wall above the bed, then jumped up and wrapped herself in a bulky robe. Last night after coming home from the laboratory she had showered and crawled into bed nude, luxuriating in the cool softness of the cotton sheets.

"Oh shit!" she mumbled when she glanced at the clock glowing a bright eight-thirty. "I overslept! Jack and the guys are waiting on me. Damn it all, I used to pull all-nighters and pop awake before the sun was over the horizon."

Feeling chagrined, Laura ran to the door and opened it to look into the devilishly happy and sparkling pale blue eyes of Jack Stoner.

"Good morning, Doc," Stoner said with a wry grin. "Or maybe I ought to say afternoon. I'm guessing you must have burned some midnight oil in that big tin can of a lab last night. We kinda hated to come and wake you but something's come up you need to know about."

Laura Masterson felt her brain cells lining up and engaging. She also realized her hair was not combed and she wore no makeup. There was no doubt in her mind that she looked a mess. Then Jack Stoner's words registered. "What happened?"

"The backhoe's broken down. Rodney can't get it started. He's a fairly good mechanic and Frank Lowry was raised on a ranch, been around diesel tractors all of his life. Neither one of them has a clue what's wrong with the thing. It's got fuel and the battery's in good shape."

"Then there won't be any more graves dug this morning?"

"Not likely, Doc. I called headquarters and they're canceling the transport crew and arranging for both a mechanic and another backhoe to come out later today. I'd venture a guess we're down for at least the rest of the day."

"Thanks for waking me," Laura realized her robe had worked itself open, attracting a furtive look from Jack Stoner. She wrapped the red terry cloth tight against her body and shook out her hair. "I can use the time in the lab." She smiled and added, "I really do appreciate you coming to tell me."

"Sure thing, Doc." Jack turned to stare at the distant yellow backhoe. "That tractor's almost new. Can't begin to figure why it would go and conk out on us like it did."

"I had a car like that once—never was a good idea to drive it off the bus route."

"Yeah, but it's still odd," Jack said over his shoulder as he began to walk away. "I'll keep you posted."

She thanked him again, closed the door, and went back into the bedroom. The day would not be wasted for her that was for certain.

Laura filled a cereal bowl with cornflakes and gave a skeptical look at a stalk of bananas that had mummified to black. She decided to use some caution. After taking the plastic half-gallon container of milk out of the refrigerator, she opened the lid and gave the contents a testing sniff. Then she gave it a second sniff and turned the container until the "sell by" date came into view. The milk went down the kitchen sink and the empty jug joined the rotted bananas in the wastebasket. There was a sack of red delicious apples in the fridge, not exactly what she wanted, but one would fill the empty hole in her stomach for a while.

Going into the bedroom to dress for the day, Laura took a moment to stare at the colorful dream catcher. While she had to admit it seemed to have stopped the nightmares, it certainly wasn't doing much to prevent strange dreams.

Early this morning she had come into the motorhome around three. When Laura had finally fallen asleep, she had had one of the most vivid dreams of her life.

She was back in the mobile laboratory viewing samples of viruses with the electron microscope. There was nothing unique about the spiked ball that identified a flu virus, except that there was only one. Then a red hand with long fingers sporting what looked like claws grabbed the ball and yanked it from view.

Across the white background of the microscope, a small red demon ran dribbling the virus like a basketball. This was one of those dreams where anything could happen, and did. The demon stopped dead and stared upward at her with evil, slanted eyes full of hate. The demon's face contorted into a grin, while its free hand flipped her the bird.

Laura remembered the demon had gone back to dribbling the virus: its rhythmic tapping on the floor of her dreamscape had melded with Jack Stoner's knocking on the door of her coach.

She gave a chuckle, remembering the dream and mumbled to herself. "And I didn't even have the liver and onions." Actually, no one did. Willie Ames had mentioned that a coyote was keeping him awake at night and offered to take the liver home and leave it out. He had said with all seriousness that he was certain it would be enough to drive the coyote into the next county, a statement which did not set well with Thelma and Sadie.

Laura finished the apple, tossed the core into a wastebasket, and gave a sigh. She knew that it was time to return to the laboratory and start over what had been a fruitless effort to recover useable genetic material. The virus was there all right, only many years of lying in the ground had desiccated the samples to the point of shriveling them to the state of being useless for cloning. What was required were viruses that had been encapsulated, protected. They were there in the Paradox cemetery, however; she knew that with every degree of scientific certainty she could muster.

If none of the samples she had extracted held useable material, Laura decided to take even more samples on the next cadavers. The modified trocar would be used to aspirate three samples from each lobe of the right lung and two from each of the left lobes. Even after becoming a medical doctor, it still was a source of amazement to her that the pair of lungs nature and evolution should have made similar were, in fact, quite different. And the material she sought could be hiding in any one of the lobes.

There was nothing to do but get dressed and resume the hunt.

The wide slice of New Mexico sky that was visible above the rugged canyon seemed even bluer, more vivid than Laura remembered it ever being when she stepped out of the motorhome. This was magnificent and gorgeous country, always changing with the light.

A quick scan of the camp showed that Buno Eberhard was still among the missing. That news was cheery, but the realization that he would be returning along with a French physician who, from now on was to handle all of her communications to the Hammond Foundation, held her spirits down.

Laura clucked her tongue and headed for the mobile lab. In the distance she could see Rodney Simms and Frank Lowry fussing with the recalcitrant backhoe. Anything mechanical, anything made by man, could prove unreliable. This thought was disturbing to Dr. Masterson as she keyed the airlock on the truck-mounted laboratory and stepped inside.

After suiting up she made careful notes of everything she had worked on to date. Only the genetic material from two of the corpses had been examined, and both had contained the virus she was seeking, but in an unusable state of deterioration. Today, without the distraction of having to work in the cemetery along with feeling refreshed, she might be able to run all of the remaining samples. Dr. Masterson once again placed her arms into the heavy rubber gloves of the containment chamber and resumed the hunt. She half expected a little red demon to appear and harass her efforts.

CHAPTER THIRTY-FOUR

While no little red demon from some surreal land of dreamscapes made an appearance to Dr. Laura Masterson that day, another all-too-real monster did.

The digital clock which was built into the powerful computer made an electronic record of its emergence at 1:58 P.M., Mountain Standard Time. The computer also registered the following data: outside temperature, 18 degrees Celsius; wind direction, SSE at three knots; humidity 39 percent.

Further data that were recorded onto both disk and handwritten notes by Laura Masterson were more detailed. The cadaver's name had been Alberto Garza, age at death, nineteen. Dr. Wheeler's death certificate gave the cause of death on November 10, 1918, as influenza with secondary pneumonia. Alberto Garza had been employed by the Bessemer Fuel and Iron Corporation for a period of sixteen months and four days. His job description was "nipper." Laura made a side note to find out what a "nipper" did around a coal mine. Did he work underground or on the surface? Every detail could become very important at some future date even though it appeared trivial at the time.

The genetic material that contained viable, encapsulated clusters of the deadly Spanish Flu virus had been extracted from the lower lobe of the left lung, from a presumably encapsulated area of infection. An autopsy would be necessary to determine the size of the encapsulation, Laura noted.

The recovered sample weighed 0.8742 grams. An amount weight of 0.0621 grams was consumed to make the slide viewable with the Jeol electron microscope. This left an amount of 0.8121 grams of viable material available for further experimentation and cloning attempts. She added to the record that it was possible that many more grams could be extracted from the subject, if she were able to do so without drawing undue attention to the process. Perhaps she could say a finding had been made of tuberculosis which needed to be verified for the record. That disease would not be liable to frighten the workers, especially when she explained that the bacteria were long dead and tuberculosis is quite curable with a course of antibiotics.

Dr. Laura Masterson looked up from her notebook to stare once again with scientific awe at the viewing screen of the electron microscope. The little spiked spheres were perfectly round. They were all solid, intact, and quite useable for the cloning process. The first step of the Paradox Project had been achieved.

A deep rumble from her stomach told Laura that the apple she had eaten for breakfast had been a little amount of food and a long time ago. There were frozen TV dinners in the freezer of the motorhome. Cans of soups and chili along with assorted box dinners filled the pantry. No, she didn't need to take the time to go to the Black Rock Grill, even though it was tempting. Thelma Ross and Sadie Helms were spoiling her with some of the most tempting and tasty home-cooked meals she had enjoyed in years. Well, possibly with the exception of the liver and onions, which had at least smelled good. But the cheeseburger she had opted for was out of this world.

Dr. Masterson used the robotic arm to move the vial containing the remaining genetic material from Alberto Garza's lung into a special receptacle in the still unused cloning preparation area. Once the virus had been placed into a plasmid, the Paradox Project would begin to enter into its second and most critical phase.

Until now there had not been much of anything found that should cause much worry or concern. The flu viruses had all been long dead, along with every bacillus that had been viewed by the microscope, especially the monicus capsulatus or streptococcus pneumoniae bacteria found in pneumonia patients. The bacteria were of much more concern than the viruses because of the ability of the more hardy rod-shaped bacteria to be able to "hibernate" for many years under ideal conditions.

Once the Satan bug of the Spanish Flu had been recreated through the cloning process, however, containment and safety protocols would become of paramount concern. The beast was being reborn solely for the purpose of developing a vaccine. The smallest amount necessary was all Laura intended to clone. Making more once the live virus was recreated would be terribly easy. In fact, Laura nearly shuddered at the thought that a single one of those little microscopic spiked balls, given a favorable medium, could replicate itself into several million in a shockingly brief time.

Laura secured the containment area, stored all of her data, and exited the mobile laboratory after following all of the required procedures. The bright New Mexico sun was already beginning to hide itself over the ragged rimrock of the canyon, causing shadows to ascend up the sandstone cliffs on the precipitous east wall.

Laura took a moment to once again allow herself to stand and gaze with awe and amazement as the grandeur of nature painted the desert with a moving kaleidoscope of changing colors. The layered sandstone cliffs shifted from reds to white beneath an azure sky that held the whitest and fluffiest of clouds. After spending hours in the cramped confines of the mobile laboratory, the openness felt like a genuine gift from Heaven.

After a while she tore herself away to proceed with the short walk around the lab to her motorhome to fix something to eat. The moment the camp came into view, Laura Masterson stopped dead still, sighed, and muttered lowly, "Oh shit."

CHAPTER THIRTY-FIVE

Buno Eberhard's shiny black and chrome Hummer was parked alongside his motorhome, stark as a festering boil.

Laura Masterson felt her appetite take wing. The bodyguard being back meant that almost assuredly the other physician from the Hammond Foundation had arrived. And damn it to hell, she had everything lined up. All was in order to proceed quickly. Now, even if the doctor was bright, competent, and amenable to work with, it would take precious, unnecessary time away from the cloning process just to fill the new physician in on the status of the project along with orientating him on the layout of the laboratory and procedures.

The longer the meeting could be postponed, the better. Laura speeded up her step in order to reach her coach quicker. It did not work. The door to Buno's motorhome swung open and the electric steps extended to latch outward with a metallic click that sounded like a gun being cocked.

"I see you're out of the lab at last," Buno Eberhard said, his voice flat and unemotional as usual. "Dr. Bettencourt is in the other coach. He told me to keep a watch for you and take you to meet him when you were available. It looks to me like you're available now."

"I was going to fix myself a late lunch," Laura said, slowly making her way to the door of her coach. "Or an early dinner. I haven't had anything to eat all day but an apple. I'll pop over and see him shortly."

"A few minutes to take care of business won't hurt you any. My orders are to take you to him. I intend to do just that."

"You have such a sweet and winning personality, Buno, I can't refuse. Lead on."

The bodyguard lowered his eyebrows, trying to decide if he had been insulted or given a compliment. After a moment, he simply nodded with a grunt then escorted her to the door of the late Dr. Singh's Prevost motorhome.

Before they were within a dozen feet of the door it swung open. A tall, slim man with shiny, silvery, almost-white hair that cascaded straight down to his shoulders jumped out and stepped over to meet them. His steel-gray eyes sparked like flint in the rays of the a dying sun.

"Doctor Laura Masterson," the silver-haired man said pleasantly, extending his hand. "I am *so* very glad to meet you at last. I have heard a great many things about your accomplishments. It is simply an honor to stand in your presence. I am Dr. Andre Bettencourt, at your service."

Laura accepted his hand. She was somewhat taken aback when he did not shake her hand, but grasped it, placed it to his lips, and pecked a small kiss on the backside.

"I am charmed, *Docteur,*" Andre said. He bowed with a flourish and clicked his heels together. "I must say that I am honored beyond measure to be here to help you with this very important undertaking."

This guy is so full of it, he probably has sideboards on his ego just to hold it all in, Laura thought, but she said, "Dr. Bettencourt, I am pleased you made it to Paradox safely. I'm sure we will enjoy working together."

"*Madame,* I shall be pleased to simply act as your assistant. My degree is only in medicine. Since you are the expert in molecular biology and also considering the fact you are already proceeding with our, ah, *goals,* I will be most happy to do only those things which will be of the most benefit to your fine efforts."

"Thank you for your understanding, Dr. Bettencourt." Laura regarded him for a moment with the scrutiny of a medical doctor. There were certainly at least some latent genes of albinism in the Bettencourt family tree. The man likely had had silver hair all of his life, along with the telltale light, steel-gray eyes. Briefly she wondered if he wore contacts or had undergone surgery to correct the almost-always present astigmatism that very often accompanied the condition. "I'm certain we'll work together quite amenably for the duration of this most-worthy project."

"I believe Dr. Masterson has yet to eat lunch," Buno Eberhard said, giving Laura cause to wonder if he was ill.

"Why, my good doctor," Andre Bettencourt waved an arm to the open door of his coach. "Your dedication to science is commendable. Most commendable. I would love to welcome you inside for a repast. Alas, I have found the pantry bare."

Buno Eberhard spoke up again, "The restaurant here does serve up good food. Why don't you two get acquainted while I go pick up some sandwiches or whatever they call the 'special' and bring your dinner back to camp."

Laura Masterson nodded in agreement. She realized the stoic guard's thoughtfulness was due to malice aforethought. He was simply following orders instead of being stricken by a case of niceness. "I think that would be an excellent idea," she gave him a glare calculated to clabber milk. "Thank you, Buno."

"Sure thing, Doc," Buno was not one to pick up subtlety, never had been. It was not part of the requirements for a member of the Master Race. "I will be back as soon as I can."

A moment later the Hummer's rapid departure left both Dr. Bettencourt and Laura Masterson standing in a cloud of red dust.

"Buno *so* tries to please," Laura said after giving a cough and blinking dust from her eyes. "He's just not always very good at it."

"I can assure you, Dr. Masterson, that he is quite loyal along with being reliable and efficient. Being on a project that could very well bring some dangerous attention our way, having someone with his skills about is desirable. That is a sad truth we who live in this dangerous world must accept." Andre Bettencourt's thin smile returned. "How rude of me. I have some cold drinks I brought over from Buno's motorhome. Please come inside and take a seat."

Laura Masterson followed him inside. She was not at all surprised when Dr. Bettencourt opened a bottle of Perrier water, poured the fizzing mineral water over ice, and set the glass in front of her.

"How much does Buno Eberhard know of our project here in Paradox?" Laura asked straight out. The time for pleasantries was over; too many lives were depending on her swift success.

Andre Betterncourt said, "Nothing of the medical details. He has been working for the Hammond Foundation long enough to not ask questions nor divulge any information. All he has been told was to take every precaution to protect you and the laboratory. And this he *will* do, at any cost, at the sacrifice of his own life if necessary."

Laura Masterson considered Dr. Bettencourt's words. "Do you have any hard evidence that some," she took a sip of the Perrier, "should I simply call them 'bad guys,' have knowledge of our operations here in Paradox and are out to steal the virus?"

Dr. Bettencourt swirled his drink, keeping his gaze on the bubbles roiling to the surface of the glass. "Specific data, Dr. Masterson, no we do not. But there are always some snippets of information we can garner through monitoring the Internet, along with *other* means. What you must keep in mind is that the Hammond Foundation's activities are *always* monitored. And the Spanish Flu virus, once it is reborn, could be a weapon of terrible mass destruction in the wrong hands. There are, sad to say, nefarious parties who exist simply to profit from instruments of death and destruction."

Dr. Masterson regarded the Frenchman in the close quarters of the Prevost. When he spoke she noticed Bettencourt's extremely white teeth were small, and filed to sharp points, making them denticulate. This caused her to wonder why a dentist had done such a thing, but it would be rude to ask. The effect however, was like looking into the mouth of a piranha.

"Yes, of course it is always better to take every possible precaution," Laura said. "I personally have a difficult time understanding how anyone could seek to profit from such a wholesale slaughter that releasing the Spanish Flu would cause."

"We are both physicians, healers. That is our calling. All we can do is recognize that there are evildoers out there who will stop at nothing to do harm and leave the handling of those people to the likes of Buno Eberhard."

"Of course, you are correct. Once you have rested, Dr. Bettencourt, I'll be happy to orient you on the layout of the project and give a medical update."

"How considerate you are, Dr. Masterson. But I have been instructed to mainly assist you in the speedy conclusion of the project. Perhaps my time here would be best spent if I continued the collecting of specimens from the cadavers, allowing you to concentrate on the recovery of viable genetic material."

"I've made some progress just today. I recovered enough genetic material to begin attempts at cloning."

Dr. Bettencourt was obviously pleased and impressed. "*Magnifiqué,* Doctor. This is indeed good news."

"If you can take care of the cemetery, I'll begin tomorrow."

"Of course. May I ask if you are opening the chest to remove specimens?"

"No. I have a modified trocar that uses bulb suction to keep the material inside the tube. The time to extract samples from a corpse is only a few minutes and it does not draw attention."

"Very astute. I am again impressed."

"There's a medical bag with everything you need. I'll leave it with you this evening."

Andre Bettencourt sat down the glass and steepled his hands. "Is the laboratory suitable—is there anything you require? I have been instructed to spare no expense on this critical project."

"All I need is time and luck. The technology of cloning viruses has not yet been perfected. It may be more time consuming and tricky than we expect."

"I shall not allow anyone or anything to divert your focus."

Dr. Masterson could not figure out if Bettencourt was being genuinely helpful or acting the part of a sycophant for other reasons. There was no choice, however, but to proceed as planned.

Laura finished her Perrier water. "I'll go over everything with you yet today. I believe Buno can show you around the camp and what there is of the town of Paradox. There's a small store still in operation that might be able to supply the refrigerator and pantry." She could not contain her curiosity. "Do you know when Michael Delvaney will be coming back from his trip? Aside from you and Buno, he's the only person from the Hammond Foundation that I've actually met."

Dr. Bettencourt's small sharp teeth flashed as he spoke. "The lawyer is spending some time at one of our facilities doing *pro bono* work."

"Michael Delvaney did not strike me as being such a compassionate man. I must have misread him."

"I can truly say that many people will benefit from his presence." Andre Bettencourt stood to open the door for Buno, who had his arms full of white Styrofoam containers. "And our dinners have arrived. Let us enjoy our repast."

"I'll help," Laura said. When she went to grab up some of the packages she wondered just why it was she felt so ill at ease. Dr.

Bettancourt was actually quite nicer than she had expected. Laura decided the gravity of her task was grating her nerves. She gave a thin smile then began setting out dinner.

CHAPTER THIRTY-SIX

The rumbling of the diesel engine echoed off the steep canyon walls, sounding like a deep growl, as the new backhoe pushed the disabled one onto the flatbed truck that had hauled it into Paradox.

Jack Stoner and Frank Lowry stood to one side watching the proceedings, while Rodney Simms expertly maneuvered the big yellow tractor.

"What I can't understand is why anyone would want to sabotage the moving of a cemetery," Lowry said shaking his head in puzzlement.

"The fuel tank had corn syrup or molasses poured into it," Jack said. "That stuff plugs up the filters and stops any diesel engine dead as hell. That backhoe won't run again until the entire fuel system has been flushed and cleaned. Whoever did that had a damn good reason in mind, there's no doubt about it."

"But they only cost us a day."

"Maybe they didn't want to stop us, only slow us down."

Frank Lowry shot a glance at the mobile laboratory that was rapidly being enveloped in shadows. "To buy a day for Dr. Masterson to work in the lab."

"That's the way I've got it figured."

"Then ol' Puno's brought in the help that's due to arrive."

Jack Stoner painted a wry smile on his tanned face. "I think I'll go find out."

"Good idea. I'll help Rodney secure everything—this backhoe has a locking fuel tank—and meet you at the Black Rock in a while."

"Yeah," Jack said, then he spun and was gone.

Laura was going over with Dr. Bettencourt the cloning procedures she planned to use with the Spanish Flu virus she had recovered when someone began knocking on the motorhome's door. Buno Eberhard had dropped off the dinners of roast turkey and dressing along with generous slices of cherry pie then excused himself and returned to the privacy of his own coach.

Laura opened the door to Jack Stoner's usual smiling face. He looked around her to study Andre Bettencourt for a brief instant. "Sorry to bother you, Doc. I know you're busy but I thought I ought to give you an update."

"No problem. Come in Jack and meet the other doctor the Cougar Canyon Development Corporation sent to help us." Laura moved aside to admit him.

The Bureau of Reclamation man stepped up and offered a handshake. "Jack Stoner at your service."

"And I, sir, am Dr. Andre Bettencourt." He gave a quick handshake, his hands were delicate and needed to be protected. "I am delighted to be here."

"Hopefully we'll have this job wrapped up in a few weeks then we can all go somewhere we'll be even more delighted to be," Jack said, turning to Laura. "We have a new backhoe on site."

"The other tractor couldn't be repaired?"

"No, something was broken in the fuel system as I understand it." He gave a shrug. "They just don't build things like they used to."

Dr. Bettencourt said, "But with what you have said, Mr. Stoner, I assume the excavation of graves will continue tomorrow. I shall be the one checking the sites for contamination. This will free Dr. Masterson to perform the necessary laboratory tests. I believe this arrangement will speed things considerably."

"I'm sure it will, Doctor. And since we'll be working together for a while, just call me Jack."

"Of course sir, as you wish. I have spent most of my life in France and all throughout Europe. I often have to remind myself that you colonists prefer an informal style. I feel certain we'll get along famously...Jack."

"I'm sure we will...Andy," Jack Stoner said.

"It is *Andre*, my friend."

"Of course, please forgive me, I must have misunderstood the pronunciation." Jack turned to Laura. "Are you going to make it over to the Black Rock for dinner tonight?"

"No," she said motioning to the empty containers on the dining room table. "We ordered in. I have a lot of things to go over with Dr. Bettencourt."

"Then I won't keep you any longer." Jack Stoner nodded to the Frenchman. "We try to get started around eight. I'll see you then." With that, he turned and left.

Laura Masterson spoke first. "Jack and his crew are actually doing an excellent job here. You'll find that most people who live in the west take a little getting used to."

Bettencourt nodded and smiled to expose his eerily sharp and small teeth. "I adjust quite rapidly, Dr. Masterson. Our very reason for being here requires focus. To obtain a living sample of the Spanish Flu virus is all that matters, is it not?"

"Yes," Laura said. She added. "And to develop a vaccine to make certain that virus never gets another chance to wrack the world with another pandemic as it did back in 1918."

"Of course, Doctor. And with your talent in the field of cloning, I feel success will be at hand very shortly."

Laura suddenly felt terribly tired and wanted to return to her own motorhome. "It's been a long day. If you don't mind, I'll get some rest and start work in the lab early. I believe that with Buno and Jack Stoner's help you'll manage just fine."

"Dr. Masterson," he said flatly. "You may rest assured that I will do the job I came here to do."

Laura Masterson took an extra long and hot shower. When she dried off, Buno Eberhard's German opera music could be heard intertwining with the mournful howling of coyotes that seemed to be moving closer to the camp. This pack sounded like it could not have been more than a hundred feet away.

She adjusted the Navajo dream catcher then slid naked between the cool, soft sheets. There had been a Carl Hiaasen book on a shelf in the living room. Laura reached over picked it up. Tomorrow she had the formidable task of attempting to revive a long-dead monster while a cemetery full of corpses were being moved.

For a while tonight, Laura decided she was going to read something to take her mind out of the crevice of concern and worry that it had fallen into. A fun story about dysfunctional criminals sounded perfect.

She began turning pages to the tune of opera and coyotes as Carl Hiaasen wove a twisted tale.

CHAPTER THIRTY-SEVEN

Rio de Janeiro, Brazil

Philip Roth lay panting on the silk sheets of his circular bed. Beside him the lithe and naked Vema was purring like a contented kitten while probing his left ear with a talented tongue. This particular girl had the most tremendous appetite for sex—kinky sex—that he had ever encountered in his experience with girls. And that experience, he was proud to remember, had been vast.

Briefly, the head of one of the world's largest pharmaceutical corporations wondered if there was some gene Vema carried in her body that caused her desires. If such was the case, it could possibly be extracted, studied, and refined into a pill. The profits from putting a drug on the market that would turn a cold woman into a raging, insatiable nymphomaniac would reap an incalculable amount of money.

A beep and flashing red light on the telephone by the bed told him that he had an important phone call. He decided to take the message in his private office, giving him some much-needed rest.

"Business must be taken care of," Philip Roth pushed the girl away to stand and wrap himself in a bathrobe. "Go take a shower."

He did not bother to look anymore at the girl. There would always be girls available. A quick glance at his Rolex gave him a good idea who was calling. The Paradox Project came before sex; making money could be even more pleasurable, especially making a *lot* of it. The caller ID on his office phone confirmed his surmise.

"Well, Andre," he said after picking up the receiver. "I assume you are in New Mexico."

"Yes sir, the trip went exactly as planned."

179

"I want you to tell me of Dr. Masterson's progress."

"The woman is apparently quite brilliant. She has already obtained some viable material. She will begin to undertake the cloning process tomorrow."

"Excellent, my friend. Tell me what your intuition says about the status of the project. I know you have an ability to feel how things are going."

"I have reason to believe everything is going according to our projections. All that remains is for us to obtain the samples of the live virus. The scientists in Rio can easily grow more and make the vaccine there."

"Yes and what of Dr. Masterson?"

"I had originally thought it best to dispose of her once our need for her services were done. Now I believe another tact may be in order."

"And why is that? You know I do not like changing plans."

"I am concerned about the American government. They are quite sensitive these days about matters of bioterrorism. The murder of a person of the stature of Dr. Masterson might cause undue attention, especially causing me problems crossing the border. I believe it may be best to simply grab the samples of virus and leave the area as quickly as possible."

"I see your point. The stupid people on site will surely spend much precious time trying to decide what to do. And the good doctor believes the benevolent Hammond Foundation is behind the whole affair. I think you should follow your instincts."

"Yes sir. When the time comes I will do just that. The vials that contain the viruses are quite small. I may be able to just put them in my pocket and fly to Rio on a commercial airline if I am unable to schedule a rendezvous with one of our private jets. The telephone reception here is atrocious. I have to drive Buno's Hummer for miles to get out of the canyon to phone."

"And you may have reason to move quickly. I understand. Do what you must. Just get the samples of live virus to our laboratory. The profits will be too immense to allow for failure."

"I will not fail."

"I know you won't, Andre. That is why you are my right-hand man." Philip Roth added, "Did our lawyer get his needed *vacation*?"

"Michael Delvaney should be drugged and in a hospital bed in Grenada as we speak. The greedy fool could not pack fast enough."

"Keep up the good work. Call me if or when possible."

Philip Roth set the phone back into its cradle. He disliked talking more than was absolutely necessary. It was a total waste of his valuable time. He opened his desk drawer took out a bottle full of blue pills, shaking out two. After washing them down with a bottle of energy drink, the pharmaceutical magnate headed back to the bedroom for some more strenuous exercise.

CHAPTER THIRTY-EIGHT

Dr. Laura Masterson had made her way to the mobile laboratory when the first red rays of a newborn sun were beginning to inch their way down the eastern cliffs that cradled the town of Paradox.

While she suited up in the white biohazard suit and ran the required safety checks, she reflected back on last evening and Dr. Bettencourt. The Frenchman could charm a snake out of its skin with his charismatic mannerisms and flowery verbiage. But on the other hand, the physician came across as competent and anxious to help. Laura had decided to focus on cloning the Spanish Flu virus and let Andre Bettencourt do his job of collecting more specimens. The technology of cloning viruses had not been perfected; it was impossible to predict how much of the virus-rich viable genetic material might be needed to reach a successful conclusion.

While Dr. Masterson actuated the robotic arm to remove the vial of dead viruses, she thought of just how little live virus it would take to begin researching a vaccine. The rate of growth in a favorable medium was fantastic.

Once viruses invade a cell, or are given a suitable substitute, they grow in exponential amounts. Given ten thousand live viruses—a meager number from a medical view—after about ten hours those would begin to double every hour or so. Ten thousand times ten thousand times ten thousand. The replication would continue unabated for as long as there were cells available to invade and control. The numbers of live viruses that could be made from an amount no larger than a drop of water would be able to expand their numbers theoretically into infinity. Of course this was never possible in the real world because of lack of suitable mediums and resistance from other sources. And any virus that does not find a suitable host within a few days dies. Viruses might be deadly, but they are not invincible.

Laura began to introduce the genetic sample into a plasmid. She took a brief and comforting glance at the blue ultraviolet lights that could bathe the containment chamber, along with the complete interior of the laboratory, with the simple flick of a handy switch, or, failing that, the lights could be activated automatically should any sensors show a breach. Exposure to blue ultraviolet light instantly kills all viruses. The demon could not be allowed out of its jar.

The concept of cloning was not new. Hans Speman of Germany had envisioned the process in a paper he published in 1938. The talented author Ira Levin had used this remarkable theory in his chilling novel, *The Boys From Brazil,* in which the DNA from Adolph Hitler had been saved and later introduced into unsuspecting women in an attempt to return a replica of the Füeher to power.

Laura Masterson knew the book was a work of fiction, but the process of cloning *could* theoretically bring back into existence the likes of Adolph Hitler, Genghis Khan, Attila the Hun, or the plague of Athens. All it would take was a viable sample of the appropriate DNA. Their essence.

And Dr. Masterson had a sample of the Spanish Flu virus. It was only mere inches away from her watchful eye. Modern science held a double-edged sword. Technology could be used on one hand to eradicate disease, enhance crops, and build more prolific herds of livestock. In the wrong hands, science could reconstruct and release past terrors that had wracked wholesale death and destruction across the face of the earth.

But the genie had already escaped from the bottle. Laura Masterson knew the outbreaks in Mexico could easily be only the tip of the iceberg, a harbinger of a worldwide pandemic that would likely kill hundreds of millions of people.

To defeat an enemy one must first understand it, learn how to vanquish it. Laura was simply employing the other side of that double-edged sword to protect the world from the most terrible and devastating disease in history—the very virus that she was manipulating at the end of a robotic arm.

THE PARADOX SYNDROME

The process of cloning the virus had been painstakingly worked out, designed, and programmed into the laboratory computer. All it would take was time to see if the monster would live.

Dr. Laura Masterson noted the time, made an entry into her notebook, then began punching the cloning sequence into the computer.

It had begun.

CHAPTER THIRTY-NINE

Clinica La Esperanza, Grenada

Slowly the fog began to clear from Michael Delvaney's muddled mind. He forced his eyes open. It was pitch black out.

At least it is still night, he thought. *I've been drugged and robbed. That is what happened. The bastards. God, my head hurts something awful.*

The lawyer remembered being picked up at the airport in the town of Sauteurs and driven by limousine to a delightful cottage called "Almost Paradise." His Spanish-style little house was set on a lovely white sand beach, alongside the swimming pool. Across the street he noticed a bar with a sign announcing it to be *The Horni Baboon, the friendliest place on the island.* Michael Delvaney couldn't resist popping over for a nice frosty gin and tonic; his appointment with the Roth people wasn't until the following afternoon.

There had been a lovely lady at the bar, a blonde with an exceptional figure. And she had naturally fallen for him. After a few drinks they were on the way to his room for some recreational activities when he felt dizzy. The blonde, he could not recall the bitch's name, helped him into a car. That was his last memory until a few moments ago.

I'm going to sue the pants off everyone who was negligent and let this happen. When I get done with those sons of bitches, I'll own Grenada.

Michael Delvaney realized with a start that he could not move. A few futile attempts told him he was either chained or tied in a spread-eagle fashion on a bed or mattress. He couldn't see a thing in the totally dark room.

I've been kidnaped. This is a shakedown for ransom. The people who took me know who I am. They know I am a wealthy attorney.

"Well, Mr. Delvaney, I see you are awake," a man's calm voice said from the darkness. "Welcome to Grenada."

"Damn you, let me go! I'll not press charges if you do."

"Why Mr. Delvaney, I am certain you realize we can't do that. You are a most valued guest."

"What do you mean *guest*?"

"Actually that term may not be altogether accurate," the voice gave a low cough. "Let me turn this recorder on, it will help you to understand."

A very loud voice began booming in his ears. The narrator began with recounting a series of figures and dates along with repeating his name. The voice was recounting every dollar Michael Delvaney had skimmed from Roth Pharmaceuticals.

"I can repay every dime," the lawyer's voice cracked when he began to plead. "Let me go. I'll pay back double. Trust me, please."

"Mr. Roth intends for you to return every dollar you stole, my good man. I really don't believe you quite yet appreciate the method of repayment. But you *will*."

"I have money, lots of it. I'll give all of it to you if you'll let me go." Michael Delvaney recognized he was nearly sobbing.

"That won't be necessary," the voice was gloating now. "There are other assets you have that are as valuable as cash."

"Huh? What do you mean?" The lawyer summoned his strength. He knew that anyone who showed weakness was always a loser. "And turn on the damn light so I can see your face. I demand you work with me, negotiate a deal."

"Ah, Mr. Delvaney," the voice sighed in the darkness. "I suppose it will be best if I come straight to the point. The light *is* on. I can see you just fine. Your eyes were removed and sold for a tidy sum. I believe a kidney will be taken next, along with the bone morrow from your legs. It might be many weeks before we have a sale for your heart. See, I told you that you had valuable assets—at least enough to pay back what you stole."

The famous trial lawyer began screaming. After a few hours the best the silver-tongued orator could muster was a whimper. In the background, the accountant's voice kept droning on, reciting lists of figures and dates. It was a recording Michael Delvaney would hear over and over for every single hour of the pain-filled weeks or months that remained before all that was left of him would be an empty, useless hulk.

CHAPTER FORTY

What Dr. Laura Masterson was attempting to accomplish in the gleaming high-tech laboratory was to create life itself, using organisms that had been long dead. The task was not only a daunting one, it brought to mind dark mental images of shadowy realms where mankind should not venture—or do so at their peril.

Laura had read, several times, Mary Shelly's timeless novel, *Frankenstein*. It stretched the imagination to realize that book had been first published back in 1818. The plot was that of the brilliant scientist, Victor Frankenstein, who recreated life from death, and did so only to have his own creation turn on him then overpower and destroy him.

Religion and science were oil and water. In all likelihood they would remain as such. Religion warned of perils, admonishing human beings to leave some things untouched, left to the realm of God. Science on the other hand saw all of creation as mathematics, a puzzle to be solved, a maze to be walked. And Laura Masterson was a true scientist.

The hemagglutinin and neuraminidase of the dead flu virus were a blueprint to reconstruct the entire organism. And once this had been accomplished, she intended to infuse it with life itself, renew its existence. This is exactly what the fictional Dr. Frankenstein had done those many years ago: Create life from death.

It amazed Laura that Mary Shelly had conceived the use of lightning, a source of electricity, for Dr. Frankenstein to bring his creature to life. In those times electricity was merely a laboratory curiosity, a frightful companion of life-giving rainstorms. Yet today it is realized that all brain and muscle function is dependent on minute electrical signals to function. How could the young wife of a poet, writing in a cold dank stone castle so long ago have known this fact?

Laura watched the digital readouts on twin viewing screens. The flashing, moving displays were giving out the combined wisdom of thousands, possibly millions of textbooks and medical papers. But the mystery of life, its *essence*, remained steadfastly in the realm of the gods. All she or science could do was the same thing Victor Frankenstein had done: use existing lifeless matter and reinfuse it with life. The ability to actually create life from base chemicals, and then turn it into a living being, was still found only in science fiction.

The advent of the electron microscope first allowed people to actually view something as tiny as a virus. Now these wonderful tools of science had been refined and improved to become unbelievably powerful instruments.

One of her professors of molecular biology had quipped, "A regular optical microscope can see a bacteria quite easily. An electron microscope can not only see the bacteria but also analyze the dirt under its fingernails." This analogy always brought a laugh from students who were all too aware that bacteria don't have hands, let alone fingernails.

It was time to focus on the moment.

Carefully, Dr. Laura Masterson used the robotic arm to remove a small glass dish from the cloning chamber to where she could access the plasmid it held. Hopefully, after all of the preparation and work, a living sample of the Spanish Flu virus was happily swimming around in the blue liquid, munching on a few bits of cellular material and enjoying its first few moments of being alive.

Laura took a few moments to look through the thick glass and admire her creation. She realized that nothing was going to wave hello or hold up a sign telling her she had done good, so Laura began the process of preparing a slide.

Several painstakingly slow minutes later, she swung around in the swivel chair and brought the electron microscope into play.

"It's time to see if the girl can cook," Laura said to herself inside of the glass face mask of the biohazzard containment suit. "The problem is, I wrote the damn recipe. Can't even blame Martha Stewart if the cake doesn't turn out."

She focused on the flat view screen now. It was a solid blue background, the color of a pristine ocean bay, the result of the stain used to highlight the viruses.

Laura pushed a single button allowing the computer to make all of the many needed adjustments. It took only scant seconds before the screen came alive with moving little tennis balls covered in spiked hair.

"Oh my God," Laura couldn't contain her elation. "It's alive. Dr. Frankenstein eat your heart out, I've done it!"

Laura Masterson watched in total awe as she observed something that no human being had ever seen: a living colony of the deadly Spanish Flu virus.

But she quickly realized something was wrong. Something was terribly wrong. All flu viruses are in a state of constant motion, a *predictable* mutational curve. This was the reason that each year a new flu vaccine had to be designed and distributed. The moving target had found a way to dodge the vaccine bullet.

But what Dr. Masterson was observing could not be happening. It was not possible. Yet it existed right in front of her trained eyes. She remembered one of the truths of science: "All biological systems are the product of evolution, not logic."

Laura added in thought, *and all biology is chaos.* She had the proof. Now what to make of the truth. The genie was out of the bottle, the monster had been reborn.

There was nothing else any true scientist *could* do. Dr. Masterson began observing, making notes and entering data into the computer. The phenomena she had created would definitely be studied and debated in professional circles for years.

The problem was for the Hammond Foundation and the fate of millions of human beings, Dr. Laura Masterson, M.D., Ph.D., one of the most trained and skilled molecular biologists in the world, didn't have a clue what to make of her creation. It was as if the strange virus was not of this earth.

CHAPTER FORTY-ONE

Dr. Laura Masterson stared with rapt awe at the flickering blue-tinted, flat-view screen. She felt like she had felt all those many years ago when her father had taken her to the zoo. In the herpetology section, there had been rows and rows of deadly poisonous snakes. All that had separated her from harm were what appeared to be a woefully thin and inadequate panes of glass. But as she found not long afterward, monsters sometimes escaped, or were not recognized until it was too late.

The clusters of Spanish Flu viruses that were on the view screen kept wildly mutating, shifting, and dividing before her eyes. These viruses were not behaving in any orderly, predictable fashion. Dr. Masterson felt as if she were staring at the quintessence of madness—and evil.

These were not normal moving targets upon which to fix a bullet of vaccine. The flu viruses that had previously been studied—*all* of them—had the decency to run in a nice straight line. And do so slowly. In comparison, the Spanish Flu viruses, at least the sample under study, were sprinting, hiding, and dodging.

Laura Masterson shivered at the realization that if this virus was let loose, there could possibly be no defense mounted. At least not until the beast had been studied for a long while. No, if this monster slipped its shackles, it would be 1918 all over again. Anyone coming down with *this* flu would either, through some unknown mechanisms, survive the disease on their own or succumb.

And there was not a damn thing medical science could do about it. Antibiotics would save some lives by acting upon the secondary bacteria. The only way to stop a flu pandemic, however, was to develop a vaccine ahead of time. Millions of doses would be required, but not for *this* strain of virus; couldn't be. At least not in any foreseeable future Dr. Masterson could envision.

Whatever fiend she was watching on the monitor, it did not fit any mold. Hell, it didn't fit in the category of any living creature. The Spanish Flu virus was behaving more like a chemical reaction. A spoonful of baking soda dropped into a dish of vinegar would be an analogy. Pure chaos. Pure madness.

Then Laura watched, spellbound, as the intertwining clusters of viruses began to slow their movements. In a matter of a few minutes, every single virus had sputtered to a complete stop. It was apparent that they had died. *But why?*

The virus mutated so wildly that it burnt itself out. The answer boomed in her mind like a loudspeaker. *Nothing can change that rapidly again and again and survive. Not even the most lethal virus in the history of the world.*

Again the age-old question of science repeated, *But why?*

Was the wild mutation process a result of the cloning? Had she done something wrong or was this normal behavior for this particular virus?

It couldn't be normal, she thought. *The stuff just died in front of your eyes after being alive only minutes.*

Dr. Masterson took a deep breath and let it out slowly. It was time to consider all of the possibilities. That was what a scientist was supposed to do. No matter how urgently results were needed, a professional never rushed to gather answers.

It was fact that the Spanish Flu had been alive and spread around the world over a period of nearly two years, with the peak coming in the fall of 1918. Perhaps the virus began to lose its grip and began to mutate wildly. That would account for the flu pandemic ceasing. The monster had simply burned itself out from changing so rapidly.

But such an event would certainly not prevent *another* such outbreak. The 1918 flu had to have come from somewhere. What Laura needed to concentrate on was the etiology. There *had* to be some common nucleus, some parallels to be drawn for a vaccine to be developed.

Perhaps, the thought jolted her, *the wild mutation is merely an end result of the infection.This virus might behave itself for some period of time in the early course of the disease.*

If the Spanish Flu viruses had a time frame in which they were moving slowly enough in their mutations, they could be shot at and stopped by a nice vaccine bullet. Also, the cadaver this specimen had come from had expired from the flu. Any viral samples would already be in the process of burnout if that theory turned out to be accurate.

But what if the rapid mutations were caused by something entirely different...such as a mineral present in the soil of the graveyard? There could also be chemical deposits in the water the person drank before they died. The rapid mutation of the virus might be limited to only this one single cadaver, not the entire spectrum of the 1918 virus strain.

The answers could only be determined by more samples from the cemetery and more tests. Dr. Masterson made certain all of the data were saved, then flooded the containment area with blue ultraviolet light. No one should ever let a monster get by with playing possum.

Laura began to consider carefully what to tell Dr. Bettencourt. Any negative information at this stage might cause undue problems. While the flamboyant Frenchman had medical knowledge, a few very technical questions she had posed proved to her satisfaction that Andre wasn't the brightest bulb on the cloning tree. It would be an easy task to stall giving no answers except that the genetic material wasn't viable—hell, it wasn't—and the testing must continue. That would buy time for more research and badly needed time.

The digital clock showed she had been inside of the mobile laboratory for twelve straight hours encased in an airtight biohazard suit. Her bladder gave the clock no argument. The time had *really* come to call it a day.

The very last thing she had to do was give a name to the header file that held and described the day's work. That required but little thought. After what she had witnessed today, the name of this remote old coal mining town fit like a hand in a glove.

Dr. Laura Masterson entered *The Paradox Syndrome* into the computer. She then began to go through the decontamination process and rushed to her motorhome as quickly as she could.

CHAPTER FORTY-TWO

Buno Eberhard stepped in front of Dr. Masterson in an attempt to stop her as she sprinted from the mobile laboratory. The Teutonic guard was shocked and surprised by the strength Laura exercised when she used an elbow to rudely push him aside and continue on her way.

"I'll be out in a few minutes," Laura Masterson said over her shoulder as she closed the door behind her. "Think happy thoughts."

Buno humped up in a rage of seething anger that was driven by humiliation. He massaged his aching arm, knowing there would be a bruise to remind him of the blunder he had made by not grabbing her first. And here he was, a member of the Master Race. To be so brusquely treated by a mere female rankled him beyond measure. All women were good for was providing breeding stock as a source of building the Aryan nation. They were innately inferior to men. Still, he reminded himself, a headstrong female could present difficulties that were hard to foresee or prepare for. They were all as unpredictable as cats. It was becoming very clear to him that Dr. Masterson had a mind of her own, along with the will to use it. The pain in his arm attested to that fact. Then the answer to the entire incident hit him harder than the woman doctor had. *She has pure Aryan blood flowing in her veins. Excellent, most excellent indeed. I am impressed.*

The guard also had to remind himself that all women, even those of good Prussian blood, measured time by a different clock than did men. He could have run to town and back and done a hundred pushups before the doctor opened the door of her motorhome and stepped out to meet him.

"Yes, Buno, what can I do for you?" Laura asked pleasantly, as if nothing untoward had occurred. This confirmed Buno's conclusion that she was a true Aryan. They *never* apologize.

"Dr. Bettencourt is having dinner in town this evening. He asked me to invite you to join him there."

Laura did not particularly want to spend time with Andre Bettencourt for a number of reasons. One was a simple gut-level feeling of dislike of the man on grounds she couldn't pin down. But it would be rude of her to refuse and she felt totally famished. "I'll be happy to join him."

Buno nodded. "Dr. Bettencourt gave me instructions to drive you to the restaurant in my Hummer."

Laura could not understand the reasoning behind this, but where the German guard was concerned, it seemed like a good idea not to cause him to have to think any more than absolutely necessary. "Thank you for the courtesy."

When Laura headed for Buno's somber Hummer she studied the town of Paradox. A few sparse lights in windows and one lone streetlight twinkled against the gathering darkness like lonely stars. The time was later than she had realized. Considering the events of the day it was understandable that the night had caught her unawares.

It was with considerable relief that Laura exited the Hummer in front of the Black Rock Bar and Grill after the blessedly short trip. She enjoyed Mozart's music, but not blasted from CD speakers loud enough to rattle the fillings in her teeth.

Buno came to her side and escorted her through the doorway. Laura was not sure if the guard was watching after her welfare or making certain she went inside. The man was an enigma, that much was for certain.

Andre Bettencourt took her aback in yet another turn of events in what had already been a very strange day. The French doctor had taken the center table of the restaurant. He was sitting alone behind a silver candelabra that held four flickering candles. A white tablecloth graced the table. A galvanized metal bucket filled with ice held two bottles of wine.

Laura Masterson could not help but be impressed by Andre's preparations. She smiled and took the lone chair across the table from him. Jack Stoner, Frank Lowry, and Rodney Simms watched with silent interest when Laura walked across the room. Aside from Willie Ames who was at the bar watching a baseball game, no one else was present.

"I am pleased you have joined me," Dr. Bettencourt said. "And I trust the day was not too terribly tiring for you."

Laura watched as Andre poured a taste of wine into his glass, swirled it, held it up to observe its legs, then took a slight sip and filled both glasses.

"No," she said. Neither of them could talk freely. "Just a routine day of testing. Nothing to report out of the ordinary."

"Ah well, the time now is to reward the body for its labors. I believe the wine to be acceptable, even though it is from a vineyard here in the state of New Mexico instead of France. I honestly never thought of the colonists as being vintners, but I must say they are learning quite well."

Laura nodded agreeably and took a drink. "It is quite good. You have an excellent palate for wine."

"Someday I hope you might allow me to introduce you to some of the more excellent French vintages, but for now let us enjoy."

Dr. Masterson and Andre Bettencourt indulged in small talk while Sadie Helms hacked her way back and forth carrying food from the kitchen. Since the cocky Frenchman had slipped the waitress a hundred dollar bill to give good service, she went out of her way to give the man his money's worth. Sadie wondered where the doctor had come up with lobster tails, but considering the fancy motorhomes and vehicles the Cougar Canyon Development Corporation had brought in, almost anything was possible. Thelma had little experience cooking lobster. The drawn butter had been made from a recipe book that hadn't been opened for years, but everything turned out just fine. Laura enjoyed the food and thoughtfulness, only she secretly wished to be able to join Jack Stoner and the Bureau of Reclamation workers at their table and drink Miller Lite while enjoying cheeseburgers and french fries.

Later, after the far-too-fancy dinner, Andre escorted Laura outside into the star-studded night. Once they were out of earshot they could talk freely.

"Have you successfully cloned the virus?" Dr. Bettencourt asked outright.

"No. The genetic material I had to work with was too degraded. More samples will be necessary."

"I trocared the chests of eight cadavers today. I have already placed the samples in the holding area of your laboratory."

"Then we will continue our efforts tomorrow as planed." Laura felt uncomfortable and wished to be away from the Frenchman who reeked of sweet cologne. "Thank you for the fine dinner," she said. "I appreciate it very much. Now I really should go back to camp, finish up some notes, and get some rest."

"Ah my dear, the night is still young," Dr. Bettencourt wrapped a dainty hand around her waist in an attempt to pull her close. Laura had been in a few Texas roadhouses before. She expertly turned to brush Andre's hand away like a piece of unwanted lint.

"Again let me thank you for the dinner," Laura stepped back, her voice firm. "But I have business to attend to." That was when she noticed Bettencourt's Hummer was there, but not Buno's. The reason she had been driven into town was clear. Her choice of getting home would be to either walk or allow the Frenchman to drive her.

The howling pack of coyotes from near the camp caused her to wonder which of the choices she faced was the most desirable. Considering the people she had met who worked for the Hammond Foundation, this encounter caused her to wonder about their hiring practices.

"Well, Laura, it looks like you might be in need of a lift."

From the dark shadow of an abandoned building, Jack Stoner came into the light grinning and using his John Wayne voice. "I reckon I'd be mighty happy to offer the little lady my services if you're amind to."

Andre Bettencourt was obviously shocked to see Jack Stoner. The man had seemingly appeared from nowhere. The doctor said, "I shall be the one to drive her."

"Well now if that's what the little lady wants, I reckon that'll be fine and dandy with me." Jack grinned in the darkness like a cat staring at a canary. "But considering that flat tire," he motioned to the Hummer that was definitely on a tilt, "I'm thinking the both of you could use a ride back to your camp. I was going to offer to change it for you, but would you believe the spare's flat, too? Sometimes if a person didn't have bad luck they'd have no luck at all."

Laura took delight in observing Bettencourt's shifting expressions. Jack Stoner had been inside the Black Rock Grill all evening. He could not have let the air out of both tires, yet she knew he was somehow responsible for two flats.

"We accept your generous offer," Dr. Bettencourt said almost pleasantly. "You are most kind. And observant."

"Just aiming to help our esteemed co-workers," Jack Stoner said motioning to his Dodge pickup. "We all have our jobs to do here in Paradox."

You don't have a clue, Laura Masterson thought. Then she began walking to Stoner's truck. "I appreciate this. Tomorrow's going to be a long day."

"They're *all* going to be long ones until we're done with what we're here for." Jack Stoner said, looking Andre straight in the face. Then he walked over to open the door for Laura.

On the short drive back, not a word was said by anyone. From the open windows of the pickup the coyotes could be plainly heard serenading the starry night. They appeared to be no longer frightened by the sound of vehicles and could definitely be seen on a rocky ledge overlooking the old cemetery.

It was as if the coyotes were being drawn by the smell of newly opened graves and the odor of old deaths that had occurred long years ago.

CHAPTER FORTY-THREE

While Laura was putting on the white biohazard suit and checking out the mobile laboratory, her mind was reflecting on events of the past evening.

It was obvious the cocky French doctor had planned and presumed to take her to bed last night. And Andre Bettencourt seemed to be used to getting his way. Laura mused that perhaps wherever he called home such tactics were acceptable, but she doubted that. In most any civilized country, a good slap in the face would be his reward for such temerity.

Thank goodness for Jack Stoner intervening to stop what could have turned into an ugly confrontation. Andre Bettencourt and she were going to have to keep working together for the good of the world. Having to smash the horny doctor's nuts with her knee could definitely cause a rift in their relationship.

But how did Jack manage to flatten two tires on Bettencourt's Hummer and then turn up in the shadows of that abandoned building? Laura could swear in court that the Bureau of Reclamation man had been in the restaurant all the time they were there. He had certainly still been in the booth when Andre and she had gone outside.

Jack might be part Indian, she surmised. Not only did he have somewhat high cheekbones, he had also mentioned spending time on the Navajo reservation. Being a Native American could account for his being able to move about so silently. In any case, the man's presence was most welcome last night. Jack had courteously escorted her to the door of her motorhome and watched over her until she was safely inside. Then she had heard through an open window when he did not *ask*, but *told* Andre Bettencourt to get back into his truck and go with him to get an air tank so they could fill the tires on the Hummer.

Now spending the night with Jack Stoner might not be that bad. Not bad at all. The man had class, manners and a sense of humor along with an air of mystery. And a girl could become lost in those deep pale blue eyes of his.

But there were monsters to slay first, a beast from a thousand nightmares. A beast she had set eyes on for the first time only yesterday. The Spanish Flu virus was far more of an enigma than she or anyone else ever expected it to be. The wild mutations gave good reason to believe this *was* the dying gasp of the virus, a violent swan song after its terrible mission of death was accomplished.

At least that was the most plausible theory Laura Masterson had to work with at the moment. The biggest problem to surmount should that theory be accurate would be obtaining a sample of viral DNA that was not in the final throes of the mutation sequence—a task that seemed nearly impossible.

The odds of obtaining from a cadaver some genetic material that had, for some reason, *any* reason, not run its course, was infinitesimal. A person had a better chance of lining up seven consecutive numbers on a Powerball game. After all, these people weren't buried until *after* the flu had already killed them. But more research was required to know if this theory was scientific fact.

Dr. Masterson completed the myriad safety checks then took a seat in the now-familiar and not very comfortable swivel chair in front of the long glass containment area. She deftly moved the robotic arm to slide in the box of samples Dr. Bettencourt had collected into the chamber. There were sixteen vials, two from each of the eight bodies that had been exhumed. One vial had been filled from each lung. From the amount and condition of the material in the vials, it was obvious that Dr. Andre Bettencourt did not employ her finesse. Every sample contained small flecks of bone from where he had jabbed ribs with the trocar. The Frenchman was dealing roughly with the corpses, that much was certain. This made her angry. Yes, the cadavers were long dead and could feel no more pain, but they were still human beings, dammit. They deserved to be treated with decency and courtesy.

No matter. The research had to continue. Andre Bettencourt was definitely a blue-ribbon winning asshole who probably spent his nights cuddled up with a picture of himself, but she had to continue working with him. There was nothing else to do but buckle down and focus on research.

Before beginning to add the genetic material to the dishes of plasmid, Dr. Masterson took a few minutes to compare the numbers on the vials to the cemetery records. It was part of good science to record everything known of the sample donor. Their age, race, and sex, along with the date and cause of death, could somehow become valuable knowledge. All of this was time consuming, but vital.

The first was an eighteen-year-old girl who had died in childbirth from what Dr. Wheeler had described as exsanguination due to *postpartum hemorrhage*. Simply stated, the poor girl had bled to death after giving birth. Not an uncommon occurrence in those days, when it was unlikely the attending physician would have had blood transfusions available.

Laura wondered what had become of the baby. Perhaps it did not survive. A small grave marked only as "infant child" might remain in the Paradox cemetery yet to be unearthed. If the baby had lived—she did the figures in her head—the person might still be alive at age 87. Doubtful but possible. Laura had interviewed a few elderly people who remembered the Spanish Flu epidemic from when they were small children.

The next set of samples were numbered R-76 and L-76, the letters referring to which lobe of the lung the samples were taken from, and the numbers matched the gravesite.

Dr. Wheeler's records referred to *"a young Mexican man, age unknown but approximately twenty years old. The deceased's name is Juan Arroyo, time of death approximately seven-thirty A.M. on November fifteenth, 1918. Cause of death, multiple rib fractures causing puncture trauma to both lungs and probably the heart and liver. No autopsy will be conducted due to the flu epidemic that is raging. The man was crushed by a falling rock in the gallery number two of the Black Beauty mine. The fatality is laid to an act of God. I find it interesting that the men who brought in the deceased mentioned that he was showing symptoms of the flu at the time of the accident and that God was determined to have his soul. May he rest in peace.*

Dr. Masterson read the entry, blinked, and read it again. If the information in Dr. Wheeler's logs was accurate then Juan Arroyo's young life may have been ended by a mine accident before the

Spanish Flu had run its course. If the man was just beginning to exhibit the first stages of the flu, his lung tissues might possibly yield a sample of the virus in its early stages before the wild mutations began.

"Girl," Laura said as she maneuvered the robotic arm to extract vials R-76 and L-76 from their containers, "if this works out like I hope it will, you definitely have to start buying some lottery tickets."

CHAPTER FORTY-FOUR

Laura sat transfixed in front of the flat view screen of the electron microscope. No other human had ever set eyes on a living example of the Spanish Flu virus, save her. And she knew exactly the significance of the newly cloned sample from Juan Arroyo's crushed chest. This specimen had come from a cluster that had been "frozen" and encapsulated when the host had been killed in a mine accident. The virus had not evolved to the end stages where wild mutations brought about its own demise. No, this virus was far more familiar and well behaved. It moved in the normal linear evolution of any influenza virus.

"Gotcha, you son of a bitch," Laura said to the screen. "It doesn't matter if you speed up like a rocket and explode like some kind of shifting antigen Roman candle after you've killed your victim. Now we can target your microscopic ass with a vaccine while you're moving nice and slow. You might think you're the toughest bugs on the block, but now you're in my crosshairs and it's only a matter of time until I pull the trigger."

Laura marveled at the odds of obtaining a sample of the virus that had been stopped and preserved by an accident before the disease had run its course of infection.

"Juan Arroyo," she murmured, "your death might just save untold millions of lives."

Dr. Masterson took time to make extra copies of all of the computer data. A crashed hard drive could not be allowed to cause a loss of time where this virus was concerned. She also made a couple of pages of handwritten notes, just to be extra careful.

Laura used the robotic arm to move the dish containing the shimmery blue of ancient death about inside of the containment area. First she weighed the sample, deducting for the dish. There were many thousands of strands of the living influenza virus available. All she wanted to do was make certain there was sufficient nutritional plasmid to keep the colony in a condition of stasis for a period of time.

No more samples would be necessary. Considering the exponential rate in which a colony of viruses can expand, only the seed amounts to fill a couple of glass vials would be necessary to obtain sufficient material to develop a vaccine. Should by any accident even a drop of the viral plasmid be let loose where a growth medium, such as human lungs, was available, the reborn Spanish Flu virus could jump from host to host and expand across the world just as it had done with awesome efficiency back in 1918. Another pandemic unleashed upon the earth. Only this plague would be completely her fault...a scenario Dr. Laura Masterson was determined to avoid at any cost.

Carefully, very carefully, Laura used the robotic arm to transfer the virus-laden plasma into two specially constructed solid black boro-silicate glass cylinders about the size and length of those seen at cigar sales counters. The lids were screwed on tight and an extra sealing of a special sterilizing tape tightly wrapped the joints.

Laura clucked her tongue from tension as she flooded the chamber with ultraviolet blue light, effectively killing every live virus not securely locked inside of the twin cylinders.

The remaining genetic material from Juan Arroyo's chest had been safely stored inside another chamber in case it might be needed at some future date. The viruses were long dead, harmless until cloned as she had successfully done with the recreated disease that was safely inside those cylinders.

Theoretically, a person could simply open the air lock on the end of the chamber, reach in with a bare hand, and carry the deadliest virus on earth away in his or her pocket. Of course that would never happen. The virus would be taken to a laboratory where there were facilities to use it to manufacture a vaccine. Many millions of doses. The cost would be untold millions of dollars, the time factor months. But it *could* be done. Hell, it *would* be done. That was what the Hammond Foundation had hired her to do. And she had done it.

Laura couldn't help but stare long and hard at the dull black cylinders. She felt just like she had as a girl, looking through panes of glass at poisonous snakes such as cobras, kraits, and rattlesnakes. If death could be said to exude an aura, those two vials were enshrouded by it, like those terrible snakes were all those years past. She suppressed a shiver. The beast was securely shackled. Now it was time to have a personal conversation with Andre Bettencourt to tell him of her findings.

For a brief moment, Laura Masterson felt more fear of the French doctor than the contents of those two vials. But the emotion was baseless, personal, it had no place in science or medicine. She began the safety procedures of exiting the biohazard level-four mobile laboratory.

CHAPTER FORTY-FIVE

The bright orange orb of a New Mexico sun was beginning to sink low in the west, painting itself into a spectacular coffin that was attended by a dark shroud of storm clouds.

Buno Eberhard sat on a finger of red sandstone jutting out above the deep canyon that sheltered the dying town of Paradox. The stoic guard held the black cell phone to his ear and grinned with satisfaction. Philip Roth was pleased with his work.

"Yes, sir," Buno said. "Dr. Masterson has successfully cloned the ah...item you wished." He did not understand many of the big words the doctors and pharmacists he worked with insisted on using. But that did not matter; he always accomplished what they sent him to do, just as he had done this time.

"Excellent, Buno," Roth said. "There will be a nice bonus for you when you return to Brazil." He hesitated a moment. "You are *certain* the item is available?"

"The computer link you had installed from Dr. Masterson's mobile laboratory to my motorhome works very good sir. I even downloaded a disk of the doctor's work and copied all her conversations. The doctor has a tendency to talk to herself."

"Now listen carefully, Buno. I want you to tell all of this to Dr. Bettencourt. In the strictest of confidence, of course. He will know what to do. Follow his instructions exactly."

"I always do, sir."

"And that is the reason I have just entrusted you with the details of why you are in New Mexico. If *anything* goes wrong, I want you to personally remove those two black cylinders from the laboratory and bring them back here to Rio. Don't worry about the contents. As long as those vials are unopened they are quite safe, I assure you.

But I command you to bring them to me at *any* cost. Do you understand?"

"I will follow your orders, sir."

"Excellent, Buno. Please do not act as if anything out of the ordinary is happening. All should appear nice and calm in Paradox."

"Of course. I will only tell Dr. Bettencourt of your instructions."

"Your diligence is commendable, Buno. I hope to see you quite soon."

The click and ensuing stone silence told Buno Eberhard the conversation had ended. He liked working for people who didn't talk too much. He could now give a chuckle over Roth's comment about a good bonus awaiting him. The manila envelope containing a quarter million dollars in cash was safely stashed in his motorhome. Now *there* was a bonus worth counting.

Buno walked back to his Hummer. He took a moment to adjust the Kelvar body armor that was pinching him. Before bending to climb inside he adjusted his pistol and hidden knives. The venomous spikes that were inside the heels of his shoes could, sadly, not be tested, only used. He was certain, however, they would work just fine.

When Buno Eberhard scooted into the plush leather driver's seat, he hoped fervently that Dr. Bettencourt's instructions would include killing Stoner. Some people deserved being snuffed out more than others. Removing Jack Stoner from the world of the living would be a real pleasure. He grinned at the thought, then keyed the ignition and sped off down the steep dirt road into the shadow-filled canyon.

Centers for Disease Control and Protection
Atlanta, Georgia

Ruben Hernandez was watching Fox News on one televison screen while monitoring over a dozen more. The computer on his desk flicked routine messages. Just another quiet night in The Tombs.

He had quit paying undue attention to monitoring the area around Tucumcari, New Mexico. All of the news from there was boring enough to cause nearly anyone to nod off. If any place on earth could be said that watching paint dry seemed exciting by comparison, Tucumcari was it.

Then he was jolted to the big screen by a sharp warning buzz. A single red light indicating a level-four biohazard alert had just flashed on. And it was located approximately forty miles northwest of Tucumcari. A biohazard level-four alert wouldn't stay secret for long.

But what the hell was it? And how did it appear out of the middle of nowhere?

Ruben began to closely monitor every single police, sheriff, and highway patrol call in that area. Everything was ominously routine.

The perplexed CDC man kept doing his job, just as the rule books laid it down. There *was* a major biohazard alert in northeast New Mexico, just exactly *what* it was obviously remained to be seen.

He mouthed a prayer that the red telephone would not ring, and kept listening intently to every communication from that area.

CHAPTER FORTY-SIX

After Laura secured the mobile laboratory, she went straight to her coach. It was pleasing to note that both Buno and the black Hummer he drove were among the missing. That was one potential problem she didn't have to deal with.

After a day when she had cloned a living batch of what was likely the most deadly virus on the planet, Laura felt unclean. A long hot shower and a change of clothes were in order. A glance at the cemetery when she had walked to her motorhome revealed that Andre Bettencourt and the Bureau of Reclamation people were still occupied with moving bodies. This gave her plenty of time before having to meet with Dr. Bettencourt. It was most important that she act as if the day had been perfectly routine, nothing out of the ordinary.

The shower and a power nap did wonders. Laura dressed in jeans and a baggy western shirt, which she decided to not tuck in. Andre Bettencourt was lecherous enough without dressing to entice him even slightly. A glance at the clock showed it was well past her dinnertime. Not too long ago she had heard Buno come roaring back from wherever he had been in his Hummer.

Giving the matter some thought, Laura decided to drive over to the Black Rock Bar & Grill for a cold beer and to eat a relaxing dinner. It would be good to see Jack Stoner and have occasion for a laugh or two before the private meeting with Dr. Bettencourt, which she was dreading.

Laura was surprised by the drop in temperature she encountered when she stepped outside. A distant rumbling along with a gathering of ominous black clouds that could be seen moving in over the rimrocks to the west told her a thunderstorm was headed their way.

Maybe Andre Bettencourt will get struck by lightning, she thought. *A person should always strive to keep an optimistic attitude.*

Buno Eberhard's glowering face stared at her through the front window of his motorcoach when Laura passed by on the way to her Suburban. The light was poor due to the storm clouds that now covered the long, narrow slot of sky over Paradox, but it appeared Buno was dressed in camouflage clothes for some odd reason. Anything that German did really should not be considered odd, she decided. Laura fought back the urge to stick out her tongue at him, then continued on to the Suburban, traipsing to the music of a Hugo Wolf opera being played much too loudly.

At the Black Rock Willie Ames was sipping whiskey and watching television from his usual barstool. The three Bureau of Reclamation men were in their regular seats alongside the wall when Laura entered. It was classic dejà vu, with the welcome exception of Dr. Andre Bettencourt, which was a pleasant though temporary reprieve.

"You're out of the lab early," Jack said with obvious delight. "Come over, have a seat, and let a government employee pad his expense account and buy you a beer."

"All right big spender," Laura said scooting up a chair to the table. "I'll take you up on that. Since you're being generous, I intend to order a name-brand beer in a real bottle instead of one of those bargain-priced drafts you've started drinking."

Frank Lowry lowered his eyebrows and looked at Jack. "I warned you the good-looking ones always have expensive tastes. Every one of my exes could have bankrupted a small country with their spending habits."

"The good doctor's going to have to lower her lifestyle," Rodney Simms said, twirling an empty mug with a sad expression on his face. "Thelma's out of bottled beer of any brand worth drinking. It's draft beer or join a group that holds meetings three times a week."

Sadie Helms hacking caught their attention before she made it out of the kitchen to set a tray of draft beers on the table.

"A buck a mug is a bargain, guys," Sadie wheezed. "The way things are looking, the last keg will blow empty about the time the cemetery's moved." She looked sadly about the big room that was nearly empty. "Then we'll all be leaving here. No reason to stick around and watch the water rise."

Laura grasped the cold handle on her mug. "Where are you and Thelma going first? There's a lot of nice country to see."

Sadie Helms gave a shrug. "We don't know for certain. That old motorhome has a lot of miles on it and needs tires and stuff. Thelma and I might not be able to afford to go too far, but hey, there's cool mountains up north and warm desert in the south in this state. That will do for the two of us."

A flash of lightning from the front windows followed by a clap of deafening thunder interrupted the moment.

"I'll miss the weather most of all," Sadie said. "It's hard to replace the weather we get here in Paradox most any place you can find other human beings."

Laura looked to the door where fat drops of rain were beginning to splatter and trickle down the windows. "This rain might give everyone a day or two off, at least everyone but Dr. Bettencourt and myself. We have quite a few things to go over." She gave a worried look. "Did he go to his coach? I halfway expected him to be here."

"Frenchy nearly ran to that fancy motorhome of his once the last body got loaded up," Lowry said. "He moved so fast, he either remembered he had a roast in the oven or came down with a case of diarrhea. Either of them will get a move on."

"We started calling him Frenchy ever since we found out it irritated him," Jack said taking a sip of beer. "Frenchmen are so easy to piss off, it would be a shame not to rankle them on most any occasion."

"Speaking of a day off," Rodney said as dime-sized hail began to beat a tattoo on the metal roof, "we might get longer than that. I understand the road down the side of the canyon turns muddy with most any rain that falls."

Sadie gave a hack then said, "Make that the slickest mud you'll ever find. Nothing on wheels goes in or out of here after even a little shower until the road dries out." She grinned and shrugged. "This is the desert. The longest we've been unable to get out of here was a couple of weeks back in nineteen seventy-seven or thereabouts. Most of the time, a day or two of sun does the trick."

"That'll put a stop to the body buggy," Lowry said. "No reason to dig up any graves if we can't ship the residents out."

Laura gave Frank a skewered look. The man had developed a black sense of humor, probably from being around Jack Stoner for too long, she decided. Then she smiled. That was why she had come here, to be around life, fun. To forget, at least for a little while, about the ancient plague that she had caused to become reborn.

The realization that she might be stuck here in Paradox, unable to get the virus transported to a laboratory to begin developing a vaccine, struck Laura like a slap to the face. She couldn't be stranded here for days on end while precious time passed like sand through an hourglass. There were helicopters, of course. But to use her cell phone, the *only* phone she had been ordered to use, required being on top of a mesa. Laura's worried thoughts began to flash across her mind like an out-of-focus movie.

"What's the matter, Laura?" Jack had noticed her spirits sag. "My mother would say that you look like someone just walked over your grave."

Laura Masterson shook her head as if to cast off bad thoughts. She took a sip of beer. "I suppose I was being concerned over the job taking longer than we expected. There are some reports I need to phone in."

Rodney Simms said, "The phone here works fine."

"The company I work for pays a fortune for my cell phone," Laura said. "They would be upset if I ran up another bill."

"Use my calling card," Rodney volunteered, reaching for his wallet. "I never use all the minutes. Long distance phone calls are really cheap these days."

Laura realized that being around generous and educated people could create its own problems.

"Thank you for the offer, Rodney," Laura said. "But I don't have my notes from the laboratory. I'll maybe call tomorrow. Looks like we'll have lots of time on our hands." *And I just might need to call out* she thought. *I'll see what Andre Bettencourt thinks. We need to move as quickly as possible.*

Sadie Helms turned away, a scowl on her wrinkled face. She gave a slight cough as she walked to stare out of the window in wide-eyed awe. "What the...I thought I heard an engine. Why, there goes that big lab truck heading out. And Buno Eberhard's following in his Hummer. Don't those idiots know they'll never make it out of this canyon with it raining and muddy?"

Jack bolted from his seat joined by Frank.

"I didn't expect them to try anything this stupid or this quick," Lowry said. He held a Glock pistol in his hand.

"We should have suspected something like this considering who and what we're dealing with." Jack held a matching pistol to Frank's.

"Oh shit!" Laura was awestruck. "Who's stealing the laboratory for God's sake?"

"Andre Bettencourt will be driving it," Jack Stoner said. "He's cocky enough to believe a little mud won't stop him."

"No use letting him get any farther than we have to." Willie Ames pushed his way past carrying a huge rifle.

"Kill both of them with a head shot if you can," Frank shouted to Willie as he ran out into the rain and hail to aim at the departing truck and Hummer.

Laura joined a puzzled Sadie in wondering why Willie Ames was planning to kill Dr. Bettencourt and Buno Eberhard.

And why was Andre Bettencourt trying to take the mobile laboratory away? Laura shivered from more than the weather when she thought of the deadliest virus on earth being inside the big black and chrome truck that was roaring up the steep road leading up to the mesa and out of the town of Paradox.

If for any reason even a drop of the living Spanish Flu virus became unleashed on the world....

CHAPTER FORTY-SEVEN

Buno Eberhard had always hated Andre Bettencourt for some reason he could not pin down. That was no longer in question; the man was an arrogant idiot. He was only one of many the New Reich would happily dispose of in some shining future.

Looking through the flipping windshield wipers of the Hummer at the rear end of the mobile laboratory, Buno shook with rage. Only his loyalty to Philip Roth had kept him from disposing of the French doctor. His anger had been compounded when the uppity physician had not given him the opportunity or time to retrieve the quarter of a million dollars from his motorcoach.

"There is a storm coming, we must move fast," the overconfident physician had commanded. "After a storm they tell me the road will become slick with mud. That will stop any pursuit."

"Why can't we simply grab the two vials from the laboratory and take off in the Hummer?" Buno had prudently asked.

Andre Bettencourt said, "No, we want to confuse everyone, make them wonder why the entire laboratory has been moved. My intent is to leave it abandoned in Tucumcari. The way the soft Americans handle potentially dangerous matters, we will be happily back in Rio De Janeiro before the morons get up the courage to even open the laboratory to find out if the virus is missing or not."

The man's words did make some sense, Buno had to admit. But to abandon all of that money so desperately needed by the New Reich in Paraguay both angered and saddened him beyond measure.

You should have cut his throat, Buno chided himself for being weak and indecisive. *Mr. Roth told me that if anything went wrong for me to grab those little black bottles and return to Brazil. I only needed to say that someone else killed Dr. Bettencourt. Hell, maybe he just had a heart attack. A quick jab from the venom spikes in the heels of my boots would have passed for a heart attack. Then I would have had the Fourth Reich's money.*

Buno Eberhard realized, as his father had wisely said, "You are crying over spilt milk." The die was cast. He was following Dr. Bettencourt as he had been told. Only the rain was coming down a lot heavier than anyone had expected it to. The big black and chrome laboratory truck began to fishtail back and forth. It looked like the idiotic Frenchman's answer was to push the accelerator to the floor. Mud and smoke flew from all eight of the rear tires to obscure Buno's vision.

Then Buno glanced at the rearview mirror. His heart did a flip-flop when he saw a man on the porch of the Black Rock Bar and Grill aiming a rifle at him.

Buno did not have even a few seconds to consider the rifleman before the laboratory spun crossways in the road in front of him and slowly came up on the driver's side wheels to overturn in the middle of the road. The blonde guard's attention had been focused on the man with the rifle.

Buno rammed the Hummer into the bottom side of the toppled laboratory just as heavy caliber bullets began slamming into back of his vehicle.

CHAPTER FORTY-EIGHT

Thelma Ross bounded from the kitchen, her reddish-purple hair streaming. She had a battered and scarred old Winchester Model 94 rifle clasped in both hands. "What the hell's all the shooting about. This is a peaceable joint and I'll put a hole in the first son of a bitch that don't agree with me."

Lowry stepped over to Thelma and placed a firm hand on her shoulder while grabbing the rifle with his other. "They're drug dealers out there, ma'am. They're trying to make a getaway that's not turning out well for them."

"How do you know so much?" Thelma saw the distant mobile laboratory lying on its side. The Black Hummer had slammed into the bottom side. "You guys work for the Bureau of Reclamation."

Jack Stoner stepped in front of Laura to stop her from going outside. Willie Ames had stopped firing, but kept the rifle pointed at the Hummer.

"Frank, Willie, and I are undercover police," Jack spoke loud enough for everyone to hear. He didn't have time to answer a lot of questions. "We've had the Cougar Canyon bunch under surveillance for a long time. Buno Eberhard and Andre Bettencourt are the ones we're after. They're trying to get away with a fortune in drugs. We're here to stop them."

Laura Masterson stared at him, aghast. She did not know who to trust. Dr. Bettencourt being a drug dealer wasn't possible. Her thoughts were muddled. The live virus in that laboratory was her concern. *If Stoner is lying, then Buno is trying to protect the Hammond Foundation along with me and the laboratory. I have a gun in my purse.*

At the scene of the collision of the Hummer and laboratory, Buno Eberhard could be seen jumping from his vehicle, then sprinting, bobbing and weaving as he headed for the shelter of the overturned laboratory.

"Don't shoot him, Willie!" Jack yelled through the open door. "It's too risky."

Willie held up two fingers to indicate that he had heard, but kept his rifle at the ready.

"Oh shit!" Jack spun to Laura, fear, stark and vivid glittered in his pale blue eyes. "Laura, grab that cell phone of yours and give it to me *now*."

Laura did not hesitate. What Stoner wanted the phone for she hadn't a clue, but the opportunity to get her hands on the pistol that was next to the cell phone wasn't a chance to be missed. She ran and grabbed the purse from under her chair at the table where a throughly stunned Rodney Simms sat, wide-eyed and speechless. A few seconds later she tossed the phone to Jack Stoner.

The government man immediately ran outside and threw the big black phone across the street where it rolled into a muddy ditch.

"Get back from the windows," Lowry yelled, waving his arms wildly to motion Sadie and Thelma into the depths of the restaurant.

A bright flash lit up the shadows, followed by a roaring boom that sent shards of glass flying from a terrific explosion that blew out every window facing the street.

Jack Stoner wiped a trickle of blood from his cheek then spun to survey first Willie and then everyone inside. No one seemed to be hurt. "If Frenchy had been quicker to think to dial a number and blow us up, we wouldn't have been so lucky. I should have thought faster."

Laura Masterson shook her head to clear the ringing from her ears. She had no idea what had just occurred, but was damn well going to find out. "Okay, Jack, what exactly are you insinuating about Dr. Bettencourt."

"Drug dealers have a bag of dirty tricks, Laura. That big black cell phone was so heavy because it was filled with a pound of plastic high explosive. Punch in the correct sequence of numbers from another phone, then hit 'send,' and—well it's plain that'll be the last phone call you'll ever receive."

Michael Delvaney's behind this, Laura Masterson's thoughts came into an angry focus. *I've been set up. But the drug dealer thing is a crock. I've just cloned the deadliest virus on earth and it's out there in that lab. It's a fact, however, that they intended to kill me. But why? Keep your mouth shut and listen girl. Jack Stoner just saved your life. Trust him, at least for now.*

Laura grabbed the Glock from her purse, making certain to hold it up for all to see.

"I understand you know how to use that gun," Jack said matter-of-factly. "Bring along extra ammo if you have any. We can't let those bastards get away. It won't take Frenchy and Buno long to figure out we're still alive. They'll have no choice but to grab what's most valuable and take off on foot. We have to stop them."

A deep rumble of thunder ominously puncuated Jack's words.

Laura Masterson decided the "government" men knew a lot more than they were letting on. The virus was far more important than any drug bust. No matter what was coming down, she owed it to the entire world to stop the release of a pandemic that could kill millions of people.

"Let's go get them," Laura said, stuffing the Glock inside of her belt. Then a few seconds later she followed Jack Stoner and Frank Lowry into the rain while Willie Ames kept his rifle pointed toward the laboratory. So far, nothing could be seen to moving about up there, but she knew that bullets could come flying at them at any second. Considering the consequence of failure, there really was no other choice but a direct attack.

Buno Eberhard knew the man who shot his tires out had hit exactly what he was aiming for. Not a single bullet came close to his person or blew out a window. They could not afford to take a chance of having a stray bullet break one of those vials Mr. Roth wanted so badly. The substance inside was deadly, he had been told, and was also very valuable. He meant to get these two tubes back to his boss and Rio at all costs. But Dr. Bettencourt had them with him in the mobile laboratory.

Buno threw open the door and rolled out of the Hummer. He kept low, bobbing and weaving from side to side, nearly slipping in the mud. The lack of any shots fired his way confirmed his theory there were more than a few people in Paradox who knew exactly what they were attempting to take away. The fact they weren't going to take any chances would be usable, maybe to their foe's downfall.

Reaching the relative safety of the overturned laboratory, Buno encountered an obviously furious Dr. Andre Bettencourt, who had just kicked out the front windshield to crawl from the wreckage. The Frenchman's face was a red mask of rage. For some reason he was attempting to punch numbers into a cell phone. Bettencourt shook from anger so badly his dainty fingers could not hit the buttons.

"You can't make a call from here, Doctor," Buno said helpfully.

"Goddamn it, I know that. I'm trying to trigger a bomb, blow them all to hell."

Buno brightened. Bombs were always a lot of fun. "I'll punch in the numbers for you, sir."

Andre Bettencourt's shaky hands kept playing on the buttons. After a few moments he gave the phone to Buno. "Punch in six-six-six, then wait five seconds and repeat the sequence."

"Yes sir." A few brief moments later his efforts were rewarded when a huge explosion from the town ripped the stormy air. He was so anxious to see the results he walked around to stand in the open.

"Well damn it all," Buno Eberhard said to Dr. Bettencourt while staring dejectedly. "They must have been expecting that. The bomb looks like it went off in that vacant lot across the street; only blew a bunch of windows out, didn't kill anyone. I hate it when things like that happen."

"Get back here you fool," Andre barked. "They'll shoot you."

"Nein," Buno shrugged, but followed his orders to return. "Those people know what we have. They won't take a chance on a bullet breaking one of those black bottles you've got in your pocket."

"That would mean the end of the world, Buno. We have to get them to Rio."

"The end of the world," Buno scratched his short blonde hair. "Exactly what's in those tubes? Mr. Roth only said it wasn't harmful unless opened, and that it's very valuable."

Dr. Bettencourt was too shaken up for subterfuge. "It is a live virus, Buno. The Spanish Flu epidemic is ready to devastate the world once again. We intend to make a vaccine for it, then sell it for a fortune once we let the flu out to run amuck."

Buno Eberhard considered the doctor's words. While he did not understand everything, the part about devastating the world was worrisome. The New Reich might be imperiled. "Then we'd better take care of all the people heading up here with guns."

Bettencourt made a careful glance around the front bumper. For once he couldn't agree more with Buno Eberhard.

CHAPTER FORTY-NINE

There was the remnant of a thick adobe wall from some long-collapsed building across the bridge where the road began its steep ascent from the canyon. Jack Stoner took a position behind the sheltering bulwark and waited, pistol held at the ready, until Laura, along with a panting Frank Lowry, joined him.

"All right, Jack," Laura's eyes sparked with a combination of both anger and concern. "Tell me what is going on here. Make it plain and make it the truth. There are a lot more dangerous things going on here than drug dealers with guns."

Before Jack could speak, Frank took a deep breath, bent over, placed both hands on his legs, and said, "You can start with telling her about your misspent youth along with how you failed a year of English back in high school. I need to catch my wind."

Jack Stoner ignored his friend. He turned to Laura. "Willie, Frank, and I work for a branch of the government you've never heard of. Never will. We take care of problems just like a surgeon; we cut them out and kill them. No one ever knows the facts of who caused what to happen. Considering there are two vials of live Spanish Flu virus and a few hundred million lives at stake here, I'd say we have to trust each other."

The shock of Jack Stoner's words hit her full force. "*You know!*"

"And so do they." He motioned with his pistol at the distant laboratory and wrecked Hummer. "Every entry you made in that computer was hacked into, along with a recording of every word you spoke. Roth Pharmaceuticals bugged your communications. Frank simply piggybacked on their hacking to keep us informed."

Laura Masterson's confusion and dismay became a maelstrom inside of her gut. "But—I quit my job with Roth. I'm doing research for the.... Hammond Foundation."

"You're still working for Philip Roth, Laura. You always have been." Jack's words hit her like a fist.

Frank stood, flicked a few small hailstones from his shirt, and said to Laura, "The Hammond Foundation doesn't even know that you or Paradox exists. That's one problem when an organization is secretive. People can use that trait to their own ends, like Michael Delvaney did with you."

"But the virus—the vaccine, must be developed. There's already an outbreak of the Spanish Flu in Mexico." Laura felt as if the world was spinning about her.

Jack shook his head. "There's no outbreak in Mexico or anywhere else. They told you what they needed to to speed up your research efforts. Roth Pharmaceuticals is in this solely for profit."

The hail and rain stopped as suddenly as it had began. A few scant red rays of a setting sun begun to creep down the side of the canyon. None of this was noticed by Laura, who was taking a moment of silent thought to line up the reality of the situation. Jack Stoner knew far too much not to trust him, as if that was a problem after her cell phone nearly blew up her along with everyone else in Paradox.

"Let me get this straight. Roth Pharmaceuticals is going to use the sample of live virus I cloned to develop a vaccine," Laura's voice was cold as the scattered hailstones. "The bastards are going to patent that vaccine, stockpile a few million doses, then release the Spanish Flu to run rampant. They're planning to kill millions and millions of people just to make a profit."

Frank gave a nod to Jack. "The little lady just got a gold star on her report card."

Laura Masterson shot both of the men a scathing look; anger had taken over her emotions. "The government and you knew what was going on. Why didn't somebody stop this before now?"

"No one at the CDC thought you'd succeed," Frank Lowry said simply. "And if you did, it'd save the government a bundle on research. This administration's pretty frugal. What we were here to do was make certain we got our hands on the virus, if it became cloned, before the Roth people could move it out of the country."

Laura cast a sour glance around the wall to the overturned mobile laboratory. "And with you men in charge, I'd say we're gone from the sublime to the ridiculous. That must come with working for the government. Guys, this isn't good. Bettencourt and Buno have to be stopped, along with the virus being recovered without any mishap."

"We know that," Jack said. "That was the reason Willie or anyone here can't go for a body shot. There's a chance one of those two thugs might have those vials in their pocket. We can't risk breaking one with a bullet."

Laura flashed another angry glance. "Why did you wait? You knew the minute I cloned that live virus. Why didn't you come in and take over right away? There was no reason to give those criminals a nice head start like the one they seem to have."

"The Centers for Disease Control will be sending a helicopter for the virus. That is, they will unless they either receive a coded call from us or...no call at all."

Laura Masterson felt a fresh chill. "Then what happens?" she asked, even though she had worked around biohazard-four laboratories long enough to already know the answer to her question.

"This administration is not only frugal, they're big on having accidents cover up problems," Frank said somberly.

Jack rolled his eyes skyward. "If no one hears from us before nine P.M., they'll assume the worst. There are six bombers loaded and fueled at Kirtland Air Force Base. At ten o'clock they will be overhead with orders to lay down napalm. A few minutes past ten, there won't be a living thing left in this canyon for miles."

"Not even a cloned virus," Laura nearly whispered. "The genie can't be allowed out of the bottle."

"The incident will be attributed to two airplanes colliding in mid air and crashing into the canyon. With everything else going on in the world, it won't make but a mention on the news," Frank said. "Only we don't intend to let that happen."

Laura flashed an angry glance up the road. The dying red rays of sunlight shooting through openings in dark storm clouds matched her attitude. "I brought that virus back to life. This is *my* responsibility."

Jack gave her a genuine smile. He chambered a round into his pistol; the metallic click echoed from the high sandstone cliffs. His John Wayne voice was back, "All right men, the bad guys have the little lady's test tube babies and won't give them back to their mommy. Let's go do what we have to do."

CHAPTER FIFTY

Andre Bettencourt ran dainty, shaking fingers through his long silver hair. He always hated it when things spun out of control. The French physician knew exactly what to do however; blame others and kill enough people to cause the survivors to see things his way. This tactic had always worked, or at least it had up until now. He decided to keep Buno around to use as a shield until he was out of harm's way. He also knew it was wise to let people know who is in charge, even if you were planing on killing them at the first opportunity.

"Mister Roth is going to be most unhappy with your performance, Buno," Dr. Bettencourt said matter-of-factly.

Buno Eberhard lowered his bushy blonde eyebrows and turned to face the physician. "What do you mean *my* performance? *You're* in charge."

"Ah, but my dear Buno, I must have fast and accurate information. You tarried too long in giving me the gist of Mr. Roth's instructions. It should have been very obvious to you to call me from out of the cemetery. Those morons wouldn't have cared less. Then we would have been out of this depressing canyon long before the rains came. I lay this failure squarely at your feet."

The henchman knew for certain that he should have removed Andre Bettencourt from this world when he had the opportunity. Now, everything had gone wrong because of the Frenchman's lack of proper planning. If nothing else, Bettencourt could be used as a decoy to allow him to escape with those valuable black tubes. Buno took a brief moment to allow his rage to settle before he said simply: "We must get the items to Rio."

"On that point Buno, we are in agreement." Andre looked around the end of the overturned truck and squinted through fading light to where that long-haired man on the front porch of the Black

Rock Bar and Grill still had a rifle aimed their direction. Dr. Bettencourt was wet and miserably cold. Night would soon be upon them. Already shadows were filling the canyon. The decision could not be put off. "The road is impassable for any vehicle." He frowned at the wrecked Hummer. "Even if we had one in running condition, the overturned laboratory truck has blocked the road."

"Yeah," Buno grumbled. "I noticed that, too."

"We are both in excellent condition, not soft like the Americans."

"They have intermarried with the Simian Jews, this makes them devious but not strong of body." Buno caught himself before he added, "like the Master Race" to his comment.

Dr. Bettencourt motioned with a thin, bony finger down the canyon. "There are undoubtedly some farms farther along the stream."

Buno shrugged indifferently. "That makes sense, but they might be a long way off. This is some of the most rugged and remote country I've ever been unfortunate enough to be in." He glowered at Dr. Bettencourt. "They call them ranches out here, not farms."

Bettencourt ignored him. "No matter what they call them, all that we require is a serviceable vehicle. We will shoot everyone who causes us problems, drive to Amarillo, Texas, take an airplane to the nearest big city, and then on to Rio de Janeiro. The virus being in glass vials won't set off metal detectors. I will simply place them in a bag with some toiletry items we can purchase. I do not expect any difficulties with the stupid American authorities. They are too busy making old women take off their shoes."

Buno had no plans for Dr. Bettencourt to have to fret over airport security. The uppity physician's troubles would be over forever once a vehicle had been obtained and he was no longer of any conceivable value. The muscular Teutonic guard kept mulling over the possibility that whatever disease was contained in those two black tubes, it might possibly infect the colony of pure Aryans in Paraguay who were rebuilding a new Reich. Buno did not have a firm plan to deal with this possibility, but intended to come up with one once the pesky Americans had been dealt with and the virus was safely in his possession. The single most important drive in his life, even more so than his loyalty to Philip Roth, was the rebuilding of the Führer's dream of a world dominated by the Master Race, as God had intended.

"We will get out of this fix, Dr. Bettencourt," Buno said, as he extracted his beloved father's Luger from its holster and jacked a round into the chamber. "It would be helpful if you joined me in shooting at our pursuers."

"I am a doctor damn it, a physician. I don't carry around a gun, that's your job."

Buno suppressed a snort. "Do you know how to use one?"

"Of course I do, you oaf. I have won honors in shooting skeet."

"*These* targets are going to be shooting back." Buno bent low and darted to the Hummer. He was somewhat surprised when he yanked open the door, grabbed up a leather case, and returned to the shelter of the huge overturned laboratory without a single shot being fired at him. What Bettencourt had said about the virus in his pocket being the end of the world must have been the truth. And the Americans who were after them knew it, too.

Then it dawned on him like an epiphany accompanied by a thunderclap. *Whoever has those two little black tubes controls the world.* Buno Eberhard knew that he alone had been chosen by fate to restore the Führer's dream. All he had to do was make it out of Paradox and deliver the items to the safe hands of the New Reich in Paraguay. He took a silent vow to do this at any cost. The future was in his hands, and any son of an SS officer would smilingly sacrifice himself for Hitler's legacy.

"What have you brought back from that bit of foolishness," Andre Bettencourt hissed. "I need you to protect me, not run out in the open like that. You might get shot."

"The Americans are very afraid of the virus—too afraid to fire and risk breaking one of the vials. I thought I would be able to get this, and we really need it."

Andre Bettencourt's glower melted into a look of glee when Buno unzipped the leather case and extracted a pair of rifles with folding stocks along with canvas pouches of clips filled with ammunition. He grabbed a rifle up and examined it. "These are, I believe, fully automatic submachine guns. It appears that the advantage of firepower is now on our side."

Buno coughed to hide a snort of disdain. "These are Heckler & Koch MP5s. They fire a 9mm Parabellum round at the rate of eight hundred per minute. The clips hold thirty rounds." He showed the doctor how to operate the slide to chamber a round and how to reload along with the location and operation of the safety. "You are correct about us having abundant firepower."

"I would believe a demonstration to that effect might buy us an edge when we move out."

"Your judgement is likely correct." Buno poked his head around the front bumper to notice Jack Stoner beginning to edge his way around a stone wall a few hundred feet down the road from their position. He doubted he would actually hit the man from this distance, but that delightful possibility did exist. The blonde henchman stepped around the front of the laboratory truck, took aim, and sent a full clip of bullets flying toward his target.

CHAPTER FIFTY-ONE

"Well *that's* not good news," Jack said as he spun back behind the bulwark while slugs of hot lead slammed into the thick wet adobe wall like fists. "First we can't get a clear head shot, now they've gotten submachine guns, dammit."

Willie Ames came puffing to join Jack, Laura, and Frank Lowry. He had barely made it behind the sheltering wall before the bullets began peppering their position. "Hey, a man's head is a mighty small target from that far away. And you *did* tell me not to shoot at their bodies."

Laura Masterson waited a moment until the hail of bullets ended to turn and ask Willie Ames: "I don't know how you could hit the side of the canyon with as much as I've seen you drink. It might be safer for everyone if you set that gun down and let us handle this."

Willie shrugged and grinned with a twinkle in his dark gray eyes. "No problem in that department, Doc. There's a little white pill a person working undercover can swallow, then drink like a fish and stay sober as a judge. Hell, even the tattoos I've got are temporary. It's all a matter of looking and acting like someone you're not. Keeps a person in my line of work from getting shot."

"Willie's a lawyer by profession," Jack said. "Then he left the dark side to get an honest job."

"Speaking of lawyers," Laura said, her tone sparked with anger. "There's one by the name of Michael Delvaney in Houston that I have a score to settle with big time."

"You can forget about him," Jack said. "We've got good Intel that he's not half the man he used to be."

Frank Lowry had been lost in serious thought. He asked Laura, "Hey Doc, just how well built are those vials and how big are they?"

"It's not like in the movies where the test tube shatters when dropped. Borosilica glass is tough enough to withstand a really hard blow. The two tubes are black, about four inches long, maybe three quarters of an inch in diameter. They're equipped with plastic screw-on caps and are double sealed. If a bullet was to strike one, however, it would almost certainly break and release the virus."

Jack Stoner chewed on his lower lip, gave a furtive glance around the end of the adobe wall, and then turned to his friends. "Buno and Frenchy have us outgunned, and you can bet what they're wanting more than killing us is to get the hell out of this canyon with that virus. If the road hadn't gotten slicker than lizard snot they'd have done it, too. The way I see it, the first option is we can charge into The Valley of the Shadow of Death and get those vials. The other alternative is to keep them pinned down and wait for the bombers." He glanced at his watch. "Hell will start popping in around here in less than two hours."

"Gee, boss," Willie Ames said, "I really like the first option better."

Frank Lowry gave a deep sigh. "The part about charging 'em does have a decidedly nicer ring to it. Too bad it's uphill."

Laura Masterson felt a wretchedness of mind she had never known before. She had been used, duped, and lied to. The virus that could kill millions existed only because of her. All that mattered was the virus. Whether it was recovered by them or destroyed in a firebombing by the military, it could not be released upon the world. "Let's go after those bastards. They have to be stopped at any cost."

"That's just what we'll do then." Frank Lowry took a deep breath and held his gun at the ready. "But let's try not to make it easy for them. I've got three ex-wives depending on me."

"Hey, boss," Willie Ames's voice sounded hopeful, "that idea about a head shot is neat, but what if we managed to plug their legs. If they're slowed down some it might help give us the advantage."

Jack Stoner gave an evil grin. "You sometimes come up with some really great ideas, Willie. Sure, put a hole in them anywhere but the torso. I'm betting that the virus is in Andre Bettencourt's front shirt pocket. Frenchy isn't one to let someone else carry the payoff."

"That would fit what I know about him," Laura said. She had a fiery, angry look that had never before been painted on the canvas of her face. "Stay low, guys," Laura Masterson elbowed a stunned

Jack Stoner aside to burst out past the wall. The second she was in the open, she began firing her Glock at the overturned mobile laboratory.

The three government men instantly bolted out to cover her. The first thing they saw was an orange ball of flame from where Laura's fusillade had ignited a puddle of spilled diesel fuel from the overturned truck. After only a few scant moments, a spiraling plume of flame and black smoke obscured the entire area where Buno Eberhard and Dr. Andre Bettencourt were holed up.

CHAPTER FIFTY-TWO

"*Zut!*" Dr. Andre Bettencourt shouted when a wall of flames erupted from the bottom of the overturned truck they were hiding behind. "The Americans are shelling us with artillery." He spun to Buno, eyes wide with fear. "We must run."

Buno did not have a clue what a "zut" was and he didn't care. But he agreed wholeheartedly with the plan of making a quick departure. Where the French idiot had come up with the idea they were being attacked by artillery, he couldn't fathom. There was spilled fuel all over the place, the smell is unmistakable. It was also a fact that once the flames reached the several hundred gallons of diesel fuel still remaining in the main tanks, their hiding place would be turned into a fireball. A really *big* fireball.

"Head for the edge. There are always game trails along the sides of hills," Buno shouted over the building roar. "We will go to the bottom of the canyon. There are many large rocks and crevices to shelter..." Out the corner of his eye he caught the movements of a very rapidly departing French doctor. Buno gave a snort of disapproval—he always hated to witness a display of cowardice—then spun to follow Andre Bettencourt over the side of the road. At least the panicky Frenchman was heading in the right direction.

A few bullets sang their way past Buno Eberhard as he dropped over the edge of the road and out of the line of fire. He had felt a slug tear through his pant leg, but did not think it had more than barely scratched him. Buno had to respect the idea of shooting at his legs. The tactic was so brilliant he realized there must be a misguided Aryan among those in pursuit of the virus. He steeled his resolve. Soon, very soon, the entire world would bow to the New Reich.

There were many game trails made by deer, grazing cattle, or other large animals crisscrossing the sides of the sandstone canyon. Buno easily caught up with the cowardly Frenchman who had stopped behind a large flat boulder to remove a small paddle of prickly pear cactus from his leg. Not far below, Cougar Creek burbled merrily along in the fading light. Buno always took special care to note his surroundings and plan escape routes before they were needed. It was an inherited trait that he felt honored to possess.

"This is painful, Buno," Andre Bettencourt bent over studying the cactus and giving it testing touches with a stick he had found. "I need my medical kit."

Buno Eberhard had had enough of the namby-pamby doctor. The man's attitude and insufferable whining was becoming intolerable. The blonde bodyguard flicked out with the toe of his boot and brushed the small piece of offending cactus from Bettencourt's leg.

"Dammit, you stupid oaf. That hurt like hell."

"We need to move on, sir," Buno spat out the word "sir" as if it was a piece of rotten food. That was when Buno realized the doctor did not have his German-made Heckler & Koch submachine gun. "Where is your weapon?" His voice had assumed a demanding tone.

Andre Bettencourt gave a dismissive, almost feminine flap of a hand. "Oh, I believe I must have left it behind. I think yours will be sufficient. I am sure we will out-distance them shortly. And look over there."

Buno Eberhard rolled his head to the direction the doctor's slim finger pointed. Across the small, easily fordable creek, no more than a half mile downstream, at least two large mine buildings sat on huge slabs of burnt red rock. The physician might be a coward, but he had found a wonderful place to hole up and fight off their pursuers. There was a large open area of flat ground on this side of the mine structures. If they could obtain a foothold there first, anyone crossing that unprotected stretch of land would be cut into bloody shreds by his bullets. It was a delightful mental image. They might even decide to spend the night there. The soft Americans would not have the courage to attack them in the dark.

"We..." Buno's words were drowned out by a dull, loud booming that shook the ground beneath their feet when the laboratory exploded on the hillside above them.

"Possibly the Americans, or at least some of them, were stupid enough to have been close when that laboratory blew up."

Buno Eberhard severely doubted anyone was that stupid, but this was not a time for talk. He took a forceful tone. "The explosion has given us a diversion. We have to take advantage of it. Follow me to those old mines you pointed out. There is no time to lose."

To Buno's amazement, Bettencourt gave a nod and kept silent, giving no complaint as they hurried downhill along the narrow game trail to ford the shimmering creek.

CHAPTER FIFTY-THREE

"I didn't mean to do that," Laura stood in the open, staring transfixed at the building flames and spiraling tower of black smoke shooting upward into the wan New Mexico twilight. As if by rote she dropped the empty clip from her Glock pistol and inserted a full one, an action that was well noted by the three men who stood by her side. "It was a state-of-the-art laboratory, millions of dollars worth of equipment."

Jack Stoner placed a firm hand on Laura's shoulder and ushered her to a more sheltered position behind a large boulder. Surely Buno and Bettencourt had other things to do than shoot at them, but when dealing with lunatics it paid to be cautious.

"The fire ought to put a move on them," Frank wheezed. "I hope they have the decency to head downhill. I'm not as young or slender as I used to be."

Willie could not help but smile. "The main fuel tank will blow any minute, I'm actually hoping they'll stick around for the barbeque."

Jack gave Laura a questioning look, his expression taut. "If those two idiots hang around too long will the heat be enough to destroy the virus?"

Laura nodded affirmatively. "Yes, they are living organisms. Any virus can only survive in a relatively narrow band of temperature, just like us. For being so deadly, a virus is actually quite fragile."

Frank clucked his tongue. "Then that lab blowing up would not only get rid of the frigging flu virus along with a couple of deserving hoodlums, it might even warm us up. I'm freezing my butt off out here."

Laura realized for the first time since she had bolted from the Black Rock Bar and Grill into a hailstorm that she was drenched from head to toe. Her hair probably resembled a drowned poodle and she was growing increasing cold. The physician had read cases of how adrenalin had kept people going for hours under dire circumstances, even when fatally wounded. This was the first time, however, that she had had the opportunity to experience firsthand such an extreme rush of the hormone. It certainly lived up to its reputation.

Willie surprised Laura when he brushed aside his long blonde pigtails and stripped off his shirt, which he handed her. "Here, Doc. Put this on. I was born and raised in Wyoming. This weather is like a hot summer day for me."

Laura could not help but focus on the ugly red scars that were plentiful on the left side of Willie's lower abdomen. There was also the telltale remnant of a colostomy that had been done not too many years past.

Willie noticed the doctor's attention and shrugged. "Sometimes the bad guys get lucky, but the end is what counts. I went to the hospital, they went to the morgue."

Laura shivered now from more than the cold. She was beginning to realize all the more just how much of a terrible and dangerous situation she had wound up in. No matter about her own safety. Those two vials of cloned virus were her doing and her responsibility. The doctor gave Willie a genuine smile, doubting his act of chivalry wasn't causing him to nearly freeze, yet not even a patch of gooseflesh showed on his tattooed skin.

"Take my shirt, Doc," Willie offered again, holding out the long-sleeved flannel shirt that was big enough for Laura to use as a jacket. "I'd really appreciate it if you did."

"Thank you," Laura said. She slipped it on and instantly relished the comfort it gave her. "I owe you one, Willie."

"What the hell!" Frank shouted, jerking his head to where a huge fireball appeared where the smoking laboratory had been. A scant second later the ground shook beneath their feet as if from an earthquake. "Oh wow. That's a *lot* more bang for the buck than I'd expected."

"The oxygen tanks blew up, too," Laura said. "Add a helping of pure oxygen to a fire and it accelerates to no end."

Jack focused on the roaring tower of flame and smoke. "Well, whatever the mixture was exactly, it sure took off nice."

"There goes one of our lovelies." From his position Willie Ames had caught a movement no one else saw. He grabbed the rifle he had laid against a rock to enable him to remove his shirt, then began sending bullets flying into an area on the downhill side of the fireball.

"Did you hit anything?" Jack asked.

Willie shook his head negatively. "I don't think so. I put all of the slugs low where I'd only hit his legs. It was Buno Eberhard I was shooting at and I didn't notice him drop. If I'd had my rifle ready, I might have been able to plug Frenchy. He ran over the edge first."

"I'm sorry," Laura said sincerely. "If you hadn't tried to help me you'd never have set your gun down."

"Don't blame yourself, Doc," Willie said, his eyes twinkling from the reflected flames. "Like I said earlier, it's the end that counts."

"And that end won't be much longer coming," Jack said, casting a glance at his watch. "One way or the other."

"We have them flushed from cover," Frank said. "And they're being nice enough to head downhill, bless their little black hearts."

"You can bet they'll get to the creek and follow it downstream," Willie said. "I say we cross back over the bridge and head down the road to where those old mines are. Those two will be slowed considerably from dodging cactus, climbing around rocks, and having to ford the steam."

"Yeah," Jack agreed. With some decent luck we might even be able to circle around and come out ahead of them, be waiting when they show up."

Frank said, "That's one meeting I'm looking forward to. Should be exciting."

"That's putting it mildly," Laura said, as she turned to face the bridge across Cougar Creek. "But let's get to it."

Jack grinned broadly at the departing doctor. "All right men, let's tag along just in case the little lady might have need of our services."

"Time's wasting," Willie said, as he cradled his rifle against his naked chest.

Scant moments later the four of them ran in front of the Black Rock Bar and Grill on their way down the canyon. From inside broken out windows a wide-eyed Thelma Ross, Sadie Helms, and Rodney Simms silently watched them scurry past. Laura Masterson, who was in the lead, raised her hand that wasn't holding a gun to give a quick wave as she ran by.

Sadie Helms stuck knotted fists on her bony hips. "It's been a long time since we've had this much excitement in Paradox."

"Not long enough, Sadie," Thelma said with a sigh. "Not long enough."

Rodney Simms gave a snort, shrugged his shoulders, and decided to go back to drinking beer. He didn't have a clue what was going on, but it appeared that things would work out just fine without him getting involved. He poured a fresh glass full of draft beer as he passed the bar, took a seat, and wondered who would live and who would die before the night was over.

CHAPTER FIFTY-FOUR

As he followed the cowardly French doctor along the steep talus slope to the bottom of the canyon, Buno Eberhard kept thinking about only one thing: the New Reich and the wonderful possibility of being able to cause his beloved Führer's legacy to be reborn.

Buno's eyes moistened and his lower lip quivered when he remembered his father telling him that Adolph Hitler had personally attended his christening. To think that the Führer had taken time from his duties at a time of war to honor the Eberhard family's new arrival was overwhelming. Such an act of veneration from the leader of the Third Reich had now become the single most driving force in his life.

Buno Eberhard, the only son of a valiant SS officer and one of the very few remaining who had been graced by the presence of the Führer—even though an infant at the time—held the future return of the New Reich in his grasp. Or at least the opportunity was as close as the front shirt pocket of a certain French doctor who had shown himself to be a coward.

Possibly the most valuable substance on earth was sealed in those two little black tubes Andre Bettencourt carried. Philip Roth had spent millions of dollars to obtain it for profit. Buno wasn't certain exactly what the substance was, but having heard it described as being "the end of the world as we know it" was cheering.

Anything that had the capacity to decimate on a global scale would make the possession of nuclear bombs pale in comparison. And soon, very soon, the glorious New Fourth Reich in Paraguay would have this substance. There were scientists there, brilliant, strong German scientists. They would know *exactly* what to do with those two glass vials.

The honor of seeing Hitler's legacy become a shining reality would be reward enough for any true Aryan. All Buno Eberhard had to do was grab those tubes and get them to South America. Nothing else mattered.

Then Buno realized that he did not have enough money to purchase airplane tickets. The arrogant Dr. Bettencourt had not allowed him time to snatch the cash he had hidden in the pantry of his motorhome. Buno realized that he might be forced to returned to Paradox and kill everyone there to obtain the means to restore Hitler's legacy. He patted his pocket to reassure himself the several fake passports Roth had supplied him were safe.

Buno felt a burning sensation on the calf of his right leg. He slowed a second to look down and noticed a bloody tear in his pants where a bullet had grazed his skin. He smiled broadly. Any member of the Master Race welcomed scars, wore them like the medals of honor they were.

Overhead, the storm clouds had moved on, giving way to an orange orb of a full moon that was rising over the high rimrocks to the mournful tune of coyotes. The night would be a bright one indeed, bringing both a blessing and a curse. While it would enable them to safely navigate the rugged chasm, the bright moonlight would also allow their pursuers to follow them with ease.

"Dammit," Bettencourt swore. The Frenchman came to a halt, turned, and waited for Buno to catch up with him. "I seem to have another piece of cactus, this one is just above my shoe. Please remove it. I am in pain."

Pain is something I can cure permanently, Buno Eberhard thought. But he said nothing as he slipped a large knife from a hidden sheath then quickly and efficiently pried loose the small piece of cholla cactus from Dr. Bettencourt's ankle.

"I hate this place," Andre spat. "I look so forward to returning to Rio."

Buno sized the opportunity. "Bettencourt, we will require funds to leave the country. Do you have enough money, or do we need to resort to, ah... *other* means to obtain our airplane tickets?"

Andre Bettencourt didn't hesitate to answer. "I have over ten thousand American dollars in my wallet along with various no-limit credit cards. Your job is to get us out of this fix and to a city with an airport. I shall do the thinking. You do the killing."

Oh, I will, Buno thought, happy that he did not have to risk returning to Paradox and encounter Jack Stoner. For some reason that man frightened him more than anyone he had encountered in his sixty-two years on this earth. *No, not frightened*, he corrected himself. *I respect him as a fellow predator.*

"Come along, Buno," Bettencourt said, his words coming across as a whine. "Let us make it to those mine buildings. I'm freezing to death out here."

"Yes sir," Buno agreed as he began following the Frenchman, staying a lot closer to him than before.

The waters of Cougar Creek were clear and cold. Dr. Bettencourt complained bitterly that his shoes, which he said were quite expensive, had been totally ruined. Buno noticed that the water had come only up to his knees. His focus was on the shadowy ground just across the creek. For some odd reason, the earth appeared black, fuzzy and...moving. He had never seen anything quite like it before and he didn't have any idea what to make of the situation. It was certain however, that Bettencourt would be walking on that moving patch of earth in a scant moment. Then he would find out what in hell was going on.

CHAPTER FIFTY-FIVE

Jack Stoner assumed the lead as Laura Masterson, Frank Lowry, and Willie Ames kept close to the edge of the road to allow the thick, fat cedar trees and juniper bushes that grew prolifically along the canyon floor to shield their movements. The last slim fingers of the dying sun's rays shimmered like blood on the high red rimrocks to the west. Very soon the only light they would have to navigate by would be from a pale, full moon that was showing in the narrow slice of heaven visible above Cougar Creek Canyon.

Just before coming to a sharp bend in the road, somewhat past where the laboratory and Hummer were in the last glow of burning up on the road high above them, Jack held an arm out sideways to signal a halt.

Frank was the first one behind him. "What is it, Jack?" he asked after catching his breath. "Do you see something?"

Stoner waited until all four of them were together to speak. "No I don't see a thing, but we need to plan. The full moon tonight's going to help both them and us. They used to call it an 'Apache Moon' because that was the only night the warriors would attack. The Apache believe that if you are killed when there's not enough light for your soul to find its way to the Spirit World, it will become lost forever."

Willie shifted his wristwatch around to be able to make out the position of the hands. "Hell, it won't be much longer before this whole friggin' canyon lights up like the Las Vegas strip. I'd say if those Apache were right, all of our souls won't have any problems finding the stairway to Heaven...or wherever."

"I'd really prefer it didn't come to that," Frank Lowry said cautiously, sticking his head around the bend. "Those two sons of bitches are so close, I can almost smell them."

"They can't be far," Laura said. "This is rugged country and I'm betting Dr. Bettencourt wasn't dressed for hiking—or in shape for it. His plan was to simply drive away with the virus in a nice warm vehicle. The laboratory turning over came as a surprise to the both of them."

Jack said, "All that matters is getting our hands on those two tubes. There's no doubt in my mind that they have them. There's too much at stake for them not to have taken them from the lab before heading out. Those two might be mean, evil, and greedy, but they're not stupid."

Frank Lowry's eyes were wide when he turned from poking his head around the bend in the road. "Guys, there's something going on here you've got to see to believe."

Willie Ames gave Laura Masterson a mischievous grin. "Frank said those exact words once in Algiers. You wouldn't guess in a thousand years what it turned out to be. This woman...."

"Not now, for Pete's sake." Jack cut him off sharply, then asked Lowry, "What's up, Frank?"

"Come and see. They won't shoot back."

All four cautiously made their way around the thick copse of juniper bushes to stare in amazement at the thick wavering carpet of large black and brown spiders that covered the road as far as they could see in the fading light.

Jack Stoner stepped a few feet ahead then bent over to allow one of the big spiders to climb onto the back of his hand. He stood and turned, smiling to his friends, while the hairy arachnid climbed up his shirt sleeve.

"This is a common occurrence in the southwest after a rain like the one we just had," Jack explained, keeping an unworried eye on the spider. "Tarantulas choose this time to mate and migrate. I've seen it before a few times and it's quite a sight to behold."

"There must be hundreds of them," Willie said in awe.

"More like thousands," Stoner said. "After a rain is when they come out. Generally they're happy to stay in their burrows. He stroked the spider on his arm with a gentle finger. "At least they're harmless. Even if you make one bite you, it's no worse than the sting of a honeybee."

"I'd prefer they weren't out here, considering everything else that's going on," Laura said with a frown. "I know they're not all that poisonous, but so many at one time is really creepy."

Willie clucked his tongue. "There are some people who freak out totally on just one spider; arachnophobia I believe it's called. If anyone suffering from that phobia was to be here now, they'd likely wind up in the booby hatch, and spend a few years of their life sucking on Valium popsicles."

Before Willie's words had died on his lips, a quarter mile further down the canyon, from possibly an ear-splitting scream rent the quiet of night in the desert. At first they thought it was a mountain lion, they had all heard them cry occasionally at night. Only this scream was higher pitched, filled with sheer terror.

Laura gave a wry grin. "I've never heard a mountain lion scream with a French accent before."

Jack turned to Laura with a knowing look when yet another scream drifted in from down the canyon. "From all of that caterwauling going on, I'd venture our two lovlies have found another patch of tarantulas all by themselves."

Frank Lowry gave a deep sigh. "I just hope the idiot doesn't step on some poor innocent spider or fall over with a heart attack and break a little glass tube he might have in his shirt pocket. I'd hate to see something like that happen, I *really* would."

"At least now we know where they are," Stoner said, as he gently placed the tarantula on a nearby rock. "There's no way they'd separate that I can think of."

It was Frank Lowry's turn to give a worried look at his wristwatch. "Let's go pay those damn virus stealers a visit."

"I'm all for that," Willie said as he took the lead down the road carrying his rifle at the ready. "Time's wasting if you're waiting on me."

Within seconds all four of the pursuers were darting in and out of bushes as they kept to cover while making their way downstream, trying to keep from stepping on tarantulas.

Each person noticed that an ominous silence had replaced the loud, terrified shrieking that they all knew had come from Dr. Andre Bettencourt.

CHAPTER FIFTY-SIX

Buno Eberhard shook with a combination of rage and shame. The cowardly French doctor had actually screamed like a woman when he discovered he was standing in the midst of a crawling carpet of big black spiders. For the man who was an executive in charge of a major worldwide pharmaceutical company to display such a total lack of courage was unforgivable. The fact that Bettencourt was his boss only added to the sad situation; to be in the company of cowards is a matter of shame.

Being of pure Teutonic blood, all Buno Eberhard could allow himself to do was watch and see how the sickening scene would play out. One thing was for certain: without a doubt their pursuers now knew where they were. The skinny Frenchman's yelling echoed from the cliffs advertising their position.

Bettencourt danced about the spiders for a moment, screaming like he was being tortured. Then he fixed his wide and wild eyes on Buno hoping he would provide a salvation from his terrible predicament. When the blonde henchman only stood staring silently at him from the edge of the creek, Bettencourt bolted and ran blindly for the safety of his bodyguard in a state of total panic.

Buno noticed the sandstone boulders that lay across each other, forming a perfect pinchers of rock the doctor was running wildly towards, but did nothing to warn him or stop his headlong plunge into certain catastrophe. The man was a coward; having him contribute to his own downfall was only right, the deserved fate of all of the weak of body or mind, just as the glorious Führer had intended.

At the speed with which Dr. Bettencourt was running when his ankle became jammed in the fork made by the two rocks, his forward motion caused his lower leg to twist and snap loudly when it broke.

Buno thought the sound, which he likened to the breaking of a dry tree limb, to be immensely satisfying.

The pain seemed to drive the panic from Dr. Bettencourt. The silver-haired man's eyes were sane but pleading when Buno Eberhard came to his aid.

"Oh Buno," Andre said. "I am so glad to see you. Those spiders, they were all over the place. It was horrible. I simply detest the things. In my hurry to get away from them"—he looked for the first time at his leg. It was bent at such an angle no one needed a medical degree to know the bone had been broken or shattered—"I seem to have accidentally injured myself and require your help."

"I will be honored to help stop your pain," Buno Eberhard bent down on his knees to look the stricken doctor square in the face. "But the main thing that must concern us is getting those two tubes in your pocket to Philip Roth in Rio de Janeiro, is it not?"

"Of course, you oaf," Bettencourt's predicament and pain had not softened his arrogance in the least. "Those vials are worth untold millions of dollars. Now help me with my leg. You must find some pieces of wood or cut some tree limbs to use as a splint. We can rip your shirt into strips to tie them with, then you will help me out of this terrible place."

Buno Eberhard acted as if he had not heard the last of the doctor's words. "You told me those little bottles contain the end of the world."

Bettencourt snorted. "They contain a living sample of the Spanish Flu virus. This is not a normal flu; it causes the immune system to turn against itself. Those who are young and have the strongest immune system are the first to die. We estimate more than one out of every ten people who catch it will die unless they have the vaccine which we will develop." A glimmer of apprehension appeared in the Frenchman's gray eyes. "Why do you need to know this? You are hired to help me, not ask questions."

"Then those samples are potentially more deadly and valuable than a nuclear bomb." Buno kept ignoring Dr. Bettencourt. His thoughts were far from here, deep in the mountains of Paraguay. "Even as a weapon of terror, the virus would be worth a fortune."

Bettencourt felt a chill that came from more than the cold of a coming night. "Buno, the vaccine is what we have to manufacture for the money. Once the virus is released, we stand to make billions of dollars and do so legally." He hastened to add, "I will see to it that your loyalty is *handsomely* rewarded. Mr. Roth and myself shall give you stock options that will make you millions of dollars, but first you have to get me out of here."

"Give me the vials," Buno Eberhard's tone was a command, not a request. The blonde grinned sardonically. "It would be a disaster should one of them become broken from your falling again."

"I will do no such thing." Bettencourt began to realize his perilous circumstance, but had been in command long enough to know how to handle men, especially sluggish brutes like Buno Eberhard. "I am ordering you to help me splint my leg. You *will* do what I tell you to do."

Buno Eberhard stood. He made an odd twisting motion with his right foot that made a metallic clicking noise. Buno squinted in the fading light to assure himself the thin stainless steel needle loaded with cobra venom had extended itself from the heel of his boot. It had.

"I promised to stop your pain," Buno said to the now-quavering French doctor. "As a German, I *always* keep my word." Then he spun and jabbed the needle into Bettencourt's upper leg with a backward kick.

The cowardly Frenchman gave one of his shrill, girly shrieks, then the venom hit his nervous system. The doctor shivered like a clubbed fish for a brief moment then arched his back and collapsed with a pathetic sigh.

"Cowards don't even die well," Buno Eberhard said with disgust. He twisted his boot hard on the ground to retract the needle, then bent over the corpse. He had to roll the body to one side to extract the much-needed wallet. Buno opened it to assure himself it did indeed hold sufficient funds to get him to Paraguay. The Frenchman had lied even about this. There was only fifty dollars in cash, but the credit cards issued to Roth Pharmaceuticals would surely be valid. Buno had used company credit cards like the one he held many times before. There would be no need to obtain other funds, which came as a relief.

Buno Eberhard's usually frozen features melted into a smile of complete satisfaction when he extracted the twin vials from Bettencourt's shirt pocket. He held them up to the yellow moonlight and studied the black tubes for a brief moment, savoring the power of the contents. But he had no time to tarry. The pursuers knew where he was. Buno slid the tubes into the front pocket of his sturdy khaki shirt and buttoned the flap closed. Not having anyone to slow his leaving was a blessing; he could move in the night with the silence of a cat on the hunt, blending into the darkness like a shadow.

Carrying the deadliest substance on earth, Buno turned and ran down the creek bed staying close to the shore where soft sand muted all sound. In a few brief days he would be in Paraguay. All he had to do was be stronger and more clever, more devious than the fools who were after him.

Buno Eberhard was a pure Aryan on a mission to rebuild the Führer's Fourth Reich. He had the means to do so in his pocket. He couldn't fail. As he ran, Buno lovingly massaged his beloved father's Luger pistol. In his mind he could picture the shining future. He wished to sing a patriotic German song, but that would have to wait—though not for much longer. All he needed to do was kill the few insignificant pests who were in pursuit of him, then he could sing all the way to Paraguay.

CHAPTER FIFTY-SEVEN

"This isn't a good omen. Not good at all." Jack Stoner's pale blue eyes darted back and forth, probing the shadow-filled canyon for any movement that could signal danger, his pistol held at the ready. "Buno Eberhard is out there and he has the virus. I can *feel* it."

Dr. Laura Masterson looked up at him, her fingers still pressed to the carotid artery on Bettencourt's neck. "He's been dead only minutes. I can still make out some muscle spasms. I'm thinking he must have been subjected to some deadly and very quick-acting neurotoxin. Dr. Bettencourt's heart has stopped beating, but not all of his body realizes it's dead yet."

Jack kept surveying the gloomy canyon. "Buno Eberhard's a professional killer. We have a dossier on him going back over thirty years. He favors cobra venom and giving lobotomies over simply shooting someone, but he's not really all that picky."

Laura gave a sigh and stood. "Cobra venom is neurotoxic and it fits Dr. Bettencourt's demise perfectly." She looked down at the still-twitching corpse. "His left leg suffered what looks to be a spiral fracture. He couldn't go on. I checked his pockets for the virus. You're right, he doesn't have the vials on him."

Willie Ames and Frank Lowry stepped from a nearby thicket of juniper bushes. Lowry's teeth clicked with anger and tension when he glared down the canyon, studying the craggy rock formations and dark patches of trees.

"Buno Eberhard having that virus is dangerous as a monkey with a hand grenade," Frank snorted. "The quicker we get it away from him the better."

Jack said, "He's single-minded, we know that for certain. Right now you can bet his goal is to get the virus out of the country as quick as he can. With Dr. Bettencourt not around to slow him down,

263

he'll make tracks fast." Jack turned to his three companions. "There's a ranch about four miles down the canyon—that'll be where Buno's heading. He'll need a vehicle, and he can steal one there."

"Yeah," Willie added. "And he'll kill everyone at that ranch the second he gets the keys."

"If Buno gets away with the virus," Laura Masterson said motioning with her Glock down the canyon, "the killings will only have started."

Jack gave her a grin. He said in his John Wayne voice, "Well pilgrims, it's up the posse to head 'em off at the pass."

Frank gave Laura a knowing nod. "Jack's a real big fan of old John Wayne movies."

"I thought he might be," Laura Masterson gave a final look to the open-eyed corpse of Dr. Andre Bettencourt then joined the three men in a desperate run to stop a professional killer who possessed the most deadly weapon on the face of the earth.

CHAPTER FIFTY-EIGHT

Buno Eberhard's keen sense of hearing picked up the footsteps of his pursuers echoing from the canyon walls hundreds of feet behind him. This came as no surprise. The embankments on both sides turned into sheer cliffs before reaching the rimrocks; they were impossible to scale without climbing equipment. His only exit, his only hope to re-build Hitler's legacy, was to follow the canyon until he found an op-portunity to obtain a vehicle. How far that would be, he could only guess. The country here in New Mexico was as remote and rugged as any he had ever encountered, even in Africa or South America.

I will not fail the Führer. Buno seared the words into his brain. The future of the New Reich was buttoned securely inside his shirt pocket. Surely God would smile upon his plight, give him aid and guidance. The Jews had killed the Christ, Adolph Hitler had merely extracted retribution with his splendid final solution. Yes, God was on his side, had been all along.

Jack Stoner was the one he had to concern himself with. Frank Lowry was old and fat; sluggish of body always meant sluggish of mind. That man presented no problem. The other man with long girl's hair and degenerate tattoos was more ludicrous than a threat. Dr. Masterson being with them—he had heard their voices carrying in the still desert air—was laughable. A woman's place was in the bedroom or the kitchen. No, once he killed Jack Stoner, which he needed to do right away, the others would likely run away or allow themselves to be eliminated without difficulty.

But how to kill Stoner? The element of surprise would be a neces-sity. Buno slowed his pace along the sandy shore of Cougar Creek. He made his way to a sheltering series of stair-stepped sandstone ledges and stopped to think. The abandoned buildings and tipple from the old coal mining operations lay just ahead, standing stark in the yellow moonlight like the skeletons of great ships that had wrecked long ago.

A glimmer of a plan flared in his mind and began to build like the crescendo of a great German opera. It was a brilliant plan, one worthy of the son of a valiant SS officer.

Buno gave a low, satisfied chuckle. In mere minutes they would *all* be dead; Stoner, the female doctor, all of them laid low in a spray of bullets from the submachine gun he held in his left hand. It would be a fitting end to their pathetic efforts to apprehend him, a member of the Master Race. They would die riddled with 9mm Parabellum slugs from a wonderful firearm manufactured in the Fatherland.

Suddenly, from the ledge only a foot or two from his face came a hiss, like that of an angry cat. There was a flash of movement in the shadows, a rough grating sound of scales and hard muscle rubbing against sandstone. The buzzing that reminded Buno of rustling dry leaves started the instant he saw the head of a huge diamondback rattlesnake draw back to strike him squarely in the face.

Buno Eberhard jerked his head back the instant the snake struck. Using reflexes indigenous of a true Aryan and honed over the years, he swatted upward with his free hand and grabbed the deadly reptile by its neck. The fangs stilled scant inches from his eyes.

The snake was huge, even by New Mexico standards, being at least six feet in length. The diamondback hissed, buzzed, and writhed with its primitive muscles of steel. It was of no avail; Buno held it with the grip of a vise. He took a moment to study the snake, admire its slitted eyes that regarded him with the purest of hate. Just as it should. Buno actually felt a kinship with the powerful hunter, a bond of sorts.

It was with a small pang of regret that Buno Eberhard yanked the rattlesnake forward, then snapped his wrist back with a hard upward jerk, breaking the hapless snake's neck instantly. Then he tossed the still-writhing reptile aside and proceeded up the slope to the coal mine. There would be more killing this night. The snake had simply been another necessary death.

CHAPTER FIFTY-NINE

"There's no doubt in my mind, Buno's heading straight for those abandoned coal mines." Jack Stoner motioned with his pistol to the adumbral forms of old, partially fallen in buildings and structures. "That area has been fenced off for years to keep people out because of danger."

"I doubt if Buno Eberhard has paid any attention to fences or signs since he dropped out of the third grade," Willie said as he came to join his companions who were crouched behind a long cedar tree, surveying the area ahead. "But it's easy to see why he's gone there."

"Yeah," Frank Lowry said. "Buno knows full well we're not going to simply let him stroll out of this canyon with that virus in his pocket. He chose that place to make his stand."

Laura Masterson understood all too well what the men were talking about. "There's not a tree or a rock for the length of a football field between here and those mine buildings."

Jack Stoner nodded his agreement. "The light's good enough. He can pop us off like ducks in a shooting gallery. What we'll need to do is for someone to try to scale those high rocks above and come out on the other side of that bastard. All we'll need then is for him to make a single shot to betray his position. Then we can catch him, or should I say his legs, in a crossfire and mow him down."

"That will require someone to act as a decoy when the time comes," Frank Lowry said with a heavy breath. "I'm in no shape to climb the cliff, so I'll draw Buno's fire when the time comes."

Laura Masterson looked at him, aghast. "Frank, you'll get killed!"

"The question is, Doc," Frank Lowry said, "how many innocent people will die if that virus makes it out of this canyon. It's a tradeoff that'll pay dividends." He gave a coarse laugh. "My ex-wives will have a ball spending the life insurance money." He glanced at his watch. "And I'm not taking a really big risk here."

"I'm off," Willie said. Without waiting for a reply he disappeared into the shadows at the base of the nearby cliff.

"Willie always has been one to take the bull by the horns," Jack Stoner said. "One of these times he's liable to get hurt."

Frank Lowry said, "Let's just hope this isn't the time."

"I'll second that motion," Laura Masterson said, scouring the old buildings for any sign of movement as best she could in the yellow wavering moonlight. Overhead, patchy clouds, remnants of the earlier storm, caused the wan light to undulate like fey spirits.

Suddenly Laura stiffened, blinked twice, then clicked the safety off of her Glock. She pointed it and steadied the weapon with two hands. "That rotten son of a bitch," Laura growled before sending a full clip of 9mm slugs flying. The shots boomed and echoed like thunder in the steep, dark canyon.

CHAPTER SIXTY

Buno Eberhard had not expected to find a barbed-wire fence surrounding the old mines where he hoped to slay his pursuers. He chuckled at the skull-and-crossbones signs along with others warning of dangerous conditions, caving ground, and so forth. The Americans had become soft, a nation of cowards. They were all destined to serve the Master Race. Damn soon.

He took out a small pair of wire cutters he carried in a leather sheath next to his largest knife. It always paid to be prepared. Buno did not concern himself with being in the open; he knew he was well ahead of those after him. Jack Stoner was burdened by a fat misfit, a degenerate and, of all things, a *woman*. There was ample time for him to prepare his plan of deadly ambush. He was bending over, cutting the last strand of wire, when the first of many slugs came blasting from out of nowhere. One of them blasted a chunk of flesh from the calf of his right leg, another smashed into the heel of his left foot.

Buno Eberhard knew he was too badly wounded to make the dash to one of the big buildings. He would surely fall in the open stretch and be shot to pieces, just as he had planned to do to them.

How did they get so close without me knowing, Buno wondered desperately. *It has to be Stoner. None of the others could possibly have been so competent.*

A quick glance to the cliff ahead showed a black maw where a sagging tunnel entrance to the old coal seams beckoned like a beacon of safety. Buno knew he could make the short distance, but first he had to deal with Stoner. He spun around and began spewing slugs from his submachine gun in the direction he thought the shots that hit him had come from.

Then, the unthinkable happened. After only a few rounds had fired from the Heckler & Koch, it jammed. The bullets were undoubtedly faulty, made in heathen China most likely. With a snort of disgust Buno tossed the worthless weapon aside, yanked out his Luger, and sent a single bullet flying to keep Stoner pinned down. He ignored the pain as he ran to the sheltering mine opening. The blood filling his left boot squished with every step.

What surprised the blonde henchman more than being shot was the hail of bullets that dogged every agonized step as he ran to the opening. The soft woman doctor was shooting at him, not Stoner. To have such a thing happen to a true Aryan was unthinkably embarrassing.

She won't shoot you in the body because of the virus, Buno realized through the red cloud of pain that grew in his legs with every footfall. *Keep hunched over, protect yourself at all costs, the New Reich is counting on you.*

A final bullet sailed past his ear scant seconds before Buno entered the shelter of the old mine tunnel. He took a deep breath, blinked his eyes into focus as best he could in the increased darkness of the tunnel, then began to weigh his options. One thing he knew, even wounded, a member of the Master Race could overcome any obstacle. The virus in his pocket would either make it to Paraguay or he vowed to release it here in this canyon and kill as many Americans as he could. Buno Eberhard would not be forgotten. Not by any stretch of the imagination.

CHAPTER SIXTY-ONE

"Well, that was exciting." Jack Stoner came running up brandishing his pistol. He turned to Laura. "None of us dreamed we'd be waiting on Buno to show up. It might have been a good idea to let the rest of us in on the fact you saw him so we could have joined in sending some slugs his direction."

Laura Masterson shrugged. "I didn't want to take a chance and miss a good shot. I think I hit him at least once."

"Buno was hobbling around like a wounded sand crab," Frank Lowry said. "There's no doubt you put some serious hurt on that man."

Willie Ames came puffing his way to their side. "Up the hill, down the hill," he wheezed. "If I keep hanging around with you guys, I can give up my gym membership."

"Buno's shot in the legs," Jack nodded to Laura, a thin smile of admiration on his face. "Laura saw him cutting the fence and disabled him."

"Now he's holed up in that old mine tunnel," Frank said. "We really need to get those little glass tubes away from him." He eyed his watch. "And the sooner the better."

"I've got an idea," Laura said.

Jack said, "Before you act on it, let the rest of us know first."

"Let's go have a chat with him," Laura said, already on her way. "As long as we stay to one side, he can't get a shot at us without coming out and exposing himself. I don't expect him to do that."

Frank turned to Jack. "Now there goes one headstrong woman with a gun. Sort of reminds me of my third wife. I expect we ought to head up there. Ole Buno's likely going to need some protecting."

CHAPTER SIXTY-TWO

Buno Eberhard relished the pain, bathed in its glory. *Any* true member of the Master Race would do the same. The waves of martyrdom that shot up his legs served to focus his thoughts, steel his resolve. As long as breath remained there was *always* a chance of victory.

Think damn it. THINK. *There has to be a way out of this. The legacy of Adolph Hitler is in your hands. Do not fail him. There are only four people out there. Your wounds are not fatal. You have the virus. All you need is the means to take it to the New Fatherland. Think!*

"Oh yoo-hoo, Mr. Puno, are you up to receiving visitors?" Jack Stoner's taunting voice from outside shook him from his thoughts.

"Step out in the open like a man," Buno Eberhard growled, flattening himself against a dry mine timber that cracked and dropped dirt in his face from the pressure. "I'll be happy to give you an answer."

"What we actually would like, Buno," the voice was a *woman's*, Dr. Masterson's, "is for you to hand over those two tubes you took from Dr. Bettencourt. If you do that, I'll treat your wounds and get you to a hospital."

Buno Eberhard could not contain a roaring laugh of disdain. To think that a mere *woman* was giving him, the son of an SS officer, an *ultimatum*.

"I believe I might open one of these tubes," Buno said loudly. "They are well sealed, but if you come any closer, I *will* smash one."

"There's no need for anyone to die here, Buno," Came Jack Stoner's voice, serious now. "But I have to tell you that the Air Force is going to bomb this canyon with napalm in a few minutes. Releasing that virus will serve no purpose."

Buno Eberhard heard more cracking timbers over his head and echoing from the deep recesses of the decrepit old tunnel. From above the dirt falling in his face and trickling down his back increased to include fist-sized rocks. For the first time he could remember, Buno didn't know what to do.

"Get out of there!" Jack Stoner's voice was edged with anxiety. "Those timbers are rotten. Any movement will cause that mine to cave in. Even from out here we can hear rocks falling."

"Run!" Laura bellowed. "We won't shoot. The whole mountain is going to fall on you!"

"Don't be an idiot!" Jack shouted. "No one has to die here!"

"The Fatherland," Buno only had time to say these two words before the weight of a mountain, a weight that had been held at bay for decades by slowly decaying wooden timbers, gave way to the forces of gravity and nature.

Before Buno Eberhard could grasp what was happening, the German, along with the two tubes of virus in his pocket, were flattened beneath hundreds of tons of settling sandstone rock. He was squashed like an annoying insect by forces stronger than any of which he had ever dreamed.

CHAPTER SIXTY-THREE

"That fellow's had a bad run of luck," Frank said, wiping dust from his eyes with a tissue. "Too bad he didn't toss those tubes out before the roof fell in on him. Sure happened fast. And Buno wasn't the sharpest tool in the shed."

Jack Stoner stood beside Laura Masterson, watching the last few rocks settle into a depression that now marked the tunnel where Buno Eberhard had taken refuge. The earth gave one final sigh, a single boulder rolled to a stop, then silence returned to night in the desert.

"It'll take a lot of heavy equipment, a lot of time to dig Buno and that virus out," Jack Stoner said. "Time we don't have."

"There's no problem," Laura Masterson said firmly. "The virus will be dead in a matter of days. In the meanwhile, it's sealed under tons of dirt and rock. The substance can't get out. We're all safe. The world is safe!"

Jack Stoner gave her a look of incredulity. "Explain what you mean, Doc."

Laura gave him a genuine smile. "I placed the living virus into the tubes with only a small amount of plasmid, enough to support it, keep it alive just long enough to allow transport to a laboratory where a vaccine could be developed. That Spanish Flu virus will die on its own and it can't spread before then. The danger has past."

Frank said to Jack, "You want to maybe give those nice flyboys over at Kirtland a call that their services won't be needed tonight. My exes will be disappointed, but they'll get over it."

Laura cocked her head in alarm. "Cell phones don't work here in this canyon! We'll have to climb to the top of the rimrocks."

Jack amazed her with his easygoing grin as he fished a small cell phone from a carrier on his belt. He flipped it open, pushed a few buttons, then said into the receiver: "This is Ironman One. Code 12.

We can cancel that delivery we ordered." After a moment of listening, he spoke a series of numbers, then closed the phone and returned it to his belt.

"No problems," Stoner said cheerfully.

Willie answered a bewildered Laura Masterson's unasked question. "We ordered a satellite moved over our position days ago. This happens all the time. Haven't you ever wondered why you can get good reception in the same spot one time but not again? The government builds little solar-powered doohickeys into a few satellites to move them around. Sure comes in handy, doesn't it?"

Jack added, "Didn't you wonder why Frenchy was able to set off that bomb in your cell phone? Everyone here has had great cellular service for some time, but they never knew it."

"What *else* don't we know," Laura said with a hint of anger. "I've been a pawn in this whole deadly game."

"There's one big difference," Jack said. "The bad guys lost. All that matters is how it plays out in the end."

Suddenly, Dr. Laura Masterson felt her anger and tension flee, to be replaced by a terrible feeling of tiredness; more than anything she wanted to take a shower and sleep for hours. Laura wondered if she might awaken to discover that Paradox and everything terrible that occurred here was but a nightmare, but she knew better.

"There's no reason to stay here any longer," Laura said.

"No, there isn't," Jack agreed.

The three men and the woman who had managed to defeat one more monster turned and walked away in the wavering yellow light of a full moon.

On the high rimrocks, coyotes sang to the heavens.

EPILOGUE

The news media gave scant attention to what was reported as a drug deal gone bad in the near ghost town of Paradox, New Mexico. One unnamed man, believed to be a French National, had died from exposure while attempting to avoid pursuing undercover policemen in inclement weather. The drug dealers had burned a mobile meth lab in an attempt to destroy evidence. The upcoming rodeo in Santa Fe, where many of the world-champion bull riders were scheduled to appear, was deemed far more important and received front-page billing in all of the local newspapers.

Six days after Jack Stoner, Frank Lowry, and Willie Ames were airlifted from the town of Paradox in a sleek, black helicopter that bore no markings, an aging 747 jet taxied down the runway of the Antonio Carlos Jobim International Airport on Governor's Island, about 20 kilometers north of Rio de Janeiro, Brazil.

Inside the fully fueled jetliner, one hundred and twenty-eight corpses of varying ages, all of whom had died either of disease or accident, were dressed neatly and strapped into their seats. The luggage bay contained suitcases filled with party clothes along with personal items needed for a nice holiday abroad.

The three men in the cockpit of the TNT Worldwide Express jet received clearance for takeoff. The 747 gained altitude, then banked sharply over the bay. If anyone had been closely watching the ill-fated flight, they might have noticed three parachutes open minutes before the huge jet crashed into the headquarters building of Roth Pharmaceuticals. Unfortunately the company was holding its annual meeting at this very time. All of the upper management, including the son of the company's founder, Philip Roth, III, were present at the time of the accident and sadly perished.

Business analysts doubt that after the loss of all of the management personnel, the company will survive. Buyers began making bids for various branches of Roth Pharmaceuticals before the fires had been fully extinguished.

Sadie Helms and Thelma Ross gladly accepted Jack Stoner's offer to take anything they could use from the pantries of the expensive Prevost motorhomes that were destined to be seized and towed off by the ATF under the RICO Act. The two silver-haired widows' skimpy retirement received a much-needed boost when, stashed behind a cannister set in the pantry of Buno Eberhard's coach, they found a fat manilla envelope stuffed with something they *really* needed.

The next day, the elderly ladies drove out of the town of Paradox for the last time in a smoking old motorhome with their cat stretched out in the front window. Neither of them turned a head to look back at the now ghost town where they had lived for so long. It was time to follow the sun at last. In style.

In the Tombs of the Centers for Disease Control in Atlanta, Georgia, Ruben Hernandez wondered briefly why the red biohazard level-four light north of Tucumcari, New Mexico, had been extinguished. For that matter, he wondered why it had been lit in the first place. He decided the whole situation was probably nothing but a computer glitch and returned to monitoring a dozen television news channels, grateful for small favors.

Dr. Laura Masterson returned to Houston, Texas, to reclaim her car and belongings. While staying in the nearby Holiday Inn Express, she received a visit from two clean-cut men in black suits who wore sunglasses indoors on a cloudy day. Less than an hour later, Laura made the decision that would change her life forever.

These days, Laura lives in Las Vegas, Nevada, and works for the government at the super-secret Area 51 north of town. Her job title is that of "medical technician," but the work she does there is of a magnitude she never imagined existed. Monsters live that have yet to be named, let alone understood. But fighting monsters is what Laura Masterson had been hired to do. And she is *very* good at her job.

Occasionally, she and Jack Stoner visit by phone and promise to get together sometime. That time has yet to come; the world keeps them too busy and they have not set eyes on each other since they left Paradox.

Every night Laura Masterson sleeps soundly beneath the Indian dream catcher she purchased in Tucumcari, New Mexico. In a dangerous world where real monsters lurk in many shadowy places, no nightmares mar Laura's peaceful dreamscapes.

that followed. I'd more or less been in the wrong place at the wrong time when a sociopathic killer had become obsessed with destroying Foxdale. He'd targeted the farm and eventually me. The only good to come of it was that he wouldn't be bothering me anymore. Wouldn't be bothering anyone.

I rested my elbows on the counter, slid my fingers into my hair, and leaned my forehead on my palms. "Jesus Christ. I never thought it would be this bad."

Ralston walked across the room and stood next to me. "He came within an inch of murdering you. What did you expect?"

"Not to be so fucked up, that's what." Anger flooded my voice. I closed my eyes.

"Have you thought about counseling?"

I shook my head. "They suggested it at the hospital. Rachel's suggested it. I don't want it."

"Why not?"

"I just don't."

"You know, cops get counseling when they need it. It doesn't mean you're incapable of handling yourself. Sometimes we all need help."

I lifted my head and looked at his reflection in the glass. He was dressed in a light gray suit, crisp white shirt, and striped tie, and he looked cool, even in the heat. "Have you ever gone in for counseling?"

"No," Ralston said. "But then, I've got my buddies to talk things through with. Cops. They know what it's like to make difficult life and death decisions, to have mind-numbing boredom turn into unmitigated terror in the blink of an eye. Dealing with death's part of the job. We all know it going in."

"I knew you'd say you hadn't." I rested my chin in my hand and stared out the window. "I knew it."

He said nothing for a moment, and it was so quiet in the loft, I could hear the clock on the stove tick off the seconds as the hand moved jerkily around the dial.

"Look, Steve. Sometimes all we need is someone to talk to, but what you went through is much worse than the typical confrontation a police officer deals with, even an atypical one. He was playing games with you. Trying to break you. None of us are meant to deal with that. You really need to get help from a professional. Someone who specializes in counseling victims, post-traumatic stress, that sort of thing."

The tractor crawled across the hill above the lake. "Maybe. I don't know." I sighed. "I just know if I spend any more time in this loft, I'll go nuts."

"How are you feeling physically? Are you able to go back?"

"Yeah. Except when I forget and move a certain way, most of the pain's gone, or at least manageable."

"Good." He rested his hand lightly on the countertop. "If you want to try and go back to Foxdale, and you want company, I'd be happy to go with you."

I turned my back to the window and stared across the loft, at the white-on-white kitchen and the broad expanse of forest green carpet beyond. At the warm knotty-pine paneling stretching to meet the ridge beam high above our heads. At the north wall that was nothing but glass. A place where tons of hay had once been stored. A place I loved. More home than anywhere else. My wonderful home turned prison.

I looked at Ralston. "I don't know."

He reached across the counter, picked up the nearly empty whiskey bottle, and examined the label as he screwed on the cap. He tossed it in the trash can by the door, and the heavy glass clattered against some empty soda cans. When he turned around, he was startled to see me smiling at him.

"I'm surprised you didn't pour that last little bit down the drain," I said.

Ralston considered me for a second or two, then pulled a card out of his wallet and handed it to me. Thomas J. McKeeman, PHD, HSSP was embossed above Mental Health Services, followed by a list of specialties.

"Give him a call, Steve. Don't put it off." He looked out the window, then back at me. "Why don't we go to Foxdale right now?"

"Now?"

"Yes. Get it over with."

I looked down at the card and shook my head.

Ralston put his hand on my shoulder. "Steve, give him a call. He's really good at what he does."

I glanced at him, then went back to fingering the card.

"And give me a call if you need somebody to talk to. Anytime." He squeezed my shoulder. "Okay?"

I nodded, and he left, closing the screen door quietly behind him.

I walked into the bathroom, turned on the shower, and looked in the mirror. No wonder Ralston thought I needed help. It was two-thirty in the afternoon, and I still hadn't gotten dressed. My normally tanned face had turned sallow after so many weeks indoors, and the dark shadows under my eyes didn't improve my look, either. Yawning, I rubbed my face and ran my fingers through hair that had grown too long.

I took a shower and was pulling on a clean pair of jeans when I heard a knock at the door. I grabbed a tee shirt and paused in the kitchen when I realized who was at my door.

Kessler was standing on my deck, his back to the door, his hands arrogantly on his hips as he looked out across the pastures. He was dressed in a salmon colored polo shirt and a pair of glaringly white jeans. He obviously hadn't come from the track, and I wondered why he had come at all.

He turned and saw me through the screen. "Can I come in?"

My jaw muscles felt stiff. I slipped on the shirt, opened the door, and stepped back. Kessler strode into the middle of the kitchen, glanced around the loft, then looked steadily at my face.

"You're tough to find, you know that? Your mother wasn't sure where you lived, and your boss wouldn't tell me."

I thought about the suit she'd had delivered to the loft and knew she'd tried to keep us apart. "My boss?"

He nodded.

"How'd you figure where I worked?"

"Your hat. It had Foxdale Farm printed on it."

He stood on the white tile, his arms still at his sides, waiting for me to respond. Outside, above the constant, lazy drone of insects, the tractor grew louder as it neared the barn. In the distance, a dog barked halfheartedly.

"Okay," he said. "I was taken off guard. Someone's been getting to my horses, and I don't know who, and I don't know how, and that was on my mind. I had you pegged as working for the opposition. What you told me was…" He shrugged, then glanced out the window. "Well, it was the farthest thing from my mind. Asking you what you wanted wasn't the most tactful, intelligent thing in the world to say, but…" He swallowed, then hooked his thumbs in his pockets. "I'm sorry. I didn't intend for it to come across the way it did. I was hoping we could put it behind us and start over."

I looked at the floor and mumbled, "We don't have to start over. We don't have to start anything."

"Is that what you want?" he said quietly.

I shook my head and looked up at him.

"Good." He walked over and perched on one of the barstools with his back toward the counter. "So, where do we start?"

I shrugged.

Kessler leaned back, rested his elbows on the edge of the counter, and laced his fingers together over his stomach. "Guess you'd like to hear how I knew your mother."

"I think I already know how."

He frowned and seemed unsure how to respond. He cleared his throat. "She and I were working on a committee together, organizing a fund-raiser to establish a transition farm for retired racehorses. Horses that were sound when they left the track were re-schooled so they'd be suitable for another career. Eventing, hunter/jumpers, dressage, that sort of thing. If they were unsound or mentally unfit, the farm gave them a permanent home or found adoptive homes." Kessler unlaced his fingers and rubbed the back of his neck.

"Your father was traveling a lot, lecturing all over the country on the angioplasty procedure he'd invented, and I don't think Patricia saw him much. Or not enough, anyway. She was lonely and bored with all that free time on her hands. My wife had died the year before, and we were…well…" He shrugged. "It's no excuse. What we did was wrong, but it happened."

He sat up straighter and rested his hands on his thighs. "She wasn't thrilled when I called her this morning, I'll give you that." He smiled briefly. "How long have you known?"

"About you?"

He nodded.

"Since Friday."

His eyes narrowed. "Since the funeral? Why in the hell'd she tell you then?"

I shook my head. "Not her. My brother." He opened his mouth to say something, but I cut him off. "So, how'd you get my address?"

He hesitated. "I pulled some strings at the MVA. A friend of mine works there. She gave me your address." He looked me up and down, then cleared his throat. "When I talked to your boss, I got the impression you haven't been to work for a while, but she wouldn't say why. As a matter of fact, she wouldn't say much of anything."

I walked over and pulled out a stool for myself. "I've been on sick leave."

He considered me, not stating the obvious, that I looked healthy enough.

"I'm ready to go back…pretty much."

"So, Patty has another boy?" he said.

"And a girl."

"I have two girls. Cassandra. She's twenty-five, lives in Michigan. Married, no kids. Abby's twenty-four. She works for me."

"Tall? Long dirty-blond hair?"

"Yeah, that's her."

The mystery woman. Abby. My sister. No. Half-sister. Running the time sequence through my head, I frowned. We seemed too close in age for what he said to be true. "I thought you said your wife died the year before you met my mother."

"That's right. She died in childbirth."

"Oh."

Kessler glanced at his watch and said, "I haven't eaten since this morning. Want to go get something to eat?"

I shrugged. "Okay."

He drove as I would have guessed, as his personality dictated. Smooth, controlled, confident, not bothering to discuss our destination ahead of time. When he pulled off the main drag that runs through Columbia and parked by the lakeside restaurant Rachel and I had gone to on one of our first dates, I almost smiled.

After we were seated, I leaned back in my chair and fiddled with the edge of my menu that lay closed on the white linen tablecloth. As I watched Kessler study the selection, it occurred to me that I hadn't truly believed Robert until I'd actually seen Kessler with my own eyes. Hadn't believed the nightmare.

He glanced up and said, "Ever eaten here before?"

"Once or twice." I opened my menu and made a pretense of examining the contents, though I had no need to. I looked up from the fancy, nearly indecipherable script and caught Kessler watching me with a gaze so intense I almost flinched.

He laid his menu near the edge of the table, and our waitress materialized at his side. She took our orders and left behind a basket of gently steaming bread. He'd been studying me, I noticed, and I found it increasingly irritating.

As soon as she was out of hearing range, he said, "I never would've guessed you'd be working in a stable. Not with your parents."

I snorted. "I gotta admit, it went over big when I told my father I was going to work on a horse farm. He kicked me out for it."

Kessler was sitting very still, his gaze steady on my face.

I looked away from him and smoothed my fingers down the cold surface of my glass of ice water, dislodging droplets of condensation. "At the time, I didn't understand why. It all makes sense now."

Kessler shook his head. "What a waste."

He was holding a butter knife in one hand, momentarily forgotten, and a hot slice of bread in the other. Above the soft murmur of voices and civilized clatter of silverware and china, the strains of one of Vivaldi's seasons tumbled and hop-scotched toward the crescendo.

"One of my owners," he said, "a patient of your father's, mentioned his accident the other day, but I was only half-listening." He laid his knife on the tablecloth, unused, and leaned back in his chair. "I'm sorry about your father, Steve. About everything, really. Life sure has a way of getting twisted around, doesn't it?"

"Yeah, I guess you could say that." I lifted the end of my napkin and watched the silverware roll onto the tablecloth. "So, what's going on with your horses?" I looked across the table at him.

There was a glimmer in his eye that told me my attempt at changing the subject hadn't gone unnoticed. "I wish to hell I knew. About eight or nine months ago, I started getting phone calls suggesting how my horses should run. If I agreed to play ball, I'd learn which longshot to put my money on, and everyone would be a winner. I told 'em to stick it, and eventually they stopped calling. I thought, then, that that would be the end of it, but right after Christmas, I got another call. He said if I didn't join them, I'd wish I had, because they were going to get what they wanted one way or the other."

"Hmm."

A tic worked at the corner of Kessler's left eye, although I doubted he was aware of it.

"But if I ran my horses to instruction," he said, "I'd make good money. At the time, it didn't occur to me that if I'd gone along with it, there was a chance I would have found out who they were."

"A slim chance," I said. "They wouldn't believe they could trust you since you'd already turned them down."

"Yeah, I guess you're right."

I tapped my fingers on the tablecloth. "If you'd pretended to go along with them, though, even for a little while, you would've gotten a feel for which trainers were in on it simply based on the horses running in the fixed races."

"True. Running their own horses gives them an edge. More control. But I was hesitant to join them, especially in a con. Who knows what they would've done when I tried to back out, or when they figured I was playing them."

He was right, of course. Risking it could have had dire consequences. "Why don't they just go to the jockeys? Why bother with trainers at all?"

"God knows that's done often enough, and it's the best way to get to a horse if the trainer doesn't want to get in on the action. But I'm lucky to have the services of a jock who's gotta be one of the straightest guys I know."

The waitress returned to our table, and Kessler watched without comment as she placed an overfilled, steaming cup of coffee in front of him. Coffee sloshed over the rim and puddled in the saucer. She gave me a Coke, smiled brightly, and left.

Kessler idly followed her progress across the room before continuing. "It's a clique running it. They just carve up the races however they want, betting heavily on the predetermined winner, lowering the odds on their own horses until they're ready to send them out so that they win big."

"Trainers and jockeys alike?"

"Not necessarily. If a trainer's willing to screw around like that, he doesn't need the jock's help. There are any number of ways to send your horse out in less than top condition. He just makes sure the horse is a little tired. Maybe he works him too hard the day before the race. Or maybe he's withheld the horse's water, then he lets him fill up just before the post. Well, he's done it without anyone else knowing."

Kessler sipped the coffee and grimaced. "I really don't understand it. If they'd put as much effort into running their horses straight as they do screwing around, they might actually make a name for themselves. It's gotta be trainers who aren't doing so well to begin with who are pulling this shit."

"Did you report the phone calls?"

"Yeah. I mentioned them to the authorities, but you see, there wasn't really anything they could do."

I frowned. "And they didn't suggest a sting of some kind?"

"No. I half-wondered if he believed me when he didn't suggest anything. Being pressured like that's a bit unusual, considering there are plenty of people willing to cheat. But then, I'd already blown it by turning the guy down. And I'm sure the stewards knew, as well as I did, that to gain their confidence, I would have actually been forced to throw a race or two. And I couldn't afford to do that. As it turns out, the bastards are getting what they want anyway, like they said they would." He bit into his bread and leaned farther back in his chair. Another inch or so, and he'd tip the damn thing over.

I cut through a chunk of butter and smoothed it across my bread. Maybe the official thought Kessler was feeding him a story to allay suspicions, but I kept that thought to myself.

"There's about a thousand different ways to stop a horse," Kessler said. "And somebody's been doing a damn good job getting at mine. For the past three months, now, I've had runners that should've buried the competition finish out of the money, all with the same symptoms. Nothing obvious, just a subtle feeling that something's not right. Their pre-race blood work's excellent. They're eating well, working well. They look good. But they go out to run, and there's nothing under the hood when the jocks call on 'em.

"They come back lethargic as hell, totally wiped out. I've had laboratory tests run from here to China and back, and nothing. Zilch. The TRPB guy's been conducting spot checks for weeks, snooping around the feed room, taking samples of the weirdest things. He—"

"TRPB?"

"Oh, yeah. You wouldn't know. The Thoroughbred Racing Protective Bureau. They run background checks and investigate anything and everything that affects the integrity of racing, from doping and race-fixing to narcotics distribution. He won't find anything, though, because there's nothing to find."

"But there must be," I said.

"Not on my end. Whatever they're using, they're bringing it in. Then there's the State Racing Commission. Their people are in charge of testing the win, place, and show horses, and any favorite that doesn't perform as expected. Needless to say, they know my horses by sight. Some days, even I wish they'd find something." He bit into his bread and mumbled, "Get some answers."

"Wouldn't you be in trouble, then?"

"Not necessarily. As long as they don't have direct evidence that I'm involved, I'd be okay. And it could point me in the right direction, knowing how it's done, even if I don't know who's behind it."

"Why don't you hire a guard?"

"Just fired one. He's the second I've canned in a month. Caught the first one smoking in the barn." He took another bite and shook his head. "Simple-minded bastard. The last one was dead asleep when I showed up one morning a little earlier than usual. Track security's even less effective, if you can believe that."

"Was Icedancer one of your poor performers?"

Kessler stopped chewing and let his chair rock back on all fours with a thud. "She sure in hell was. They called last week and told me she'd better be off her game. How'd you know?" he said, and I had a feeling he was once again suspicious.

"I was there, remember? She fits the profile."

At that moment, our waitress arrived with a tray balanced on her left hand. She asked who had ordered the eggplant rata-touille. Kessler sat motionless and didn't answer. I indicated what went where, and she laid out our plates and asked if there was anything else she could get for us.

No one answered.

After an extended pause, she shrugged, and as she turned to leave, I caught a quizzical expression on her face.

"Damn." Kessler looked down at his plate as if he were just then aware of its existence. "Too bad you're going back to Foxdale. I sure could use you at the barn."

"What do you mean?"

"Snooping around. Watching. Trying to find out who's getting to the horses and how." He gestured toward me with his fork. "You know horses. You'd fit right in. And there's no chance you're already working for the opposition, like I often thought might happen if I tried to hire someone who's worked on the backside. Wouldn't that be a crock? Hiring someone to investigate, and they're already in on it."

He absentmindedly stabbed a chunk of tomato with his fork. "Your boss acted real strange, like she didn't trust me, like she didn't even want to talk about you. It was weird." He paused, his fork halfway to his mouth. "What's her problem anyway?" He grinned suddenly. "You didn't go out and murder somebody, now, did you?"

My stomach knotted into a ball. I looked down at my plate and cleared my throat. "She's just overly cautious."

"It's a shame you can't extend your leave for a couple more weeks. I think you'd find the track...interesting." Around a mouthful of crepe, he said, "Were you hurt on the job?"

"What?"

Kessler surveyed his plate with the enthusiasm of the starving, then gestured with his fork. "Your time off."

"Oh. Yeah."

"We have a lot of that. Time off because of injuries, even with all the precautions we take. Horses are so unpredictable." He swallowed. "That's one thing in life you can count on."

I sliced through my crepe, folded a section filled with shrimp onto my fork, and stared at my plate. If I went to the track for a week or two, maybe I'd be ready to go back to work afterward. It would be an adventure of sorts, and it sure as hell beat sitting in the loft, staring at the walls. And I'd learn more about Kessler. I rested the fork on my plate. Try as I might, I still couldn't see myself at Foxdale. Not yet.

God. I closed my eyes. Why was I such a coward?

"Something wrong with your food?"

I opened my eyes and shook my head. "No. It's fine."

"Huh," he said. "Could've fooled me."

I looked him straight in the eye, and his grin faded. I said, "I could do it for a week or two. Maybe three."

"Do what?"

"The track."

"I wouldn't want you to lose your job."

"I won't. So soon after the funeral, she won't expect me back right away."

I ate the rest of my meal with growing enthusiasm as we discussed the mechanics of our proposed operation. While Kessler thought out strategies, filled me in on the numerous scams that had been tried in the past, and identified possible suspects, I listened lightheartedly to a plan that could quite possibly be dangerous and felt the chains of the past few weeks dissolve and drift away like mist on a lake.

Chapter 5

At five-thirty the next morning, with a gym bag crammed full of clothes lying on the seat beside me, I drove past the guard post at Washington Park and was officially hired by Christopher J. Kessler, proprietor of the west side of barn sixteen, third on the list of *Jockey and Trainers Standings* with sixty-two starts, fourteen wins, and earnings just topping two hundred thousand. My father. A virtual stranger.

I paused in the shedrow near Kessler's office and waited while a gray filly was led round the corner on the soft loam and sawdust track that circled the interior row of back-to-back stalls. In the short aisle just beyond the office, Kessler had both hands braced on either side of a doorway, elbows bent as he leaned into the room and talked with someone.

I waited until the filly reached the far corner, then I walked down the aisle and stood next to Kessler.

He glanced over his shoulder. "Oh, Steve." He looked back into the room.

It wasn't an office, as I'd thought, but a well-equipped tack room.

"Abby." Kessler gestured to me as he stepped into the room, and I noticed the corner of his mouth twitch. "This is Steve. He starts today. He'll be walking hots."

Abby frowned. "We need another..." she began as she turned toward the doorway with a saddle cloth draped over her arm and irritation clearly in her voice and on her face, "...hotwalker?"

She looked from her father to me, then seemed to pause in mid-thought. The lines of irritation around her eyes softened and disappeared altogether as she stared openly at me. I doubted whether she heard her father's response and wondered if she saw, as I did, the obvious resemblance between us.

Whether or not to tell her had been a sticking point in our conversation the evening before. Kessler had complete and unwavering faith in her and had, without hesitation, wanted to tell her who I was and what we were doing. I, on the other hand, had been concerned that she might tell someone in confidence.

I had sat through an uncensored, highly derogatory commentary on Abby's current boyfriend—an exercise rider who, according to Kessler, had a major chip on his shoulder and an insatiable desire for the green stuff which he spent as fast as he earned. Eventually, after considering her level of infatuation with him, Kessler had agreed with me.

"Good morning," I said formally.

She stared at me with a blank expression, then turned to face a pegboard hung with an assortment of bits and gadgets, several of which I'd never seen before. "So, Dad, do you want me to change Dancer's bit?"

Kessler lifted his eyebrows in surprise and glanced at me before answering.

I leaned against the doorjamb and watched her as they discussed tack changes and strategies for the morning's work. Her actions were precise, and outwardly, she seemed totally focused on their conversation. Yet on another level, I had an overwhelming feeling that she was highly attuned to my presence.

Abby was my height, thin, and athletic-looking, and unlike the last time I'd seen her at the races, she had made no effort at femininity in preparation for the morning routine. Her sandy brown hair was brushed straight back from her face and secured in a plain ponytail. No ribbons, no jewelry, no makeup. She was dressed much as I was, wearing jeans that were dirty at the knees, a plain gray tee shirt, and work boots. And she looked younger than she had at the races. More her age.

Behind me, a skinny guy, with scraggly blond hair and jeans three sizes too large, led the gray on yet another circuit. Just around the corner, someone whistled as he clattered around in a stall. Kessler reached up and wiped off a section of white board with a cloth, then made notations in a column alongside each horse's name. "Steve," he said without turning around. "Come over here."

I stepped into the room.

Kessler jerked his head. "Grab a shank off the wall over there, and Abby will get you started."

I lifted a chain shank off one of the hooks.

"What outfit were you with last?" Abby said.

"I haven't worked here before."

She pursed her lips and frowned as she glanced at her father's back. "You mean you've never worked on the track?"

"That's right."

"Do you know anything about horses?"

"A bit."

"Racehorses?"

"Not much."

Abby sighed and all but rolled her eyes. "When the horses come back from their morning workouts, their grooms take them to their stalls and untack them. That means removing their saddles and bridles," she added as she crossed her arms. "The groom does this, not you. Then you have to hold the horse while it gets a bath. After that's done, you walk them around the shedrow until they're cooled out. Counterclockwise," she said. "Always counterclockwise."

Kessler looked at his daughter's back, then he looked over her shoulder at me and shrugged.

"Before you start, the groom will show you where he's set up a water bucket. Each circuit around the barn, you can let the horse have two or three swallows at a time. No more."

She frowned slightly, and I imagined she was sorely dreading the prospect of breaking in someone new, especially since they didn't need the help.

"Either myself or the horse's groom will tell you when to put the horse back in its stall. Got it?"

I nodded.

"Oh, and when you're walking a horse in the shedrow, and you have to stop, you need to yell 'ho back.' Understand?"

"'Ho back'?"

"Yes. And keep at least a length between your horse and the horse in front, otherwise you'll end up getting kicked, or worse, your horse might get hurt."

Charming girl, Abby.

She strode into the aisle and said to the air in front of her, "Ace is back. You can start with him."

I slid my hands into my pockets, and as I stepped out of the room, I glanced over my shoulder. Kessler was looking after us with a perplexed expression on his face. I followed her down the shedrow, wondering what I'd gotten myself into.

Even though the sun had yet to rise above the horizon, the day had already heated up, and the air was so laden with moisture, I felt like I was breathing through a sponge.

Ace, it turned out, was Devil's Ace, the same horse that had run in the second race on Monday afternoon, less than forty-eight hours ago, and had proven too much for his jockey. He'd outpaced the field early on, then run out of steam when it counted. Just two days ago. It seemed a lifetime.

"Got 'im, Abby," a voice behind us said. I turned as the black groom I'd seen on my first day at the races stepped out of a stall. Abby introduced him simply as Jay. He took hold of Ace's bridle and glanced at me without comment or recognition. Sweat glistened on his bald head and trickled down the back of his neck. His biceps were as thick as fence posts.

Ace's exercise rider, an old, wiry guy with deeply wrinkled skin and a crooked nose, slid lightly to the ground. "Pig propped on me and swung around at the gap. Damn near got me off." He spat on the ground. "Damn horse got a mouth like a rhinoceros's backside."

Abby crouched down and smoothed her hand along the back of the gelding's leg, between the knee and fetlock. Ace flinched at her touch. "He sound?" Abby said.

"Can't hardly tell with him carrying on and all, but I think he's okay."

Ace snatched up his leg, and his hoof almost grazed Abby's face. She steadied him without fuss, and when she was satisfied that he'd come out of the workout sound, she stood and signaled to Jay to get on with it. I followed them into the stall.

Ace was a difficult horse. He shied at everything, tried to sink his teeth into my arm at every opportunity, and basically did his level best to make life miserable for everyone around him. I was thankful when the time came to put him back in his stall for the day. Abby's baptism by fire, I guessed. She probably figured if I could handle Ace, I could handle any of them. And I didn't think it a highly intelligent method of operation, considering the consequences if I hadn't been up to the job.

By eleven o'clock, the morning stable routine had come to an end, and all of the crew had gone home. Except for the constant drone of fans, the barns were quiet, the hustle and urgency of the day spent or at least temporarily suspended until the afternoon's racing.

I had cooled out six horses and was exhausted. I had learned the names of half the employees and not quite a third of the horses. I had noticed nothing out of the ordinary, remotely suspicious, or even moderately informative. If the days to come proceeded as this one had, the entire endeavor would be a complete waste of time.

I walked slowly down the shedrow. With nothing to see or do, many of the horses stood toward the backs of their stalls, quietly dozing, their eyes half-closed, ears at half-mast. Some picked at their hay nets. Only a few watched me with any interest at all.

As prearranged, I found Kessler in his office.

I collapsed into the stiff-backed chair alongside his desk.

"You all right?" he said.

"Yeah. Just tired. Guess I underestimated what it would be like to walk in a circle in this heat for six hours straight." I slid my spine lower in the chair, leaned my head against the hard plastic, and closed my eyes. "It would be helpful if you'd give me a diagram of the barn, indicating which horses are stalled where, who their grooms are, the names of your hotwalkers…stuff like that." I opened my eyes. "Who works out of the other side of the barn?"

"Two trainers. David Reece and Larry McCormick."

"McCormick?"

Kessler nodded.

"I thought so. I recognized one of his grooms from Monday, but I didn't see McCormick."

"He's in Kentucky. Horse hunting, I think. His assistant trainer's over there, though."

"McCormick and Reece. They weren't on your list of suspects."

"No, but…and I hate to say it, but a small portion of the seventy or so trainers working out of Washington are involved in some kind of scam at one time or another. Some are borderline legal, some definitely are not, and some are downright wicked. It's the nature of the game."

"Some game," I said more forcefully than I'd intended.

Kessler paused. He laid the pencil he had been absentmindedly rolling between his fingers on the desk blotter and leaned back in his chair. "True. In any endeavor where there's the hope of easy money, there's a game. It's human nature." When I didn't respond, he opened a desk drawer. "Speaking of money, here's the check I promised."

Kessler leaned across the desk, his arm outstretched. "Take it, Steve. I don't want you doing this otherwise."

In addition to the usual salary, a sum that had me appreciating Foxdale more and more, he had insisted that I be compensated for my…extracurricular duties.

I folded the check and slid it into my pocket. The medical bills that had been flooding my mailbox since the stint in the hospital were threatening to undermine my independence altogether. "Thank you."

"Is there anything else I can get for you?" Kessler said.

I shook my head.

"We have a runner in the ninth, today. If you still want to see what the routine's like, I'll need you here by six-fifteen."

"Fine."

"Good. I already told Ray not to come in."

"Blond hair, skinny, baggy jeans? Everybody calls him Stingray?"

"That's him."

"Weird nickname."

Kessler shrugged. "He's from Florida. Guess he got it there."

I closed my eyes and heard my stomach rumble. "How long's he worked for you?"

"Four, maybe five months. I'd have to look it up."

"Could you include that kind of thing on your list and anything else you can think of? You never know what might be useful," I mumbled. When he said nothing, I opened my eyes.

"Are you sure you're up to this? You look ill."

I nodded.

"How were you hurt?"

I stared blankly at the wall above the filing cabinets, not wanting him to read anything in my eyes. "I had surgery," I said. "Recovering's taking longer than I'd expected."

Kessler stood abruptly and walked across the room. "It isn't going to work." He turned around. "You're in no shape for this."

"I can do it. If I can't, I can't. There's no harm in trying. I'll give the check back if I have to quit."

He shrugged that off and sat down. "Do you think grooming would be easier on you?"

I exhaled and felt as if I weren't breathing properly. I pushed myself upright. "Maybe, but like you said last night, I'll have more flexibility hotwalking instead of being stuck with the horses I groom."

"All right. We'll continue, but if it gets to be too much, let me know, okay? I don't want you ruining your health over this."

I smiled faintly. Hotwalking could in no way, shape, or form compare to getting shot. I would be fine as long as I was careful. And going back to Foxdale could wait. A nice, neat way of postponing the vivid memories I knew I'd have to deal with once I went back… "to the scene of the crime," as Ralston might have said. But, I still dreamt about it, and in that netherworld, halfway between sleep and consciousness, the nightmares were annoyingly real.

Kessler leaned back in his chair just short of tipping it over. "You need to go over to the Racing Commission office and fill out your paperwork, then you ought to try and get some sleep if you're going to stay up tonight."

"Yeah. You're right." I stood and stretched and felt the familiar ache cut through my chest.

I filled out a stack of forms, was photographed, fingerprinted, given a housing assignment and a key to go with it, and finally made it to my room by way of the track kitchen and a hefty lunch that tasted better than it looked.

The housing units were two-story rectangular buildings, and each contained fourteen rooms and two common bathrooms. I climbed the steps to the second level balcony and stood in front of a green wooden door with peeling paint and a plastic number four dangling from a rusted nail. I slid my key into the lock and pushed the door inward.

A blast of heat and a strong unidentifiable odor hit my face, and I stepped back. After a minute, I unenthusiastically walked into the small room and looked around. A metal-framed bed, little more than a cot, had been shoved against the wall to my right. In the corner directly opposite from where I stood, a twisted hanger dangled from a length of clothesline. It moved in a current of stale air.

I glanced at the window. Sometime in the past, an industrious boarder had looped a length of baling twine around the faded floral curtains and tied them back to let in the light. And that was it as far as accommodations went.

I walked over to the bed and dumped my gym bag on the mattress.

"Ain't the fuckin' Hilton, is it?"

I turned around. Gordi, one of Kessler's grooms, stood in the doorway. "No," I said. "It sure the hell ain't."

"They say they gonna build us new dormitories during the break when we at Pimlico." He strolled the three paces necessary to cross the room, sat his behind comfortably on the bed, and leaned against the wall. "A rec-room and a laundry, TV, all kinds a shit. Private bathrooms, too." He crossed his legs and flicked a dead fly off the mattress. "Me…I'll believe it when I see it. If you ain't noticed, the horses have it better'n we do."

Kessler had mentioned that Gordi was one of his best grooms, yet I found him to be a jumble of contradictions. Black, lean, and clean-cut (although that could have had as much to do with the fact that he was too young to be anything else) he looked like he should have been modeling clothes instead of mucking out stalls. He was also hard-working, industrious, and smart. Yet, I had an overwhelming impression that he had little ambition to do anything else.

I fiddled with the air-conditioner under the window.

"Hate to tell you this, but it's broken," Gordi said. "That's why this room's empty most of the time."

"Great." I pulled the curtain back, with the intention of opening the window, and a roach the size of my little finger scurried across the windowsill and dropped to the floor. It disappeared in a crack along the baseboard where the linoleum had curled up at the edge thanks to one too many rainstorms blowing in through the window.

I shook the curtain. Two more roaches fell to the floor and followed their cousin into darkness.

"Be thankful you ain't downstairs," Gordi said to my back as I cranked the window open. "Down there, besides them motherfuckers, they got water bugs the size of horse turds."

"Shit."

He chuckled. "Sting and I entertain ourselves by sneakin' into the john at night, real quiet like, switchin' on the lights, and seein' how many of 'em fuckers we can stomp on."

"Stingray?" I said, thinking it wasn't my idea of a fun pastime.

"Yep."

"Does he live downstairs?"

"Sure does. So you can imagine, he ain't too fond of 'em. He's right next to the girls' bathroom, though." Gordi grinned. "The motherfucker be trying to drill a hole through the fuckin' wall, but the cement keeps crumblin' and shit, and he's scared it'll do that when he gets to the other side. If he don't perfect his technique, he gonna end up makin' a big fuckin' hole you could put your goddamn head through. Then everybody'll know what he up to, and they'll ship his ass back to Florida."

"Florida? Why'd he come up here?"

Gordi shook his head. "Said it was too fuckin' hot, but I got the feeling he weren't talkin' 'bout no weather."

I couldn't think of anything else to ask without arousing Gordi's suspicions, so I said, "Where's your room?"

"Right next to yours. Number five. Home sweet home." Gordi eyed me for a moment, then said, "I got some good weed right now, wanna come over?"

I shook my head and yawned. "I'm gonna catch a nap. I'm not used to getting up so early."

"You ain't use to gettin' up? I thought you come from another outfit, seeing's how you knew what you was doin'."

"No, I worked at a show barn before this."

"No kidding? You handled Ace okay, the stupid pig. I'm glad he ain't mine. Jay can have 'im for all I care, even if he starts winnin' like Mr. K hopes."

I started to lean against the wall and thought better of it. Jay. Who the hell was Jay? Then I realized he meant the black guy with the muscles and shaved head.

"Trainer that had Ace before Mr. K waited too long to cut the sonofabitch. All the horse got on 'is mind is gettin' laid."

I peeled my damp shirt away from my chest. "Like the rest of us, huh?"

Gordi hooted. "Fuck, yeah." He shook his head and languidly pushed himself off the bed. "Good luck takin' a nap in this hole. You better be gettin' youself a fan." He looked down at my gym bag. "This all the shit you got?"

"Kind of."

Gordi shook his head and headed for the door. "Fuck. And I thought I was poor."

After Gordi left, I looked down at the thin, filthy mattress and reconsidered my decision to stay at the track. But driving back and forth to the loft would use up valuable time. I peered under the bed. No bugs. Nothing alive, anyway.

I spread a clean tee shirt on the mattress, lay on my back, and laced my fingers behind my head. I was staring at the ceiling, thinking that I was too tired and too sore to sleep when the alarm on my watch beeped spasmodically. I squinted at the numbers. Six o'clock.

"Christ." It was time to get up, and I hadn't even realized I'd fallen asleep. Hadn't enjoyed the luxury of drifting off.

I levered myself out of bed and rolled my shoulders. In the past, this job would have been a piece of cake. I grabbed a change of clothes and headed to the showers.

The common bathroom was worse than I'd imagined. A single cracked mirror and narrow metal shelf were tacked above two rust-stained porcelain sinks. On the other side of a long wooden bench, a corroded shower head dripped into a drain in the sloped concrete floor. The loft was looking better and better.

Despite the dreary conditions, I felt human again after showering. I walked down the paved road, past barn eighteen and seventeen, and down the length of sixteen. Blue feed tubs hung face down along the exterior waist high wall, and hanging baskets, overflowing with yellow flowers I didn't recognize, decorated the roof overhang every twelve feet or so. I paused outside the entrance.

A wooden sign with "Kessler Racing Stable" carved into the grain was centered on the wall to my right. Someone had planted some shrubs and blue and yellow flowers in a neat, organized garden. Abby's work, I guessed.

I ran my fingers through my hair, which had already dried in the gradually diminishing heat, and walked into the shedrow.

The ninth race was uneventful in every respect. A maiden special weight for two-year-old fillies, the outcome of the race had been anyone's guess. In any case, Kessler hadn't expected to win, and he didn't.

I had overheard his instructions to his jockey, which were basically to keep out of trouble and let the filly settle into her job.

The filly had been bathed and cooled out. Her legs had been rubbed and wrapped, and she was now back in her stall, contentedly eating her hay. Karen, her groom, had already left for the night. Across the track, lights blazed in the grandstand, even though the crowd had long since departed.

I was sitting on an overturned bucket, wondering where best to set up for the night, when Kessler came out of his office. He flicked off the light and closed and locked the door behind him in one smooth, practiced motion.

He handed me an envelope. "Here's the information you asked for. I wrote down which horses have races in the next couple days, too, so you'll know who to focus on."

"Great."

He glanced at his watch. "Would you mind taking Abby home? Her car's in the shop, and I told her I'd give her a ride, but I forgot about a meeting with a potential client at nine, and I'll be late if I don't head out now."

"Sure."

"Thanks. I told her I was going to ask you." He glanced down the shedrow. "She'll be along any minute now."

We said goodnight, and I watched him slide behind the wheel of his gold Lincoln LS. The tires crunched over the stone dust, then Kessler turned onto the access road, and the car glided silently around the corner. Only after hours did anyone dare park between the barns. The car suited him, I thought as I rested my head against the wall and closed my eyes. So did the color.

I was contemplating the lucrativeness of racehorse training when I heard soft footsteps approaching. I opened my eyes.

Abby stopped in front of me and rested her hands on her hips. "Ready, then?"

Except for directions, which she gave in short, monosyllabic sentences, we drove to her house in silence. I pulled up alongside the curb, switched off the engine, and opened my door. When she didn't move to get out, I looked over at her.

She stared stonily out the windshield and said, "Where'd Dad find you?"

I let the door swing back against the frame, and the overhead light clicked off. "What do you mean?"

"How'd he find you?"

"I don't know what you mean. I applied for a job, and he hired me."

"We didn't need another hotwalker." She smoothed a few strands of hair off her forehead. "Though I have to admit, the day was easier all around with an extra person. But he never mentioned he was going to hire more help." She swiveled in her seat and looked straight at me.

Even in the dusky light, I could see the tightness in her jaw and tension in the way she held her shoulders.

"He always tells me stuff like that. Even though I'm just a foreman, I do most of the stuff an assistant trainer would do." She fiddled with the zipper on her fanny pack. "He hates Jeff. I figure he hired you so I'd...get interested in someone else."

"I doubt it," I said and tried to keep the surprise I felt out of my face and voice. "But if that's what he had in mind, he's out of luck."

Abby lifted her chin, and I realized that I'd insulted her.

"Eh…I didn't mean it like that. It's just that I already have a girlfriend."

"Oh."

When she put her hand on the door handle, I touched her arm. "You ought to have your keys ready before you get out."

Sensible advice, I knew, but ridiculous-sounding all the same. I'd been given loads of similar instruction in the past. Being cautious had become a habit.

"You've gotta be kidding." she said as she pushed open the door with exaggeration and stepped onto the sidewalk.

Abby lived in a quiet residential neighborhood not far from the main drag. Red brick townhouses lined both sides of the street, but they were staggered in such a way that their facades weren't flush with each other. The overall effect created an unexpected air of individuality.

As I stepped onto the curb, Abby was halfway down the sidewalk leading to a corner unit. The front porch was recessed from its neighbor, dark and quiet. She hadn't left on any lights. Not even the porch light. The lawn had been mown recently, the sidewalks edged, the gardens tidy. The only thing out of place was a small boat trailer that someone had tucked half under the branches of an overgrown hedge that butted up against the neighboring house.

Thinking that keeping the boss's daughter safe was a number one priority, and knowing she'd resent even the idea of it, I followed her down the sidewalk.

Abby stepped onto the front porch, and as she bowed her head and fumbled in her pack, I watched in disbelief as two dark figures crept out from the bushes with hunched shoulders and maliciousness clearly their intent.

Chapter 6

I couldn't move fast enough. I ran toward them and screamed at Abby to get in the house, fearful of them. Fearful of what they might do. Instead, she turned toward me, and it seemed as if she were moving in slow motion.

The questioning look on her face turned to one of disbelief as the man nearer to her leapt onto the porch in one quick stride. I hit the one on the sidewalk with a flying tackle that took both of us crashing into a tangle of rosebushes. He took the brunt of the fall full in the face and bellowed with rage. And pain.

I shoved him deeper into the branches, then lunged toward the porch.

I pulled my knife out and unfolded the blade.

He held Abby in front of him like a shield. His left arm was clenched around her throat, and I noticed for the first time that he had a nylon stocking pulled down over his face. He glared at me through the fabric, his eyes black and hateful.

Abby was on tiptoe, her back arched, her hands gripping his arm as she tried to keep from being lifted off her feet. She wasn't saying anything, wasn't yelling, and it suddenly occurred to me that she couldn't.

"Let her go," I yelled.

His gaze shifted to a spot above my head.

Instinctively, I pivoted and raised my arm.

A chain arced through the air, its links glinting in the dark. It glanced off my forearm and crashed into my shoulder with such force, my breath was knocked out of my lungs. I moaned in surprise and almost went down to my knees.

As the chain slid off, I latched onto it with my left hand. More than anything, I did not want him using it again. Not if I could help it.

I jerked him toward me and jammed the point of my knife under his chin. His eyes widened in surprise. His face had suffered significant damage from the rosebushes, and I hoped he was thinking of the further damage I might inflict with my knife.

He swallowed hard. His Adam's apple jerked upward, and the nylon stretched across his nose and mouth moved spasmodically with each ragged breath.

I pressed the point of the blade deeper into his flesh. "Tell your friend to let her go."

He glanced over his shoulder toward his buddy.

In the end, it was Abby's neighbor who helped him make up his mind when a light switched on above our heads, and a window creaked opened.

"You, there. What are you doing? I'm calling the police."

Her high-pitched voice and threat were enough to unnerve my guy completely. He let go of the chain and bolted.

I turned back to the guy who held Abby. "Let her go." I said it slowly, trying to put as much weight into my voice as possible.

He glanced after his partner, then looked steadily at me, and it was his calmness that I found most disturbing. "I'll get you," he said quietly. No threats screamed in anger, no emotion. More a statement of fact. He shoved Abby, and she slammed into me as he vaulted the banister and cut across the front yard.

I closed my eyes and gritted my teeth and listened to the old woman as she anxiously called to Abby. Listened while Abby convinced her that she was okay, and that, no, I wasn't one of the thugs. I straightened and looked despondently at my knife, lying where I'd dropped it, and at the length of deadly chain.

When the old woman reluctantly closed her window, Abby touched my arm. Her hand was trembling. "You okay?"

I nodded.

She peered at my face. "No, you're not. You're hurt." She scanned the porch. "My purse. He took my purse. I don't have my keys." Her voice cracked.

Abby yanked open the screen door and tried the doorknob. It was locked. "Oh, God." She leaned on the doorjamb.

"You won't want to stay here tonight, anyway," I said but couldn't get enough breath behind the words.

"Oh, wait a minute. There's a key…" She let the screen door slam and strode down the porch with her head held high, her back unnaturally straight, her neck stretched with tension.

She tilted over a flowerpot full of sick-looking geraniums, slid the toe of her boot beneath the pot, and nudged a key into the open.

"Thank God." She clutched the key to her chest and hurried back to the door.

Her voice, her actions, even her posture, were animated. An attempt to maintain composure, I supposed, and I decided it took a lot to rattle Abigail Kessler.

She pushed open the door and switched on the lights inside and out. I followed her into the living room. When she went into the kitchen to call the police, I perched on the sofa's armrest and wiped my forehead with the back of my hand. As I steadied my breathing, I could feel the rhythm of my pulse strumming through my veins.

After the attention to detail evident at the barn, Abby's home wasn't what I'd expected. The living room was cluttered with mismatched furniture, all of it old and worn, just this side of a landfill. The sofa I was sitting on was a patriotic red, white, and blue plaid, and I couldn't imagine it looking any better new. Across the room, under the bay window, a bile-colored velvet sofa sagged heavily in the middle. Other assorted armchairs and miscellaneous junk were crammed into the corners.

Abby caught me looking. "I have three roommates. We all brought furniture from where we lived before. None of us make much so," she gestured around the room, "this is it."

"I didn't say anything."

"No, but…" She shrugged, then crossed the room and sat on the sofa under the bay window. We waited in silence until the sound of a vehicle moving slowly down the street drifted through the screen.

"The police." Abby jumped up and ran to the front door.

A cruiser glided to the curb as she pushed open the door and stepped outside. I followed more slowly. A second patrol car idled down the road from the opposite direction.

Abby took the lead and gave the officer a statement but hesitated over the descriptions.

"The guy who had Abby," I said, "was white, six-two or -three, medium build but muscular. He weighed around one-ninety. They both had nylons pulled over their heads, so I couldn't tell much about his face except that he has a long, thin nose and short hair. He was wearing a navy or black tee shirt, black jeans, black sneakers. Couldn't tell his age."

"His arms were hairy," Abby mumbled. The officer and I both looked at her, he calmly, me with jolting surprise.

She was leaning against the brick wall, hugging herself. Her face looked colorless in the glare of the porch light.

The officer turned back to me, his pen poised. I continued, all the while watching my sister. "The guy who had the chain…" I thought back and saw his eyes clearly in my memory, as if he were standing before me. "He was five-ten or -eleven, two hundred pounds. Short hair. He was wearing blue jeans, a white muscle shirt with a Nike logo on the front, and white sneakers with black diagonal stripes on the side."

"White?"

"Yeah. Oh, and his face is scratched and bleeding."

He looked up from his notepad, and I explained about the rosebush.

"You didn't see a vehicle?" He looked from me to Abby.

We both shook our heads.

The officer keyed his mike and broadcasted their descriptions, then continued with our statements while the other cop took off, presumably to search for the bad guys. We went back inside, and even though the room was well lit, he unhooked his flashlight and examined the welts on my arm.

"Let's see your back."

I hesitated.

Abby looked up from the plaid sofa where she had curled into a tight ball. Even though it was hotter than hell, she'd wrapped a navy afghan around her shoulders. She must have sensed my unease, because she announced that she had to use the bathroom and went upstairs with the afghan trailing behind her.

I tugged my shirt out of my jeans and started to raise my arms. Pain stabbed across my upper back. I sucked in some air. My muscles felt weak and unresponsive, as if they had seized up altogether.

"You've got blood on your shirt." He pulled a pair of blue latex gloves out of a back pocket. "The chain must have broken skin."

"Um."

He lifted the back of my shirt. "When were you shot?"

"Eight weeks ago," I said and wondered if he thought I was some kind of punk. "It happened where I work."

He let the fabric fall back into place. "Do you want the medics to have a look?"

I turned to face him and shook my head. "Nothing's broken."

"Yeah, but—"

"I can't afford it," I said bluntly.

He retrieved a Polaroid camera from his cruiser, photographed my injuries, and had me sign a statement.

Abby asked about fingerprints, but the porch railing was too rough to yield prints, and the chain wasn't any good, either. When he was ready to leave, I thanked him and found Abby in the kitchen, leaving a shaky message on her father's answering machine. A message that would galvanize Kessler into action or, at the very least, high anxiety.

When she hung up and turned toward me, I saw that she was trembling. "Thanks." She swallowed. "Thanks for...coming to the rescue." She smiled weakly. "I didn't even realize you were following me."

"Father's orders," I said.

"Hmm." She wrapped the afghan tighter round her shoulders. "Well, thanks anyway. I'll be all right, now," she added, indirectly giving me permission to leave.

"Abby," I said. "You don't want to stay here tonight."

"Why?"

I hesitated. "They have your keys."

She tensed and reflexively looked toward the kitchen door. "Oh, God." She pressed a hand over her mouth. "You're right."

"Where are your roommates?"

"Working, vacation, boyfriend's apartments. We never know who's going to be home from one minute to the next."

"How about your father's house? I can drop you there."

"Okay." She hurried toward the living room as if the demons were poised to burst into the house that very second.

I glanced at the back door myself, unable to shake an underlying feeling of foreboding. Nothing there but uninformative squares of glass, the night pressing blackly against the panes. I rubbed a hand across my face, then left a note of warning for the roommates.

Abby was waiting by the front door. She had replaced the afghan with a hooded sweatshirt. Her arms were wrapped around her waist, and she was bouncing her leg, reminding me of a little kid who'd waited too long to use the bathroom.

"Great. Let's get out—"

Behind us, the phone rang.

"Dad!" She ran back into the kitchen.

I leaned against the wall by the front door and closed my eyes. I was wondering how I was going to get through the next twenty-four hours when I realized I could no longer hear Abby's voice, only an unnatural, lengthening silence. As I pushed off the wall, I heard something clatter on the kitchen floor. I sprinted around the corner.

Abby was standing by the counter, staring at the phone lying at her feet, and she was crying. As I skidded to a stop, she looked up at me with wide, unblinking eyes.

I glanced around the empty room, glanced at the window, at the door firmly shut. "What's wrong?"

"It was them."

"What?"

"Them!" she screamed. "He said they'd come back if Dad didn't do what they wanted next time. What did he mean by that?" she asked, not expecting an answer. Not from me, anyway.

She shuddered. "He said I wouldn't like it if they did, or maybe I would, depending on what kind of girl I am."

Abby spun around, ran across the mottled yellow linoleum, and pushed against a door in the far corner of the room. She slammed and locked the door, and in a minute, I heard the toilet flush.

"Christ." I picked the phone off the floor, hung it up, and crossed the room. "Abby, you okay?"

No answer.

Eventually the doorknob rattled and she stepped back into the kitchen.

I touched her arm. "Do you have a key to your dad's house?"

She shook her head. "No. The only one I had was on my key chain. It's almost eleven, though. He'll be home soon." She looked at the phone hanging innocently on the kitchen wall. "Could you try his number again? Maybe he's home and just hasn't checked his messages yet."

I made the call and listened to Kessler's disembodied voice on his answering machine, inviting me to leave a message. "He's not home," I said and hung up. "What about his cell phone?"

She shook her head. "If he's still with a client, I don't want to interrupt them." She bit her lower lip and gathered her too-big sweatshirt more tightly round her shoulders. "Let's leave, anyway. We can wait in the parking lot if we have to."

She looked forlorn and devastatingly vulnerable, and I unexpectedly needed to put my arms around her, to protect her. Keep her safe. Instead, I escorted her out the door and across the empty street. In fact, to her, I was just a stranger, not a brother, not a friend, and I suddenly felt guilty about the deception. It had been a mistake not to tell her.

I slid behind the wheel and, without thinking, leaned normally against the backrest. There was nothing normal about the reaction I got. I grimaced and sat up straighter. It would be awhile before I'd be sleeping on my back.

Abby directed me through a maze of deserted side streets until we were on the main drag, heading east toward the track. She told me to get in the right lane. A white Corvette, which had been rapidly closing the distance between us on the otherwise empty street, passed on the right. I changed lanes and saw that Abby had turned in her seat and was watching me.

"What do you think he meant about Dad doing what he said?"

"I don't know. You'll have to ask your father." I glanced at the speedometer and let my foot off the gas a bit. "Abby?"

"Hmm?"

"When the detective does his follow-up interview, you ought to tell him about the phone call." In my peripheral vision, I saw her nod.

"After I talk to Dad first." She looked down at her hands. "I don't know what they were talking about, but I don't want to say something that will get him in trouble."

I glanced at her. She looked close to tears, and I imagined this was the first time she'd given any consideration to the fact that everything wasn't as simple and straightforward as it appeared. That there were hardships and struggles she could only guess at and more to her father's job than she'd ever contemplated, and I admired her all the more for her concern.

Up ahead, a streetlight flashed red, a late-night concession to diminished traffic. I took my foot off the gas and coasted to a stop.

"He had a hard-on," Abby said.

I twisted around and stared at her. She clutched the sleeves of her sweatshirt, jammed her fists against her thighs, and began to sob.

"What did you say?"

"The man who grabbed me." She shuddered. "I could feel it. And what he said on the phone...the way he said it, I know he'd do it." She sniffed and wiped the heavy cotton sleeve under her nose.

"Abby, I'm so sorry."

Behind us, someone laid on his horn, and we both jumped. We continued the journey in near silence, Abby giving directions where needed, and what I mostly wanted was to have that moment in time over again. I would have caught him and pounded him into the ground, the goddamned pervert.

"Turn here," Abby said.

I braked hard and pulled into a modern-looking apartment complex. Not at all what I had expected. I had envisioned Kessler living in a large, comfortable home, not an apartment.

We both saw the sleek, golden sedan slip into a spot at the far end of the lot.

"Dad!" Abby unbuckled her seat belt and reached for the door handle with tension and relief jumbled together in ragged movements and growing impatience.

I accelerated across the pavement and jerked the truck to a stop alongside the Lincoln's back bumper as Kessler climbed from behind the wheel. He turned toward us, and his expression changed to one of concern when he saw Abby bounding out of the truck. She wrapped her arms around his waist and buried her head against his neck. He put his arms around her and looked over her head at me, questioning.

Abby said something, then, because he bent his head down to hers and smoothed a hand through her hair. From the racking of her shoulders, I imagined she was crying. Kessler started to step toward me, bringing Abby along with him, but she clutched at him and shook her head. He looked back at me and signaled that I could go.

Although Kessler's apartment was minutes from the track, it was close to one before I drove past the guard post. I had detoured by way of the loft and nearly gave in to the temptation of my bed with its clean sheets and soft pillow. Instead, I picked up what little pain medication I had left from the hospital and headed back.

I parked by the perimeter fence and strolled down the length of barn sixteen. Nothing looked suspicious or out of place, so I detoured once again, this time for the soda machine below my living quarters. I bought a Coke, swallowed two pills, and headed back to the barn, knowing that in another twenty minutes, I wouldn't be feeling anything at all.

I slipped into the stall belonging to Kessler's next runner, a horse named Russian Roulette, barn name Ruskie. One of Gordi's. I'd seen him in the sand pen Monday morning. He pricked his ears and moved toward me. His hooves rustled through the straw as he stepped from the deeper shadows at the back of the stall. I ran my hand down his face, and he sniffed my palm, looking for a treat I hadn't thought to bring.

"Sorry, boy. I don't have anything," I said and thought how easy it would be to walk in there and feed him a treat laced with drugs. Simple.

I scratched between his massive jawbones, and he tilted his head in appreciation. When I grew tired of it, apparently long before he did, he nudged me with his big chestnut head.

He left me alone for the next two hours, but around three-thirty, he came over to where I sat in the corner of the stall and nuzzled the top of my head. I had been sitting in the straw with my legs drawn up, arms wrapped around my shins, head on my knees, trying to stay awake. I pushed him away, and in a minute or so, he came back. He lowered his head and sniffed. His hot breath tickled my ear and slid across my neck, sending a chill down my spine.

"All right. All right, already."

It was time to head out, anyway. I hadn't yet come up with a story to explain away my presence if I got caught in his stall. Not at that time in the morning. Trying to guard the damaged muscles in my shoulder, I rose stiffly to my feet and walked over to the door.

The electric fan that hung above the doorway, as they hung in every stall in the barn, blocked out way too much noise, but I couldn't think of a solution. Maybe I could find a better place to hide. But where? The hayloft wasn't practical. In the stall, they'd just about have to step over me.

I left Ruskie's stall and noticed that all of the horses had grown restive. Nothing wrong with their clocks. Nothing at all.

Outside the office, I leaned against the wall and wondered what Kessler would do next, considering the attack on his daughter, when a fat little terrier bounded around the corner at high speed. He bounced to a stop, tentatively wagged his tail, then trotted over to me.

I crouched down and scratched him behind his ears. "Who do you belong to? Huh, boy?"

His tail wagged faster.

Kessler and Abby walked into the barn. Both looked as if they hadn't slept. Abby was still wearing her sweatshirt, although to my mind the air was uncomfortably warm, boding ill for the coming day.

"Steve." Kessler switched on the lights, and every horse in the barn reacted by nickering or pawing or otherwise expressing eagerness to be fed. He didn't seem to notice.

I stood up, much to the terrier's disgust. "Sir?"

"I can't thank you enough for what you did."

I glanced at Abby. She had dropped her gaze and was staring at the ground between us, uncomfortable, I expected, with the shared memory. "No problem...Mr. K," I added, belatedly remembering how his crew addressed him.

A slight grin twitched the corner of his mouth. We both needed to work at this cloak and dagger stuff.

"All the same," he said. "I'm indebted to you. Abby, too."

Abby glanced at me, then said to her father, "I'm gonna get started, Dad."

She walked unenthusiastically down the shedrow, unhooking feed tubs and dropping them on the ground in front of each stall, her every move watched by intent equine eyes.

I whispered, "How's she doing?"

"I don't know. It really shook her up." He looked back toward his daughter, suddenly angry. "I can't believe they've stooped so low, the goddamn bastards. Going after Abby like that. I swear to God, if I find out who they are, they'll regret it for the rest of their lives." His hands were clenched into fists, though I doubted he was aware of it.

"I wanted her to take a break, stay away for awhile. A little vacation." Kessler's shoulders were stooped with tiredness, his eyes bloodshot. "We argued about it half the night, but she wouldn't hear of it. I couldn't even talk her into spending the morning at the apartment."

I looked toward the feed room.

"She's so damn headstrong," Kessler said.

Overhead lights blazed from the identical, evenly spaced stall doors, making the shedrow appear longer than it actually was. Abby balanced a jug of tonic on the feed cart's wide metal rim and scanned a clipboard before measuring out a second supplement. She dumped both into a feed tub that still sat on the ground outside a stall. A variety of pails hung from the sides of the cart, easily accessible. It was an efficient system, one I could use at Foxdale.

Use at Foxdale. The thought was at once disturbing yet welcomed.

"And how about you?"

"What?" I looked back at Kessler. Behind him, across the alley, the lights in barn seventeen snapped on, accompanied by the familiar whinnies and nickers of a bunch of hungry, anxious horses.

"Abby said one of them hit you…with a chain," he said, clearly disturbed, and I decided he was pretty much an idealist. Honest, hardworking, finding such behavior incomprehensible, and I doubted that Abby had told him everything.

"I'm okay," I said.

"You didn't look it when you stood up just now, and you've got a nasty bruise on your arm."

"I'll live."

He shook his head. "Take the morning off. Come back at six."

"It's not nec—"

"Yes it is. Come back later."

"Okay."

"And thanks," he said. "You have no idea how grateful I am. Whether or not you find any evidence of doping, after last night, you've earned every cent of that check."

Fourteen hours, I thought as I walked into the alley. Fourteen hours before he needed me back. I left the dreary little room to the cockroaches and went home to the loft. To a big breakfast, a clean shower, and a soft bed.

Chapter 7

When I returned to the track, I was on the mend. My shoulders had lost the deep cutting ache that had made every movement painful. The only disappointment of the day was that I hadn't gotten hold of Rachel. I'd called her office, and the nasal female voice on the other end of the line stated with boredom that she was at a seminar and couldn't be reached. In the afternoon, I called her parents' house and didn't get an answer. She was probably at Foxdale, as she rode her horse most days after work, but I hesitated calling there. Mrs. Hill would have answered, and she would have wanted to know when I was coming back.

I walked into Kessler's office.

He looked up from a pile of paperwork, then glanced at his watch. "Damn. Didn't realize it was so late." He laid his pen in the crease of an open folder, leaned back in his chair, and yawned. "Feeling better?"

"Ready for another night."

Kessler nodded.

The office was close, the heat and humidity nearly unbearable. An inefficient fan was balanced on the corner of a filing cabinet, doing little more than stirring the hot air.

Kessler waved his hand. "Sit down."

I angled the chair so I would be facing him and sat carefully on the hard plastic. Kessler's terrier walked over and nudged my hand. "Where's Abby?" I said.

"Out with Jeff. She seems all right. Getting back to work ended up being the best thing, I guess."

"Hmm." I shifted in my seat.

It struck me that Abby had known instinctively what Kessler hadn't. What I hadn't. That getting back to her usual routine, striving for a sense of normalcy, in fact, achieved it. What I wished I had known after I'd been shot. Going back to work and facing the memories head-on would have sped up the process of getting my life together. The longer I waited, the harder it became, so that now, I was to the point of not wanting to go back at all. The waiting had actually helped the memories take on a life of their own. But physically, I hadn't been able to go back right away. I'd been too busy trying to stay alive.

The terrier pressed against my leg, and his ribcage vibrated with his panting.

"Is she going to have the locks changed?" I said.

"I had it done this morning."

"Good."

He picked up his pen and absentmindedly turned it end over end, tapping the tip on the desk blotter with each rotation. "I still can't believe they went after her. Every time I think about it…I could just strangle them."

I dropped my arm over the edge of the armrest, and the dog came over and stood beneath my hand. I obliged and patted the top of his head.

"Thank God you were with her."

"Um. What about your apartment?" I said. "Since they took Abby's keys, they now have a way in, and I wouldn't put it past them to cause you more trouble, or worse."

Kessler stared at me blankly, the pen frozen in his hand. "Jesus," he muttered under his breath.

"And about last night. Because the barn was unprotected for several hours, I was wondering if there would have been obvious signs if Ruskie had been…tampered with?"

"They didn't." He tossed the pen on a stack of papers. "For one thing, they never called and told me to hold him back.

Anyway, when a horse is drugged and is just standing around in the stall, you can't really tell, but I'm confident they didn't get to him because he was sharp this morning. Juan had a hard time holding him back. If he'd been doped, he would've been sluggish."

"Juan?"

"His regular jockey, Juan Garcia."

"Oh."

"He's worked him most mornings for the last two months now, and that's another reason I think no one got to him. They don't know how good he is. No one expects him to win tomorrow but me," he grinned, "and Juan." Kessler leaned back in his chair and pulled his shirt away from his chest. "He's got a lot more horse under him than he had just two weeks ago."

I hadn't recognized Garcia during my first morning hotwalking, but I hadn't cooled out Ruskie, either. "Any particular reason why you're using Juan instead of Jeff?"

Kessler made a face. "Juan works all the horses at one point or another. Schooling them, getting used to them, evaluating them. In Ruskie's case, with all the improvement he's been making, I didn't trust Jeff to keep his mouth shut. His odds won't stay long if everyone knows how good he is. Even with all the precautions we've taken, it's hard to keep a secret around here. So don't slack off tonight. You still need to be vigilant."

I nodded. "Who owns him?"

"I do. Claimed him off John Greenfield last February. The horse was so high strung, he was losing all his races in the paddock. But he's got world-class breeding and the conformation to match. He has speed he hasn't even tapped yet.

"I've made concessions for him." Kessler gestured toward the access road. "The sand pen, for instance, and hand-grazing in the afternoon. I've adjusted and readjusted his diet. He's really blossoming, settling down. I don't think the clockers have made him, either." Kessler grinned mischievously. "We snuck in two fantastic works recently, when the track first opened, and it was so hazy and dark, the clockers had trouble identifying any of the horses. They didn't get his times, and I don't think anyone's picked up on his potential. That's what I'm counting on tomorrow." He dragged the sleeve of his shirt across his forehead. "I usually don't bet much, but tomorrow…"

I studied his face. His eyes glistened with the anticipation of victory, with confidence born from the knowledge that he'd done all he could. All the preparations and strategies, all the hard work and sweat. It was now up to the horse, and I saw, too, that part of the excitement was the rush one got from being in on a secret.

I said, "At dinner the other day, you said something that made me think you'd already tried to find out who's behind the dopings."

Kessler grunted. "I hired a PI firm from Baltimore. They didn't work out, and with the fee they charge, they were destroying my profit margin and then some. They put a guy here, undercover." He rolled his eyes at the memory. "Some geek. The guy didn't know horses. He was scared shitless. Afraid every time a horse did something unexpected which, as you know, is about every other second. Two horses got loose from him in one day, so I cut him loose." He smiled faintly at his little play on words. "It was a goddamn waste of time…and money."

"Did they use surveillance cameras?"

"Yeah. Infra-red, night-vision, whatever you call it. A motion detector with an audio alarm feature. The works. Nothing ever came of it, but then they weren't here all that long."

I leaned forward, peeled my shirt off my shoulders, and let it drop back down. With luck, the storm that was building in the west would wash some of the humidity from the air and cool things off. The temperature gauge that was nailed to the wall outside Kessler's office read ninety-eight. And that was in the shade.

"How'd they have it set up?" I asked.

"They had a camera at each end of the shedrow with a split-screen monitor here." He waved his hand toward the row of filing cabinets. "The guy sat at my desk, and the monitor would beep every time it picked up movement, so there was no chance he'd miss anything." Kessler paused, then added as an afterthought, "If he stayed awake."

"How noticeable were the cameras?"

"Well, they started off with pinhole cameras. They were recessed, see? They drilled right into the rafters, and the cameras were tiny. No one would have seen them, but the environment was too dusty. The lens got covered with dirt the first night. You couldn't make out anything on the monitor. So they replaced them with regular cameras. They were visible to anyone paying the least bit attention, but they handled the dust better."

"Any chance you could get them set up again?"

"Sure. Why?"

"The fans are too loud. Last night in Ruskie's stall, I wouldn't have known what was going on at the other end of the shedrow, and if someone sneaks up on me, I won't know until the last second."

"Not a very comforting thought, huh?"

"No. Not very."

"Okay, sure. I'll give them a call."

"And you'd have evidence if someone comes."

"I hope so. The picture was passable, definitely not great." He leaned back in his chair, and the terrier took it as an invitation. He jumped into Kessler's lap. "With the holiday and all, I doubt they'll be out until Monday at the earliest."

"That's fine."

"Speaking of the Fourth," Kessler said. "You probably didn't hear, but right after morning stables, we're having a cookout. Damn." Kessler looked down at the terrier. "It's too damn hot for this. Get down."

The dog ignored him.

"Come on, get off." Kessler jerked his head.

The terrier hopped to the floor, walked around the desk, and rested his head on my knee.

"Just ignore him," Kessler said as the dog worked his jowls and gazed at me expectantly. I pretended I didn't notice.

"Anyway, feel free to invite someone if you like."

"Okay," I said but didn't mean it.

I wouldn't bring Rachel within spitting distance of the track. I didn't want anyone to know who she was. Not her name. Nothing. The last time I'd gotten involved in something that had become dangerous, she'd almost become a target herself.

"What time's Ruskie's race tomorrow?" I said as the terrier gave up and sprawled out on the concrete with a sigh.

"He's running in the ninth. Since it's a holiday, the schedule's the same as it is on weekends. Post time's five-oh-five." Kessler looked thoughtfully across the desk at me. "With the cookout and the schedule change, you aren't going to have much time to sleep tomorrow afternoon. You ought to hold off coming in until late tomorrow night. Abby and I'll be here all afternoon, anyway."

I said flatly, "I want to see him run."

Kessler grinned. "You aren't getting hooked now, are you, Steve?"

"Nah, not me." But I could see that getting wrapped up in this world was easy enough. During the last two days, it seemed to me that everyone who worked on the backside lived and breathed it, the hopes and the dreams along with the shattering disappointments, until the work itself became a way of life, all consuming.

"Want me to put on a bet for you while I'm frontside?"

"Sure."

"How much?"

I tapped my fingers on the chair's armrest and figured out how much cash I had left. Yesterday, I'd been too tired and sore to mess with going to the bank to cash Kessler's check.

I pulled out a thin wad of folded bills, damp like everything else with the humidity, peeled off two twenties, and tossed them on the desk. "Forty'll do."

"To win?" he said, and I could see the humor in his eyes.

"Of course."

Kessler reached over and picked up the bills.

"This how you make all your money, Kessler?" someone said from the doorway. "'Cause you sure aren't training many winners right about now, are you?"

The dog jumped to his feet, and Kessler looked up, slightly startled, definitely annoyed, and said nothing.

I turned in my seat as the guy strolled into the office with his hands in his pockets.

He looked at me with cool, emotionless eyes and said, "Would you excuse us, please?"

When I looked back at Kessler, he nodded. I jammed the rest of my cash into my pocket, walked around the chair, and waited for the guy to move out of my way, which he did slowly and deliberately, watching me leave and making sure I knew it.

I strolled into the alley and leaned against the wall next to Abby's garden. There was something familiar about him. An underlying arrogance. But I didn't know him. He was tall and lean, with professionally styled black hair, going gray at the sides. He looked distinguished and gentlemanly, except for the hardness around his eyes.

Two minutes later, he strode out of the barn, took four or five steps, and stopped. He spun around. His instincts were highly tuned, as I was standing in the long, cool shadow of the barn where he couldn't easily see me. The muscles in his jaw tightened, but other than that, he didn't react. He turned without speaking and headed toward his transportation, a golf cart with Washington Park's logo painted on the side in green and maroon. I watched him drive down the alley and turn right onto the smooth asphalt.

Back in the office, Kessler was on his feet, shuffling papers into untidy piles, closing folders and stacking them into heaps that, to my eye, looked as unstable as the storm clouds building in the west. The terrier was on his feet, as well. His tail wagged furiously as he gazed up at his master with anticipation.

"Who was that?"

Kessler looked up from his desk. "Dennis Hurp, Thoroughbred Racing Protective Bureau, and a major-league asshole."

Anybody, I thought, could see that, but I said, "In what way?"

Kessler shrugged. "The guy thinks he's Clint Eastwood, and everybody's guilty until proven innocent. He probably couldn't make it as a real cop and ended up working here, instead." He ran his fingers through his hair. "Anyway, the post-race blood work on Icedancer came back negative."

"Oh."

He looked down at the terrier and jerked his head. "Come on, Runt."

The dog wriggled with excitement, his nails clicking the concrete. Kessler turned off the fan and glanced around the office. When he pulled his keys out of his pocket, the dog shot through the doorway like a cork from a shaken bottle of Dom Perignon.

"How'd Runt get his name?"

Kessler shrugged. "Just started calling him that. The barn next to ours at Gulfstream cleared out and left him behind. I couldn't see just leaving him to starve, so he came with us."

"Hmm." I stepped into the aisle and waited while Kessler closed and locked the door. "Besides the PI firm, have you done anything else to find out who's been stopping your horses?"

He shook his head. "Oh, yeah. Only nothing came of it. An old buddy of mine looked into it before I got desperate enough to hire that PI firm."

"Can I talk to him, ask him what he did?"

"'Fraid not," Kessler said. "'Cause he's dead."

I felt like the ground had just opened up beneath my feet.

"Shit, Steve, nothing like that," he added, undoubtedly seeing the color drain from my face. "He died of a heart attack. What'd you think, that he got killed?"

"Something like that."

Kessler shook his head. "Even after what happened last night, I can't believe anyone would actually kill over this. Nobody's that crazy."

"You're talking about a substantial amount of money, aren't you?"

"Well, yeah."

"Some people kill for a lot less."

Kessler shook his head. "How'd you get so cynical?"

"Practice." I grinned, but it didn't feel right.

I piled some extra straw in the corner of Ruskie's stall and settled into position for the night, thinking uncomfortable thoughts. The man was looking into the dopings, and he died. So what? Nobody could induce a heart attack, could they? No, not without some very specific knowledge. It was simply a coincidence, and I was being paranoid. Paranoid and cynical, two qualities that weren't necessarily detrimental in the sleuthing business.

The sleuthing business. I could hardly believe I'd gotten myself into this so soon after Foxdale, and when Rachel had listened to my plans, she'd been dumbfounded, then angry. "Why don't you just come back to work?" she'd wanted to know. But Kessler wasn't at Foxdale. Working at the track, I had been handed a unique opportunity to learn about him. In a sense, I'd been given a window into another world, for the backside was indeed a world unto itself, separated as much by the ten-foot-high chain-link fence that surrounded the place as by the uniqueness of the lifestyle inherent to the job. The long, hard hours, the sacrifices and dedication, the plans and the schemes, the underlying current of excitement. All were as tangible as the horses themselves.

I rubbed my face, leaned against the wall's wooden planks, and wondered if I would be able to stay awake through the long, boring hours. Last night had been easy by comparison.

Well before the official beginning of the Fourth of July, nature got a head start with fireworks of her own. I heard the thunder long before the storm hit. When the rain finally came, starting slowly, with widely spaced, huge drops, I left Ruskie's stall and stood in the aisle.

The rain came harder, then. It pelted the barn roof and poured off the eaves in a solid wall of water. The runoff flooded the gully between the barns, carrying wisps of straw and debris along in the current. I watched lightning streak across the sky and felt the rain against my skin as the wind changed direction and pushed a cooling breeze through the doorway.

Other than the storm, the night was uneventful. By nine o'clock the next morning, the coolness of the evening before was a long forgotten memory as the heat and humidity skyrocketed. I was walking my fourth horse of the day, and my clothes and hair were soaked with sweat.

I was halfway down the shedrow with horse number four, when Gordi stuck his head out of a stall. "Hold up, Steve."

I stopped and called out the required ho back as Gordi cut in front of us. He casually ran his hand across the filly's chest. She gnashed her teeth.

Gordi had good reflexes. He jerked his arm out of range and grinned. "She loves it when I touch her there. Just like a woman, huh, Steve?" He turned and saw that Abby had caught his comment.

She put her hands on her hips and glared at him. "Boys."

I cleared my throat to keep from laughing and received a glare equal to, if not greater than, Gordi's. As Abby turned away, he raised his eyebrows and mouthed "boys?" and I almost choked.

Abby brushed against me as she stepped over a pile of dirty leg wraps and said over her shoulder, "Gordi, you wouldn't know what to do with a real woman."

Gordi hooted and slapped his leg, and the chestnut filly flattened her ears. He cleared his throat. "Put her up, Steve. You don't need to hold her, though, 'cause I gotta scrounge up some clean leg wraps."

I led the filly into her freshly bedded stall, hooked up the stall guard, slipped the chain shank off her halter, and gave her a departing pat on the neck. She didn't like that, either.

As I ducked beneath the stall guard, Marcus, one of Kessler's hotwalkers, stepped in front of the doorway, and I nearly lost my balance trying to straighten up. He spread his legs and folded his meaty arms above his fat beer belly. His undershirt was dingy and gray, and the fabric was stretched so tightly, it was almost transparent.

"Christ, Marcus, move outta the way." He had a habit of being in the way. It went along with his habit of being slow, unhelpful, and generally scornful of everyone around him.

"What'ja do to keep your job, Blondie, suck up to the boss?"

My shoulders tensed. "Screw you, Marcus."

I tried to sidestep him, but he moved with me. I stopped and waited. Waited for him to move, to get tired of it. I wasn't going to put my hands on him, not if I could help it, especially since that was what he wanted most.

He didn't move, and I couldn't. I waited. Behind him, Sting led a bay down the aisle, oblivious to the stand-off.

A bead of sweat trickled down Marcus's bloated face, laying an irregular track through the stubble on his cheeks. His eyes appeared recessed, dwarfed by his massive face, and their yellow color confirmed the rumors that he drank himself into a stupor most nights.

"Missin' your second day a work like that, your ass'd be fried if you was a nigger."

I gritted my teeth, looked at his face and the anger within, and held my tongue.

"Ain't that right, Blondie?"

I knocked against his shoulder as I squeezed around him and felt his gaze on my back. Outside, I leaned against the wall. The coolness within the concrete block seeped through my shirt as I worked to slow my breathing.

I didn't know much about Kessler, but I was sure Marcus was at least half right. The barn couldn't function with employees showing up when they felt like it. Under different circumstances, I would have fully expected to have been fired, no matter my skin color.

As I waited for my next horse, I wondered what to do about Marcus. What looked like developing into a feud of sorts wasn't an option, unless I could somehow use it to advantage. Maybe developing a reputation as a hard-ass would attract attention from the doping ring.

I tilted my head back and closed my eyes. What was I thinking? Kessler would never put up with a lousy employee. Abby definitely wouldn't. I smiled at the image of Abby facing off with someone like Marcus. She would have laid into him so hard, he wouldn't have known which way was up. And he knew it, too. He had been careful to express his opinion when no one was watching.

I walked over to the spigot and turned it on. I doubled over, cupped my hands beneath the stream of water, and rinsed the sweat off my face.

Someone walked behind me.

"Steve, bath time's over. Your next horse is here." Abby's voice, cool and serious with a trace of sarcasm, or maybe it was just my imagination.

She ran a tight ship. You didn't even have time to piss. The guys back at Foxdale didn't know how good they had it. I tightened the faucet until it stopped dripping. That was sarcasm, all right. My next horse was Ace, Abby's baptism by fire, part two, no matter that I'd saved her ass.

The exercise rider, a different one from the previous morning, unbuckled his chin strap and dropped the reins. Someone had taken a pair of scissors to his shirt. The sleeves, neck line, and at least twelve inches of material around the waist had been chopped off, forming ragged gaping holes, and I wondered why he had bothered with it in the first place. He smiled down at Abby as he swung his leg forward over the horse's withers and slid to the ground. From the way she gazed into his eyes, my bet was on his being the stuck-up, money-grubbing Jeff Truitt.

Normally the horses were ridden right into the barn, a practice that was frowned upon at Foxdale, but apparently, Jeff wasn't compelled to do it like everyone else. I walked out to meet them.

"How'd he go?" Abby asked as she slipped the reins over Ace's head.

Truitt pulled off his helmet and ran his fingers through curly black hair wet with sweat. "Good. Thanks to this fucking heat, he actually gave me a decent work for a change," he looked from her to me without missing a beat, "instead of fartin' around and fighting me every step of the way."

Abby held out the reins for me and, keeping her gaze on my face, said, "Jeff, this is Steve."

"Hey, man, thanks for helping Abby the other night." Truitt held out his hand, and contrary to his words, there was little friendliness in his pale gray eyes.

Mindful of Ace's teeth, I switched the reins to my left hand and shook his hand.

"I owe you one," Truitt said. "Wish I'd been there. I would've beat the crap out of them, the goddamn bastards."

I glanced at Abby and saw she was watching me, checking for a reaction I supposed, and I wondered what she thought of her boyfriend's bravado. It was easy enough, standing there in relative safety, to imagine all the brave things one might do when faced with danger. I'd done it myself, but the reality was quite different.

Working with horses was inherently dangerous, but that danger was easy to deal with, unexpected and accidental, not calculated and malicious. Not deliberate.

"One thing's for sure," Jeff continued, "they'd be locked up in a goddamned cell where they belong, not out on the street."

"Oh, come on, Jeff," Abby said. "You have no idea what it was like. It wasn't that simple." Abby absentmindedly stroked Ace's face, then paused and looked at me. "How's your shoulder, anyway?"

"Fine." I glanced at Truitt, saw the frustration in his eyes, and decided it was time to leave.

I led Ace into the barn and found Jay in the horse's stall with his back to the door. He was using a broom to knock down the cobwebs that had formed between the joists.

"Can I bring him in?" I said.

With the broom still pointed toward the ceiling, he glanced over his shoulder. He took one last swipe down the back wall. "Yeah, bring 'im in, and mind the door." Ace had a habit of bolting through tight spaces.

I guided Ace into the stall without incident and held him. "What's this horse's problem, anyway?" I said.

For answer, Jay shrugged. As far as I could tell, he wasn't necessarily unfriendly. He just didn't talk much. He was quick and efficient, wasting as little time as he did words, and instinctively, I liked him.

According to the scribbled, borderline illegible notes Kessler had given me the other day, once Jay was told what was expected of him, he required zero supervision. He never complained, which Kessler thought unusual, and was always polite to Abby. He knew his job inside out, despite the fact that he had been away from the track for seven and a half years. What he had done for work in the interim was anyone's guess, and that did bother me.

Jay unbuckled Ace's girth. "Abby pissed I weren't out there to get 'im?"

"Not that I noticed."

He shot me a quick glance, then nodded as if reaching a decision of some sort. "Good."

Chapter 8

After Ace's bath, I led the gelding into the barn and started the tedious job of cooling him out. By our fifth lap, it was so damn hot, my sweat-soaked clothes hung heavily on my body, and I wished I had worn a shirt with sleeves, if only to use them to wipe the sting out of my eyes. The only plus, as far as the heat was concerned, was that Ace was on his best behavior. He'd only tried to nail me once, right after we started on our first circuit down the sawdust and loam path. So far, he hadn't even bothered with the fake shying he liked to do in the corners.

There was a noticeable increase in the level of activity on Kessler's side of the barn, which probably had something to do with the mouth-watering aroma of grilled chicken carried on a trail of mesquite smoke.

Two wagons from Corridor Catering had parked alongside the grassy verge by the perimeter fence a half hour earlier, and the crew, wearing immaculate white hats and aprons over worn jeans and tee shirts, had unloaded a huge portable grill. I'd seen the menu lying on Kessler's desk the evening before. Chicken, hot dogs, hamburgers, corn on the cob, potato salad, watermelon, cake, all the makings of a traditional Fourth of July cookout.

I ran the palm of my hand down Ace's neck and checked his temperature. He was nowhere near being cool enough to go back to his stall. I decided to concentrate on what I knew about the people in barn sixteen, if only to keep my mind off the food and the ache that had spread across my shoulders since the pain medication had worn off.

Ace and I approached the entryway at the northwest corner of the barn as Karen stretched on tip-toe and wiped down a bridle that hung from a tack hook in the doorway. Cleaning tack was just about the last chore done in the morning, besides raking the aisle. She would be finished soon, and she wouldn't be back until the following day. She was enrolled in architectural courses at a local college and usually arranged to groom horses that weren't actively racing. Kessler obliged her as often as possible. Even still, she frequently showed up in the mornings, riding in on her bicycle, weather permitting, looking like death, bleary-eyed and pale.

At twenty-three, she lived in town with her mother, paid her own tuition, and kept mostly to herself. She had worked for Kessler for the last three years, and unless she was extremely clever at deception, I didn't consider her a suspect. Scraping together money for tuition might be motive enough to get wrapped up in a doping scam, but she wasn't on the backside long enough to get the job done. The more I thought about it, the more certain I was that whoever was behind the dopings lived at the track.

We rounded the corner by the open door to Kessler's office. Ace skittered forward halfheartedly, and I chuckled to myself. He had to put up some pretense of being tough. The oscillating fan blew across an empty desk. Runt was asleep, stretched out on the cool floor, oblivious to his surroundings.

As we passed the doorway to the tack room, Ace craned his neck at the sound of plastic rustling. Hector was doubled over, gathering together a disorganized pile of saddle cloths, leg wraps, and girth covers and stuffing them into a large plastic trash bag. It was his week for laundry duty. He glanced up as we walked by, but if he reacted, smiled, waved, grimaced at the prospect of the job that lay ahead, or any other kind of acknowledgment, I didn't see it as we had already moved out of his line of sight.

I knew very little about Hector. According to Kessler's notes, thirteen months ago, Hector had left California and headed east with his wife and two little girls in tow. And he had worked for Kessler ever since. He smiled a lot, nervously it seemed to me, and seemed perpetually worried that he might do something wrong, as if he had spent most of his life being hounded by some form of authority or other. He came to work with a harried expression on his face, did his job, and left immediately afterward. He never hung around and bullshitted like many of the employees who lived at the track, and his English was so heavily accented, I understood little of what he said.

Grooms made slightly more than hotwalkers and, based on my pay scale, making ends meet had to be difficult with a young family to care for. He had the motive, but he didn't strike me as the type.

So far, none of Kessler's employees struck me as the type. Well, I wouldn't have put it past Marcus with his angry-at-the-world attitude, but I didn't think he was smart enough, and alcoholic stupors didn't bode well for sneaking around at night, doping horses.

Next on my self-guided tour, as I tried to ignore the rumbling in my stomach, we passed David Reece's feed room, followed by his sparsely furnished office. He was a marginally successful trainer who rented seven stalls from Washington Park. Two were presently empty. A wiry, older man, bordering on emaciated, he got along with as little help as humanly possible. It was not unusual to see him circling the shedrow as he cooled out one of his horses.

Rumor had it that Larry McCormick, the other trainer on the east side of barn sixteen, who had gloated when his horse had beat out Kessler's on Monday afternoon, was taking over Reece's empty stalls.

Reece was outside, raking the sawdust that had been kicked into the alley by the constant parade of horses. As he bowed his head and concentrated on the task, his shoulder blades cut lines into the thin cotton of his shirt. His jeans hung loosely from his hips. As far as I could determine, his employees had left for the day. No catered picnic lunch for them, and I appreciated Kessler's management practices more and more.

Kessler dealt with his employees fairly and calmly. Unlike Mr. McCormick, whose loud voice was often heard over the clamor of a lot of people doing a difficult job, he treated them with respect. Hector probably thanked his lucky stars every night that he hadn't been hired by Larry McCormick.

As we turned the corner and started down the shedrow, leaving Reece and his rake behind, I heard McCormick before I saw him. True to form, he was yelling at one of his grooms. Ace's ears swiveled back and forth in irritation, and it suddenly occurred to me that he usually shied there. He wasn't doing it out of silliness or aggression but out of nervousness and fear. I wondered why I hadn't noticed the pattern before.

As we approached McCormick, he was carrying on about leg wraps not being done up right, and he didn't like how his groom had bedded the stall, either. She nodded and kept her gaze fixed on the floor. Although her back was to me, I was fairly certain she was sobbing. McCormick's other employees kept their heads down and tried to remain as inconspicuous as possible, only occasionally sneaking sidelong glances at what was, for them, an everyday occurrence.

Ace and I had almost passed McCormick when he looked up and caught me staring.

His scowl deepened. "What're you lookin' at?"

To answer or not? He wasn't my boss. I didn't owe him an answer. I certainly didn't owe him respect. However, attracting attention to myself was not part of the game plan, and not answering would do just that. All the same, I did not like him, and I'd had enough bad attitudes for one day.

I kept my mouth shut and looked straight ahead. Didn't meekly say "Nothing, sir."

As I walked past, McCormick's struggle to control his temper vibrated in the air between us.

I didn't look back.

By the time we reached the corner by his office, I was pissed. I wasn't going to do well with this sleuthing business if I kept drawing attention to myself. In little more than half an hour, I had managed to alienate myself twice. I was supposed to remain as invisible as possible. Fat chance. Not if I couldn't control *my* temper.

We passed McCormick's office, and the steady tremor of an overtaxed air-conditioner hummed faintly through the shut door. He kept it running day and night. Whenever he wasn't in the shedrow yelling at the help, he was shut in his office, cool and comfortable, not sweating at his desk under an inefficient fan, worrying that someone was going to get to his horses. Beyond the office, the door to McCormick's feed room was closed and double locked, but the tack room door had been left ajar.

As we left McCormick's side of the barn, Ace pricked his ears. Kessler's feed room was up next, and any activity within was cause for intent equine attention. Abby was in there, standing with her back to the aisle. A fifty-pound bag of carrots, slit down the middle, lay on the workbench along the back wall. She rhythmically fed carrots into an industrial-sized food processor, filling plastic tubs with the orange mash that would be added to the rations of finicky eaters. Bushel baskets of apples had been shoved against the side wall alongside bags of beet pulp, sacks of linseed meal, and fifty-pound bags of steamed, crimped oats stacked high on a wooden pallet. The shelving above the workbench overflowed with supplements.

I must have slowed down, because Ace stopped altogether, his attention riveted on the feed room. I jiggled his lead, and he lunged forward and almost ran into the alley before I got control of his head. He jackknifed around, his hind hooves scattering sawdust across the ground before he came to a stop, half in the barn, half out. His nostrils flared, and his ears periscoped back and forth, certain that some terrifying, horse-eating monster was going to sneak up on him.

You stupid son of a bitch, I thought as I stepped to his shoulder. He was beginning to believe his own line. If you looked for demons around every corner, you would eventually find them. Real or imagined.

I patted his neck and said, "Come on, ol' boy, time to get moving."

He lowered his head and exhaled. His soft black nostrils fluttered, sending a spray of vapor into the air. He took a tentative step forward, and I got him going in the right direction. He was a spoiled brat, and I hoped, for his sake, that one of these days he'd settle down and get his mind on his job.

I lifted my head and had a straight shot down the shedrow into Kessler's office. The stalls, identical as they were, were lined up on my left, and to my right, the waist-high wall stretched down the building's length with only one human-sized opening midway down the aisle.

Jay had peeked out of a stall at the sound of the commotion. When he saw that everything was under control, relatively speaking, he ducked back inside. I looked in as we passed. He was crouched in the straw, rubbing the left foreleg of a chestnut colt and whistling under his breath. Each of Kessler's grooms cared for four horses and attended to minute details far beyond grooming and mucking out.

Jay lived on the track, although I didn't know which unit. He didn't seem to have any friends, not on Kessler's crew, anyway. I had no idea what he did in his free time, of which there seemed to be a great deal. He got off at eleven and didn't need to be back in the barn until four the next morning, unless he was scheduled for afternoon feeding or had a runner. Come to think of it, I couldn't remember ever seeing him after hours. As much as I liked him, he looked like a good suspect.

Next down the aisle after Jay's four, we passed Karen's horses. They were settled in their stalls for the day with legs done up in bright blue bandages. Bulging hay nets hung outside each stall door, a practice that encouraged the horses to eat with their heads in the aisle so they would stay interested in their environment. With so many hours spent in their stalls, I had learned that keeping them from becoming bored was a number one priority.

Karen was nowhere in sight and was presumably biking her way
home in order to study or sleep. I yawned at the thought of bed
and noticed Ace eyeing the hay nets.

"Hey, bud, you still gotta cool out some more."

His ears flicked at the sound of my voice, and he tossed his
head, no doubt expressing disgust with me in particular and the
world in general. Endless grassy fields under a wide blue sky and
a herd of mares to go with it, this was not.

Next, we came to Trudy's four charges, and I almost didn't see
her. She was standing toward the back of the stall, polishing an
already gleaming coat with a soft brush in one hand and cotton
cloth in the other. A bay with a delicate, noble head. Icedancer.
Trudy was talking to the mare in a soft, sing-song voice. No way
could she be involved with the dopings. She loved her horses
and treated them like children.

Kessler had told me that he assigned her horses that were
timid and needed a quiet hand and voice. She fit the bill perfectly. Trudy, with her fine blond hair and delicate features, was,
by my estimation, as timid as the horses she cared for. What
she seemed to lack in herself she gave to them. I scratched her
off my list.

Ace and I passed Trudy's bunch, and I looked in on Hector's
horses. Up ahead, Sting led a gray filly into the barn, fresh from
her bath. He had caught the last hot of the day, something
everyone liked to avoid. He would still be cooling her out while
everyone but the horse's groom and Kessler packed up and went
home. I smiled to myself. Except for today. Today, everyone
would be heading to the picnic, getting first dibs on the food.

William J. Ray, eighteen, had dropped out of school in the
tenth grade. No wonder he liked being called Stingray. I could
just hear his mom calling, Billy Ray, where've you been? He had
walked hots for Kessler for five months. I knew very little about
him other than the fact that he was from Florida (where he may
or may not have gotten himself into trouble), lived in my housing
unit, and killed water bugs as a form of entertainment.

The other two hotwalkers, Marcus and Allen, were conspicuously absent. Outside, Hector had abandoned his laundry and was raking the sawdust that had spilled into the alley while Gordi rinsed out the bucket he had used to bathe the gray.

In the second to last stall, Kessler was holding Ruskie. A tall, thin man, wearing thick-framed black glasses and a blue lab coat, stood along the side wall with his arms crossed over his chest. He was studying the horse with concentration. Kessler's vet, I guessed and hoped nothing was wrong.

After ten more mind-numbing laps around the shedrow, Jay told me to put the gelding up. When I unclipped his lead and stepped out of his stall, Ace collapsed in the thick bed of straw, energetically rolled onto his back, and flailed his black legs in the air. He was a striking horse. Too bad his mind was screwed.

"Hey, Steve." Someone clapped me on the back.

I smiled at the sound of his voice and thought it would be too much if I was wrong about him, and he was involved in the dopings.

"Let's get some grub," Gordi said. "I'm starving."

"Me, too." I gestured toward Ace. "Doesn't he have to be done up?"

"Nah. Jay'll rub 'im down in a bit. The ornery pig can't wear bandages in front. He tears 'em off and chews on hisself if you try to do 'im up right."

We cut across the aisle. As we slipped through the narrow opening in the wall, Sting came around the corner with the gray.

"Man," Sting said. "You bastards better leave me somethin' to eat."

We grinned at him.

Sting had nothing to worry about. Platters stacked with chicken, hamburgers, and hot dogs weighed down the table, and the cook was arranging more on the grill with a pair of long-handled tongs. I stood in line behind Gordi.

Except for Karen and Hector, everyone had stayed for the free meal. Down at the far end of the table, Jeff wiped his fingers with a napkin as he leaned over and whispered in Abby's ear. She had been stirring her iced tea with concentration. She grinned and turned to face him, her hand idly holding the straw, the ice cubes still swirling in her glass. Jeff leaned closer. His curly black hair brushed against her blond bangs as he slid his hand across the small of her back. He said something else, and she giggled.

I looked beyond them and saw Kessler on the road, talking to an elderly man with yellowed gray hair. Maybe his problem with Jeff lay more with the thought of losing his daughter than with any moral deficit on Jeff's part. He would be struggling with the inevitable, that one day, in a sense, he would lose her to someone else. If Jeff had been around after the attack, whether Abby would have gone to her father or Jeff was anyone's guess. And Kessler must have known it, as well.

I turned back toward the picnic table and caught Jay watching me. He held my gaze as he unhurriedly laid a half-eaten drumstick on his plate. Then he picked up his fork and looked across the table at Allen and Trudy. Allen had swiveled around on the bench and was talking to Trudy while she gazed shyly at her plate. A breeze drifted through the branches of a nearby oak, and the dappled sunlight flitted across her blond hair and bare shoulders. She was holding an ear of corn between her fingers and seemed to be waiting for him to stop talking before she even thought about eating. No wonder she was so thin.

Gordi moved farther down the line. I picked up a plate, then glanced over my shoulder. The old man Kessler had been talking to stood behind me, clasping an empty plate with both hands and holding it to his chest. He grinned widely, and if he had ten teeth in his mouth, I would have been amazed. I nodded, then looked beyond him at Kessler, who promptly winked at me. I turned away from him and got busy filling my plate.

I sat next to Gordi and was thankful Marcus was at the other end of the table. Even as hungry as I was, he would have been enough to kill my appetite.

Gordi eyed my plate. "Whoa there, Steve. By chance you hungry?"

I leaned toward him and whispered, "Well, you know what Abby said. We're just boys, and growing boys gotta eat."

He snorted. "Boys. That girl don't know what she talkin' 'bout. We ain't no boys. Guess cause we ain't over the hill like ol' Jeff over there, she might be thinkin' we boys."

I glanced at Jeff. He didn't look over the hill to me.

"Now there's a guy that over the hill and then some."

I followed Gordi's gaze. The old man was shuffling across the street in carefully measured steps, his plate balanced in both hands. He turned into the alley, and a stray breeze lifted wisps of thin, yellow hair from his scalp.

"Guy gotta be ninety if he a day."

"Who is he?"

"Some ol' geezer be workin' here since before time. Use to be a pretty good trainer back in the fifties. Had a bunch a good horses. Won some big races, real regular like. Then he went an' lost his license. Got caught red-handed, hoppin' some horse with amphetamines."

When he didn't continue, I said, "Not much has changed, has it?" But he didn't pick it up. He was too busy wolfing down his food.

Kessler stopped at the far end of the table and rested his plate and drink on the checked tablecloth. When he didn't sit down, the various conversations died down one by one.

He cleared his throat. "I have these little dinners every now and then, in appreciation for your hard work, and I've got to say, we have an excellent crew right now. Every one of you has been doing a good job. I know it's hard work, especially in this heat, and it gets monotonous sometimes, but your attention to detail makes for a successful, winning team. We've done well this year, and with luck, we'll continue to do so. But all the luck in the world won't make one bit of difference without your hard work. Thank you."

"You're welcome, Mr. K." Allen.

"No problem." Jay.

A jumble of murmured responses.

Abby smiled at her father. A strand of blond hair fell forward across her cheek, and she smoothed it back behind her ear.

Gordi leaned toward me. "He the only guy round here gives a shit about us grunts."

Kessler picked up his plate and drink and headed back to the barn. After he was out of sight, Marcus got up and strolled toward the buffet table for seconds.

As he walked behind Gordi and me, he slowed and mumbled, "Can't eat with us niggers, though, can he?"

Gordi and I swiveled around on the bench.

Gordi said, "Man. Guy like you, ain't no surprise somebody came up with the word nigger."

I chuckled, and Marcus removed his fat-lidded squint from Gordi and leveled it on me. "White boys. They all stick together."

"Ain't no blamin' anybody, they don't wanna buddy up to you," Gordi said.

Marcus grunted and turned away from us.

I slid back around and rested my forearms on the table. I was halfway through a second plateful, when Sting crossed the road with a bounce in his stride.

He paused at the end of the table and said to Gordi, "Mr. K. said you need to check on that filly when you're done eatin', and if she's heated up again, you gotta walk her out yourself."

"What? You go complainin' to the boss?"

Sting rolled his eyes and said, "No-o-o," in a long, drawn out tone that sounded more like a whine than anything else. "I don't get paid near enough to do this shit while you fucks are stuffin' your faces. Plus, I got plans. I'm gonna meet Sandy, that little blonde works in barn twenty, and with any luck—"

Abby nudged him as she walked around the table, and he closed his mouth with a snap. She paused behind me, and I could hear the ice cubes in her drink clink gently against the glass.

"What kind of plans, Sting?" Abby said.

He grinned nastily. "Nothing I'd be tellin' the boss's daughter."

Gordi smothered a laugh with a mouthful of food.

"Steve," Abby said. "How's your back?"

I shifted in my seat and glanced at her. "Fine." I turned back around and stabbed a chunk of potato salad with my fork. Tried to change the subject. "When does Ruskie's race go off?"

"Back?" Gordi's eyebrows arched as he looked from Abby to me. "What's wrong with your back?"

I began to shake my head, to tell him nothing, but Abby cut me off.

"Steve gave me a ride home the other night, and we got jumped. They stole my purse and beat Steve with a chain."

"A chain?" Gordi mumbled.

While I mostly stared at my plate, Abby launched into a slightly edited account of the attack. Sting plopped his plate on the table and sat heavily on the bench across from us. Out of the corner of my eye, I saw Gordi staring with his mouth open, and it seemed to me that everyone around the table had become suddenly quiet, intent on hearing each morbid detail.

I glanced down the row of curious faces and cringed when I came to Jeff's. He balled a napkin in his fist, then threw it onto his plate, and I imagined he wished he was in my place. As far as I was concerned, he was welcome to it.

"You oughta hit Mr. K for a bonus," Sting said as he rotated an ear of corn in a puddle of melted butter on his plate. "Seein' that you're pullin' extra duty being Abby's personal bodyguard, and all. The man's gotta be grateful, savin' his daughter like that." He looked up at me and grinned, but the smile never made it to his eyes.

"You askin' me," Marcus said, "he oughta be glad he still got a job. Gets in a little scrap and missin' his second day a work like 'at."

"Ain't nobody askin' you, Marcus," Gordi said. He turned back to me. "Well, well, well. Our homeboy here's a real pistol. Guess it true what they say. You gotta watch the quiet ones."

Sting snorted at that, and I felt sick. So much for blending into the background.

I distractedly picked at my food and was thankful when the conversation drifted back, as it always did, to the ever-present topic of horses—which horse from our barn had the fastest workout that morning, which ones were sore or off their feed and practically had to be spoon fed, which one was the biggest pain in the ass to work with (my vote went to Ace). Predictably, the most pressing concern on everyone's mind was how Ruskie would handle the competition.

"I be puttin' half my pay packet on the ol' boy," Gordi said.

"What the hell makes you think he'll win?" Sting said. "Just 'cause you're rubbin' him don't mean he's gonna all the sudden transform into Secretariat."

I looked up at the sharpness in Sting's voice.

Gordi wiped his mouth with the back of his hand. "Yeah. Well the jocks better be wearin' their sunglasses, 'cause all they're gonna see is that shiny chestnut ass of his."

Sting leaned forward and looked down the table. "Whadaya think, Jeff?"

"How the hell should I know? I haven't worked him for a month."

Sting settled back into his seat.

"What's wrong?" I said. "Don't you want him to win?"

"Fuck off." He looked at Gordi. "You really think he'll do it?"

I sensed more than saw Gordi's nod, because I was watching Sting's face, and even though I didn't understand it, if anything, he looked worried.

When the talk eventually worked its way around to baseball, I drained my glass and stood up. Sweat trickled down the center of my back. How well Ruskie performed, in part, would depend on how he handled the damn heat.

"Leavin' already?" Gordi swiveled around on the bench, and I noticed his gaze flick over the bruising on my arm. "You ain't had any dessert, yet."

"I gotta make a phone call."

"Later, then," he said, and I saw the amusement in his eyes, "Mr. Bodyguard."

I nudged his shoulder. "Shut up, Gordi."

As I started across the grass, Sting made some lewd comment about guarding Abby's body that I only half caught, and Gordi's high-pitched laugh drowned out whatever anyone else might have said.

I walked down the road, past the rows of long, cement-block barns with tan roofs and faded green doors. Almost noon. Siesta time on the backside. Except for the low, throaty rumble of a trash truck idling in the next block of barns, it was quiet. Each afternoon they hauled away bins loaded with straw and manure and left empty ones in their place. Diesel fumes mingled with the strong odor of horse, and the air hung so heavily, nothing stirred.

I detoured across the lawn in front of the track kitchen and stopped in front of a pair of pay phones. The sounds of garbled voices and clattering dishes floated through the double doors as a steady stream of track employees pushed their way into the cafeteria-style lunchroom. I punched in the familiar number and listened as the phone rang once, twice, three times. By the tenth ring, I was preparing to hang up when I heard a breathless hello. Rachel's voice, sweet and welcomed.

"Hi."

"You still at the track?"

"Uh-huh."

When she didn't say anything, I said, "Rachel?"

"How's it going?" A distinct element of the Arctic in her voice.

"Good." I listened to her breathing and realized we were picking up where we'd left off. "I miss you," I said.

Another pause. "I miss you, too." And this time she sounded frustrated. "Do you really have to be doing this?"

"Just for a while longer."

She sighed. "What's it like there?"

I told her about the horses and the hours and the heat. I told her about Gordi and Stingray and Hector, but I didn't tell her about the bugs and the filthy bathroom, or that getting buzzed was the backside's pastime of choice. When an automated voice interrupted us, I fed more coins into the slot and told her about Kessler and what I thought of him, and how I liked him, and when I finished, she'd come around to her usual cheerful self.

"What are you doing for the Fourth?" I said.

"Besides missing you?"

I grinned. "Yeah, besides missing me."

"I'm going with Mom and Dad to a cookout at my aunt's house, and after that…"

I fiddled with the phone cord and pictured how I'd seen her last, naked, getting out of my bed, needing to get home so she wouldn't be late for work Monday morning. Monday. Only five days ago.

"Steve, are you listening?"

"Uh-huh," I mumbled and couldn't recall what she'd said last.

"And I wish I was going with you, instead."

"Me, too," I said, though I had no idea what I'd just agreed with.

"Fireworks over the lake would be so romantic."

"Yeah, it would."

"When do you think you'll be coming back to work? Marty says he's going to drag you back, kicking and screaming, if he has to, because he's fed up with doing your job. And he says Mrs. Hill's been irritable, but I have to admit, that isn't exactly how he put it."

"I'll bet it isn't."

"And some of the boarders have been complaining about how the farm's being run, though I don't see much wrong. Even Dave's grumpier than usual, according to Marty, that is." When I didn't answer right away, she said, "You're not planning on coming back, are you?"

"I didn't say that."

"No, but that's what you're thinking." Her voice trailed off, and after a moment, she said, "I understand that you want to know more about your…father, but you don't have to work for him to do it, and you certainly don't have to help him figure out who's been drugging his horses. That's his problem, not yours."

"I know. I don't think I'm going to have much luck finding that out, anyway."

"So, why not come back?" she said. "I miss you."

"I miss you, too, but—"

Another cut-in, and before I could feed more coins into the slot, Rachel said she had to go and hung up.

I stared at the Verizon sign, then slowly cradled the receiver. If I had any sense at all, I would make arrangements for a night off. The sooner the better. I rubbed my face and looked toward the kitchen as one of McCormick's grooms loped down the steps two at a time. Scratches crisscrossed his chin and forehead, and there was a gash under his right eye. He turned left and cut across the lawn toward the men's room.

I bolted down the sidewalk, grabbed his shoulder, and spun him around.

"What the fu—" He looked at the anger in my face and shut his mouth. "What's the problem?" he said, taking half a step backward.

"You're the problem," I yelled. "You and your pervert friend going after Abby."

"Wha—?"

"You son of a bitch!" I slammed my hands against his chest and shoved him backward.

He caught his balance. "I don't know what you're talking about. I didn't do anything to Abby," he whined. He glanced to his left and saw that we were attracting a crowd, mildly curious with nothing better to do.

"Then what happened to your face?"

"I was in a wreck."

I looked more closely. He had two black eyes, and the bridge of his nose and left side of his face were bruised and swollen. He was the right height, the right build, but the guy on Abby's porch wouldn't have had that kind of damage.

"Oh."

"'Oh'? That's all you got to say is 'oh'?"

"Sorry."

I glanced at his hands. They were clenched into fists. A muscle twitched in his jaw, and I braced myself, half-expecting him to take a swing at me.

His eyes briefly focused over my shoulder, then he looked back at me and muttered, "Go fuck yourself."

I was thinking about commenting on his originality when he spun on his heel and strode down the sidewalk with short, jerky strides. I glanced at his shoes. Not shoes. Cowboy boots. Gaudy, with way too much tooling. No white sneakers with diagonal stripes on the side. No muscle shirt with a Nike logo, either. Only a rumpled tee shirt and Wrangler blue jeans, the official uniform of the backside.

I consciously loosened the muscles in my back and headed in the opposite direction. I had taken several steps before I noticed Dennis Hurp, the TRPB's version of Clint Eastwood, standing at the base of the stairs. He was blocking traffic and seemed unaware of the irritated glances from the men and women squeezing their way into the kitchen. From the expression on his face, he had caught at least part of the confrontation. Not necessarily the words, but the underlying antagonism. I ignored his stare as I walked past.

Chapter 9

I almost missed Ruskie's race.

The wash from the fan slid coolly across my skin. I opened my eyes and wondered why I was awake in the first place. The alarm hadn't gone off, and as tired as I was, I had been worried that I would oversleep. Then I heard it. A distant clicking sound. I lifted my head off the pillow and looked toward my feet, refocused my eyes on the source of the sound, something on my chest. The brown lump came into focus. A large cockroach stared into my face, its long brown antennae rotating as it tested the air.

"Fuck."

I swiped at it as I scrambled off the bed. It bounced off the wall with a hollow thud, landed back on the sheet, then scurried across the mattress and dropped down into the gap between the bed and wall. The thought of those suckers crawling over me as I slept made the hairs on my arms stand on end. It hadn't been the first time, and I hated it.

I glanced at my watch and realized I'd slept straight through the alarm's shrill beeping. I was late, and if I didn't hurry, I wouldn't make it. I yanked my jeans off the clothesline where I'd left them to air out and inspected them for bugs, then pulled them on. They were still damp from the morning, and I hated that, too.

I slipped through the gap to the track just as the attendant swung the gate closed behind the procession of horses heading toward the parade ring and the ninth race of the day. Midway down the field, I could make out Ruskie's broad chestnut rump. As I watched, he tossed his head, but he wasn't jigging. He wasn't curled around Gordi's hold, trotting sideways, tense and edgy. It looked as if Kessler's management practices were paying off.

When I reached the path to the parade ring, I slipped through the barricade and stood by the railing. Kessler was leaning against a post in the saddling stalls with his arms crossed over his chest. His face was tight with concentration as he watched Ruskie stride down the far side of the ring. On some subconscious level, he must have felt that he was being watched because he looked across the ring. When he caught sight of me, he grinned mischievously and winked. Not at all the demeanor befitting a trainer toward his employee.

I glanced at Abby. She hadn't noticed. Neither had the other trainers and grooms who were concentrating on their pre-race preparations. I exhaled slowly and ran my fingers through my hair.

When the horses were led into the stalls, I watched Kessler tack up Ruskie and couldn't help but wonder what it would have been like to have had him for a father. To have grown up in a family that genuinely cared for each other instead of being farmed out. Sent to this camp or that program.

The memory of being dropped off that first summer, a week after my eleventh birthday, was still vivid. I had stood on the lodge's rustic porch as Father's car glided down the rutted drive, moving silently from bright sunlight to dappled shade, leaving me behind. And I'd blinked back tears as I waited for him to look over his shoulder. To wave.

He had done neither.

I tried to think of it as an adventure, a test of sorts, but was dismayed when, week after week, the other kids went home, and I didn't. If it hadn't been for Gus, the head wrangler at the riding stable, I don't know what I would have done.

By the second week, I was spending most of my day at the barn, arriving well before daybreak to help feed and groom the horses, then riding out with the rest of the guests. After a quick lunch, I would hang out with him while he did his afternoon chores. Quite often, we would ride high into the mountains, checking the fence line for breaks. Only years later did I realize the chore probably hadn't been necessary, that he was doing it for me. The following year, the camp had been converted into a ski resort. Gus was long gone, the horses sold.

Sherri had been oblivious to the tension between our parents. She had apprenticed and eventually received a scholarship to the Maryland Academy of the Arts, where she enthusiastically honed her musical skills. Her passion had saved her, allowing her to grow up whole and healthy, whereas Robert had become bitter and spiteful.

And me? I had mostly grown up feeling unloved. I wondered how my life would have been different if I had known the truth. Would it have helped? Maybe. At least I would have had some sort of explanation for Father's miserable behavior, for his constantly wanting to get away from us. From me. Maybe I could have accepted it, even if I couldn't forgive it. Forgive him.

"Hey, Steve?"

I blinked, then caught sight of Gordi seconds before he disappeared behind Ruskie's tall frame.

"Cheer up, man," he shouted over the horse's withers. "Lookin' at ya, you'd think we was at a funeral instead of a horse race."

I dropped my gaze. Ruskie's polished hooves stepped soundlessly across the loam, giving the impression of weightlessness, the dark chestnut tail swinging rhythmically with each long-legged stride.

As he marched past, I looked up and came face to face with Kessler. He was staring at me from across the ring, and I realized he had overheard Gordi's comment. Abby was saying something to him, and when he didn't respond, she reached out and touched his arm. When he looked toward her, I turned away, surprised and confused by what I felt.

I walked away from them, down the narrow concrete path, then sat on a bench and stared through the chain-link fence at the dirt track until my vision blurred. Through no fault of my own, I had been cheated out of a happy life. Cheated by my mother's indiscretion. And Kessler's. Cheated because my father hadn't been able to look past my parentage to see me for the kid I was. A kid who needed him. Cheated by the distance he put between us. That we both did.

Cheated by his death.

I propped my elbows on my knees, clasped my hands together, and stared at the ground, at the crushed soft drink cups and discarded programs that littered the walkway. I had done absolutely nothing wrong.

At that moment, I think I hated him more than I'd hated anyone in my entire life. He wasn't, anymore, just a poor excuse for a father. A stuck-up, self-centered snob who cared only for himself. No. He was capable of knowingly and purposefully alienating a child because he couldn't deal with the truth. Without any thought of the consequences, he had shut me out.

It had only been a week. Just one week to the day, and I still found it hard to believe he was dead. By the time the semi's driver had noticed that the cars in front of him had come to a stop, it was too late. The impact had been so violent, the cab had actually mounted the Mercedes' bumper and rolled forward onto the roof. My father's heavy tank of a car had been no match for twenty-seven tons of rolling steel.

The casket had been closed. I wasn't so sure I had wanted to see him, but not seeing made it less real. I unclamped my fingers and looked dispassionately at the half-moon impressions my nails had dug into my skin.

My mother hadn't been any better. For as long as I could remember, she'd been too absorbed with her charities and committees to bother with anything as mundane as parenting. That job had been left to a procession of nannies. I wondered why they hadn't divorced, why they'd had kids in the first place, but I already knew the answer. Image was everything.

Even though the entire length of the bench was empty, someone sat down next to me, and I didn't have to see the halter and shank dangling from his hand to know it was Gordi. I rubbed my eyes and turned to look at him.

He had an exaggerated grin plastered on his face. I shook my head, looked back at my hands, and smiled despite myself.

"That's more like it, man." Gordi laid the halter on the bench. "So. What's up?"

I straightened my spine and looked to where the horses were warming up under the late afternoon sun. "Nothing."

"Nothing? I know nothin' when I see it, and this ain't no nothin'. What's the deal? You don't got no money for a bet? 'Cause if that's it, I can spot you a twenty. You still got time to put it on if you hurry." Gordi reached into his pocket.

"No. Thanks, Gordi. I have a bet on."

"Oh." He frowned, then looked toward the track. "Hey, they at the gate."

Gordi hopped onto the bench for a better view. I stood and stretched, then stepped onto the bench alongside him.

As the starter's assistants loaded the last few horses into the gate, I glanced at the board. "Gordi, what's his number?"

"Huh?"

"Ruskie's number?"

"Oh. He drew the six slot."

I looked back at the columns of numbers. He was going off at 20 to one. Based on his mediocre past performance, there was no doubt in my mind that if he'd come out of a lesser-known barn, his odds would have been a lot longer.

The bell sounded. The gates sprung open.

I couldn't sort him out in the jumble of movement and color. It wasn't until the field neared the turn that I caught sight of him. With a sinking feeling, I watched the bright chestnut horse with the blue and yellow colors stride along the rail, trapped behind a wall of horses.

"Shit."

"He got time." Gordi's voice was tense, belying his words.

"Yeah, but is he gonna get the chance?"

As the field swept into the turn, I lost sight of him. When the horses entered the stretch, the sound of their hooves pounding the ground suddenly intensified, and I felt the reflexive, familiar rush of adrenaline. I squinted and scanned the field.

I glanced at Gordi. "Where is he?"

He began to shake his head, then his eyes widened. "There he is!" Gordi's fingers clamped around my arm. "Comin' up on the inside."

The leaders must have drifted out in the turn, allowing Garcia the opening he needed. Sandwiched alongside the rail, Ruskie shot past a pair of horses as if they were moving in slow motion. He pricked his ears forward, focused on the leader, then began to close the gap with guts and determination and pure heart.

Now was the time for that big, intelligent horse to show everyone what he was capable of. To prove Kessler right.

The jockey on the lead horse glanced over his shoulder, then went to his whip.

It didn't matter. Ruskie flew past him in two strides. Effortlessly. A thousand pounds of muscle and tendon and bone striding across the ground in a relentless desire to run. To be first.

"My God," I muttered under my breath.

Gordi's fingers dug deeper into my skin, and the bench vibrated under my feet as he bounced up and down. His voice was hoarse with screaming. Ruskie didn't need any encouragement. The big chestnut horse was doing what he was bred for. The product of hundreds of years of instinct and breeding. And courage.

Behind us, through the heavy plate glass, I heard the crowd in the stands yelling. They may not have bet on him, but they knew class when they saw it.

Gordi jerked my arm. "That big red sonofabitch did it. Four lengths, going away."

I jumped off the bench as a man walked in front of us, and I almost knocked into him.

"Sorry," I said when he spun around.

"Watch what you're doing," he said gruffly, and I was startled because I knew him. Larry McCormick, who could frequently be heard over the whir of barn fans, yelling at his help. His eyes narrowed with recognition as he looked from me to Gordi, and I noticed that his puffy cheeks were flushed with emotion. With anger.

The trainer turned abruptly on his heel and strode stiffly down the concrete path toward the parade ring.

I picked up a discarded program and thumbed through the pages until I came to the ninth race. McCormick didn't have a runner.

"Come on, Steve. They comin' back."

I flipped through the program as I followed Gordi onto the track. McCormick didn't have any runners that day, which led to the obvious question. Why was he there, and more important, what was he so angry about?

I looked up from the program as Abby skipped through the opening in the fence.

"Congratulations, Mr. K," Gordi said as Kessler joined us, and I suddenly felt awkward, out of place. Trapped in the deception.

I slipped the program into my back pocket and listened to Kessler telling Gordi what an excellent job he had done with the horse. He didn't feel like an employer to me, and God knows, he didn't feel like a father.

Calling him Mr. K didn't feel right, either. At that moment, nothing did, and I wondered what I would call him when the investigation was over. Kessler certainly wouldn't do.

Would I call him Chris, or Dad, like Abby did?

"Congratulations, sir," I mumbled.

Kessler nodded in acknowledgment, and I think that only I noticed the concern in his eyes. He was conscious, I was certain, of the awkwardness I felt. Awkwardness at playing a role, one that was both complicated by our relationship and deceptive.

Under the hot afternoon sun, Ruskie trotted back to a smattering of applause. When Gordi and Abby led him toward the winner's circle, Kessler whispered, "You okay, Steve?"

I nodded.

"Go on in and stand next to Gordi for the photo."

"Yes, sir."

Abby watched us cross the finely raked sawdust with a puzzled expression on her face. Apparently hotwalkers were not generally included in the ritual. I stood slightly behind Gordi and felt more alienated and out of place than ever.

After the photo, Kessler sent us back to the barn, while he and Abby headed for the grandstand.

I looked at Ruskie's sides as we neared the gap and said, "He's already quit blowing."

"Yeah. He just finished runnin', and here I be gettin' all outta breath just walkin' in this shit."

"I know what you mean." And it was true. The track's deep loam and sand mix was heavy going. When Gordi took Ruskie through the gap and turned right, I said, "Where you goin'?"

"To the spit box." Gordi glanced over his shoulder. "This the first winner you walked?"

"Yeah."

"Right. I keep forgettin' you ain't been here long. Anyway, this guy gotta get his piss and blood checked 'cause he won."

"You're kidding?"

"Nope. They check everything. All the pokin' and proddin' we do to 'em, you'd think they'd just plain wanna stop winnin'."

At the barn's entrance, a fat security guard was tipped back in a metal folding chair so that only the back legs made contact with the ground. He looked up at our approach, then tucked his chin against his chest, balanced a clipboard on his huge belly, and made a notation.

"Take 'im into the second stall," he said to Gordi, then he yelled down the shedrow, "Got a horse in two."

Gordi led Ruskie into the stall and turned him around so that he was facing the door.

"Latch the stall guard and help me get on his halter."

We had just finished exchanging bridle for halter when two men in blue lab coats bustled through the doorway.

The tall one consulted his clipboard. "Number?"

"Six," Gordi said as he adjusted the chain where it crossed over Ruskie's nose.

He looked up from his paperwork. "Russian Roulette, Kessler's horse? Came in first?"

Gordi finished straightening the colt's halter. "He the one."

I read his ID as he jotted information onto several oversized tags. Fred Brewer, DVM, one of the track veterinarians. He propped the clipboard against the wall, and as he approached Ruskie, the colt flicked his ears back and forth, and the skin above his eyes wrinkled with worry.

I stepped to Ruskie's side, casually grasped his halter, and helped Gordi steady the gelding's head as the vet pulled two vacutainers from his pocket.

"Who runs the test?" I said.

"The Maryland Racing Commission."

"Do you always collect two samples?"

He glanced at me with clear, intelligent eyes behind dark-rimmed glasses. "When there's special interest in a horse or when the trainer or owner requests it."

"Which is it this time?"

He tilted his head and considered his answer. "Both, I'd say."

"Hey, Doc," Gordi said. "What the name of that horse was trying to kill you last week? A gray, I think."

"Safety Deposit," the vet said. "That colt didn't want nothing to do with this."

"I could hear 'im halfway down the shedrow," Gordi said, "kickin' and throwin' hisself against the wall like some kinda idiot."

"Yeah. He was a pain all right."

Someone moved behind us, and I glanced over my shoulder. Dennis Hurp stood in the doorway with his shoulders framed by the worn oak posts. His suit hung damply from his shoulders, and the first two buttons of his shirt were undone. He had loosened his tie, which now hung cockeyed. All in all, he looked hotter than hell, except for his cold gaze, which he fixed on me in a lengthy stare.

He had a good line in subtle intimidation, and I was determined that he wouldn't get the best of me. I didn't look away, didn't blink, didn't flinch, and on some level, it seemed to irritate him. His eyes narrowed a fraction. "Fred, when you're done in here, I need to talk to you."

Fred grunted.

"I'll be in your office," Hurp said, and he seemed reluctant to go. Reluctant to be the first one to break eye contact.

Even though I'd been careful not to react, his mouth tightened with irritation as he pivoted around and strode down the aisle. After witnessing my confrontation with McCormick's groom, he probably figured I was a troublemaker, but then, he probably thought everyone was up to something.

I refocused on what I was supposed to be paying attention to as the veterinarian removed the first vacutainer from the plastic housing. He slid a second container into the sleeve and pushed it in until the needle penetrated the purple, rubber seal. A thin stream of dark red blood from Ruskie's jugular spurted into the test tube-like vial. In a couple of seconds, it was three-quarters full. The vet removed the vial, slid the needle out of Ruskie's neck, labeled the tubes, and handed them to Gordi for his initials.

When they left, Gordi said, "Take 'im round the shedrow once, and by then, I be ready to give him his bath."

I nodded, then took Ruskie out of the stall.

Compared to a typical training barn, this one was quiet and lacked the lived-in touches of color-coordinated feed tubs and stall guards, bulging hay nets, and neatly rolled leg wraps stacked outside each stall. Without a loft full of hay and straw and a constant population of equine residents, the barn even smelled different. More sterile but with an underlying odor of mustiness.

Ruskie got his bath and settled into his walk around the unfamiliar shedrow. When I next saw Gordi, he'd scrounged a chair from somewhere and was sitting next to the guard with his legs stretched out in front of him. His head rested against the concrete block wall, and his eyes were closed.

I wondered what it was like to do this job day in and day out, three hundred and sixty-five days a year. It had its attractions. But it also had its drawbacks. My room for one. It had taken me two days to get used to the smell, but it would have taken me a lifetime to get used to the oppressiveness of the track's living quarters.

We were halfway down the path when I noticed Kessler and Abby standing by the entrance. Abby was watching the horse, and Kessler was watching me, and I wished Gordi had kept his mouth shut in the parade ring.

"Bring him out here, Steve," Kessler said as we approached the doorway.

I led Ruskie outside and saw that Gordi had been more aware of his surroundings than I'd thought. He bounded to a stop next to me and inhaled deeply. When he caught my look, his lips twitched with suppressed amusement.

Kessler examined Ruskie's legs, then straightened and patted the horse's neck. "Looks like he came out of it good. Steve, take him around again, and this time, when you get to that corner," he pointed to where the guard was sitting, "jog him down to us."

"Yes, sir."

Ruskie jogged as sound as any horse ever had, and both of them were pleased.

While Abby stroked the colt's neck and told him what a great boy he was, Kessler glanced around, then reached into his pocket and casually handed me a wad of bills. "Your winnings," he whispered.

I jammed them into my pocket and grinned at him.

He held out a set of keys. "These are for you. They open up everything in the barn. Office, tack room, feed room."

"Thanks," I said and dropped them in my pocket.

◇◇◇

We were finally allowed to return to home base after Ruskie obliged, and one of the track employees caught a urine sample. Not the vet, I noticed. He evidently reserved his skills for drawing blood.

That evening, a party atmosphere as thick and heavy as the day's humidity descended over barn sixteen. Stragglers stopped by to congratulate Kessler. Gordi, Sting, and Allen picked apart the race stride for stride, celebrated their winnings, talked about the future. Trudy and a girl from the other side of the barn sat on the waist-high wall, sipping sodas and giggling.

I leaned against the wall outside Kessler's office and halfheartedly listened to their animated conversation. I pulled the creased program from my back pocket and peeled the damp pages apart until I came to the ninth race.

It hadn't been just any race. First place brought in a tidy piece of change.

Thirteen grand, six-eighty.

Not bad, and I wondered how much of it would be profit after five months of training expenses. Although I supposed the real windfall would come from whatever Kessler had made at the pari-mutuel window. From this point on, Ruskie's odds would be significantly shorter.

I looked to my right when someone walked through the doorway on McCormick's side of the barn. David Reece bent forward and concentrated on unlocking his office door with a trembling hand. He got the key halfway in before the tremors racking his hand, his entire body, in fact, caused the key ring to slip out of his fingers and land in the dirt.

As he scooped them up, I pushed away from the wall and walked toward him. "Mr. Reece, are you all right?"

He spun around. "What?"

His eyes were bloodshot, and his skin was unusually blanched and covered with a sheen of perspiration.

"Can I help you, sir?"

He frowned at me, but it was clear his thoughts were elsewhere. Without speaking, he turned his back to me, forcefully rammed the key home, and fumbled with the doorknob.

I watched him stumble into his office and turn to shut the door. "Mr. Reece—"

"Go away." He slammed the door so hard it rattled in the frame.

I returned to Kessler's side of the barn, listened to the banter, and tried unsuccessfully to get into the spirit of the day. By eight-thirty, almost everyone had left. I walked outside and leaned against the wall. The last rays of sunlight cut horizontally across the track and glinted off the sheer glass of the grandstand, bathing the wall in iridescent pink. As I watched, the sun slipped below the horizon. Cooler grays replaced the pink, and I hoped the weather would follow suit.

Abby and Jeff had stayed behind so they could leave with Kessler, and though I knew he wanted to talk to me, I was relieved when he never got the chance. I was fairly certain he would ask what was bothering me, and I didn't want to talk about it.

Not with him. Not then.

They left together, and before starting my familiar, oftentimes boring routine, I walked down the aisle to Mr. Reece's office. No light shone through the crack under the door. He was gone.

Chapter 10

Monday night, just before midnight, I was beginning to wonder if I would ever uncover anything, assuming there was something to uncover in the first place. At no time in the past had drugs been detected in the blood tests to indicate that someone had interfered with Kessler's horses. Maybe it was all in his head.

Horses performed unexpectedly all the time. Maybe the symptoms of exhaustion he'd described were innocent, accidental, not connected to some clandestine scheme. Maybe the intimidation and threats were as far as the attempt to control had gone. Finding a drug that would reliably slow a horse, yet avoid detection, couldn't be easy.

Behind me, one of Hector's horses in the next stall groaned as he dropped heavily to the ground. His hoof knocked into the wall and sent a wave of concussion down the plank I was leaning against. I shifted my weight, stretched my legs, and leaned back against the wall.

The weekend had passed without incident, with no one even mildly curious in Kessler's runners. He'd had a winner and a second on Saturday, another winner on Sunday, and no runners today. Tomorrow, the track would be closed, as it is every Tuesday, and Kessler and I had debated whether or not I should even bother staking out the barn with no runners scheduled until Thursday.

In the end, I had decided to continue as planned. After all, if I hadn't been at the track, Kessler would have already hired another night watchman. To leave the barn unattended seemed foolish, yet, I had to admit, I was getting bored with the routine and found it increasingly difficult to stay awake with each passing night.

Unlike Ruskie, the horse I was watching tonight did not appreciate my being in her stall, intruding in her space. She stood with her rump toward me and made no attempt to socialize or investigate my somewhat unusual presence.

I wrapped my arms around my knees, rested my chin on my arms, and as I closed my eyes, pictured all the James Bond movies I'd watched in the past and thought about how they never showed the long empty hours. The energy-sapping, mind-numbing boredom. And there wasn't any sex, either.

And that had been the biggest disappointment of the weekend. I had hoped to see Rachel on Sunday, but she had stayed at her aunt's for the weekend. Nothing like getting the cold shoulder when it's hotter than hell outside, and all you can think about is how damn sexy her skin looks under a fine sheen of perspiration.

I jerked my eyes open when I heard a hoof slam into a wall on McCormick's side of the barn, then another, followed by a series of scrambling blows. As I jumped to my feet, the mare I'd been baby-sitting bumped into the wall in an effort to get away from me. I ducked under the stall guard, grabbed a lead rope, and ran to the other side of the barn. At the corner formed by the walls of the end stall, I ran my hand along the rough planks until I found the light switches. When I flipped them on, the sudden light caused the horse to struggle even more.

I found his stall easily enough. His was the only door that didn't have a concerned equine head peering out of it. I looked in at him. The bay colt had rolled too close to a wall and had become wedged in the angle between the wall and floor. Thrashing in his effort to get up, he had dug himself in deeper. His panic infected the rest of the herd. As I stood there, tense, high-pitched whinnies echoed throughout the barn.

I scanned the alley. No one was around to help, and if I left him too long, he just might snap one of those long, slender legs. I slipped into his stall.

"Easy there, boy. You're gonna be all right. Just be still and let me help you."

Getting him up, and doing it safely, was a risky procedure, best done with help. Even though I'd done it by myself often enough, the prospect made me sweat. It was just too easy to get kicked, especially when horses were panicked. And this one was panicked. I checked the alley one last time, then stepped toward him.

His spine was closest to me, his head to my right. All four legs scrambled uselessly against the solid oak planks. He didn't have enough purchase to push off and roll over, and he didn't have enough room to get his legs underneath him so he could heave himself to his feet.

"Steady, boy. Take it easy, now." I stepped closer.

I needed to wrap the lead rope around his hind leg, the one closest to the ground, and rock him over. The difficulty lay in getting close enough. He suddenly lashed out with both hind legs. Light glinted off a hind hoof. He was wearing shoes behind.

"Easy now." I stretched across him and lowered the rope down along the wall. "I'm not gonna hurt you. Take it easy now, boy."

When his leg moved into position, I pulled the rope tight and tried to roll him toward me. He kicked out. A hoof brushed my forearm, and the lead rope wrenched out of my hand. I stepped back, rearranged the rope, and caught my breath.

I tried again. This time, we gained some ground before he flexed his legs and the rope slipped off. On the third try, the rope caught good and tight. I hauled on the rope.

He teetered on the sharp edge of his withers, then rolled toward me. Four long, black legs arced through the air. I jumped into the corner at the back of the stall and watched as he drew his legs beneath him and scrambled to his feet. Once there, he pivoted around to face me. He took a single step toward me and nickered softly. I grinned when I heard the reaction in the barn. The excited whinnies had turned to reassuring nickers when they heard his voice. It always happened like that, and I found it amazing. They might be big, dumb animals, whose brains were no larger than an apple, but they had feelings and emotions we rarely considered.

When I stepped to his side and patted his hot, sweat-soaked skin, he turned his head and regarded me with a soft, brown eye, and I wondered if on some level he was thankful. Or was I just being whimsical? I ran my hands down his near fore and checked for damage. The colt lowered his head and nuzzled my waist. When I felt him open his mouth and go after the belt loop on my jeans, I nudged him with my elbow. Typical coltish behavior. They could never keep their mouths to themselves.

When I was satisfied that he wasn't hurt, I switched off the lights and headed back to Kessler's side of the barn.

As I rounded the corner, I nearly jumped out of my skin. Trudy was standing there, and she did jump.

"Oh, Steve." She lowered her hand from her mouth and touched the crucifix that hung around her neck. "You scared me. What are you doing here?"

"Sorry. One of Mr. Reece's horses got cast—"

"Which one?" She cut around me and headed down the short aisle.

"I don't know," I said to her back. "A bay colt in the third stall."

"Is he okay?"

"Yeah. Looks like it."

I caught up with Trudy outside the colt's stall.

She hadn't bothered with the lights, knowing that switching them on would be more disturbing to the inmates than leaving them off. But there was enough light to see by, thanks to an almost full moon hanging low in the sky. Kessler's side was pitch black, but on McCormick's side, moonlight streaked through the doorway and cut across the cinder-block wall at an acute angle, as if someone were spotlighting the barn with a giant flashlight. The stall fronts were bathed in the milky light, and so was Trudy.

Her skin looked paler than ever, her legs more so. Though, I had to admit, they were nice legs, long and shapely, even if thin, the thinness making them seem longer.

"Oh. This is one of Mr. Reece's new two-year-olds."

The colt stretched his neck over the stall guard and extended his nose toward Trudy. She rubbed his face, and he lowered his head appreciatively.

She cradled the horse's head in her arms. "You're just a baby, aren't you?"

Trudy pushed her tousled blond hair out of her face. Her skimpy tank top rode up with the movement, revealing a lot of pale waist. The fabric was paper thin and clingy, lying smoothly against the curves of her body. No wrinkles or lines, no indication that she had anything on underneath but skin. The matching shorts were cut high, and I passed the time imagining how she'd look if she bent over. I rubbed my face. Damn, I needed to get my mind out of the gutter. As it was, I was becoming privy to a lot of details otherwise left to the imagination.

Trudy murmured softly as she ran her fingers down the colt's face in long, gentle strokes.

I shifted my feet and jammed my hands in my pockets.

The bay had his face pressed against her body then, with his eyes half closed. She turned and looked at me through the tangle of bangs that had fallen back across her face. "The poor guy's still hot."

"Um." I swallowed.

She returned her attention to the horse and said in her soft, singsong voice, "You're so sweet, aren't you? Poor guy, getting stuck in your stall like that." She smoothed the palms of her hands across the flat, angular planes of his face. "You need to be careful, silly. We don't want you to hurt yourself."

The colt suddenly raised his head. His nose slid up the center of Trudy's chest, and the movement pulled her shirt up, revealing a white half moon of breast. Trudy leaned away from him.

The fabric slipped back into place, and I wondered if she knew I had seen. The colt pressed his nose against her, just above her breasts.

"Be careful," I said, and my voice sounded thick. "He's mouthy."

"Oh, he's okay. He's so gentle."

I wouldn't bet on it, but I kept my thoughts to myself.

As I watched, she cupped her hands under his chin and whispered to him. He lowered his head again, and I noticed that his ears were at half-mast, his eyes half-closed, and he was working his mouth. All in all, one totally relaxed horse.

I cleared my throat. "What were you doing in the barn?"

The colt nudged her. Trudy patted his neck, then turned toward me. "I woke up and couldn't go back to sleep, it's so hot. So I decided to check on the horses." She walked down the aisle, and I forced myself to look at her face. "What about you?"

"Same thing, pretty much. The heat, I mean. I wasn't checking on the horses, but when I went outside to get a soda, I decided to take a walk, and that's when I heard all the commotion."

"Oh." She looked at the ground, and my gaze slid down her body. She had the kind of build that accentuated her crotch, a narrow waist, long legs, a nice gap between her thighs. And the fact that she wasn't wearing anything under that thin fabric slammed into my brain.

I jerked my gaze upward when she looked back at my face. The shyness had come back strong now that she was dealing with a human. Or maybe it was dealing with the opposite sex that she had trouble with.

The rest of the night was hell. Tuesday morning wasn't much better. Every time I saw her in the shedrow, all I could think about was that flimsy tank top and her too-short shorts and what lay beneath. I was thankful when the morning shift was finally over.

I took a shower, ran the towel over my hair one last time, and pulled on a clean pair of jeans. Pulled on socks and sneakers and combed my hair. The restroom smelled musty and dank, and I would be glad when I…

I lowered the comb and stared at my reflection. Was I really all that eager to get back to the loft? Back to Foxdale? No, I wasn't.

"See anybody you know?"

I shifted my gaze. Gordi was standing inside the doorway, frowning at my reflection.

"No," I said, and the scary part was, I was only half-joking.

Shaking his head, he crossed the room and straddled the bench. The worn wood creaked as he lowered his weight onto the plank. "You in the mood for some spic food? Best this side a Meck-e-ko."

I turned to face him.

"Or you gonna make like Houdini and disappear like you do every damn afternoon?

I slipped my comb in my pocket. "Mexican sounds good. We can take my truck." I lifted my shirt off the bench and saw that Gordi was shaking his head. "Sure we can," I said. "I'll—"

"Nah. We can't ride together, not 'nless you wanna hang around and watch the spin cycle all fucking afternoon."

I smiled. "You got laundry duty?"

"Yeah. If it ain't my goddamned week."

I followed Gordi into town and squeezed the Chevy into a too narrow space in a too small parking lot that was jammed with more vehicles than the designer had intended. I caught up with Gordi alongside his dented, rust-pitted Cavalier.

I indicated his car with a jerk of my head. "This where you had your body work done?"

He snorted.

"They should put up a sign—Park at Your Own Risk. This place is a zoo."

"That's because—"

"Yeah, yeah, yeah. I know. This side of Meck-e-ko, and all."

"You'll see."

We crossed the lot strewn with pebbles that had worn through an eroded layer of asphalt. When my pace slowed, Gordi looked over his shoulder.

"It's a dive." My voice rose an octave. "We're gonna eat here?"

He grinned broadly. "Sure are, my man. Remember, they got the best food…this side of Meck-e-ko." We said the last in unison, and Gordi chuckled.

Inside was cool, and that was the only positive thing I could say about the joint. The space clearly had not started out as a restaurant but as a mid-sized business in a cramped three-store strip mall.

Modifications had been minimal. The view into the kitchen was unobstructed, and attempts at atmosphere bordered on childlike. A desert scene, complete with cacti and three sombrero-clad figures riding off into the sunset, sprawled across the pink-washed walls.

Gordi chose an empty table alongside the plate-glass window. I brushed some crumbs off my seat and sat down. A menu was wedged between the salt and pepper shakers and a large plastic squirt bottle with a glob of taco sauce hardened around the nozzle. I grimaced as I peeled apart the pages. "What's good?"

"You ain't lived 'til you tried their chile con queso. Stuff so hot, it'll make your ears burn."

"Okay. Chile con queso it is. What else? I'm starving."

"All their shit's good. I like their beef enchiladas. The tacos, too."

The place may have been a dump, but the service was fast, and the food was surprisingly good.

Gordi looked up from his enchilada. "Well?"

I wiped my mouth with a napkin. "Great." I nodded. "Really good."

"Told'ja."

"So you did." I laid my taco on its square of waxed paper, loaded a chip with queso, took a bite, then another. It didn't seem all that hot, and I was beginning to wonder about Gordi when my mouth started to burn. I grabbed my Coke.

"Ah-ha," he said. "Don't worry. You get use to it."

I took another swallow. "In what lifetime?"

Gordi snorted.

"My eyes are watering," I said, incredulous.

I propped my elbows on the table and rotated my cup, sloshing the Coke around the crushed ice. Directly opposite from where we sat, a group of men erupted in laughter. I looked up and recognized one of them.

He worked in one of the barns near my unit. A groom, or maybe a foreman. He was often there after hours, doing odd jobs or holding a horse for the farrier. I glanced at the next table and caught the profile of one of the men as he turned in response to the laughter. I knew him, too. McCormick's groom.

His companion leaned toward him and spoke as if he didn't want his conversation overheard. As I watched, he passed an envelope to the groom, and he took it and slipped it into the waistband of his jeans.

A simple exchange.

Nothing unusual about it, except they had done it under the table.

Chapter 11

I sat up straighter, glanced at Gordi, then looked back across the room. McCormick's groom checked to make sure the guys at the next table weren't paying attention, then he pulled an envelope from his back pocket and handed it to his companion. I checked the time. Twelve-fifty. Tuesday.

I bit into my taco and tried not to stare. Ate some more queso. Drank some Coke. The man leaned back in his chair, slipped the envelope into his pocket, then stood.

I snapped the plastic lid onto the queso's Styrofoam container and dumped the chips into my bag.

Gordi looked up from his enchilada. "What'ja doin'?"

"I forgot something." I pulled a twenty out of my pocket and handed it to Gordi as the groom's friend walked toward the doorway. "I've gotta go. Could you pay for me?"

He shrugged, then folded the bill and tucked it in his pocket. "Sure."

"Thanks, Gordi." I stood and followed the man out into the parking lot.

Heat radiated from the asphalt as the sunlight glinted off glass and metal. I squinted against the glare and saw that my target was halfway across the lot.

The clandestine exchange of envelopes could have meant anything. Yet, instinct told me it was somehow connected to what was happening with Kessler's horses.

Toward the far end of the parking lot, he cut through a row of cars and stopped alongside a silver Pontiac Grand Prix. As he slid the key into the lock, he looked across the roof of his car, straight at me.

I dropped my gaze, cradled the white paper bag containing the remains of my lunch between my forearm and waist, and slipped my hand into my pocket for my keys. When I risked another glance in his direction, he was already behind the wheel, pulling the seat belt across his chest. I picked up my pace and made it to the Chevy as he nosed his car toward the exit.

He lucked out and hit a break in traffic. The Pontiac's back tires kicked up a spray of gravel as he pulled onto the street, a one-way three-laner. I threw the bag onto the seat and squeezed into the truck.

It took forever to back out of the narrow slot, and by the time I pulled onto 198, I could no longer see his car. I moved into the center lane and scanned the vehicles as they slowed to a stop at the intersection of 198 and US 1. No Pontiac. Not unless he was tucked out of sight in front of a Wonder Bread delivery van or a FedEx truck. I glanced at the line of vehicles to my right as they merged onto US 1. A gray mini-van, a red Mustang, and a late-model GMC truck. No silver Pontiac.

As I slowed down, I realized I should have left room to change lanes, just in case. I jammed my foot down on the brake pedal. Tires squealed as the driver behind me slammed on his brakes. I glanced in the rearview mirror, and he flipped me the bird.

This tailing shit wasn't as easy as it looked. Not like on TV, and I sure as hell wasn't any James Bond. No high-tech gadgets for me. No fancy cars or hot babes. No sex, either. Just a big fuck you from the guy in the black sports car.

The light turned green. I tensed as the line of vehicles moved into the intersection. As the FedEx truck inched its way into the turn, I caught sight of the silver Pontiac nestled between his front bumper and a blue van. I looked over my shoulder, gunned the engine, and yanked on the steering wheel. Ignoring the horn blast from an approaching car, I shot into the left lane and accelerated.

The light turned yellow, and for a split second, I thought the guy in front of me was going to stop. Maybe it was the sight of my truck's grillwork bearing down on him in his rearview mirror that caused him to make a dash for it. Whatever the cause, he sped up, and I followed on his bumper as the light turned red. When the Pontiac moved over, I cut into the right-hand lane.

After a mile or two, I rolled my shoulders and leaned against the backrest. Without realizing it, I had been hunched forward, white-knuckling the steering wheel. Up ahead, he pulled into a shopping center. I kept my distance, and when he parked beside a lamppost near the outermost fringe of the lot, I slipped into a space next to a utility van and switched off the engine. I drank some Coke and watched him walk past two rows away. When he'd gone about fifty feet, I wedged my soda between the dash and windshield and followed him on foot. Despite the heat, he kept up a brisk pace as he headed toward a cluster of stores that surrounded a small courtyard.

He was in his mid to late thirties, about my height, and even though he wasn't carrying any excess body fat, he didn't appear physically fit. His pale arms were scrawny beneath his short-sleeved dress shirt, and I doubted he worked at the track. Not in the barns, anyway. When he entered the courtyard and disappeared behind a massive support column, I quickened my pace.

I walked around the column and hesitated. He was not more than three paces away, standing in front of an ATM with his back toward me. He glanced over his shoulder, then shifted position to ensure privacy. I walked past him and pushed open the door to a drug store. I hesitated, then crossed over to the magazine section and stood where I had a clear shot of him through a window plastered with Back to School advertisements. I picked up a PC magazine and flipped through the pages.

He straightened and tucked his wallet into a back pocket, then walked into the drug store. I raised the magazine and studied an article on hotsyncs and conduits as if I knew what I was reading. After a half-minute or so, I slipped the magazine back into the rack and walked down the aisle toward the center of the store.

I turned into the main aisle that parallelled the front of the store and walked down its length. I didn't see him, and I wondered if he had realized I was following him and had found another way out. It seemed unlikely. I was looking toward the back of the store when a woman's voice called a name over the PA system.

My shoulder knocked against a rack positioned in the middle of the aisle, jostling a display of designer sunglasses. I grabbed the upright support and steadied the rows of swaying aviators and Ray Bans. He wasn't a customer. He was an employee. And the implications were staggering.

He was standing behind a counter on the elevated floor of the pharmacy with a crisp white lab coat buttoned over his striped shirt and trousers. He looked alternately from the blue glow of a computer monitor to a keyboard out of sight behind a display of nicotine gum, patches, and cigarettes. I waited until his partner, who had been scanning the shelves of medicine, answered the phone before I walked over and stood beneath the Pick-up sign.

"Be with you in a moment," he said over his shoulder.

His fingers hovered over the keyboard as he pecked in additional information, then he hit a button with finality. Somewhere out of sight, a printer hummed to life. He walked over and placed his left hand on the counter. Short, clean nails, wide pores, reddish brown hair sprinkled over pale skin, no wedding band.

"Can I help you?" Friendly voice. Soft. A trace of boredom.

I held my breath and dragged my gaze up to his face, afraid that when we made eye contact, he'd recognize me. "Yes," I mumbled.

His moist-looking skin was extremely clean-shaven, and he had the watery red-rimmed eyes of someone who suffers from allergies. His receding hairline was topped with curly brown hair combed straight back and kept tidily short. I glanced at his name tag. Nathan Green.

He waited for me to continue, his expression blank.

I cleared my throat. "Is the prescription for Martin Cline ready, yet?"

"Let me check."

I watched him walk to the back wall and flip through the envelopes in the "K" bin, which was just as well.

He had access to all kinds of drugs and an intimate knowledge of their actions. Medications for horses, even medical procedures and techniques, were largely adapted from human medicine. His only difficulty would be in getting the dosage right, and even that might be easier than I imagined. Many drugs were prescribed based on weight. All it would take was a little experimenting.

He conferred with his partner, who was now off the phone, pouring distilled water into a graduated beaker. She shook her head, and he walked over to the computer and keyed in the name, scanned the screen, then returned to the counter.

"That name's not in our computer, and I don't have any record of a prescription being dropped off or phoned in."

"Oh, thanks. I must have the wrong store." I turned to leave.

"What's the name of the physician? I'll give him a call."

I shrugged. "I don't know. I was just sent to pick it up."

"You can use my phone."

"Eh…No, thanks." I headed toward the exit. As I rounded the corner next to the sunglasses, I glanced over my shoulder. He looked from me back to his computer screen, and I hoped he hadn't remembered me from the restaurant.

I cut through the snack food aisle and picked up a bag of pretzels, two rolls of Life Savers, and a box of butterscotch Tastykakes. Missing meals like I'd been, my jeans were getting baggier when I needed to be gaining weight, not losing it. At the checkout counter, I purchased a penlight and a packet of AA batteries.

Outside, the oppressive humidity clung heavily to my skin. Five straight days of temperatures creeping into the triple digits and no end in sight. I climbed into the truck, popped the lid off the container of queso, and ate some chips. I swallowed the last of the Coke, now diluted and unappealingly warm, and considered the significance of Green's being a pharmacist.

Not only would he know what drugs would slow down a horse, or speed it up, he might know how to combine them to avoid detection. He might even know, if he was smart enough, how to affect the horse by choosing drugs that mimicked natural body chemistry. He could pick something no one would ever think of testing for. I scraped the last of the queso from the bottom of the container, finished the chips, and licked my fingers.

After a moment's hesitation, I crumpled the bag and tossed it on the floorboard, then I pulled alongside Green's silver Grand Prix.

I hopped out, cupped my hands around my face to cut down the glare, and peered through the Grand Prix's tinted windows. Nothing on the dash. Nothing on the seats. Not even spare change in the console. I walked around to the back. Maryland tags, valid until April of the following year. I memorized the number and scanned the bumper for stickers. Nothing. The car was clean inside and out, and I wondered if I would be neater if my vehicle were nicer. Newer. Not a ten-year-old, worn-out pickup with peeling paint. As it was, I could fill a trash bag with the junk that cluttered the cab.

On impulse, I tried the door. It clicked open.

I looked around and saw that no one was paying any attention. Trying to look as if I had every right to be there, I reached in and opened the glove compartment. Nothing but a pen and an owner's manual.

Several documents were bound to the underside of the manual with a rubber band. I inhaled deeply and removed the packet. I pushed the door to, stopping short before it clicked shut, and walked over to my truck. I copied his address and, for the hell of it, his insurance information, wrote down the tag number before I forgot it, then returned the packet to its rightful place.

As I'd gone that far, I figured I might as well finish the job. I leaned into the car and looked under the front passenger seat. Except for a fine layer of dust, the space was empty. I walked around to the driver's side, opened the door, and ducked under the steering wheel. Nothing under the driver's seat but a scattering of gray pebbles embedded in the carpet and an ice scraper.

He wouldn't be needing that anytime soon.

An engine accelerated close by. I straightened too fast and hit my head on the underside of the steering column.

"Damn."

I rubbed the back of my head as an old, souped-up Nova peeled out of a doughnut and sped toward the exit. I turned back to the car and flipped down the sun visor. Nothing there, either. I popped the trunk release and poked around the wheel wells. Peered under the carpet. But I might just as well have not bothered. The trunk was a damn sight neater than my apartment and just as empty.

I left his car as I'd found it.

I hadn't done too badly, though. I had a name, Nathan J. Green; an occupation, pharmacist; an address; a vehicle description and a license plate number to go with it. I drove to the nearest gas station, bought an *ADC Street Map*, and eventually pulled up in front of his residence, a squat, brick ranch house with green shutters, a green front door with a brass kick plate, and a small fenced-in backyard.

The grass needed cutting. A few scraggly shrubs near the front porch hadn't been trimmed in the past year, and the guy apparently didn't know what a weed-whacker was for. Foot-high grass grew through the chain-link fence, hopelessly entwined in the metal links.

No children's toys lay scattered in the yard. No swing set. No evidence of a dog. All the shades were drawn. The place was as dreary and unwelcoming as a morgue.

I wondered if he left his house unlocked, too. He was safely occupied at work, but it didn't matter. I wasn't that brave. Or stupid.

I clocked the mileage back to my parking spot by the perimeter fence. Mr. Green lived exactly three and a half miles from the track. I rolled up the windows, locked the doors, and walked into barn sixteen.

Someone was sweeping out the tack room. I strolled past the open door to Kessler's office.

"Hey, Steve."

I backtracked.

Kessler was sitting behind his desk. A condition book lay open in front of him, weighted down with a slab of quartz that had been carved into the shape of a horse's head. A pad of paper lay to one side, and his training calendar sprawled across the rest of the blotter space.

He glanced at his watch. "What are you doing here?"

When I walked into the office and stood by Kessler's desk, Runt jumped up and planted his paws on my knee. He zeroed in on the plastic bag I still held in my hand, undoubtedly picking up on the scent of food.

"I've found out something." And I couldn't suppress the excitement I felt at finally getting somewhere. It was a start, anyway.

"Hold on a sec." Kessler left the room.

I looked out the doorway in time to see him pull a ten from his wallet and hand it to the yellow-haired old man. The ex-trainer. The old guy nodded his head and grinned his toothless grin. He took the bill in a hand that visibly trembled, then leaned the broom against the wall. When he turned and shuffled toward the exit, Kessler put the broom back where it belonged and closed and locked the door. I ducked back into the office, and in a second or two, Kessler returned to his desk.

"Okay," he smiled, "what's got you champing at the bit?"

"Got a phone book?" I said.

He jerked his head toward the file cabinets.

I balanced my bag of provisions on top of a pile of folders, pulled the directory out from under a stack of binders, and flipped through the pages until I came to the listing for Green, Nathan J. I copied his phone number into my notepad alongside his car registration statistics, ripped out the page, and handed it to Kessler.

As he scanned the information, I said, "Do you know him?"

Kessler shook his head. "Never heard of him." He straightened his arm, ready to drop the slip of paper onto the open calendar.

"I think he's the one who's been supplying whatever drug they're using on your horses."

His hand froze, and he narrowed his eyes. "What?"

I told him about my afternoon, or most of it.

"The groom he gave the envelope to, you said he works for McCormick?"

I nodded.

Kessler shrugged. "He could just be a runner for this guy," he peered at my writing, "Green."

"What's a runner?"

He gestured with the paper. "Running bets. You know? The guy's at work. He wants to back a horse, but he can't get away. So he gets a groom to put the bet on for him. Do you know the groom's name?"

"No." I described him.

Kessler's brow furrowed as he tapped his pen on the pad of paper. "Ron. No, Randy. Don't know his last name, but I can find out."

"And his face is messed up," I said. "Like he's been in a fight."

Kessler's head snapped up. "You don't think?"

"Yes, I do. I bet he was one of the assholes on Abby's porch. It all fits. Easy access to your horses, the bruises, missing a couple days work, passing envelopes. And now, a pharmaceutical connection."

"Damn." Kessler stood abruptly, and his chair rocked backward. When he began to pace, Runt jumped to his feet and tentatively wagged his tail.

"I bet McCormick's in on it, too," I said.

He turned around. "Do you think he was the other man on the porch?"

I shook my head. "No. He's too short. And fat. It was someone else. The weird thing is, I asked Randy about his face, and he said he was in an accident. At the time, I thought he was telling the truth because his face was worse than it would have been from being shoved into a rosebush."

"He's the right build?"

"Yeah. I think he was the one with the chain."

"Christ. What about Green? Do you think he was one of them?"

I bit my lower lip and shook my head. "I don't think so. He's lean, but he's not tall enough. Green's my height, and the guy who had hold of Abby was six-two, easy."

Kessler absentmindedly rubbed his chin. "Did the police recover any fingerprints? Any evidence?"

"No. The surfaces were all wrong for prints."

The terrier sprawled back on the floor with a sigh and lowered his head onto his paws.

Kessler walked across the room and glanced at the crumpled slip of paper in his hand. His shirt was damp down the center of his back from so many hours sitting in his airless office.

"Tyson," Kessler said. "That's his name. Randy Tyson."

Runt reluctantly pushed himself to his feet, walked over to Kessler, and gazed up at his master. He shifted his weight and lowered his hindquarters to the floor. His stub of a tail moved rapidly back and forth across the floor. You couldn't beat a dog when it came to loyalty.

Kessler looked up suddenly, and I saw he was gripping the paper tightly in his hand. "How'd you get this," he pointed with his finger, "his insurance information?"

"I...ah. I looked in his glove compartment."

"You what?"

"Nobody saw me."

"What if they had?"

I shifted my weight and didn't answer.

"What if you'd been arrested? That stunt could have ruined your future. Don't do it again, Steve. I don't want you getting into trouble." He paused, and I imagined him saying *for me.* "All right?"

I hesitated.

"Steve?"

"Okay," I said and knew full well I would do it again. Or at least try.

Kessler sat wearily in his shabby chair and leaned against the backrest. "So," he fingered the sheet of loose-leaf, "what are we going to do with this information now that we have it?"

I shrugged and sat in the plastic seat alongside the desk.

Kessler tossed the paper on top of the calendar. "The police won't do anything with it except question how I got it in the first place." He propped his elbows on the desk. "I'll give it to the TRPB."

"You mean Hurp?"

"Sure. He's the one who's most interested in my horses."

"But I thought you said he thinks everyone's guilty?"

He smiled faintly. "He has that attitude, doesn't he? The 'us versus them' syndrome. But to an extent, they all do. Guess it comes with the job."

I rubbed my palms on my jeans. "I was wondering, and don't take this wrong, but if the track authorities believe you're doping your horses, how come they haven't…taken action?"

"Without evidence, they're reluctant to do anything. There's an odd sort of symbiotic relationship that exists between us, anyway. Without good trainers and their stables full of decent horses to run on their track, they'd have nothing, just like I'd be out of a job without good owners. One thing's certain, though." He leaned back in his chair. "I'd be feeling a lot more heat if the track patrons got antsy. Cause the public to lose faith, and there's no faster way to get kicked out of this job. The stewards would find a way to get me out, one way or another."

"Speaking of getting kicked out, what's the deal with that old guy? The one who was sweeping out the tack room? If he lost his license, why's he still here?"

Kessler shrugged. "Back then, attitudes were different. He was allowed to stay on, doing odd jobs. Out of pity, I guess." He smiled faintly, and I thought about the ten bucks he'd given him. "That would never happen if he'd been caught today."

"Gordi said he…'hopped' some horses."

"Yeah. Got the dosage wrong. Got one of his runners wired so tight, it went berserk in the parade ring, crashed through the railing, and broke its leg. Hurt a couple spectators, too. If that hadn't happened, I doubt he would have lost his license. Not back then, when chemical help was as common as horse feed."

"Any chance he's helping someone continue in his footsteps?"

"Nah. The guy survives on handouts and the bottle. I don't see him doing anything nowadays. Maybe twenty years ago, but not now. And, see this?" He stretched back and hefted a book off the top shelf of a bookcase. *A Guide to Pharmaceuticals and Biologicals—With a Therapeutic Index* was printed on the spine. "I'd bet every trainer on the backside has a copy. Hell, some of 'em probably know more about what's available than the vets do."

"Why do you have one?"

Something moved in his eyes, and I realized he could hear the disgust in my voice. "When Charles, my vet, recommends a drug I'm not familiar with, I read up on it. And it doesn't hurt to know what the competition's up to."

"Oh."

"I got the report back on Ray," Kessler said, smoothly changing the subject, and it took me half a second to figure out he was referring to Stingray. "The trouble he got into in Florida had nothing to do with horses. He got caught messing around with his neighbor's fourteen-year-old daughter. The girl's father, who just so happens to be a 300-pound trucker, didn't think jail was punishment enough and went after Ray with a baseball bat."

"Geez. Does he have a warrant out on him?"

"Not that I could find. I heard about it from the barn foreman Ray used to work for." Kessler looked at his watch. "It's already three. Instead of coming in at nine like we planned, why don't you wait until eleven-thirty. The PI firm called this afternoon. They're going to install the cameras tonight, and I told them I'd be here."

"They install them at night?"

"Yeah. Fewer people around to see them do it."

"Oh, yeah," I said. "That makes sense."

"While they're here, they can show you how everything's set up."

"Okay."

I leaned forward and propped my elbows on my knees. It had been a week since the attack on Abby's porch, and the muscles in my back had finally healed.

"Do you know," I said, "it isn't unusual for some of your grooms to check on their horses in the middle of the night?"

"Really? Who?"

"Trudy checked on hers Friday night. And last night, Gordi looked in on his," I said, and he hadn't known I was there.

"I guess I'm not surprised. Did they see you?"

"Trudy did," I said and couldn't keep the amusement out of my voice.

"What?" he said.

I shook my head and told him about Reece's horse getting cast.

"You don't think either one of them is involved, do you?"

"No."

"Me, either, and with someone like Tyson in the same barn, they wouldn't need one of my crew helping them."

There was a trace of relief in his voice, and it occurred to me that finding a traitor among his own employees would have stung. Randy Tyson was something else altogether.

Kessler leaned farther back in his chair and rolled a pencil between his fingers. He was staring at his desk, but it was obvious his thoughts weren't on the paperwork that lay scattered across the blotter. I shifted in my seat.

"Steve?"

"Hmm?" I met his gaze, steady on my face.

"Are you all right? The other day, you seemed—"

"Yeah," I said. "Fine."

He sighed and let his chair drop forward onto all fours. "I'm so caught up with the horses all the time, I keep forgetting it's only been a little over a week since the funeral. It must be hard..."

I looked down at Runt and cleared my throat. "Being here gives me something to do." The dog was stretched out, fast asleep. "I'm okay."

"He was a lucky man."

I jerked my head up. "What?"

"Your father," Kessler said. "He was lucky to have had a son like you. You're a hard worker. You're smart and considerate and, despite looking in that guy's car today, moral."

I grinned at that and looked back at the dog.

"The other night at dinner, you said that he kicked you out when you applied for a job at, eh..."

"Foxdale," I mumbled.

"That was because of me?"

"I suppose."

He sighed heavily. "How long had he known?"

"Probably since I was ten. Maybe eleven." I glanced at Kessler.

He had the kind of open, honest face I had always valued. Unpretentious. He wasn't embarrassed by strong emotions, his or someone else's.

I let my gaze settle on the rows of photographs that lined the back wall. "He didn't think he was so lucky." I stood up, and Kessler did also. "I gotta get some sleep." I pivoted on my heel.

"Wait."

I turned to face him.

"I'm sorry, Steve."

"I know."

Outside, the mid-afternoon sun glared off the crushed stone in the alley.

Why couldn't my old man just have accepted me for me?

I stopped at the soda machine, slid the coins into the slot, and pressed the Coke button.

I really didn't understand it, because the more I thought about it, the more I remembered how much he had loved me before he'd found Mother out. Why couldn't he have held onto that?

When I passed Gordi's door, I saw that he was still out. His door was shut tight. If he'd been home, an ugly paisley bed sheet would have been hanging in the doorway. Gordi's version of air-conditioning.

I downed the Coke, stretched out on the bed, and closed my eyes. I tried not to think. Not about Father. Or Kessler.

Someone knocked on the door.

"Just a minute." I pulled on my jeans, and when I touched the doorknob, the door swung inward before I'd even turned the lock. The damn thing was falling apart.

"You forgot this." Kessler held out the plastic bag from the drug store.

"Oh, yeah."

"Thought you might need it."

"Thanks," I mumbled.

Kessler glanced past me and took in the dingy room before refocusing on my face. "Your father did you a great disservice, kicking you out like he did, and based on that, I imagine he made a lot of other mistakes, too. But, you've got to remember, his actions don't in any way reflect on you but on his own short-comings. You're a good kid, and like I said, I'm sorry you've lost him. I'm also sorry for how what Patti and I did has affected you, but on the other hand, I'm thankful I've had the chance to know you." He paused, then said, "I've always wanted a son."

He turned and walked toward the steps, leaving me speech-less.

Chapter 12

Early Wednesday morning, the monitor beeped for the ump-teenth time. I jerked my head off my arms and blinked at the screen. Something moved at the base of the picture, then disappeared. A person's head? If so, he was close to the—

The doorknob to Kessler's office rattled as a key was worked into the lock. I jumped to my feet and squinted at my watch. Four-fifteen. Kessler. And, damn it. If Abby was with him, she'd want to know what in the hell I was doing in her father's office, and I didn't have an answer.

The door creaked open, and Kessler grinned when he saw my expression. "Relax, Steve. She's not here yet." He wiggled the key out of the lock and pushed the door fully open.

"God." I rubbed a hand over my face.

He dropped his briefcase on the desk blotter and popped the tabs. "How'd it work out?"

I shrugged and watched him lift a pile of folders from the case and sort them on the desk into neat piles. I knew from past observation that they would deteriorate into a jumbled mess by late morning. "I don't know if it's smart, my staying in here. I had a hard time staying awake. It was too comfortable."

"Well, the beeps will wake you if somebody comes."

"I guess so." I stretched. "I may switch back and forth. There's no chance I'll miss them if I'm in the stall."

"It's up to you. Work it any way you like."

I yawned.

A VCR and split screen monitor that provided two views of the aisle from opposite ends of the barn had been set up in Kessler's office. The guy who had installed the system had been cheerful and informative, providing thorough but easy to understand instructions. He'd filled my head with terms like wireless transmitters, parabolic microphones, direct line of sight, quad cams, time-lapse recorders, field parameters.... For whatever reason, he had felt compelled to give me a mini lesson in the fine art of surveillance.

During the night, the alarm had gone off more often than I would have liked, causing a resultant quickening of the pulse. The only culprits, however, had been an assortment of barn cats on the prowl, a rat (predator and prey never met as far as I could determine), and in the early morning hours, a pigeon scratching in the dirt. It was no surprise that Kessler had found his night watchman asleep. Listening to an alarm beeping every other minute would surely, and in quick order, render the surveiller immune.

"Oh," Kessler said. "Ray's going to cool out today's runners this afternoon. He's been asking and asking. Needs the extra money, and since I usually rotate who cools out after the races, he'll be suspicious if I keep using you."

"Okay."

He closed the briefcase and straightened to his full height. "Look, Steve, I know your hours have been hell. Why don't you take off this morning? Get away from here for a bit."

I thought about Rachel. "How about Saturday or Sunday, instead?"

"Sure. That'll work. Allen or Ray, either one of them would be up for earning some extra money."

"Great. How do you think today's runners will do?"

"Both have a good shot. Plus, Speedwell's entered in an allowance race tomorrow, and I expect he'll win."

"Hector's gray colt?"

Kessler nodded, then glanced at his watch. "Go get some breakfast."

I walked down to the track kitchen, worked my way down the glass-fronted food bar, then parked my tray on the cheery red-and-white checked table cloth across from Gordi.

He looked up from his plate, and his eyes widened. "Well, if it ain't the man hisself."

"How's it goin'?" I said.

"Better'n most." Gordi swallowed some orange juice, then leaned back in his chair and studied my face. "You beatin' it outta the taco joint like you did yesterday and disappearin' into your room every damn afternoon," Gordi said, "I been thinkin' you some kinda vampire with a fucked-up sense of time."

I forked up a pile of scrambled egg. "A fucked-up sense of timing, maybe. I'd forgotten that I'd promised my girlfriend a phone call right after work, and I knew if I missed her—"

"Your ass'd be toast, huh?"

"You could say that."

"Well, we wouldn't want that, now, would we?" Gordi said.

"No. We most certainly would not."

"She be pissed at you, and all, and you wouldn't be gettin' any piece of it." He leaned to the side and pulled some folded bills out of his back pocket. "Your change."

"Thanks," I said and was disturbed by how easily lying came to me. I had always prided myself on being honest, and now I was lying all the time. Lied to the guard at the gate and to Kessler. A standing lie to Abby. And now Gordi. My presence at the track was one big lie. But, when I thought about it, my entire life had been a goddamned lie.

Gordi wiped his face with the back of his hand. "You disappearin' like Houdini and all, always seemin' like you got somethin' on your mind, Sting be thinkin' you a undercover cop."

I swallowed hard and, between coughs, managed to choke out, "What?"

"And seein' that you been shot like you has—"

"Gordi." I stared at him in dismay.

"Come on, man. I know what *that* looks like, and whether you wanna admit it or not, you been shot."

I shook my head. "Yeah, but he's crazy if he thinks I'm a cop. I'm only twenty-two, for Christ's sake."

"That what I told the dude."

I paused and considered him. "Why would he even think a thing like that, anyway?"

Gordi shrugged. "The word be somebody messin' with Mr. K's horses, so ain't no surprise somebody snoopin' round."

"Who says?"

Gordi shrugged. "Everybody."

"Any idea who's behind it?" I said.

"Not a clue, Holmes." He grinned.

"You and Sting got your wires crossed."

"So, bro, how'd you catch it?"

"Catch what?"

He gestured toward my chest. "A bullet."

I looked down at my plate and pushed around a clump of hash browns. The fork's tines scraped hollowly across the china. "It's a long story."

"I got time."

I shook my head and felt the walls close in around me.

"That bad, huh?"

I shrugged.

"I knowed six people shot back home. Only two of 'em round to talk about it. That's why I come here. Ain't none a that shit round here."

I ate a slice of bacon. Whether I wanted to or not, I had to eat. The days in the shedrow were long and hot and energy-sapping.

"Where's home?" I said.

"Baltimore."

He'd slurred the word like so many natives do, so that it came out sounding like Bawlmar.

"My momma and two sisters still livin' in a dump on Pratt Street. My brother went and signed up with the Army." Gordi shook his head and grinned. "Man, I ain't that stupid."

"What about your dad?" I mumbled around a mouthful of toast and jam.

"Don't know where he at. For all I know, he dead."

I paused and lowered my fork. Gordi was always cheerful and upbeat, joking around, pulling pranks. Apparently life without a father didn't faze him one little bit.

"Doesn't that bother you?" I said. "Not knowing where he is."

"Shit, no."

"You don't miss him?"

"Miss him?" Gordi arched his eyebrows, and the smooth skin across his forehead crinkled. "Man, I wouldn't recognize that son of a bitch if he came trompin' in here and sat his sorry ass in that chair." He gestured to the empty seat next to mine.

"When did you see him last?"

Gordi shrugged. "I was six, maybe. Don't rightly remember." He gulped down the last of his orange juice. "Who I be got nothin' to do with him."

I looked down at my plate.

Who I be got nothin' to do with him.

Gordi dragged a napkin across his mouth and stood up. He balled the napkin in his fist, then dropped it on his tray. He looked at my plate and frowned. "Get a move on, Steve, else you be gettin' youself in trouble with the boss."

Five minutes later, I trailed Gordi into the barn and glanced at the surveillance camera tucked under the eaves just outside Kessler's office. It and its mate, hanging above the feed room door, were obvious once you knew where to look but wouldn't be noticed by the casual observer.

I led Icedancer around the corner on our third lap of the morning. As we turned the corner, Trudy and Abby were standing in the doorway to the mare's stall, whispering with their heads bent toward each other.

As we drew closer, Trudy looked at the ground. Her hands were clasped in front of her, and her face was flushed. Abby watched me openly. Nothing wrong with her confidence.

"Steve." Abby stepped into the aisle. "Let her have a drink."

I stopped, and the mare dipped her nose into the water bucket.

Abby stood close beside me. "You forgot something."

"What?"

She arched her eyebrows. "Ho back?"

"Oh, sorry."

Eye shadow softened her eyes, and a trace of blush colored her fair skin. She'd curled her hair, too, and pulled it up into a loose ponytail. Long blond curls cascaded down her neck, mixing with a tangle of multicolored ribbons.

"That's okay," Abby said. "Just don't forget next time."

I glanced at Trudy. She stood partly concealed behind Abby, and she was smiling as if at a joke. I felt my face getting warm.

I looked back at the horse and tugged gently on the lead. "Come on, girl. You've had enough."

We walked off, and I heard their muted voices behind me. "...not like Jeff," Abby said. Trudy's response was indistinct, and both girls giggled.

The morning wouldn't end soon enough.

Shortly after midnight, I slipped out of Kessler's office and locked the door. My breath quickened with each step down the shedrow. When I turned the corner and was out of sight of both cameras, I stood still and stared down the short aisle toward McCormick's office. My heart was pounding so hard, I felt my pulse throbbing along my spine. Ridiculous. I hadn't even done anything.

Not yet, anyway.

As I listened to the monotonous hum of forty fans, I took a deep breath. This was much riskier than looking in Green's car.

But if I didn't try, I would always wonder what I might have discovered.

The night was thickly black, difficult even to see your feet on the ground, but in the east, the sky was clearing. My window of opportunity was narrowing with each passing second. In no time at all, the moon would slip above the horizon.

I rubbed my hands on my jeans, walked silently over to McCormick's office, and tried the doorknob.

It was locked. I would have been surprised if it had been any other way. I didn't know a thing about picking locks and hoped it wouldn't matter. I inched over to the barn entrance and studied the alley. Except for a rattling bucket in the next barn, the backside was quiet. No movement anywhere. Not even a cat. I checked that the overturned bucket I'd placed under McCormick's office window earlier in the day was still there and slipped my knife out of my pocket.

Like the casement window in my room, this one was cheap and flimsy, no one's idea of secure. I shoved the blade between the edge of the window and the thin metal frame and tripped the latch. I tugged on the window, and it stuck at the top, stiffened by layers of paint and rust. I yanked harder, and the seal gave. I scanned the alley, then fully extended the window, cringing at the high-pitched squeal the handle made as it rotated in the housing.

I stood on the bucket and popped the screen. Oat bags, the backside's answer for curtains, had been tacked to the window frame. I pushed them out of the way, and a wall of chilled air hit my face. As I peered into the quiet darkness, with the cool air washing across my skin, I had a sudden impression of standing at the mouth of a tomb. But I didn't believe in premonitions or ESP or ghosts. It was only the office of a grumpy, moderately successful trainer, for Christ's sake.

I squeezed through the opening and balanced on top of an old, squat bookcase. As I hopped to the floor, a stack of magazines toppled over and slithered across the linoleum. I cursed under my breath. I wasn't cut out for this shit. Double-oh-seven could keep it as far as I was concerned.

I slipped my hand under the frayed edge of the oat bag and pulled the window inward until it was flush with the sill.

No matter that the room was as cold as a meat locker, sweat prickled on my skin. I pressed a button on my watch and checked the time. If I didn't find anything in fifteen minutes, I was out of there.

I slipped the penlight out of my back pocket and flicked it on. Perfect. The narrow beam provided enough light but wouldn't be obvious to anyone passing by outside. All the same, I hunkered down, eased around the desk, and tried the center drawer.

The damn thing was locked. So were the rest of the drawers. I contented myself with searching the desktop. I fingered through the paper clip well. Felt among the pens and pencils. Looked under a heavy paperweight. I lifted the edge of the blotter and shone the light across the polished desktop.

No key. No secret papers. Nothing.

The guy did not want anyone messing with his stuff.

I pried the blade between the drawer and the heavy slab of wood and attempted to slip the latch.

Behind me, something clicked. Metal against metal.

I froze.

The air-conditioner vibrated to life. I exhaled slowly and wiped the sweat off my forehead. I should have expected it. The damn thing ran most of the time.

My hands were still shaking as I worked the knife, and after a moment or two, I gave it up and began a systematic search of the room while the air-conditioner hummed loudly under the back window. I started with the bookcase behind McCormick's desk, scanning titles on equine diseases and their treatments, conditioning, and lameness.

On the second shelf, I found the infamous *Guide to Pharmaceuticals and Biologicals*. I flipped through the pages of the heavy, green book and paused when I came to a scrap of paper marking page 379. Printed in small capital letters, the note read,

GIVE 4 CC PTX IM 12 TO 20 HRS. BEFORE POST, 6 CC IF NECESSARY, COMBINED WITH LSX. I slipped the paper back into position and replaced the book where I'd found it.

When I reached a pair of file cabinets, I glanced at my watch. Sixteen minutes, and I was only half finished. The cabinets were locked, but I had read somewhere that they could be opened by jimmying a rod that ran down the length of the cabinet. I aimed the narrow beam of light at a bronze statue centered on the otherwise bare surface, lifted it, and set it on the floor. I tipped the metal cabinet until the back edge hit the wall, then I squatted and curled my fingers beneath the cool metal frame. My fingertips brushed against cobwebs but no metal rod. No mechanism of any sort. I let the cabinet rock back into place. It hit the linoleum with an unexpectedly loud thud.

I held my breath and listened. For a fleeting second, I thought I heard a muffled sound somewhere within the bowels of the barn, then nothing except my pulse pounding in my ears over the hum of the air-conditioner. I centered the statue on the cabinet and continued down the room.

I scanned files and flipped through notebooks and found nothing out of the ordinary. As a matter of fact, there wasn't much difference between McCormick's office and Kessler's. The same assortment of books, calendars, old condition books, pedigree information, dog-eared auction programs. The same procession of photographs on the walls. The only difference lay in neatness.

The entire endeavor had been a waste of time. An unnecessary risk. Suddenly, I couldn't stay in that room another minute. I shone the flashlight on my watch and was startled to see that I'd been in the office twenty-four minutes.

I scooped the magazines off the floor, pocketed my penlight, and lifted the oat bag away from the window. The alley was flooded in the moon's pearly light. Across the way, the bulk of barn fifteen cast a rectangular shadow over the ground, and the window I was about to climb out of was spotlighted. Exactly what I had hoped to avoid and the reason I had chickened out the night before when the sky had remained clear.

I pushed the window open a few inches. Except for the high-pitched whine of a truck engine straining as it accelerated out on the main road, the night was eerily still. I stepped onto the bookcase, pushed the oat bag aside, and fully extended the window.

A hand streaked out, and strong fingers latched around my wrist.

I opened my mouth, but before I could say anything, he grabbed my shirt and yanked me through the window.

I landed hard on my side. The impact knocked the breath out of my lungs. He rolled me onto my stomach and pinned my wrist between my shoulder blades. I gasped for air as his knee dug into the small of my back. He patted down my back pockets and waistband, then rolled me over.

Jay squatted beside me and looked as surprised as I felt.

"What the hell?" he said. "Christ, man. What you doin' in McCormick's office?"

He yanked me to my feet. His grip was a tight band around my arm.

I leaned forward, rested my free hand on my thigh, and tried to catch my breath.

"Whatju doin', man?" Jay said.

I shook my head.

He reached behind me and closed the window, then glanced toward the access road. "You stealin', man?"

"No." I inhaled and felt my lungs expand. When I straightened, Jay tightened his grip. "I wasn't stealing," I said. "Just lookin' around."

"For what?" Moonlight glinted off his shaved head, yet his eyes were in shadow, unreadable. "Well?" he said.

"I can't say."

"I'm gonna have to tell Mr. K."

"Please don't," I said in a rush. "It's important that he…" I shook my head. "I didn't take anything. I swear."

"I find out you runnin' game on me, man, you'll regret it."

"I'm not lying, man. I promise."

He frowned and took his time thinking it over. "All right. But I gotta check your pockets to make sure."

"Fine. No problem."

Jay clumsily patted me down, as if he were embarrassed with the procedure. When he found nothing to object to, he said, "I catch you doin' anything you shouldn't, anything, and I'll tell Mr. K. You understand?"

I swallowed. "I understand."

He brushed grit off his knees, then walked briskly toward the access road. When he disappeared around the corner of the barn, I sagged against the concrete block and stared at the moon-washed sky. The screen. I'd left the damn screen out. I yanked the window open, grabbed the screen, and slipped it back into place. I closed the window and checked the time.

I'd been out of the barn for half an hour. I pushed myself upright, rubbed a hand over my face, and walked slowly back into the shedrow. I passed McCormick's office door without giving it a second look. Stared at the ground instead and scuffed my feet through the dirt.

I shivered, a short, spasmodic jerk up my spine. What was I thinking, breaking into his office like that? I could have been on my way to jail, and that thought twisted my gut into a knot.

As I neared the door to Kessler's feed room, I paused. In the sawdust by the exit, light reflected weakly off a small disk-shaped object. I bent over to pick it up and froze.

It wasn't just any stray piece of trash. Jagged shards of plastic lay scattered across the aisle. Flat, black planes, smooth and hard against the soft, loamy footing. Crumpled pieces of metal half-embedded in the sawdust.

Remains of the video camera.

I jerked upright and looked at the ceiling by the eaves. The bracket hung crookedly. Mangled and empty.

I spun around and sprinted to Speedwell's stall.

The colt started when I skidded to a stop outside his door. His neck muscles tensed, and he raised his head defensively. He was alone, and it appeared that, except for my hasty approach, he was otherwise unconcerned.

I continued down the length of the shedrow. The camera that hung outside Kessler's office had been similarly destroyed. Not simply disabled, but smashed to bits, and someone had expended a good deal of energy doing it.

Cursing under my breath, I returned to Speedwell's stall and flicked on my penlight. I pressed my hand on his shoulder and murmured to him, trying to calm him when all he could read from me was frustrated anger. I shone the narrow beam along the colt's dappled gray coat.

He eyed me suspiciously, tense, as if the light itself was a physical sensation on his skin. I could find no sign that he had been injected, no trickle of dried blood among the short, fine hairs. I played the beam across his lips and found no indication that he'd been medicated orally. No trace of powder or unexpected saliva.

I absentmindedly patted him and felt a lump midway down his neck, centered in the triangular-shaped area typically used for intramuscular injections.

"Goddamn it."

He had been drugged. And whoever had injected him had known what he was doing. He'd pinched the skin before inserting the needle, so that afterward, when the needle was withdrawn, the skin would retract and leave no path for the blood to follow.

I clenched my fists and whirled away from him. The penlight's beam arced wildly across the stall. Out of the corner of my eye, I glimpsed something out of place. Something white. A piece of trash? I angled the light across the straw until the beam bounced off the object.

Long, narrow, whitish. A syringe lay half-hidden in the tangle of golden, sweet-smelling straw. I crouched down to pick it up and hesitated. What if there were fingerprints?

I flicked off the beam. The stall slipped into blackness, Speedwell's bulk light against the darker walls. In Kessler's office, I ignored the staticky snow on the monitor's screen as I searched through his desk. I found a manila envelope, then snatched two pencils off the blotter.

Back in the colt's stall, I gripped the penlight in my teeth and crimped the envelope until it stayed open, then I grasped the syringe with the pencils and levered it into the envelope.

It was better than nothing.

In Kessler's office, I pulled a folded slip of paper out of my pocket and smoothed it flat on the desk blotter. The blue ink had bled after so many hours in clothes damp with sweat, but I could still read the numbers printed in Kessler's ragged hand. I snatched up the cordless phone and punched in his home number.

I listened to the recording on his answering machine, and after the beep shrilled in my ear, I said, half-expecting him to pick up in mid-message, "This is Steve. I have a problem...." No pick up, just a hollow silence on the line. "They destroyed the video cameras and got to Speedwell. I found a syringe. If I don't hear from you by..." I glanced at my watch. "If I don't hear from you by one, I'm gonna come by your place. I don't feel comfortable leaving it here." After a pause, I mumbled "Sorry" and hung up.

I sat on the edge of the desk and stared at the monitor. I rubbed the back of my neck. Maybe all was not lost. I hopped off the desk and pressed the rewind button. A low, mechanical whir filled the empty silence as the tape wound back into the cassette. After several minutes, I stopped the machine and hit the play button. The split screen image of the shedrow flicked on with a hiccup, grainy green and slightly blurred. The aisle was empty.

I propped a hip against the desk and waited. I looked at my watch. Rubbed my face.

Damn it, why hadn't I just stayed in the horse's stall?

I depressed the fast forward button and held my finger lightly on the smooth plastic, feeling a slight vibration as the reels spun beneath the housing. I watched as first one horse then another and another poked their heads over their stall guards, then disappeared abruptly back into the stalls' depths. The sped-up image would have been comical under different circumstances.

Then he came.

I slammed the stop button down, rewound the tape for a second or two, then hit PLAY.

The audio alarm beeped as he entered the barn down by the feed room. He pressed close to the wall so that the camera above his head wouldn't pick up his image as he moved into position. Only the camera by Kessler's office recorded his actions, and with a distance of approximately 300 feet, the picture was useless. Even still, he was careful to keep his back to the office camera as he lifted his arms above his head and swung. It wasn't until then that I realized he had been holding something in his hands. A baseball bat? Maybe. The picture was so poor, it was difficult to be certain.

His first swing missed, but the second connected, and the picture shifted abruptly. A blurred close-up of the barn overhang filled half the screen. He swung again, and this time the picture undulated and broke into wavy lines before disintegrating into static. He left the barn quickly, and in a second, the camera nestled among the eaves by Kessler's office went black before the snowy static took over.

The timing had been too fast for one person. There had to have been two of them, one at each end of the barn, both prepared to take out the cameras quickly and efficiently.

I pressed the eject button, and the tape slid smoothly into my palm. All the picture showed was a man, medium build, wearing jeans, a tee shirt, and a baseball cap. Christ. That fit most of the population. Straightening, I stretched my spine, picked up the envelope, and glanced around the room before turning off the lights and locking the door.

I paused outside Speedwell's door. What did they give you, boy?

He lifted his head as if he'd heard my thought.

"You try your best, don't you, boy? Run your guts out to be first, and they do this to you."

Watching him watch me with his soft liquid eyes and sleek ears pointed my way, I felt the first stirrings of a deepening anger. Anger at them. Anger at myself for being so stupid. For thinking I was going to step right in and solve everything. Be the hero. All because I wanted Kessler to be proud of me.

I should have known better.

I turned away from him and walked out to my truck. As I pulled into Kessler's apartment complex and cut the engine, it occurred to me that I didn't even know which apartment was his. I scanned the parking lot.

Kessler's Lincoln wasn't there, so I walked toward the building closest to where he'd parked the other night. Heavy iron lampposts cast yellow pools of light across the sidewalk, and the open-air foyers were well lit. Good for security. I strolled into unit 1709 and scanned the row of mailboxes.

Kessler's name was printed alongside 2B. I climbed the steps, then leaned on the buzzer for a good five seconds before giving it a rest. After a minute, I tried again. Still no response. I slammed my fist into the door. Where the hell was he?

I stood there for a second or two and stared at the door like I was going to find the solution to all my problems in the smooth, teal paint. Damn it. I had really screwed up.

When I got back to the track, I looked in on Speedwell. He turned his head when I stepped into his doorway, and a stray beam of light glinted off his half-closed eye. I checked my watch. One-thirty-five. The quiet hours before dawn when most of the horses were relaxed enough to sleep. And I felt like copying them. The damage was done, and as far as I could determine, there was nothing else I could do. After locking the tape and syringe in Kessler's office, I walked back to my room and fiddled with the doorknob. The plate in the doorframe was so loose, I could have

yanked it out with my fingers. I pushed the door to, turned the
fan on high, then stripped to my underwear. I flopped on the
bed, wrapped my arms around the pillow, and closed my eyes.
The air flowed across my back, cool and refreshing, the motor's
hum lulling me to sleep.

I gradually became conscious of my breathing. Slow, deep
breaths, indicative of sleep, then a subtle shifting of air currents
that set off an alarm somewhere in my brain. I told it to shut
up and slipped back into blissful oblivion, only to be awakened
by a tickling sensation on the back of my neck, like a shirt tag
that had twisted out of place.

When I remembered I wasn't wearing a shirt, I came fully
awake.

Chapter 13

A hand clamped down on my neck.

I opened my mouth to yell, and he shoved my face into the pillow, the sound getting lost in the foam stuffing. I swung wildly at him and was surprised when he let go. As I pushed upward, I heard a click. Something touched my lower back.

Pain jolted through my spine and slammed me against the mattress. Sharp, brutal pain. Air shot out of my lungs. A scream.

My scream.

Fingers twisted into my hair, and he held my face against the pillow.

"That was just a taste," a voice above my head whispered, "so you know I mean business."

Spasms racked my arms and legs. A million burning needles. Nerve endings firing uncontrollably.

I was dimly aware of the mattress depressing as he climbed onto the bed and straddled me, and I couldn't do a thing to stop him. He yanked my head backward, and somewhere among the confused jumble of thoughts bouncing around inside my brain, I thought that I should scream for help. Yell at the top of my lungs. Do something. But the thought never made it to my mouth or anywhere else. A hand came around in front of my face and slapped something across my lips.

"What if he vomits like the other one?" someone mumbled. Nervous. Distant. Close to the door. "He'll choke."

"Shut up," the one on top of me said. More like a growl than a voice. Low. Under his breath.

He let go of my hair then, and my head dropped back onto the pillow. Somewhere overhead, the sound of ripping. He jerked my head off the pillow and pressed something over my eyes. I tried to open my mouth, and this time I felt a response. The correct impulse traveling along the right nerve. Muscles trying to move. But my lips were stuck together.

Tape. It had to be tape.

He bound my wrists with it.

"Look at this."

The words jarred me into the present. Not the nervous voice by the door. Not the one who had put the tape on my face, either. A younger voice. Casual.

"You were right," he said. "He's got background info on everyone in Kessler's outfit. And look at this." Papers rustled. "This ain't no kinda paycheck I ever seen."

He must have found the check I hadn't gotten around to depositing. The one Kessler had given me for my...extracurricular duties, which meant they were conducting a thorough search. I'd tucked it into an inner pocket in my duffel bag.

"Let me see, and get his license," the gruff one said. The one I had come to think of as their leader.

Footsteps crossed the room, and I thanked my lucky stars I had already given Green's information to Kessler.

"All right. Let's get this over with." He leaned forward, and his weight over my hips lightened as he pressed his hand between my shoulder blades. "Listen up, Steve. You don't want me to zap you again. Just give me what I want, and we're outta here. But," he inhaled deeply, "if I think you've figured out who I am, if you somehow manage to see me, I'll kill you."

The room was deeply quiet, and it was his calmness that scared me most.

"Do you understand?"

I nodded.

"Good." His breath slid across the side of my face. Stale and warm, smelling of cigarettes. "All you have to do is tell me where the syringe is. That's all I want. I'm going to take the tape off your mouth, and you're going to tell me where it is. Nice and easy. Understand?"

I wondered if Gordi would hear me if I called out. Wondered if anyone would.

"Understand?"

I grunted.

He hopped off the bed and anchored his fingers in my hair. "I don't want to hurt you, so be quiet."

He yanked my head around so that I was facing the wall, then he peeled the tape off my mouth.

I screamed Gordi's name at the top of my lungs.

He must have expected it. Must have anticipated my reaction, because I didn't get one syllable out before he clamped the tape back down over my mouth.

"You fuck."

He pushed off me, and I knew what was coming. Heard the click and, for the first time, the crackling hiss. He pressed the stun gun between my shoulder blades, against tensed muscles and skin soaked with sweat, and this time I was screaming from pain. The sound getting nowhere. Caught in my throat. Muffled beneath the tape.

My body jerked uncontrollably on the damp sheets, and I briefly wondered when it would let up, and after a moment or two, I wasn't wondering anything at all.

◇◇◇

I heard the low purr of an engine close by. The sound of tires moving across smooth asphalt.

A sharp smell of dust filled my nostrils, and I gradually realized I was lying on my stomach, and I was damn uncomfortable. Beneath me, a bulge of some sort dug into my gut, and something hard pressed into my back, pinning me to the ground.

Everywhere was pitch black, the darkness so complete, I couldn't tell whether my eyes were open or closed. I couldn't remember where I was or how I had gotten there. Couldn't string two coherent thoughts together if I tried.

I stopped trying.

After a time, when thought drifted disconnected through my skull, disjointed, like garbled images in a dream, I decided I ought to find out where I was. I tried to move my arms but couldn't. The aborted attempt caused my muscles to spasm, and the pain kicked my memory into gear.

Were they still with me? I couldn't tell. And where the hell was I?

The ground suddenly lurched beneath me, and I half rolled onto my side. The sensation crystallized an image in my mind.

The car I heard wasn't just driving by. I was in it. On the floorboard. The bulge that dug into my stomach was simply the housing for the drive shaft. I moved my legs and found that they had fastened my ankles together as well. My toes brushed against the door's ribbed upholstery.

The front bumper dipped suddenly, and the car left the asphalt. I felt a strong drag on the tires. Sand or loose dirt. The track? Were we on the track or someplace farther away? I hadn't a clue because, even though I didn't think I'd been out long, my sense of time seemed hopelessly skewed. The car swung into a turn, then the driver shifted into reverse, backed up, and braked to a stop. He cut the engine, and in the sudden quiet, someone cleared his throat.

"Is he conscious yet?" the gruff voice whispered. The driver.

"Yeah." The younger voice was close above me, and I realized it was his shoes that were digging into my back. "Your stun gun ain't workin' too good. Nobody'll hear us back here. Want me to beat it out of him?"

"We don't have time for that," the driver said. The front door opened, and the car rocked slightly as he climbed out. The front passenger got out, too.

"Here." I heard as much as felt the driver lean into the car. "Zap him if he gives you any trouble."

The young guy cleared his throat. "How long—"

"Whisper," the leader said under his breath.

"How long's this gonna take?"

"Depends." He clicked the door shut.

I thought about the significance of what they'd said. If no one could hear us, then why whisper? Back in my room, I had thought they were whispering to avoid waking my neighbors. But now, it seemed they were whispering because they were afraid I would recognize their voices, which meant I knew them. One of them, at least.

And I prayed that it also meant they weren't planning on killing me.

Did I know them? Like them?

I thought about everyone I had met in the last eight days, starting, for lack of a better place, with Gordi. No. It couldn't be him. Whispering or not, he wasn't one of these bastards because he didn't talk like they did. I eliminated Hector for the same reason.

What about Jay? He'd been around the barn when Speedwell was drugged, but for various reasons, I hoped he wasn't involved. One, I liked the guy, and two, he could snap every bone in my body without breaking a sweat. If he was one of these guys, and they decided to lay into me, I was in deep shit.

Then there was Marcus with his fat beer gut and angry-at-the-world attitude. Maybe. Even if I didn't think much of his intellect, I assumed he could follow orders.

Allen? I had no idea. Kessler's background information on him had been useless. Stingray was more interested in getting laid than anything else. And even though I had never suspected them, I could now safely eliminate the girls in the barn.

And what about Abby's Jeff? He was romancing her despite Kessler's disapproval. Although he seemed to enjoy making his living galloping horses, and the image that went with it, he wasn't satisfied with his earnings. He was a possibility, I supposed, if he was immoral enough. And deceitful.

Next, I came to Mr. McCormick. Winning races legitimately might not be enough for him, and because of the envelope exchange, I put my money on his being one of the men in the car. His groom, too. Randy Tyson. If he *was* one of the goons on Abby's porch, it made sense that he'd be a part of this, too.

Although I hadn't recognized their voices, I still considered them prime—

The front passenger's door opened and someone slid clumsily onto the seat.

The younger guy shifted, and his feet jarred my shoulder. "Switch on—"

"Shh. Whisper," the nervous guy said. "We're suppose to whisper."

"Don't get yourself in a tizzy," he said. "Open the damn windows. It's a fucking oven in here."

I listened as the guy in front turned the key and momentarily triggered the alarm in the steering column. The electric windows slid smoothly on their tracks. Warm air currents eddied through the open windows and moved across my bare skin.

A click echoed in the dark, followed by the distinct sizzle of an arcing current.

I tensed my muscles and waited for the jolt.

He clicked it off, then on, then off. Playing with it. He was just playing with it. I exhaled slowly through my nose and unclenched my jaw.

There was nothing like pain to produce a conditioned reflexive response. I was beginning to feel like one of Pavlov's damn dogs.

The night was unusually quiet. No traffic sounds, no insect noise. Just a breeze rustling through some nearby trees. I tried to picture where we were, but I had no idea how long I'd been out. Without that knowledge, I couldn't begin to guess at our location.

Eventually, a car approached, slowed, then idled to a stop. The guy in the front passenger seat climbed out, and after a minute or two, the other vehicle moved off at a fast clip with its tires whining on asphalt.

When the driver's door opened, I tensed.

"You ready?" the leader asked.

"Yeah." The nervous guy was at the passenger's door, and I imagined him leaning into the car. "If I have to," he said, "but I'm not used to doing it to a human."

"He won't complain." A muffled chuckle.

"Well, you're going to have to pull him out. I can't do it in here."

The leader grunted.

"Time to go." The guy above me jabbed my arm with the heel of his boot.

Boot. Why did that seem significant? A thought flickered in the back of my mind but fizzled out at the sound of the door by my head creaking open. I swallowed. A sour taste coated the back of my throat.

The young guy clambered over on top of me, grabbed my arm, and dragged me out of the car.

"Damn, he's sweaty."

The leader chuckled. "You'd be, too, if you were in his place."

I lay on my side, on the cool, moist dirt, instinctively balled into a fetal position.

I had given up on trying to yell. Sometime earlier, they'd replaced or reinforced the tape on my mouth. I could smell the adhesive with every breath, and it was tighter than before. Yelling, I was certain, would get me nowhere.

One of them moved behind me, grabbed my shoulder, and tried to shove me onto my stomach. "Come on," he grunted.

Two of them shoved, and pushed, and pinched, and prodded, and when they finally got me pinned to the ground, everyone was panting, and I wished I could breathe through my mouth.

Something tightened around my upper arm. A needle pricked the skin inside my elbow, and I felt his fingers shaking.

A warm rush spread up my arm. Through my entire body. I was floating. Was certain I could feel the Earth spinning on its axis.

◇◇◇

I opened my eyes. My vision cleared slowly as I focused on my hand, inches from my face, fingers curled and lax, half buried in the sawdust. I squinted and looked beyond them at the white concrete block wall.

My arms and legs were anchored to the ground. Dead weight. Useless. I was overcome with the sensation that I was sunk into the ground, not simply lying on top of it.

I lifted my head, and that simple movement sent my brain spinning. The floor seemed to drop out from beneath me, and I felt myself falling.

Saliva flooded my mouth. I swallowed and willed myself not to get sick. After a minute or two, the sensation faded, and it was then that I realized I was in the short aisle not far from Kessler's office.

I groaned and rolled onto my side. My arm bumped against something smooth and hard. A whiskey bottle lay in the sawdust. The liquid sloshed against the glass. A sharp odor of alcohol permeated my nostrils, stronger than the prevailing smell of horse.

I licked my lips with a tongue that felt sluggish, like my brain, and tasted liquor on the back of my teeth. But I had no memory of drinking it.

I reached over and sat the bottle upright. It was three-quarters empty. I couldn't have drunk that much and not remember, could I?

And then I remembered the needle and everything else.

I rolled onto my back and stared at the roof overhang. A subtle lightening tinted the sky. I fumbled with the button on my watch. My brain felt fuzzy, every muscle in my body hopelessly drained of energy.

I finally pressed the right button. The dial glowed blue-green in the dark. No wonder they'd been worried about the time. It was already three-thirty. In half an hour, the backside would wake up. Lights flicking on, horses whinnying, voices mumbling, thick with sleep.

Sleep. That's what I needed.

I clambered to my feet and stumbled into Kessler's office.

I held onto the desk for support as I edged around to the back and plopped down in the chair. Air wheezed through a tear in the cushion, and I wondered if Kessler had ever noticed that his chair farted every time he sat down. I braced my hand on the edge of the desktop and opened the lower right-hand drawer. The videotape and syringe were gone.

"God damn it."

I couldn't remember telling them, but I must have. I shoved the drawer closed, crossed my arms on the blotter, and rested my forehead on my arms. Closed my eyes. The whirling in my head increased. Any other time, I would have enjoyed the feeling of release.

I stopped fighting it. Relaxed into it.

The damage was done, and I couldn't change that now. At least I was alive. Alive and in one piece, all things considered. I didn't actually feel drunk, but I was high. I wondered what they'd given me and decided that the relief that came with being safe was as intoxicating as any drug.

The door creaked.

I jerked my head up and flung my arms outward. The quartz horse head toppled over, and a stack of folders tipped off the blotter and slithered across the floor.

Kessler was standing in the doorway, a broken piece of camera in one hand, the whiskey bottle in the other. "What the hell's going on?"

He glared at me when I giggled, and I clamped my mouth shut. I tried to think of some kind of coherent answer. Tried to keep a straight face and knew I was failing miserably.

"I...ah. They got to Speedy-boy. Did you hear? On the recording, I mean."

I reached out to pick up the paperweight and ended up knocking over a container of pencils and pens. They scattered across the blotter, and half of them rolled off the desk and landed on top of the folders. I righted the container. It was a metal can, the kind used for vegetables or fruit. Someone had covered it with brightly colored slivers of paper, pasted then laminated. I bet Abby had made it in grade school and—

"Where are your clothes?" Kessler asked, incredulous. He had crossed the room and was staring down at me.

I hung my head and noticed for the first time that my legs were bare. I giggled.

"You're drunk." His voice held a mixture of disgust and anger.

I turned toward him too fast, and the walls tilted abruptly. I grabbed the edge of the desk and mumbled, "No, I'm not. They did it."

His jaw muscles bunched as if he were clenching his teeth, and his cheeks were flushed. "Did what?" he said.

"Made me this way." I giggled again because it sounded so fucking lame. Like saying the devil made me—

"What are you talking about, and who are 'they'?"

I squinted up at him. "I don't know. I couldn't see them." For the first time, I noticed the slur in my voice. "They drugged Speedy, ah, Speedwell, and stole the syringe and," I peered at the inside of my arm, "shot something into me." My head lulled back, and I closed my eyes. "I haven't been drinking."

"Je-sus Christ."

He thunked the whiskey bottle on his desktop, and it wobbled before coming to rest solidly on its base.

"Wait here."

I watched him leave and couldn't tell if he believed me. Eventually, the low purr of an engine echoed in the short corridor. A car door opened, and in a moment, Kessler came back into the office and grabbed my arm. He heaved me to my feet.

He looked me over and crinkled his nose. "Christ. You're filthy."

"Yeah? Well you'd be, too, after being dumped in the dirt and held down."

Kessler guided me out of the office. "What are you talking about?"

"That's where they gave it to me."

"Gave what to you?"

"I told you. I don't know."

"Who are you talking about, anyway?"

I shrugged.

"Would you recognize them if you saw them again?"

I shook my head. "I couldn't see them."

He sighed in response. As we stepped into the alley and headed toward the Lincoln's back bumper, I stepped on something sharp.

"Ouch!"

He put his arm around my waist. "Why couldn't you see them, Steve?"

"Just couldn't," I mumbled.

He propped me against the side of the car, opened the front passenger door, and shoved me inside. I sagged against the seat and leaned my head against the headrest.

The upholstery was soft and supple, smelling faintly of leather. Refined. Not the strong odor of tack, which I liked more.

Kessler slid behind the wheel and eyed me with speculation. His hair was damp from his shower. He must have sped things up when he got my message, and I wondered where he'd been the entire fucking night.

"Where've you—"

"What's today?" Kessler asked.

"Huh?"

"The day. What day is it?"

"Wednesday." I rolled my head to the side and peered at him. It must not have been Wednesday. Working through the nights like I'd been, the days bled together. "Thursday, I mean."

"What's six times nine?"

I giggled. "What's this? A test?"

"Just answer the question."

"Fifty-four."

"Which horses raced yesterday?"

It took me a minute, but I got that right, too, even though I hadn't cooled them out.

"Okay." It was as much a sigh as a word. He shifted the car into drive, pulled around to my unit, and parked at the base of the steps. "I'm going to leave you in your room for a while. You gonna be okay?"

I nodded.

He helped me up the stairs, and when we got to my room, I pushed against the door, and it swung silently inward. Kessler switched on the light. Suspended from the ceiling, the glare from the naked bulb shone into the deepest corners of the dingy room. Roaches darted across the floor. The fan had been tipped over and lay flat on the linoleum, the motor straining.

My room was trashed. Completely and thoroughly trashed. Clothes had been dumped out of my duffel bag, food stepped on and squished, everything strewn in a jumbled mess across the floor.

"I'll have to have a word with housekeeping," I said.

"Christ." Kessler glanced at his watch. "Do you want me to take you home, instead?"

"Nah."

I stumbled across the debris and flopped onto the bed. The mattress was crooked on the metal frame, and I suddenly knew why. I rolled off the bed and lifted the edge of the mattress as Kessler picked up the fan and pointed it in my direction.

"What are you doing?" he said.

I felt along the joint where two of the metal angle irons met. "Damn. The bastards found my money from Ruskie's win. Around eight hundred bucks." I shoved the mattress back where it belonged. "God damn it!"

Kessler whistled under his breath. "I'll call security."

I crawled back onto the mattress and wrapped my arms around the pillow. "Don't bother," I mumbled.

He sighed. "I'll get Abby started with the workouts, then we'll talk."

I flapped my hand at him, and he left.

Chapter 14

I didn't see him leave. As a matter of fact, I didn't see anything else until much later in the day when I woke up with a dull ache behind my eyes and a ringing in my ears. I stretched, then crossed my arms behind my head.

The fog in my brain had dissolved, leaving behind a lingering feeling of unease. Like a bad taste in the mouth. I had been lucky, and the temptation was strong to give it up and go home. But I had been doing way too much of that lately. Giving up. Running away.

I rubbed my face.

When the old man had kicked me out for leaving college, I'd done everything I could to block him out. I'd immersed myself in my job at Foxdale. If it didn't have to do with horses, then it had no place in my life. And it was ironic because, as the hard work paid off, and the farm's reputation skyrocketed, I'd become the target of a sociopathic killer. When things went bad there, I ran away from that, too.

Ran to the track. To Kessler, really. And although it hadn't occurred to me at the time, I had been running away from myself.

Someday, I'd have to stop.

Like Gordi, I had to…No. I needed to accept the fact that life wasn't fair and make the best of it.

I pulled on my jeans, jammed my feet into a pair of sneakers, and grabbed some clean clothes, a towel, and a bottle of shampoo on my way out the door.

Outside, a wall of heat and glare assaulted the senses. In the distance, the announcer's voice clattered over the PA system as he called a race, his words coming fast with excitement. I looked at my watch. Race number four.

Horses doing what came naturally while the men associated with them were willing to inflict excruciating pain, even terror, to get the right horse under the wire first. A mental shiver went down my spine.

I walked into the men's room and stopped in my tracks when I saw my reflection in the mirror. Dirt and sawdust still clung to my skin, and my hair was caked with it. It was a wonder Kessler had even put me in his fancy car.

At four-thirty, shaved and showered and looking halfway respectable, I rounded the corner of barn sixteen just as Abby walked briskly out of the shedrow. She changed course when she saw me.

"Feeling better?" she said.

"Eh…" Not knowing what Kessler may have told her, I simply said, "Yes."

"Didn't know a bug was going round."

"Must have been something I ate," I said.

"Oh."

She tucked a loose strand of hair behind her ear. A gold hoop glinted in the sunlight, and I was surprised to see she was wearing shorts and a blouse instead of the usual tee shirt and jeans. I glanced at her legs. They were pale but muscular, and considering her job, neither was a surprise.

"Could you walk me to my car, Steve? Since the *incident* on my porch, Dad doesn't like me going anywhere by myself." She scanned the alley and made an odd little gesture with her hand. "Even here."

"Sure."

When we rounded the corner of the barn, Mr. McCormick and a man I didn't recognize were standing across the street, engaged in animated conversation. McCormick nodded in response to something that was said and smoothed a hand across his scalp. He held a cigarette between his lips, and the smoke curled upward in the still air between the two men. The other guy had his arms crossed over his chest, and he was squinting as if the smoke bothered him. Or the sun.

"Well, you tell that little Puerto Rican," he said to McCormick, "he better—"

McCormick caught sight of us and cut the man off with a flap of his hand. They watched us walk past in silence. Abby stopped talking, as well, and I thought how secrecy was a big part of the game on the backside.

When we passed the next barn, Abby continued. "Dad thinks the bastards who jumped us might live at the track."

"Maybe."

Abby glanced at me, then said, "I can't believe someone's trying to get at our horses. Did you hear what happened last night?"

"No."

"Somebody destroyed the surveillance cameras Dad had installed the other day, and he thinks they drugged Speedwell."

"No kidding."

"I wish I was. He pink-slipped him first thing this morning."

"Pink-slipped?"

"Scratched him." She shook her head. "The colt looked okay to me, but Dad was sure somebody'd got to him. He had Charles run a complete work-up."

Thinking back, I remembered Charles was Kessler's vet. "Did he find anything?"

"Nothing he could put his finger on. The blood work won't be back for a day or two. Dad had a hell of a time convincing the stewards to scratch him, but they finally gave in. And I'm surprised they did, too, because they hate taking them off the card this late. But Mr. Hurp talked to them, and they changed their minds."

"Mr. Hurp?" I said.

"Yeah. He's been helping Dad find out who's behind the dopings. God," she said. "What a morning." Abby stopped alongside her little black car and unlocked the door.

A child's stuffed toy was lying on the rear deck. A bay horse with a blaze and four white socks, legs splayed, face pressed against the glass.

"I'm going shopping," Abby said. "I've gotta get away from here for awhile. Do something that has absolutely nothing to do with horses." She opened the door and waited for the heat to dissipate. "The whole thing's so scary. Why are they doing this to us?" she said.

"Maybe you and your father aren't the only targets. Is anyone else having trouble?"

She smoothed her fingertips beneath her eyes and wiped away a fine sheen of perspiration. A light dusting of freckles that I hadn't noticed before was scattered across her cheeks and the bridge of her nose.

"Oh, sure," she said. "But there's always rumors like that going round the barns. All the time. About bribes and race-fixing and horses being drugged. There's never a shortage of gossip. Everybody's always trying to cheat somebody out of something. You stick around long enough, you'll see that racetrackers are the most paranoid group of people on the face of the earth. A horse has an off day, and everybody thinks somebody got to it."

She exhaled sharply. "God, I hate this. Dad works so hard and…" Her voice trailed off.

"How certain are you that they're being drugged?"

"At first, it was just a suspicion, a gut feeling that something was wrong. But after a while, a pattern became obvious. When they're your own, you just know."

"Where's Jeff?" I said.

She regarded me with those clear hazel eyes of hers. "Jeff and I aren't joined at the hip, you know? Or anywhere else for that matter."

We looked at each other without speaking, and I wondered if the recent change in her appearance was an outward sign of trouble between them.

She turned away from me and slid gingerly onto the seat. "Anyway, Steve, thanks for the escort."

I stood back as she pulled the door to, started the engine, and drove off. The little Taurus SE bumped onto the access road and disappeared behind a row of barns.

If something bad happened to Kessler, if his reputation was irreparably damaged, it would hurt her as much as him. She was devoted to him, of that I had no doubt, and I guessed he was doubly important to her since she had grown up without a mother. I wondered which hurt more, losing someone through death or rejection.

I headed back to the barn and shook myself out of that line of thought. Self-pity would get me nowhere.

I paused at the mouth of the alley and looked toward the track. The air vibrated with the heat. In the distance, haze blanketed the grandstand, dampening the noise of the crowd and distorting the smooth, clean lines of the roof. I walked out of the glare and into the darkness of the barn, wondering if this place would still be here in a hundred years. Would anyone even care about racing, then?

But today, they cared. Cared so much, they were willing to twist the odds around in their favor.

I stopped in the doorway to Kessler's office. The room was empty, but the fan was running on high. Lined, yellow pages of a legal pad lifted in the artificial breeze and curled over the binding. Everything else that typically cluttered the desk had been stacked into a neat pile and was weighted down by the quartz horse head. Droplets had condensed on the outside of a half-empty cup from Burger King and were seeping into the blotter.

I strolled down the shedrow and stopped in front of Speed-well's stall. The gray colt pricked his ears and stretched his nose toward me. I cupped my hands around his muzzle. When he discovered that I didn't have anything for him to eat, he lost interest and went back to picking at his hay net. As I listened to the rhythmic grind of his teeth, it occurred to me that Hector would have held back his hay if he hadn't been scratched.

Another missed opportunity. Kessler had been certain of his chances, and apparently he hadn't been the only one.

I heard footsteps on the gravel and turned as Kessler walked into the barn.

He paused just inside the doorway. "So, you're back in the land of the living. I was wondering where you'd gotten to. I just now came from your room."

I slipped my hands in my pockets, walked back down the shedrow, and stopped a pace or two in front of him. "I took a shower," I said, and it sounded stupid, all things considered.

"I couldn't wake you, you know? I was beginning to wonder if I should call the medics, but your pulse and respiration seemed normal enough."

He crossed the aisle and lifted a chain shank off the junction box. Someone had slotted a hay hook behind the metal conduit, and it fell on the ground. Kessler picked it up and looked at it as if he'd never seen one before, then he walked around the corner and hooked it on the ladder to the hayloft.

"So, you're all right?" It was half question, half statement.

"Yeah."

He walked past me, undid Ruskie's stall guard, and slotted the chain through the rings on the colt's halter. When he turned around, his face was carefully neutral, but he couldn't keep what he was feeling out of his eyes.

Frustration, confusion? Anger?

He led Ruskie into the aisle and said over his shoulder, "While I graze him, you can tell me about last night."

In silence, I followed them down the alley and across the road. Kessler stopped when he reached a shady spot under a sprawling maple, and Ruskie didn't need to be told what he was there for. He greedily lowered his head and snatched a mouthful of grass.

"Okay," Kessler said. "What happened? In the first place, how'd they get to Speedwell without you seeing them? Where were you? Did you fall asleep, go to the bathroom…or what?"

Or what? He'd said it with weight, as if it were the crux of the whole fucking mess. Like he was already convinced I'd been falling down drunk.

"I wasn't in the barn," I said and tried to keep the bite out of my voice. "When I came back and saw that the cameras had been smashed, I checked on Speedwell and found the welt on his neck." I rubbed a hand over my face. "Then I found the syringe, so I left a message on your machine, and while I was waiting for you to call back, I watched the tape."

His gaze sharpened on my face. "Where is it? It wasn't in the VCR."

He was hopeful, and I realized the video equipment had probably been the first thing he'd checked after dropping me off.

"They came back later and took it."

"Did you see who—"

"The picture wasn't good enough," I said. "You could see the shape of a man, but that was about it. And the way they operated, it was obvious they knew the cameras were there. They came prepared."

"How do you mean?"

"The guy on the tape had a bat or something else heavy that he used to smash the cameras."

"You keep saying 'they.' Were they both on the tape?"

I shook my head. "There were three actually, but I didn't find that out until later, after I stopped by your apartment. When I saw you weren't home, I put the tape and syringe in your desk."

"I don't get it," he said. "How'd they know where to look, and how'd they get into the office? The lock wasn't forced. I checked."

"Uh…"

He could see I didn't want to go there. "Back up a minute. Where were you when they got to the colt?"

I wanted to go there even less. "I…uh. Oh, shit." I looked away from him. "I broke into McCormick's office and looked around, all right?"

"You what?"

Ruskie lifted his head in response to Kessler's raised voice.

"I know you said not to do anything like that, but I was certain I'd find something to link him to the dopings."

"And did you?"

"No," I said half under my breath.

"Look, Steve. I don't know what you're trying to prove…" Kessler looked at the ground and rubbed the back of his neck. "You don't need to prove yourself to me."

"I know."

He exhaled sharply through his nose. "I'm not certain you do. If anyone has to prove something around here, it's me to you, not the other way around."

When I didn't respond, he said, "Look. I can't have you working for me if you're going to pull this shit. Going off half-cocked like that, you're only going to get yourself in trouble. It's not worth it. It would be nice to catch them. Hell, it would be great. But breaking the law? Well, I just can't have it." When I didn't respond, he said, "I need your word."

He was studying me with concentration, and I knew I'd be out if I messed up again.

"All right. You've got it. I won't do anything else that's even remotely illegal, okay?"

"Okay."

A truck out on the road ground its gears.

"What happened next?"

"After I put the tape and syringe in your desk—"

"Did you lock the door?" Kessler said.

"Yeah. I went back to my room. Guess I fell asleep pretty quick."

"How'd they know where to find the syringe? Do you think they were following you, or saw where you put it?"

"No." I walked over to the base of the tree and sat cross-legged on the grass. "They didn't know where it was." I leaned against the smooth trunk and closed my eyes.

"How'd they get it, then?"

I opened my eyes and focused on Ruskie. The chain clinked rhythmically against the metal on his halter every time he wrenched a mouthful of grass from the lawn.

"They came into my room," I said. "While I was asleep. They had a stun gun."

"Shit." A sharp, short exclamation. Under his breath.

"At the time, it was pretty much incapacitating, but I didn't tell them where it was. Not then, anyway."

"Oh, Jesus."

I glanced at him, then looked at the ground. His mouth hung slackly open, his eyes round with shock, but what disturbed me most was the pity I saw in his face. I bent my left leg and draped my arm over my knee. I didn't want pity. Didn't deserve it. If I hadn't fucked up, none of it would have happened.

"Are you still in pain?"

I shook my head. "No. It hurt like hell when they were using it, but the effect's temporary."

"Then what?" His voice was hoarse.

"I couldn't see them because it was dark, and they put tape over my eyes and mouth." I cleared my throat. "They took me in a car somewhere, and when I still wouldn't tell them, they stuck a needle in my arm, and after that, I don't really remember much, except waking up in the shedrow not long before you showed up."

"And the whiskey bottle?" He'd asked it carefully, his voice neutral, without blame.

"They must have planted it."

"A ploy," he said more to himself than to me. "And it worked. I did think you were drunk, you know?"

"Yeah. That was pretty smart of them. If circumstances had been different, and I was just some kid off the street, you wouldn't have given me the benefit of the doubt."

"No. Even so." His voice was apologetic. "It almost worked."

I smiled.

"Well, that's it," Kessler said. "It's over."

I looked up, startled by the finality in his voice. "I can't quit now." When he didn't say anything further, I said, "That would be running away."

"Yeah, that's what a sane person would do."

"Would you?"

"Of course." He'd said it quickly, without thinking. Then more slowly, with less conviction once he'd given it some thought. "Of course I would."

I grunted.

Ruskie splayed his front legs, twisted around, and scratched his neck with a hind hoof. The horse's coat was the color of a newly minted penny and gleamed in the dappled shade. Sharply defined muscles moved smoothly beneath his skin like a well-oiled machine, symmetrical and pleasing to the eye.

Kessler ran his fingers through his hair, then absentmindedly rubbed the back of his neck. "I can't risk it, and neither can you. I'll hire a professional, like before."

"No." I stood up. "I don't want to quit."

"You've got to. Obviously it's too dangerous. I should have known better after they went after Abby. Last night, what happened…" He shook slightly as if from a chill, though it was hotter than hell outside, even in the shade. "Anyway, it's not going to happen again. I'm not giving them another chance."

"But if I hadn't been snooping around in McCormick's office, none of this would have happened."

"You've got to be kidding. What in the hell do you think they would have done if they'd found you in Speedwell's stall? Said, 'Nice to meet you. Now, would you excuse us while we drug this horse?'"

He rolled his shoulders as if he was trying to ease the tension in his neck.

"Come on, Steve. They could just as easily have used that bat on your head. Anyway, they know what we're up to now, so it won't work. Even if I was stupid enough to let you keep trying."

"But I don't want to quit. I need to stay with it more for myself than for you."

"What do you mean?"

"Look," I said. "The cameras didn't stop them, and when I think about it, they must have figured out ahead of time that I was watching the barn. Otherwise, they wouldn't have come after me."

"Maybe, maybe not. When they realized they'd dropped the syringe and went back for it, they could have seen you in the barn and guessed you'd found it. Then they followed you to your room, or they already knew where you lived."

"I think they already knew." I looked up at Kessler and said, "Have you told anyone that I've been watching the horses? Abby, maybe?"

"No. I haven't told anyone except Charles."

"Your vet?"

He nodded. "And I didn't tell him until this morning when I needed to convince him that Speedwell'd been drugged. And Hurp. I had to tell him, too. He stopped by shortly after I'd tried to withdraw Speedwell, wanting to know why I was so sure someone had doped him. He actually helped talk the stewards into scratching him."

"I know," I said. "Abby told me. But he didn't know before this morning?"

"No. He couldn't have."

"I wonder how they knew?"

"Maybe they just lucked out, but it doesn't matter, because you're off the case."

"Look." I began to pace. "I don't want out. I've been quitting too much lately. I've got to stick with this, or I'll start believing I can't finish anything."

He shook his head and held my gaze with the strength of his conviction. "You didn't see what you looked like this morning," he said. "You were a mess. You probably still are. I don't think you're thinking straight even now. Whatever they gave you, it's clouded your thinking. Somehow, it's made what happened seem like it wasn't all that dangerous. But it was. I see that now, and I'm not going to let them have a second chance."

I sat back on the grass and was wondering what would change his mind when tires skidded off the pavement behind us and churned through the loose gravel at the edge of the road.

Ruskie jerked his head up and leapt sideways.

A Washington Park golf cart lurched to a stop, and Dennis Hurp climbed out of the vehicle and crossed the street.

I groaned as I watched his arrogant swagger and thought that he might actually think he was Dirty Harry. A Dirty Harry wannabe, more like. I turned away and let my gaze settle on the scrub land that butted up against the perimeter fence.

I wondered why I disliked the man. Maybe because most people on the backside were more considerate around the equine residents. Cautious, anyway. That Ruskie hadn't shied more violently at the sudden unexpected noise was a tribute to the improvement he'd made under Kessler's care.

Hurp strolled across the grass and stopped so close, I had to tilt my head back in order to see him properly. It was a psychological ploy on his part, I figured, but all it did was piss me off.

He settled into a wide-legged stance, crossed his arms over his chest, and cleared his throat. "So, the stupor's worn off."

He'd said it as a statement, and I had the distinct impression he was directing his observation to Kessler, not me.

I looked sharply at the detective and didn't like his tone or, come to think of it, anything else about the man.

"He wasn't drunk," Kessler said.

Hurp ignored Kessler's comment and spoke as if I weren't sitting in front of him. "He's supposed to watch the barn every night?"

"That's right," Kessler said.

"Must be hard," he said to me, "walking hots and staying up all night."

I didn't answer.

"He does fine," Kessler said.

"I don't call lapsing into an alcohol-induced stupor fine."

"He wasn't drunk," Kessler repeated.

"He sure looked drunk when you tried to wake him," Hurp said, "flat passed out like he was."

I looked down at my hands, and a creepy-crawly sensation prickled my neck at the thought of his being in my room without my knowing it.

Hurp pulled a small spiral-bound notebook from his trouser pocket, removed a ballpoint pen from the breast pocket of his button-down Oxford, and flipped over the first couple of pages.

"State your full name." When I didn't answer, he looked up from the blank page. "Name?"

"Stephen Cline."

"Date of birth?" I told him, and he asked to see my license.

"Which one, Mr. Hurp?"

"It's 'Agent' Hurp." He paused, and when I didn't correct myself, he said, "Track."

I tossed him the photo ID that allowed me to work on the backside.

"Tell me what you know about last night, that is, if you can remember last night. In particular, anything regarding the alleged drugging of Mr. Kessler's horse, Speedwell."

"Alleged?"

He shrugged and dropped my license in my lap. "The tests haven't come back, yet."

The guy was a prick, plain and simple. If he wanted to be so damned technical, I could bury him in pile of stinking useless information.

"I left the barn for a couple minutes," I said. "Upon my return at approximately twelve-thirty-five a.m., I discovered that the surveillance cameras Mr. Kessler had installed two days previous had been destroyed. I then proceeded to check on Speedwell, the gray three-year-old colt in stall number fourteen, sired by Foxhound, out of a Wolf Power mare and scheduled to run in the sixth race, a one-and-one-eighth mile allowance for three-year-olds and up, later that same day."

Hurp stood very still, the pen motionless in his hand.

"After examining the colt," I said, "I determined that he had been interfered with. In other words, given an injection, IM, left side of the neck, further substantiated by the discovery of a ten cc hypodermic syringe, complete with a twenty gauge by one-inch needle. It had been dropped in the horse's stall a foot from the front wall and approximately two feet west of the stall door."

Beside me, Kessler cleared his throat.

I leaned back against the tree and continued. "I collected the syringe along with the surveillance tape and attempted to deliver the evidence to Mr. Kessler, which proved unsuccessful as he was unavailable. Consequently, I secured the above stated evidence in the lower right-hand drawer of Mr. Kessler's desk, closed and locked the office door, and returned to my quarters at exactly one-forty-two a.m."

Hurp's face was flushed, and the tips of his ears had turned red.

"Anything else you want to know?" I asked.

Hurp loosened his jaw. "Did you see anyone hanging around the barns?"

I thought about Jay and said, "No."

"And when did you get drunk, before, during, or after finding that the horse had been drugged?"

"You mean 'allegedly drugged,' don't you?"

He squinted with irritation down his long aristocratic nose.

"I wasn't drunk," I said.

"Stoned, then."

"I don't do drugs."

Hurp turned to Kessler. "Do yourself a favor and fire this smartass. Drinking on the job *and* leaving his post. You can't count on him for anything." He looked back at me. "And just where the hell were you?"

"Where I was has nothing to do with what happened and is none of your business."

Hurp snapped his notepad shut and shoved it in his back pocket. He kept his gaze on me and spoke to Kessler. "You've probably found your doper right here."

I stood up. "And how can that be?" I said. "I've only been in the barn a week, but the dopings have been going on for—"

"Maybe you just changed outfits to get closer to the horses you need to drug. Make it easier on yourself."

"If you'd done your homework, you would've found out that I haven't been with any other outfit because I've only been at the track for a week."

"All the same," he said to Kessler without looking at him, "you'd be wise to fire him."

"I don't have any intention of doing that. What you don't know is that he's my—"

"Couldn't make it as a real cop, could you?" I interrupted. "So you wound up with some half-ass job. A security guard's more a cop than you."

Hurp stepped toward me. I was careful not to move. I could smell his perspiration and the faint odor of cigarette smoke that lingered in his clothes.

"You get out of line, and I'll haul your butt in so fast, you won't have time to blink." A muscle above his left eye began to twitch, and I could feel his breath on my face. "So watch yourself."

"Yeah, and who's gonna watch you, Mr. Detective?"

He opened his mouth to say something, then glanced at Kessler and changed his mind.

I could feel his anger crossing the short distance between us in a palpable shock wave.

He turned abruptly, and his arm knocked into my shoulder.

I watched him stride across the grass.

"Good job, Steve," Kessler said as Hurp climbed into the golf cart and drove away without a backward glance. "He might have helped us, given the chance."

"The guy's an asshole."

Ruskie raised his head suddenly and pricked his ears. The next race had begun. His nostrils fluttered as he looked toward the grandstand with a faraway look in his sharp, intelligent eyes.

"Whatever happened to innocent until proven guilty?" I said.

"There's no such thing," Kessler said.

Chapter 15

"Randy, do your snooping somewhere else."

I looked up at Abby's comment. Randy Tyson stood near the feed room door, squinting at something across the alley.

Wordlessly, he left the shade of the roof overhang and stood on the hard-packed ground. Hot sunlight bore down on his scalp, and his short bristly hair looked like wire.

Since I was between horses, I followed Abby. Midway down the shedrow, she unclipped the lower portion of a stall guard, ducked beneath it, and disappeared into one of Trudy's stalls. I paused in the aisle as she crouched down in the straw next to a nervous chestnut filly with a wide star on her forehead. Abby smoothed her hand down the deep flexor tendon at the back of the horse's leg, feeling for heat. As I moved closer, the filly pivoted her big loppy ears with alarm. She stepped sideways, away from Abby.

Abby must have sensed my presence, because she looked toward the doorway. "Here, Steve. Hold her for me."

I went into the stall and clipped my shank to the filly's halter. "What was Randy doing?"

"What?" She frowned with concentration as she reached around and cupped her hand over the filly's hoof.

"Randy. You told him to do his snooping somewhere else."

"Oh." She wiped the sweat off her forehead with the back of her hand. "Did you notice that black colt over in seventeen, coming back from the track, the one with the shadow roll on?"

"Yeah," I said.

It was hard to ignore the goings-on around barn seventeen. An exclusively Jamaican outfit, they liked their music loud and approached the day's work with a casualness that would never fly in Kessler's barn. Although, to give them their due, they stayed later than anyone else. I'd often seen them sitting on overturned buckets, eating their lunches in the shade of the shedrow long after the other crews had cleared out. And I could set my watch by the roosters they kept (someone had told me) for luck.

"He just had a pipe opener," Abby said. "A workout at racing speed. Anyway, Miguel's got him entered in a claiming race later in the week. Randy was scopin' him out for Mr. McCormick. You know? Seeing if the colt came out of his work good and sound."

"Why would he do that?"

She compressed her lips. "You really don't know much about the track, do you?"

"Not really."

"Well, Randy'll report back, and Mr. McCormick will decide whether or not he wants to claim the colt off Miguel. Claiming barns are forever snoopin' around, looking for a good horse they can snatch up. Catch a horse just right, win a few purses, then sell it before it starts to slide. As far as I'm concerned, they're a bunch of vultures." She shrugged a shoulder. "Most of 'em, anyway."

"Didn't Ace run in a claiming race?" I asked in a flat voice, which I hoped sounded neutral.

Abby's hand paused over the filly's ankle, and she glanced up at me. "Yeah, sure. Dad's going to dump him. The owner wants it, and I guess, come to think of it, so does Dad. He's done all he can to get that colt turned around, and nothing's worked."

I considered what I knew about Ace. When he wasn't screwing around, he was an excellent mover, well put-together with the uphill conformation dressage riders covet. And he was gorgeous, too. I assumed some horses never took to racing, and it seemed to me that being confined to a stall twenty-three hours a day was simply too much for him.

"Dad puts a lot of hard work into his horses," Abby continued, "but sometimes it just isn't meant to be."

"Do you know how much they want for him. Because I know a woman who's always looking for dressage prospects. And she likes Thoroughbreds. Additional turnout might be just what he needs."

Abby sat back on her haunches. "You'll have to ask Dad, but if he can move him quickly, I'm sure the owner will take less than he's worth just to avoid further training fees."

Abby ducked under the filly's neck and began her examination of the off fore.

As I watched her, my thoughts drifted to the previous evening. Kessler had been disappointed when I'd flatly refused to report anything but a burglary to the cops. Although the stun gun had left red, circular blotches on my skin, marks that looked like burns more than anything else, the duct tape they'd used to tie me with was gone. And by the time I'd become halfway lucid, any hope of finding tire tracks had been obliterated by a day's worth of heavy traffic—human, horse, and vehicular.

At Kessler's insistence, the cops had gone over my room and his office, but the only fingerprints they found belonged there. By the time they had packed up their equipment and driven away, Kessler and I had reached an impasse. I wanted to stay. He wanted me off the job.

The fact that he didn't have a runner that afternoon was probably the only reason he had let me stay another night, and I fully expected that today would be my last day at the track. So far this morning we hadn't had a chance to talk, and I'd been unable to read him one way or the other.

I would know soon enough.

Abby straightened. "It's enough to break your heart."

"What?"

"The horses. Losing them."

"But you like the job."

Abby rested her hand lightly on the filly's smooth coat and looked at me with those clear hazel eyes of hers. "I wouldn't want to work in a claiming barn, but love it? Yes. God, yes. They're beautiful, generous, big-hearted creatures."

She shook her head. "The sport has its seedier side, but these animals would be here whether I am or not, and I know my effort and caring make their lives that much better."

She turned back to the filly and smoothed her palm down the sleek, muscled neck. The filly reached around and touched Abby's arm with her muzzle, curious and, in her own equine way, capable of affection.

"Yeah," Abby continued. "I love it. I wouldn't give it up for anything in the world. I've wanted to do this for as long as I can remember."

She stepped around me in the tight space, and the soft roundness of her breast brushed against my back. She paused in the doorway, and I turned around to see what she was doing.

We were standing in the cooling wash from the overhead fan. Loose wisps of Abby's blond hair billowed forward across her face. She reached up and brushed the hair out of her eyes. "And what do you want, Steve, more than anything in the world?"

I looked back at the horse. I didn't have an answer. Nothing I could tell her. When I next turned around, she'd already left.

The next hot, one of Gordi's, came back from the track then, and I got to work. Another chestnut. They looked much alike, except this one had normal-sized ears.

"Yo, man," Gordi said as he dunked a sponge into a bucket of water laced with Vetrolin. "Heard somebody off and stole your stash, man."

"You heard right."

"How much they get?"

"Around eight hundred."

Gordi whistled. "No wonder you was sick. That happen to me, I be down, man. Deeper than the deepest whale shit at the bottom of the deepest crack in the ocean."

I grinned.

"Somebody got to Hector's colt, too," Gordi said. "You hear 'bout that?"

"Yeah."

"Hector was PO'd big time 'cause he ain't gonna get no bonus now."

"Bonus?"

"You know, man. Groom a winner, you get a hundred bucks for a job well done. More if the owner slips you somethin' on the side. But shit, man, I keep forgettin' you ain't been here long. You work real hard, maybe you'll get a couple horses to rub."

When Gordi slopped the sponge down the mare's chest, she ground her teeth. I tightened the hold I had on her halter.

"Who do you think did it?" I said.

"No tellin'."

Gordi dunked the sponge back into the bucket and agitated the water. The minty aroma mixed with the underlying odors of horse and hay, and I realized how much I liked working with them. How much working outside suited me.

I might not want to do this kind of work forever, but I now realized a desk job would kill me. If Kessler was going to make me quit, I'd have to go back to Foxdale. Maybe now I was finally ready.

Gordi straightened and ran the sponge across the mare's back. "Rumors flyin' round here. Everybody think they know who done it, and nobody knows shit."

Including me. There had to be a way to force their hand, but I couldn't think of one. And then again, it might not matter, depending on what Kessler decided.

"Well," I said. "It pisses me off, knowing they're getting away with it."

"It all part of the game, Steve. When you bet on a race, the horse's ability ain't the only thing you bettin' on. The real gamble be which jock's got it in the bag before the post, or which trainer be tryin' his best to make his horse look better than it really is so he can claim it off on some poor sucker. Or which horse be hopped or stopped." Gordi chuckled. "'Hopped or stopped.'

That what they oughta call *The Morning Line.* '*Hopped or Stopped.*'"

"And it don't get to you?" Geez. I was beginning to talk like Gordi.

"It ain't like I don't care, man. I just know I ain't gonna be makin' no difference, is all. So why sweat it?"

"You hear anything, let me know," I said.

Gordi shook his head and sponged between the mare's hind legs. "Okay, Holmes."

I watched her expression and saw that she didn't mind and wasn't going to offer any resistance.

"Whew, she really hot, man. You gonna be a long time coolin' her out. Speakin' a hot…" Gordi looked up and waited for me to bite.

"What?"

"Boss's daughter got the hots for one skinny-assed blond dude."

"Who?"

Gordi rolled his eyes. "You, man. She be down with you in half a second."

"You don't know what you're talking about."

"Awh, come on. You got blinders on?" He dropped the sponge in the bucket and pulled a sweat scraper out of his back pocket. "She hotter'n this mare."

Gordi's assessment about the mare, at least, was accurate.

I stopped the chestnut on McCormick's side of the barn, and we waited for the horse in front to get a drink. We'd been walking for fifteen long minutes, which worked out to roughly ten laps around the shedrow. Fifteen minutes to think, and I still didn't have a plan.

Because the horses were taking so long to cool out, the shed-row was congested, and the colt immediately behind us was giving his handler a rough time. I was thinking that I would take my mare outside at the next opportunity when Randy backed out of the stall to my left. He turned and hesitated when he saw me.

He narrowed his eyes and a muscle along his jaw twitched before he spun around and headed down the shedrow. I decided to check his reaction.

"You have fun Thursday morning, Randy?" I said to his back.

He paused, then looked over his shoulder. "What?"

"You know," I said. "'Your stun gun ain't working too good. Want me to beat it out of him?'"

His face became very still, as if the muscles had frozen, and I wondered if he was holding his breath.

I continued. "Ever hear of the Theory of Transfer?"

He didn't answer.

"It's a police forensics thing. Basically, it means that wherever you go, whatever you do, you leave something of yourself behind. In other words, trace evidence. And wherever you go, whatever you do, some trace of the environment is left on you."

He spun around, walked down the aisle, and stumbled on the uneven ground as he sidestepped the hotwalker in front of us.

"Wait. There's more," I yelled. "Don't you want to hear?"

With a jumble of emotions, I watched Randy walk outside and disappear around the corner of the barn.

The bastard knew what I was talking about. He'd been there, and I didn't have a clue how to prove it. The line began to move, and when we reached Kessler's side of the barn, I took the mare outside and waited for the fractious colt to pass by.

When the last hot had been cooled out and rubbed down and tucked into its stall, and the barn had emptied, I headed to the office to find out if I still had a job.

Dennis "It's Agent to You" Hurp stood alongside Kessler's desk. He was leaning toward Kessler with his foot planted in the visitor's chair and a forearm propped on his thigh. Neither man was speaking, and because of Hurp's position, I couldn't see Kessler's face. I was thinking about detouring to the track kitchen when Hurp straightened, said something I couldn't hear, and turned around.

He peered down his long nose at me. "You always eavesdrop on other people's conversations?"

I kept my mouth shut, and Hurp brushed past me as he left the office. Runt trotted over, pressed his wet nose against my knee, and wagged his stump of a tail.

I crouched down and scratched behind his ears. "You don't like him either, do you, boy?"

His tail wagged faster.

Kessler pushed away from his desk and walked toward the doorway.

I straightened and spoke before he had a chance. "Even if you fire me, you can't stop me from going after them."

Kessler opened his mouth to say something, but I cut him off.

"After what they did the other night, I'm entitled. If you don't let me stay, I'll find another way. I'll stake out Green or bluff him into—"

"It's all—"

"—thinking I know more than I do or that I have proof of his involvement. He's connected. I'm sure of it. I bet he supplied whatever drug it was they used on me."

Kessler held up his hands, and I closed my mouth.

"I was trying to tell you...." He smoothed a hand across his hair. "You can stay and keep with the surveillance if you want, except now you'll have some help."

I frowned. "From who?"

Kessler exhaled slowly, and I figured I wasn't going to like his answer. "Hurp's going to—"

"Oh, man. I knew it."

"Settle down, Steve. He's not going to be personally involved, if that's what you're worried about. His employees will be running the surveillance."

"How?"

"Set up their own cameras. Take shifts watching the monitor."

"In your office?"

"I think so."

"Why the change of heart?" I said. "Did the drug test come back positive?"

"No. It was clean. Same as the others."

"Then why?"

"He didn't say exactly, but I got the feeling it had something to do with pressure from the stewards." Kessler walked around behind his desk and sat down. "It helps to have friends in high places."

I grunted.

"You still want in?"

"Of course I do."

Kessler leaned back in his chair. "There's really no reason for you to stay in the barn at night."

"True, but I might keep with it," I said not out of any desire to be a martyr but out of self-preservation. My door still wouldn't lock properly, and then there were the bugs to consider. There were plenty in the stalls, but the cockroaches seemed to prefer the living quarters, and I'd just as soon avoid them. "What about this weekend? Can I still have a day off?"

"I don't see why not."

"Any day in particular?"

"We don't have any runners Sunday, so that would work best."

Chapter 16

Friday evening, Hurp's people arrived promptly at eight. They installed a pair of pinhole cameras, despite the fact that Kessler had told them they wouldn't hold up with all the dust, and spent their shift lounging in the office with the door closed. I spent the night in a stall, one of Jay's, but I'd smartened up. I arranged two bales of straw along a side wall and balled up a horse blanket at one end to serve as a pillow. It was better than nothing.

We followed the same routine Saturday, and after an uneventful night, I hopped into the Chevy in the early morning darkness and sped north on I-95 with the windows down. Cool air eddied through the cab, and my spirits rose with each passing mile.

I unlocked the door to the loft, tossed a handful of mail onto the kitchen counter, and threw open the windows. The stale heat couldn't dim my enthusiasm at being home where the expanse of gleaming white tile, forest green carpet, and warm honey-colored paneling filled my eyes. A world away from the bug-infested room at the track. I dropped a garbage bag stuffed with laundry on the closet floor, stripped, and showered, scrubbing every inch of my skin and wondering if I would still smell like a muck heap. I shaved with care and brushed my teeth. When I walked back into the closet, it occurred to me that my room at the track wasn't much bigger.

I pulled on a pair of clean white socks that smelled strongly of laundry soap, not horse. I flipped through my shirts, looking for something suitable for the day ahead. When my hand brushed against a silky fabric, I pushed back a handful of shirts. The suit I'd worn to the funeral swayed on its hanger.

I was suddenly back on that sunny hillside, listening to the creaking seats and hushed voices dampened by humidity so heavy it was difficult to breath. Feeling the cheap carpet, slippery under my new shoes. Staring at the white roses, stark against the casket's dark mahogany.

My throat tightened convulsively. I sat abruptly, sliding my back down the doorjamb, and hugged my knees. I squeezed my eyes shut. It was impossible. Impossible to think I would never see him again. Would never understand the man behind those cold blue eyes. I yanked a shirt off a nearby hanger and wiped my face.

As hard as it was to believe, he was gone forever, and it felt as if a vast emptiness had spread within me, and soon there'd be nothing left.

I took a ragged breath, clambered to my feet, and walked into the bathroom. I squinted at the mirror with bloodshot eyes. After eleven days at the track, I was no longer pale, but I had lost weight I couldn't afford to lose. Not so much from the work, but from the odd hours and a screwed-up appetite. Half the time I couldn't finish what I started.

I smirked at my reflection. Drop the self-pity, Cline. You're gonna spend the day with Rachel. What more could you want? I cupped my hands under the faucet and splashed cold water on my face until my skin stung.

Forty-five minutes later, she opened the door to my knock.

"Je-sus." I let my gaze travel slowly down her body. Well known. Well loved. Familiar. Provocative. "Why don't we just scrap our plans and spend the day in bed?"

"Huh. You gotta earn it, buddy-boy. Plus, I'm sadistic. I like to see you sweat."

"More like drool."

"That, too. Just make sure you keep your tongue in your mouth." She brushed past me and headed down the wide stone staircase with a bounce in her stride.

"Awh. Come on, Rachel." I took the steps two at a time. "That'll ruin all the fun."

She giggled. "Well, maybe later, then." When we reached the driveway, she said over her shoulder, "My car or your truck?"

"The Chevy," I said.

Rachel slid a picnic basket off the front seat of her little car and turned to face me. She held the basket with both hands, arms stiff, elbows locked, the wicker pressed against her thighs. Her toes were pointed toward each other, her heels splayed, and as I approached, she grinned mischievously. Standing there like that, she reminded me of a little kid. Well, almost. I smoothed my hand across hers, took the basket from her grasp, and hefted it into the bed of my truck.

"What do you have in here, bricks?"

"Ha. I've seen you eat, remember? I don't know where you put it all." She watched me wedge the basket between a spare tire and a broken jump standard I hadn't gotten around to unloading. "It's unfair, you know? Your metabolism."

I turned to look at her, and she smoothed a hand across my chest.

Keeping her eyes lowered, she said, "You're so lean and brown...and hard."

I slipped my arm around her waist and pulled her against me. Her breath was hot against my skin as I bent down to kiss her. I slid my hands down the small of her back, then farther still. She had on a pair of turquoise shorts that I particularly liked because of their length or, rather, lack thereof. I uncupped my hands, smoothed my fingers down her thighs, and curled them upward, slipping them beneath the fabric, beneath the elastic of her underwear. I felt a grin on her lips, then she disengaged.

"Good grief. I thought you said you were going to keep your tongue to yourself."

"That was your idea. If it were up to me—"

"Geez. If it were up to you, we'd be doing it right here on the seat, in broad daylight, with Dad getting ready to come out the front door on his way to work."

"Ha," I said as she climbed into the cab. I pushed the door to. "I'm not that far gone."

She smiled up at me, feigning innocence. I leaned through the window and kissed her again. As I drew my thumb across her jaw and inched my fingertips down the line of her throat, she must have read my mind because she swatted at my hand.

"God." She caught her breath. "Don't you, uh…you know? Don't you do it, you know…by yourself?"

"What?" I straightened. "Err…It's not the same." I let my gaze travel down her body. "Not even close."

She rolled her eyes. "Apparently not."

We headed south, abandoning highways clogged with rush hour traffic, and sped down narrow back roads toward our destination, losing our way only once. I pulled into a parking lot that was empty, except for an old station wagon and a Wrangler Jeep, and backed the truck into a spot in the shade. We started down a path to the river. With luck, the shade wouldn't shift too far and leave the Chevy baking in the sun.

As the path wound farther downhill, we heard the river before we saw it. A sign posted just before the observation platform warned people to stay off the rocks. "Twenty-three people have lost their lives…" it read. Lost their lives to the Potomac where it pounded over the monstrous granite boulders of Great Falls. Although Maryland was in the midst of a heat wave, the river was swollen thanks to an unusually wet spring.

We stood on the platform and peered over the railing at the roiling brown water. It tumbled and churned over the boulders, the roar filling our ears, the swirling movement hypnotic. Death just yards away. Fall in there, and you'd be sucked under, pummeled by tons of bone-crushing water. Twenty-three people hadn't taken the threat seriously. Twenty-three people had thought they were invincible.

A fine mist floated up from the chasm, and the air temperature was a good ten degrees cooler there than in the parking lot. I folded my arms on the railing. The churning water was the color of chocolate milk, and I wondered how far downstream it had to travel before the sediment drifted to the bottom.

Rachel touched my arm. "What are you thinking?" She had to raise her voice to be heard over the noise.

I straightened and turned to look at her.

"What's wrong?" she said.

"Nothing." I took her hand in mine. "Let's go on that hike."

We hiked and picnicked, and I didn't again think about death or dying or how none of us were insulated from pain. It came to us all. The key was in going on. Living each day to the fullest.

Toward evening, we drove into D.C., dined at a French restaurant a couple of blocks from the Mall, and arrived back at the loft as the last light of day seeped from the horizon.

"Let's take a swim."

Rachel arched an eyebrow. "And just what do you propose I wear?"

I grinned. "Skin would do nicely."

"How come I knew you'd say that?"

"Lucky, I guess."

"Huh. And what would Susan and Greg think? Us skinny-dipping in their pool, among other things?"

"They're on vacation, and when they're away, I have full run of the pool. Perks of having a rich landlord."

"No kidding."

"So, whaddya say?"

She gripped her lower lip between her teeth. "I suppose so."

While Rachel made use of the bathroom, I rinsed off a bunch of grapes, sliced some cheese, and uncorked a bottle of Lafite-Rothschild that I'd smuggled out of my parents' house and had never drunk. The door creaked open behind me, and Rachel strode into the kitchen with a bundle of towels in her arms.

"Ready?" she said.

"Almost." I grabbed two wineglasses and a box of crackers, and we headed out the door.

We followed the gravel drive, mindful of the footing once we were out of range of the security light that glared down on the parking lot behind the foaling barn. The day's heat and humidity hadn't abated, and the night air was alive with the sounds of crickets and tree frogs and whatever other insect life becomes active after the sun sets. In the pasture to our left, a horse snorted. Somewhere closer, the brass fittings on a halter jingled. As we neared the end of the fence row, heavy footfalls rustled through the grass as the horses moved past, unseen by us, their dark forms merging with the night.

I unlatched the gate to the backyard, switched on the lights in the cabana, and laid out the food.

Rachel eyed the house's darkened windows as I filled our glasses. "You're sure they're away?"

"Yep. Greg left me a note with my mail."

"Hmm." She dropped the towels on a chair, kicked off her sneakers, and walked to the edge of the pool.

I turned off the lights and flicked on the pool's underwater lamps. Waves of light and shadow rippled across the back of the house when Rachel balanced on one foot and dipped her toes in the water. There was a hesitancy to her actions that made me think she regretted her decision.

I moved alongside her and held out her drink. She shook her head.

"You could always swim in your underwear," I said. "Or we could do something else."

A smile touched her lips. "Who said I'm wearing underwear." Her smile broadened at the expression on my face. "I left them in your bathroom."

"Oh, you did, did you?"

She faced me straight on, grasped the hem of her tank top, and wriggled it over her head. She dropped it on the ground as my gaze settled on her breasts. Before I could react, she stepped out of her shorts and dove into the pool.

"Man," I said under my breath.

I set our drinks by my feet and fumbled out of my clothes. When I slipped into the water, Rachel went back under and hovered near the bottom. Waiting. Watching me glide toward her in that silent world. Her hair had spread out from her scalp and moved languidly in the current like seaweed shifting in the tide, dark and alive in the pool's liquid light. I reached her and pulled her against me, then we rose to the surface, locked together. Rachel breathed deeply and laughed, then flipped her hair out of her face, spraying droplets in an arc across the shimmering water. The daytime temperature had been so high during the past two weeks, the pool water had heated up and felt warmer than the humid night air. Like bath water.

She brushed her hand across my crotch. "You don't take long to get with the program, do you?"

"Hell, no."

I went back under and slid my palms over her hips and down her firm thighs as she tread water in smooth, economical strokes. Her normally tanned skin looked pale in the blue light, contrasting nicely with the black tangle of hair between her legs. I sank toward the bottom, then swam around her, taking in the full roundness of her ass, noticing the smooth muscling along her spine, circling around and rising until I was level with her breasts. I cupped my hand under her breast, slid my tongue across her nipple, and took her in my mouth.

She gripped my shoulders when I moved my mouth down over her belly and slipped my fingers between her legs.

I needed to breathe.

I broke through the surface and gulped a lungful of air, resentful that I needed it when I wanted her more. Her smile was gone, and she was breathing through her mouth. I wrapped my arm around her waist and propelled her through the water until her shoulders touched the pool's side. I pressed her against the concrete, gripped the edge, and wedged my knees between hers. Rachel spread her thighs and locked her ankles behind me, then she smoothed her hand down my abdomen. She tried to guide me into her, but with each thrust, she bobbed toward the surface like a cork, and I imagined making love to a jellyfish wouldn't have been much different.

"Let's use the steps."

Rachel glanced at the house. The pool's blue light reflected in her eyes, and her cheeks were flushed. "We'll be more visible."

"Come on, Rachel. No one's home."

"All right." She hesitated. "It's just that I feel like someone's watching us."

"Only the horses out back." I took her hand. "Come on."

She twisted around and pushed off the wall, diving deeper as she angled toward the shallow end. I slipped beneath the surface and followed her, watching her move gracefully through the water with slow rhythmic kicks, and I don't think I've ever seen anything more sensual. Midway down the length of the pool, she took a breath and continued with the breaststroke until she reached the steps on the far side.

She rolled over and lay on the steps with her hair draped behind her. Where the strands dipped into the water, the tips fanned out in all directions. Waves lapped around her breasts and eddied through the trough formed between the gentle rise of her stomach and her pubic bone. As I approached, she spread her legs, and I groaned.

I kissed the inside of her thigh, and as I took a fold of skin between my teeth, I could smell her scent faintly above the permeating odor of chlorine. She shuddered and arched her back when I smoothed my fingertips farther up her thigh and spread her lips.

She slammed her knee into my shoulder and bolted upright, then she scrambled off the steps and slipped into the water.

I swam over to her. "What are you doing?"

"Steve," she whispered, "someone's by the fence."

She was staring past my shoulder at the gate that led to the front yard.

I spun around.

The fence that bordered the yard was the same type that surrounded the pasture, four-board, painted white, but Greg had added a hedge along the stretch that faced the road, and it topped out at five feet. I couldn't see a damn thing.

"Someone was standing by the gate," Rachel said again.

In the field behind the yard, a horse snorted, and I felt the first stirrings of apprehension.

"Are you sure?" I said.

"I think so." She studied my face. "You aren't surprised. Are you?" When I didn't respond, something changed in her eyes. She pushed away from me and swam over to where she'd dropped her clothes.

I followed.

She gripped the side of the pool, bounced upward onto locked arms, and levered herself onto the concrete in one coordinated movement bred from countless similar maneuvers onto her horse's back. She wrapped a towel around her body and watched me climb out, albeit less gracefully.

She tossed me a towel, then I pushed the gate open and walked around the side of the house. When I returned without seeing anyone, she said, "You're doing it again, aren't you? You're getting mixed up with something that you know is dangerous, and you don't care. You don't care about me or my feelings, either, because if you did, you wouldn't be doing this."

"That's not true. And it's not dangerous," I lied.

She dragged her shorts up her wet legs and wiggled into them. "Then how'd you get those bruises on your back? I saw them when you turned around just now."

When I didn't respond, she said, "I *hated* what happened to you before, and I'm not going to let you put me through that again." She pulled her shirt over her head and tugged the hem down to her waist, then yanked the towel out from beneath the fabric. "Take me home."

"But, Rachel—"

"I can't take this. Call me when you decide to grow up, Steve." She crossed her arms under her breasts and waited.

"But, I love you," I said softly.

"If you loved me, you wouldn't be putting me through hell. You have no idea what it was like, seeing you in that hospital bed with tubes and machines and monitors everywhere. Seeing the pain you were in that you pretended didn't exist."

"But none of that was my fault."

"It wasn't? You kept digging and digging until he came after you." She flipped her hair off her forehead. "And I need someone who's not afraid to share his feelings, Steve. You don't. You keep yours locked away like you're ashamed of them. Like they're a weakness. Well, they're not." Her lower lip trembled. "I need someone who isn't afraid to be human."

I clenched my hands. "That's not fair, Rachel. Your life's been so...sheltered. You have no idea how it feels to be ignored by your own parents. Now I have a chance to know my real father."

"He's not your father. He's just some," she flapped her hand, "guy. He didn't raise you."

"So what? Maybe I need him, Rachel. Did you ever stop to consider that?" I struggled into my jeans, jammed my feet into my sneakers, and looked up as a tear spilled from her eye and tracked down her cheek.

She brushed it away. "Take me home, please."

"Fine." I flipped the pool lamps off and walked past her to the gate.

"Aren't you going to take these?"

I glanced over my shoulder, and she gestured to the wine and cheese. "What the hell for?" I cleared my throat. "I'll get them later."

I opened the gate and, despite my earlier check, looked around. The front yard was deserted and probably had been all along.

The drive to her parents' house was hell. She didn't speak, and neither did I. Not even when I swung the Chevy into her driveway. I lifted the picnic basket out of the bed and handed it to her, then watched her climb the steps to the front porch. She opened the front door, and the foyer's light spilled onto her shoulders as she stepped inside and pulled the door to without looking back.

I cranked the radio up, backed onto the road, and slammed the transmission into drive. The Chevy's back tires slewed around on some loose gravel at the side of the road before the tread gripped pavement, and I gunned it out of there. I made it home in record time.

Rachel was the one who needed to grow up, not me. The screen door thumped closed as I flipped on the lights and opened the cabinet by the kitchen sink. A half-empty fifth of Gordon's vodka was tucked behind a two-liter Coke. I hated vodka, but it was the only alcohol in the joint. Marty had left it after one of his drink-'til-you-drop gigs awhile back. I looked in the fridge.

She wasn't in a position to judge me. As far as I knew, she'd always had a good relationship with her parents and didn't have a clue what it felt like to be alienated from your own family.

I opened a carton of orange juice and sniffed. Not bad, but the date was a month old. There was always the wine I'd left at the pool. I chucked the carton in the sink, cracked open the vodka instead, and swallowed a mouthful.

I'd shared my feelings with her, damn it. What more did she want?

I powered up the stereo system, wandered past my bed, and looked out the bank of windows that faced the road. Technically, thanks to Hurp's men, I didn't have to go back to the track until morning, but everything in the loft reminded me of Rachel. The Matchbox 20 bass thrumming through the floorboards was one she'd chosen. I took another swig and this time didn't notice the battery acid taste.

And now she was gone.

I thunked the vodka bottle onto the kitchen counter, threw some clean clothes into a trash bag, and headed south on 95, back to the track. I slept like the dead, sprawled on a horse blanket that I'd stretched over a couple of bales along the back of a stall. A party could have taken place in the barn, and I wouldn't have noticed. I walked my hots Monday morning, ate lunch, went to my room, and lay down. Drinking had become my preferred method of avoidance, but sleeping came in as a useful second and had the added benefit of catching me up on some much needed sleep.

Chapter 17

Waking up was a matter of stages. In one of the rooms downstairs, Run-DMC cranked from a tinny boom box. Sporadic traffic noise drifted through the open window above the whir of the fan. The humidity pressed down on my bare skin and worked its way into my lungs with each breath until I felt I could suffocate on it.

I stretched and opened my eyes. As the grime-streaked walls of my dingy little room came into focus in the day's fading light, a nagging feeling solidified into thought as clearly as if someone had spoken aloud. I sat up, yanked on some clothes, and went in search of Kessler.

One of Hurp's men, who'd already set up in Kessler's office, told me he'd gone home half an hour earlier. When I called him and got a busy signal, I went out to eat, then tried again. The line was still busy. I checked my watch. Nine o'clock. It was getting late, and if I didn't talk to him soon, he'd be turning in for the night. I hopped in the Chevy and drove to his apartment.

I knocked, and before I could lower my hand, the door opened.

"Steve?" Kessler's hair was tousled, and even though he was barefoot and without a shirt, it was obvious he'd been expecting someone.

"Mind if I come in?"

He moved to the side. "Of course not. Is everything okay?"

"Yeah. I just have some questions."

Kessler closed the door behind me, and I followed him into the living room where the conditioned air washed over my skin and trickled through my damp hair. The room was stunningly modern with a broad expanse of thick, bronze-colored carpet underfoot and gleaming glass end tables nestled among plush upholstered furniture. Above a marbled gas fireplace, track lighting spotlighted an abstract close-up of a racehorse painted in bold slashes of brilliant color. The apartment was spotless, a far cry from his office.

"What's up?" he said.

I scanned the apartment again. "Where's Runt?"

"Abby's got him, but surely, that's not why—"

I shook my head. "No. I've been thinking. Remember—"

We both turned at the sound of a female's voice calling from the back of the apartment. "He's here, already?"

"No, hon," Kessler said. "You've got a few minutes."

Oh, great. I shifted my weight from one foot to the other. "Want me to come back?"

Kessler smiled and shook his head. "She's on her way to the airport."

The *she* in question walked into the living room, pulling a small suitcase behind her. She wore the dark conservative uniform of a flight attendant, but there was nothing conservative about the rest of her. Her auburn hair fell in ringlets to the middle of her back, and her eyes were a stunning blue that took my breath away. She smiled at me, and my heart rate quickened a notch.

"Here, I'll get that." Kessler scooped up her suitcase and introduced us. Linda offered her hand, and I shook it. She had long, slender fingers and expertly manicured nails, and her smooth skin felt cool against mine.

After a second or two, it dawned on me that I'd been holding her hand a bit longer than necessary. As I relaxed my grip and lowered my hand, Linda smiled sweetly, fully aware of the effect she had on me, that I imagined she had on every male who drew breath.

A horn sounded in the parking lot.

She turned to Kessler. "See you Friday, then?"

"I'll be there." Kessler slipped his free arm around her waist, and I walked across the room and stared out the sliding glass doors that opened onto a balcony. The night was so humid, moisture had condensed on the outside of the cool glass. A tree frog had climbed part way up the door, dislodging water droplets that slid down the glass.

As Kessler opened the front door, the glass in the sliding doors shuddered with the break in suction. He walked her out to the parking lot, and when he returned, he asked me what was going on.

"Way back when we started this thing," I said, "and I asked if you'd hired anyone else to investigate the dopings, you said you'd asked an old buddy of yours to look into it before you went with the PI firm. I need to know more about him. His name. Where he lived. And the circumstances surrounding his death."

"But why? He never found out anything."

"Maybe he did," I said.

"He would of told me."

"Maybe he didn't have a chance."

Kessler ran his fingers through his hair, then gestured toward the sofa. "Why don't you sit down and tell me what you've got on your mind."

"I'll stand," I said, considering how filthy my jeans were. "I remembered something that I'd overheard when those guys were in my room. One of them said something like, 'what if he vomits like the other one?' Then I think he was going to say that I'd choke. I know it's a stretch, but what if they were talking about your friend?"

"Look, Steve. Dan was an old man, and his health was shot. He had emphysema, but he kept smoking anyway. No one was surprised when he died."

The sweat on my skin had evaporated so quickly in the apartment's chilled air that my damp clothes felt clammy against my skin. "What was the cause of death?"

"I never heard."

"Did they perform an autopsy?"

"Not that I know of."

"What was his name?"

Kessler sat on the edge of the recliner and rested his elbows on his knees. "Daniel Albert," he said. "He was seventy-two."

Seventy-two? Man, that was older than I'd imagined.

"We met in Florida when I was starting out. He was a good trainer. Knew horses better than most, but he was hopeless when it came to managing the paperwork that goes with the job. He owed everyone. The feed suppliers, farrier, exercise riders. Everybody. Eventually, no one would extend him credit, and he got squeezed out. When he moved back here, he needed money to make the rent, so I paid him for his time."

"Where'd he live."

"A motel on US 1, near Laurel Lakes Shopping Center." Kessler gestured toward the kitchen. "You want something to drink?"

I shook my head. "Which motel?"

"The Briarwood, I think."

"When did he die?"

He leaned back in the chair and thought. "The memorial service was held on St. Patrick's Day, but he'd died a couple days before they found him, maybe a week."

"He wasn't buried?"

"No. Cremated."

Shit. Any evidence of a murder would have been destroyed. I rubbed my hand over my face. "Who's running next?"

"Contrail. She's entered in the fourth race on Thursday."

"Trudy's horse, CT? The chestnut with the loppy ears?"

Kessler nodded. "With luck, she'll win."

◇◇◇

When I woke up in CT's stall Tuesday morning, something had changed, and after a moment, I realized that the change was internal, and more than that, welcomed. After thirteen days at the track, my body had finally adjusted to the workload, and I felt fit for the first time since I'd left Foxdale. Fit and strong and rested, and only then did I realize just how run down I'd been.

And the weather had changed, too. A cold front had blown in during the night, scrubbing the humidity from the air. I said hello to Phil, one of Hurp's men who'd spent the night in Kessler's office, and since I had time, I headed to the track kitchen. The place was hopping, despite the early hour. I loaded down my tray with scrambled eggs and bacon and a batch of hash browns. I grabbed two biscuits and a tall glass of milk and found an empty seat alongside the windows that faced the track. As I settled back into my chair, the sounds of clinking china, laughter, and voices eddied around me.

"...got claimed off Corey, and the colt's been on the board ever since."

"No shit."

The guy behind me bumped against my arm as he pushed his chair away from the table. "New filly I got, I whirlpooled and mudded her, packed her feet good, and she still can't run a lick."

"Ain't nothin' gonna help 'em if they waddle like a duck."

The sky was still dark, and the occasional set of headlights swept across the freshly harrowed track as vehicles turned off the road and drove past the guard post. When I'd finished eating, I scooped up my tray, and as I headed for the exit, I caught sight of Randy. He was sitting at a table near the center of the room with a group from McCormick's outfit. I set my tray down, skirted around a couple of tables, and stood behind him. Tuesdays happened to be a popular day on the backside, since the track wasn't open for racing, so it was no surprise that they were discussing how they were going to spend their afternoon off.

I stood quietly behind Randy, and when the conversations died down one by one, I gripped the back of his chair with my left hand, leaned forward, and braced my right hand on the red and white checkered table cloth. He stiffened when he recognized me and swallowed the mouthful of sausage he'd been chewing on.

"Tell me, Randy. How'd it feel when you watched them kill Daniel Albert? Were you scared, or did you get off on it?"

Across the table, someone inhaled sharply, but I was certain Randy had stopped breathing altogether.

"If you know what's good for you," I said, "you'll tell the cops what happened. They'll cut you a deal, and you won't spend as much time in the joint. But you better act fast, before your pharmacist buddy, Mr. Nathan Green, talks to them first. Then you'll be the one gettin' screwed."

Randy's face had blanched, and beneath his cropped hair, his scalp glistened with perspiration in the harsh glare of the fluorescent lights.

"What was it like when he choked on his own vomit, Randy? Did you have to hold him down?"

Randy stood up so fast, he knocked into me, and his chair skittered across the tile. "You're crazy!" he screamed, then he bolted for the door.

Voices and the clatter of silverware died away to nothing as Randy pushed through the double doors, and I saw as well as felt everyone's attention turn from the exit to me. I kept my gaze straight ahead and ignored the curious stares as I walked past the last row of tables and stepped outside.

One down, one to go.

Randy was curiously absent from the morning stable routine. I walked my hots, and as soon as my last horse was cooled out and put away, I used the pay phone by the track kitchen and called Detective James Ralston. I asked him if he could get a copy of an autopsy report on Daniel Albert.

"What've you gotten yourself into, now?" he said.

"Hey, I'm just working at the racetrack. Minding my own business. Keeping my nose clean."

"Uh-huh."

"Really." I heard him sigh, then I said, "I'm calling on behalf of my father," I said, and the word felt odd rolling off my tongue. "The guy was a friend of his, and I want to know the cause of death."

Ralston asked me when and where he had died, and I told him what I knew. "All right," he said. "I'll run it down. What's your number there?"

"I'm usually not around a phone. I'll have to call you."

I took a shower and, for the first time in recent memory, didn't start sweating the instant I switched off the water. I tightened the faucet until the spray cut off, then I ran a towel through my hair. As I pulled it across my back, I sensed that I was no longer alone and glanced over my shoulder.

Marcus had walked into the room, and he was standing six feet away. I lowered the towel and tied it around my waist, then I turned around. His puffy face dwarfed his bloodshot eyes, and the sclera was a sickly yellow. His nostrils flared with each labored breath, as if he'd just climbed a flight of stairs.

"You ain't even been here two weeks, and you already missed three days a work. Must be nice, white boy."

"Awh, come on, Marcus. Give it a rest."

He sucked in a lungful of air, and a glob of mucus rattled in the back of his throat. My gaze dropped to his meaty hands as he clenched and unclenched them, and I began to worry. He might have been out of shape, but the bastard outweighed me by a good hundred pounds. And he was effectively blocking the only way out of the room.

Marcus stepped closer.

"What? Are you gay?" I said. "Get the fuck away from me."

He took another step, and I caught a whiff of cheap whiskey on his breath and assumed he'd gotten a head start on lunch.

"I ain't gonna fuck with you, boy. I'm gonna beat the living shit out of you."

The guy generally moved like a heavy Sherman tank, slow and lumbering, guided by an equally dim-witted mind. But I'd lost any advantage I might have had by allowing him to get so close.

Marcus lunged forward, and instead of taking a swing at me, as I'd expected, he wrapped his arms around me, hauled me off my feet, and pinned me against the wall. He threw his head back, then wrenched his neck forward, and his forehead filled my field of vision as he tried to head butt me. I twisted at the last second, and his skull slammed into the side of my face. My cheekbone felt as if it had splintered into pieces, and a ringing filled my head.

He clamped his thick arms more tightly around mine, and his heavy rolls of fat pressed against my chest. His foul body odor filled my nostrils and coated the back of my throat as he tilted his head back for another go. I squirmed and yelled, and Marcus suddenly toppled backward. I landed on my feet, then overbalanced as he pulled me along with him.

Jay caught me by the shoulder and effortlessly shoved Marcus on his ass. He landed hard, and the concussion forced the air from his lungs. Marcus rolled onto his stomach, grabbed the bench, and clambered to his feet. When he spun around and got a look at who'd tossed him on his butt, he froze.

"You bother him again," Jay said, "and you'll answer to me."

Marcus stepped backward and caught the bench with his knee. He swayed, then continued backward until his shoulder hit the divider by the door. He scrambled around the corner.

Jay looked at my cheek and said, "You okay, man?"

"Yeah," I said. "And, thanks."

"Better get some ice, 'cause it's already startin' to swell." With that, he turned to leave.

"Hey," I said, and he paused. "Is Marcus friends with McCormick's groom, Tyson?"

"Far as I know, Marcus ain't friends with nobody."

He left, and after a moment, I switched on the shower again and stood under the spray until I could no longer smell Marcus's stink on my skin.

I dumped my stuff in my room, got an ice pack from the first aid station, and headed into town.

Green's pharmacy was packed with office workers running errands on their lunch hour and mothers trying to shop while their little kids whined or asked questions nonstop, and elderly people waiting for their prescriptions to be filled. And I figured all that traffic could work to my advantage.

I stood in line under a sign that read *Consultations*, and when the woman in front of me left, I stepped up to the counter. Mr. Green rested his hand lightly on the Formica and asked if he could help me.

"Actually…no," I said. "You're the one who's going to need help if you don't listen up."

Green frowned.

"Your buddies at the track are getting a bit antsy, and pretty soon, they're gonna start pointing fingers. And I have no doubt they're going to implicate you in their race-fixing scheme, seeing that you've been supplying them with the drugs they've been using to slow the opposition."

Green's hand flinched on the counter. "What are you talking about?" he asked, reasonably enough.

He wasn't rattled. As a matter of fact, he was behaving as an innocent man would. Irritated but not panicked. Not yet, anyway.

"But then, racketeering's the least of your worries. Now, murder," I said, "that's a whole different flavor, isn't it? You do serious time for aiding and abetting in a murder case."

Someone stood in line behind me, and Green flicked them a nervous glance.

"The cops are going to put it together soon enough, and your buddy, Randy Tyson, he's coming apart. I don't think he'll last another day before he turns himself in, and he sure as shit's gonna tell them who he's been getting the drugs from."

The mention of Tyson's name tipped him closer to the edge.

Green pressed both hands palm down on the counter until his fingertips blanched. "I'm sorry. I don't know what you're talking about," he said softly, but I saw that he did.

"Was the drug you gave them back in March meant to kill Daniel Albert, or were they just trying to get information out of him like they did with me Wednesday night?"

One of the other pharmacists, a middle-aged woman who'd been standing behind Green, dropping completed orders in the alphabetized bins, had paused and now stared openly at us.

"Who are you?" His voice had risen an octave, but outwardly, he appeared calm.

"Must have been an inconvenience," I said, "having to run the drug out to them in the middle of the night like that. Risky, too. Anyone could have seen you, just like you were seen exchanging envelopes with Tyson in that Mexican restaurant last week." I glanced at my watch. "A week ago today, as a matter of fact."

The female pharmacist moved alongside Green, and his shoulders tensed under his lab coat. "Is everything okay, Nate?" she said.

I gestured toward Green and took a breath. "That depends on Nathan, here," I said. "You might want to talk some sense into him, considering he's been supplying drugs out of your pharmacy to some unscrupulous guys at the track. Drugs used to slow horses and murder an old man."

She stared at me as if I'd sprouted an extra eyeball, but when she checked Green for his reaction and saw the fear in his eyes, her expression changed. "Who are you?" she said.

I ignored her. "Go to the cops, Nathan. Turn yourself in, and they'll cut you a deal."

When I turned to leave, I saw that the line behind me had grown and most if not all of the customers had overheard at least part of our conversation. Every one of them stared at me as I threaded my way past them. Although I'd planned on buying some necessities on the way out, things like Tastykakes and Cheetos, and Utz potato chips, I bypassed the cashier at the front counter and walked to the parking lot. The temperature had crept back into the low nineties, but a strong westerly breeze had pushed the humidity over the Atlantic where it belonged.

On the way in, I'd spotted Green's silver Grand Prix and had parked where I could keep an eye on it and still see the pharmacy's front door. I slid behind the Chevy's steering wheel and picked up the ice pack. It was still cold, so I scrunched down on the bench seat to get comfortable and held the pack against my cheek.

It bothered me that I didn't know all the players. I was fairly confident that Tyson had been the one in the back seat of the car that night with his boot jammed into my spine. The one who'd played with the stun gun and had offered to beat it out of me. And they'd had to wait for the drug that they'd pumped into my system, so it made sense that they'd been waiting on Green.

So, who were the two in the front seat? One had sounded worried when they were in my room, like he didn't have the nerve for the job. And I was pretty sure he was the one who'd injected me. What had he said? Something about not being used to doing it to a human. He wasn't used to injecting humans, but he was used to injecting…horses? Maybe he was a vet, but hell, I'd given hundreds of injections at Foxdale. Trainers probably did it all the time, as well. No. The guy wasn't a vet because then they wouldn't need Green to get their hands on the drugs. Was the nervous guy McCormick? Maybe, even though I'd never thought of him as being anything less than self-assured. And arrogant.

Next, I considered the driver. The gang's leader. He was so controlled and calm and cold, he scared the hell out of me. I pictured him trying to manage the growing dissension in his troops and wondered what he'd do next. As for his identity, I didn't have a fucking clue.

I changed gears and thought about the night on Abby's porch. I was fairly certain the leader was the one who'd grabbed Abby. And he'd had a hard-on. My fingers tightened on the ice pack, and I laid it on the dash. I thought about his threatening phone call to Abby and heard his voice in my mind as he calmly stated that he would get me. The guy didn't have any nerves.

Tyson had been there, too, despite the extra bruising I'd seen on his face when he walked out of the track kitchen later in the week. Maybe the leader didn't like his guys running out on him.

◇◇◇

I jerked awake at the sound of a horn blaring, and it took me half a second to remember why I was sitting in the Chevy and not lying on the cot in my room. I checked that Green's little silver car was parked where it was supposed to be, then I glanced at my watch. Three o'clock. The sky had clouded over, and the temperature had dropped into the eighties. I leaned back in the seat and yawned, switched on the ignition, fiddled with the radio, flipped it off, checked my watch. Surveillance had to be the most boring job on earth. I was starving, and worse, I had to take a leak. When Green hadn't left the store by three-twenty, I gambled that his shift didn't end until four. I took a chance and drove to McDonald's, used the restroom, and ordered a Big Mac and fries.

At four-ten, Green left the pharmacy at headed straight home. As I drove past his house, he'd already driven his Grand Prix into the garage and was stooped over, scooping mail out of his mailbox. I pulled into someone's driveway a block and a half down the street, turned around, and parked where I could see the northeast corner of his house. He was nowhere in sight, but as I switched off the engine, his garage door shuddered, then glided down the tracks and jarred closed as it touched the asphalt.

I finished my lunch and felt pretty good until sometime after five when my eyelids became heavy and my breathing slowed, and I could barely stay awake. I rested my arm on the pickup's doorframe and propped my head on my hand and tried to keep my eyes open. A middle-aged woman, dressed in shorts and a fluorescent pink tank top, pulled a Lawn-Boy out of her garage, cranked the engine to life, and pushed the mower along the edge of the garden that ran the length of the house's foundation. She circled the front yard twice, then started cutting diagonal swaths across the lawn. I'd hoped that the noise would keep me awake, but it had the opposite effect, drowning out the rest of the neighborhood sounds and effectively shutting down my senses.

When my head lulled forward, I sat up straighter and rubbed my face. The woman stared at me as she pivoted the mower and started back across the lawn. She didn't seem too keen on having a stranger camped out in front of her house. The next time she swung around and headed toward me, I looked at my watch like I'd been waiting for someone, started up the Chevy, and drove off. I studied Green's house as I cruised past. The blinds were drawn, and the place looked as dead as it had the first time I'd seen it. I turned onto the main drag, U-turned in a gas station parking lot, and pulled back onto Green's street. I parked before I reached his house, then stretched and settled against the backrest.

By nine o'clock, the light had bled from the sky. Three doors down from Green's house, one of his neighbors had had a cookout, and the breeze that trickled through the pickup's open window carried the mingled smells of cut grass, exhaust, and barbecue. Farther down the street, three kids were playing horse. I listened to their voices and the ball thudding hollowly on the driveway and the backboard rattling when one of them made a shot. A dog yapped somewhere in the distance. Life in the suburbs.

I opened my eyes at the sound of Rollerbladers gliding down the middle of the street. Two girls, both blond and slim with creamy pale skin that seemed to glow in the fading light. Sisters, I assumed, and both were wearing sports bras and very short shorts that, in combination, exposed an awful lot of skin. One was young, maybe fifteen, but the one closest to the truck was nearer my age. She slowed as she passed the side mirror. When she drew level with the Chevy's front bumper, she spread her legs to keep her balance, bent from the waist, and adjusted the buckle over her right ankle, a maneuver that would have put me on my head. As it was, the view was enough to knock me over.

She gracefully straightened to her full height, pushed off with her left skate, and caught up with the other girl. Okay. Maybe life in the suburbs wasn't so bad, after all.

I glanced toward Green's house and did a double take. The front porch light was lit, and I could think of only three reasons for switching it on: he wanted to deter burglars, which seemed unlikely, he was going out, or he was expecting someone. I checked the windows. The blinds were still drawn, but a light burned in one of the front rooms.

I tapped my fingers on the steering wheel. Since I'd been forced to move from my original parking spot, I no longer faced the main road. If Green had visitors, following them when they left would be difficult, not to mention the fact that they would drive right past me on the way in. I decided to move. As I reached out and put my hand on the ignition, headlights swept across the cars parked on the opposite side of the street as a vehicle turned off the main road. I ducked and listened as it moved slowly past, then pulled into Green's driveway. The engine cut off, and a door slammed, then another.

I lifted my head until I could see over the dash, and when I saw that they weren't looking in my direction, I straightened up behind the wheel. The driver was thin and stooped, and I didn't recognize him until he stepped into the porch light's yellow glare and turned his head to the left, looking for the doorbell.

David Reece, the trainer on the east side of barn sixteen, extended his arm and pressed the button with his fingertip.

I didn't have any trouble recognizing the passenger. Randy Tyson had strode around the hood of the car and followed Reece onto the porch in his long loping stride and now stood, bouncing on his heels with his hands clasped behind his back. Green opened the door and said something, then the three of them disappeared inside, and as far as I could tell, they didn't have a clue they were being watched.

Reece surprised me. He seemed like such a nervous, ineffectual little man, but as I went back over the night when they'd drugged Speedwell, he fit what I already knew. Reece must have been the nervous guy in my room and the one who'd stuck the needle in my arm. And he certainly fit Kessler's description of a mediocre trainer. So who was the leader? McCormick? I didn't think so. I had no trouble casting him as one of the gang, but his hot temper and loud voice didn't match the leader's quiet, restrained arrogance.

I checked the time. Nine-sixteen, which was damned late to be socializing, considering they got up well before daybreak every single day of the week. I started the Chevy, drove past Green's house, doubled back, and parked behind a souped-up Mustang with Virginia tags. Reece drove a big old boat of a car, an old, four-door Chrysler, and that fit, too. The pieces of the puzzle were falling into place, all except one.

Half an hour later, they left. As Reece backed onto the street, I grabbed a pen off the dash and wrote his tag number on the empty McDonald's bag. He drove directly to the track, where he dropped Tyson off at the gate, then he picked up US 1 and headed south. On the other side of town, he slowed, then pulled into a pothole-ridden parking lot that belonged to a raggedy-looking hotel. A vacancy sign blinked below a gaudy neon sign with several letters missing. It read, The Br-arw-od M-tel. I tore my gaze from the sign and corrected the Chevy's drift to the left. The Briarwood Motel was where Daniel Albert had spent the last night of his life.

Chapter 18

I U-turned and parked and eventually determined that Reece had gone into unit four. Ten minutes later, his lights switched off, and after an hour of quiet, I ate dinner at a local Denny's, then drove back to the track.

My room looked as unappealing as ever, so I cut over to the barn and carried a bale of straw to CT's stall. She tensed her neck when I slipped under the stall guard, so after I positioned the bale along the wall, I smoothed my hand down her neck and told her she was a good girl. She didn't race until Thursday, so that gave her two nights to get used to my unorthodox presence. Staying in the horses' stalls was ideal as far as security went, but the practice would backfire if they didn't relax.

On my way to get another bale, I waved at the camera. When Phil didn't come out of Kessler's office or acknowledge that he'd seen me, I wondered if he'd fallen asleep. I slipped the second bale under the stall guard and dumped it on the first when CT nickered and stepped toward the door. I looked over my shoulder.

Trudy was standing in the doorway with her hands clasped lightly around the top edge of the stall guard. "Steve, is that you?"

I stepped forward so she could see me.

"What are you doing?" she said, and her voice was so low, I could barely hear her over the whir of the fan.

At this point, I didn't think there'd be any harm in telling her, so I said, "Security."

"Mr. K knows?"

I nodded and stepped closer.

Light from the dusk to dawn lamp that was mounted on the far end of barn seventeen cut across the waist-high wall and sliced through the thin fabric of Trudy's shorts. They looked like the same pair she'd worn the last time I'd seen her in the barn at night, and I thought about how sexy she'd looked, standing in the moonlight. And I remembered the curve of her bare breast and wondered once again whether she'd known that I'd seen. I dragged my gaze to her face.

I figured she slept in those shorts, and an image of her spread out on her mattress filled my mind. She was wearing a different top tonight. An extra-large basketball jersey hung loosely from her slim shoulders. She'd cut off the bottom of the shirt so that the silky fabric ended at her waist.

"What are you doing here?" I said.

She shrugged, then she lifted her fine blond hair off the back of her neck and twisted it into a knot. Her jersey rode up with the movement, tightening beneath her breasts and bunching into folds above them. "Oh, I don't know," she said. "I couldn't sleep for some reason."

I slid my gaze down her legs. She'd spread them slightly to keep her balance since the ground was uneven where the stall floor met the dirt ridge that had formed from so many horses tromping down the shedrow. Her thighs were creamy white in the dark and blended smoothly into the swell of her ass, and I could just make out the soft bulge of her pubic bone beneath the papery-thin fabric.

"You always check on your horses when you can't sleep?" I said, and my voice sounded thick.

She nodded, then said something I couldn't hear. I stepped closer, and she reached up and clasped her hands behind my neck.

"I thought I might find you, too," she whispered so softly, I wondered if I'd heard right.

Even though the fan's wash slid across my shoulders and down my back, it was hotter than hell, standing in that stall. I reached over the stall guard and flattened my hands on her sides and was briefly startled when my palms touched bare skin until I remembered the low cut of her shirt.

Her flesh felt warm and smooth beneath my fingers. As I bent down to kiss her, she tilted her chin up and parted her lips. I slipped my tongue into her mouth and tasted toothpaste on her teeth. She responded with a kiss that was at once practiced and sweet, and I figured she wasn't as shy as she let on. She arched her back and pressed against my crotch, and I realized that I'd read her wrong in more ways than one.

As I slid my hand upward and felt the side of her breast against my palm, I imagined pulling her into the stall and pressing her against the wall. I imagined yanking down her shorts and fucking her, then I thought about everything else I'd like to do to her and just about came in my pants.

When I broke the kiss, she moved her lips down my throat and bit my skin. I clamped my left arm around the small of her back and slid my right hand toward the center of her chest, dragging the shirt across her breast until it was exposed. I cupped my hand under her breast and smoothed my thumb across her nipple, and she bit down so hard, I thought she might draw blood.

Trudy suddenly disengaged, and I reluctantly dropped my hand and wondered what she would do next. She stood there for a second, making no move to cover herself. Then, just as suddenly, she ducked under the stall guard, and I backed deeper into the stall. When she reached the center of the stall, she crossed her arms, grasped the hem of her shirt, and peeled it over her head. She bent over and placed it carefully on the straw bale, then she turned her head and looked at me.

She looked absolutely stunning as she gazed over her shoulder at me through a tangle of bangs that had fallen across her eyes. The golden crucifix that she wore around her neck swayed gently in front of her breasts, and when she blinked, a wisp of hair caught on her eyelashes. Her lips were parted, and she was breathing through her mouth.

She stood and faced me, and it seemed to me there was a hint of challenge in the way she held herself.

I yanked my shirt off, dropped it on the ground, and ran my hands over her breasts, then I turned her around. Trudy placed her hands on the rough-hewn stall planks and spread her legs like someone who was about to be frisked. I pressed against her and grabbed her breasts, and before I realized that I was doing it, I was rubbing against her. I was so goddamned horny, I was in deep shit.

I dropped my grip to her hips, backed her away from the wall, and gently pressed my hand between her shoulder blades. She knew what I wanted. She bent over and braced her hands on the bale, then spread her legs.

When I tugged her shorts down to her ankles, she tilted her ass higher, and I groaned. I dropped my jeans, and when I guided myself into her, she gasped. After about three thrusts, I came.

Trudy said, "Stay in me and use your hand," and her voice sounded strained.

I reached around and touched her, and she came almost as fast as I had. She shuddered, then she stepped away and pulled up her shorts. She wriggled into her jersey, and I was still standing there with my jeans puddled around my boots, trying to catch my breath.

She glanced down at me and smiled as I touched her hair. It had fallen out of its knot sometime in the past couple minutes.

"See ya," she whispered.

"Hey?" I said as she pivoted and left the stall.

I pulled up my jeans and noticed the horse for the first time since Trudy had stood in the doorway. The mare was standing along the far wall, staring at me with what I could only describe as a perplexed expression.

"What? You never seen people fuck before?" I said as I zipped up my pants. And that pretty much described it. A fantastic release of tension, sans commitment or emotion.

CT pivoted her loppy ears at the sound of my voice and watched me with a curious eye while I finished getting dressed. The wash from the fan swirled and eddied around us and smelled sweetly of straw and hay and horse. I stepped over to the mare, slipped my fingers into her mane, and scratched her withers. She lowered her head and curled her neck until her nose pressed against my thigh, then she wriggled her upper lip along the seam of my jeans. Well, that was a good sign. She felt bold enough to touch me, so she was beginning to relax. I smoothed my right hand down her wide forehead, then along the bridge of her nose, and when I cupped my hand beneath her lips, her ears swiveled forward. Her eyes widened as she sniffed my hand, and I realized that she smelled Trudy on my fingers, and probably me, and I wondered what her primitive instincts told her. Was she simply curious about an unfamiliar smell, or did she understand the smell of another species' sex?

As I looked at my hand and rubbed my fingertips together, a warm tide of guilt and shame washed over me, followed by a sudden feeling of loss that settled in the pit of my stomach when I remembered that I had nothing to feel guilty about. Rachel and I were history.

You're a goddamned bastard, Cline. The minute you're no longer with Rachel, you're screwing around.

I tilted my head back and closed my eyes. A bastard. God. What an understatement. I rubbed my face and unclipped the stall guard. As I stepped into the aisle, the realization of how close CT's stall was to the end of the barn sank in, and I wondered how much Phil had seen because of the damned cameras stuck under the eaves. I checked the angle. He couldn't have seen into the stall, but he sure as hell would have had an eyeful while Trudy stood in the aisle.

"Shit."

I rubbed my hand over my face, then headed toward the tack room. I needed a horse blanket if I was going to sleep on those bales, and it was all I could do to walk down that aisle without looking up at the camera. As I neared the last stall, the office door jarred, then swung in on its hinges.

Light spilled down the shedrow, and I stopped short when I realized that the man standing in the doorway wasn't Phil, after all, but Dennis Hurp.

He leaned against the doorjamb and crossed one ankle in front of the other, then he crossed his arms over his chest and smirked. His face was puffy from lack of sleep and drawn at the same time, as if someone had tightened a sheet around a lumpy down pillow.

"Kessler thinks you're such a go-getter, hotwalking and working nights," he said. "Guess he doesn't know about the perks."

"Where's Phil, *Agent* Hurp?"

"Sick." Hurp's eyes glistened with something bordering on malice as he took in the wisps of straw clinging to my rumpled, damp clothes, and when his gaze settled on the mark I'm sure Trudy had left on my neck, the skin along my spine prickled. "She a good fuck, Cline?" he said as I walked past.

He was fishing for a reaction, and even knowing that, I almost pulled up and got into it with him. I gritted my teeth and unlocked the tack room, instead. I slung a blanket over my shoulder and stepped back into the aisle. Hurp was still leaning against the doorjamb.

"One of these days," he said as I drew closer, "your choices are gonna catch up with you."

"Wow, Hurp. That's mighty profound."

As I walked back to CT's stall, I hoped to hell he was wrong. Like an idiot, I hadn't even considered using a condom. Not that I had one handy, but the fact that I hadn't even given it a thought scared the shit out of me.

◇◇◇

Someone spoke my name out loud, and I looked up and saw Rachel sitting on her horse, bareback. She stared down at me as if she'd asked a question and was waiting for an answer. We were in the lounge at Foxdale, and people pressed around us, wanting to hear what was said next. I heard their breathing and their murmured voices, but their faces were blurry, without definition. I glanced down and saw that I was naked. The tile floor felt cold beneath my feet.

I looked back at Rachel, but my father was sitting on the horse, instead. He was speaking to me, and as I leaned forward to hear his words, he smoothed his hand down his chest, and a swath of blood spread across his scrubs. He did it again and again, and with each pass, the smear grew wider until I wanted to scream at him to stop.

Rachel's gelding nudged my arm, and when I reached up to steady his head, something warm and sticky seeped between my fingers. I was afraid to look, terrified of what I would see.

The horse's head flopped against my shoulder, and as I turned toward him, a deep gash opened in his neck. A thick cord of blood seeped out of the tissue and snaked between the gelding's pectoral muscles like a foul, black river. It tracked down the inside of the horse's leg and coiled around its hoof.

I said something, and my father touched my shoulder. His fingers were coated with blood, and his touch was cold. A dead man's touch that pulled the heat from my body.

"Steve," the voice said, louder this time, and I jerked my eyes open and sat up.

I'd been asleep in CT's stall, and Kessler was stooped over me with his hand on my shoulder. He rocked back on his heels when I started, and CT skittered away from us.

"Shit," I said as I swiveled around and put my feet on the ground. While Kessler settled the horse, I wiped the sweat off my forehead and ran my fingers through my hair. The stall light was on, and the shedrow was lit up. "What time is it?" I lifted my head when Kessler didn't answer.

He had hold of the horse's halter, and he was squinting at me. "What happened?"

I touched my neck. "I, eh…"

"What happened to your face?"

"Oh." I shrugged. "I was careless."

Kessler waited for me to elaborate.

I'd debated what to do about Marcus and had decided to do nothing at all. The guy was a fat, lazy bigot, but since Kessler hadn't minded putting up with him, I didn't see why I should cause him to lose his job. My presence at the track was temporary, and once I was gone, if he found something else to gripe about, Kessler could deal with that.

"It's nothing," I said and told Kessler I needed to talk to him in depth. We agreed to meet that afternoon.

When I walked into the tack room to get a lead shank, Abby was on tiptoe, stretching to reach a double twisted-wire snaffle that hung from a peg above her head. Her hair was curled and hung down the center of her back in a loose ponytail. The morning was still cool, and she was wearing a thin nylon jacket.

I stepped to her side. "Here. Let me get that."

Abby smiled softly and rocked back on her heels. As she turned toward me, I held out the bit, and she slowly extended her hand as her gaze settled on my bruised face, then lingered over the mark on my neck. Her smile dissolved. She took the bit and absentmindedly gathered together the bridle and running martingale that she had draped over her arm. A look of confusion filled her eyes, followed by disappointment, then anger.

She blinked, and for a brief second, I thought she was on the verge of tears. But not Abby. She was too tough.

"You okay?" I said.

She turned away and lifted a saddle cloth off the pile that was stacked on a tack trunk and added it to the gear she already cradled in her arms. "Go see Gordi," she said. "Ruskie will be back any minute now."

"What's wrong?"

She shook her head but wouldn't turn around. "Just go."

As I grabbed a lead shank off the hook by the door, Abby rushed past me and headed in the opposite direction. I walked down to Ruskie's stall, wondering what in the hell was going on.

Gordi had already cleaned the stall and was bedding it down. He was stooped over, picking up the last two flakes of straw. As he straightened and held out his arms to shake them out, he caught sight of me in the doorway.

He whistled. "Looks like you got run over by a fucking bus."

"Awh, come on. It's not that bad."

He flicked the last of the straw across the stall floor and stepped closer. "Yeah, you right. Looks more like a mini van."

I yawned and rolled my eyes. "You have any idea what's wrong with Abby this morning?"

"Shit, almost always somethin' wrong with that girl. But damn, she hangin' with a guy like Jeff, no wonder she fucked. Macho guy like him, he too busy admiring hisself to notice her."

Gordi unclipped Ruskie's water bucket, and as I backed out of his way, he did a double-take. "Man, oh man, Jeff catch you in bed with her?"

I resisted the urge to touch my neck. "You gotta be kidding."

"She see that motherfucker?"

I shrugged.

"Guess I know what wrong with her, then."

I was beginning to feel like I was back in high school. "What in the hell are you talking about?"

"Like I told you. The girl got the hots for you, man."

Gordi hauled the bucket out of the barn, and I strolled after him. He swiped a scrub brush around the rim a couple of times, then he dumped the water in the alley. I glanced toward the access road, made sure Ruskie wasn't on his way back from the track, then I looked toward the shedrow just as Abby barged out of CT's stall. Trudy grabbed the stall guard before it swung into the doorframe and looked after Abby as Gordi said in my ear, "So, Steve. Anybody I know?"

My first thought was that something was wrong with the horse, then I realized that Abby wasn't worried. She was pissed.

Gordi followed the direction of my stare and said, "Uh-oh. Don't tell me you be doing the wild thing with Trudy?"

I glanced at Gordi, then watched Trudy disappear back into the stall. She looked mad and smug and worried all at the same time.

"Um, um, um." Gordi shook his head. "You gone and picked the wrong horse to ride. Those two might be close, but they girls, and you know what girls do more than anything?" When I didn't answer, Gordi said, "Compete. And the boss's daughter ain't gonna be too happy she came in second."

"Christ."

Gordi chuckled. "Place like this, where everybody knows everybody else and everybody sick to death of each other, it like a soap opera, man. They oughta call it Washington Place."

Hooves scrunched on the ground behind us, and we turned toward the access road in time to see Ruskie stride into the alley. He paused and pricked his ears, taking in the surroundings as if he were in charge, and I appreciated Juan's savvy more than ever. He didn't pester the colt to move on but allowed him the leeway to take charge of the little things, and that would foster confidence when it came to the important stuff, like winning races. The sun was still low in the eastern sky, and the steam that rose from Ruskie's body in the cool morning air shimmered like gold. He looked like he was on fire. An aberration.

After Ruskie's bath, Gordi draped a lightweight wool cooler over the colt's back and tied it under his neck. "Be careful, Steve. Change in the weather like this, and he be wired, plus he don't like having blankets and shit on his back. Thinks it some kinda big blue monster chasing his ass, so watch him. Especially in the corners."

I led Ruskie over to the barn entrance, and we waited for Marcus to pass by with one of Karen's horses. Marcus kept his yellow-eyed gaze fixed on me until the filly blocked his line of sight as they rounded the corner. Ever since I'd seen him walk into the barn earlier in the morning, he'd watched me like he was waiting for me to rat him out.

After they'd gone down the short aisle a few paces, I took a step, intending to take Ruskie into the shedrow, and caught sight of Abby as she stood in the doorway to her father's office. She had her arms crossed under her breasts, and when I looked her way, she spun around and walked back into the room.

This was just great. Rachel was disgusted with me. Abby hated my guts. Hurp had me pegged as a punk. Ralston figured I was being impetuous, *again*, and he was probably right. Kessler, more than likely, thought the same thing. And who in the hell knew what was going on in Trudy's head.

Ruskie skittered around the corner near McCormick's office, then he settled into a loose, relaxed stride. He lowered his head a fraction, and out of the corner of my eye, I could see his back swinging rhythmically with each step he took. On our third lap, I noticed Mr. Reece standing in the middle of the alley, talking to a woman he routinely hired to exercise his horses. She was sitting on a little bay colt with a crooked blaze down his forehead, and I thought he might have been the colt who'd gotten himself cast a week earlier. Apparently, he'd come out of it sound.

Reece grasped the reins and moved to the horse's side. As he prepared to hook his lead onto its bridle, he caught sight of us as we approached the doorway, and the muscles in his face seemed to stiffen. Only his eyes moved as he tracked us through the corner. The woman on his colt spoke to him, but whether he heard or not was anyone's guess. That got me looking for Randy Tyson. So far, I hadn't seen him, and that made two days in a row.

Around eight o'clock, I took a break and used the pay phones outside the track kitchen to call Detective Ralston.

"They didn't do an autopsy," he said when I got him on the line.

"Why not?"

"His death was listed as natural."

"But—"

"Look, Steve. He was an elderly person with a documented medical history of advanced emphysema. Inhalers and oxygen were found in his room to support his condition, and there was nothing suspicious about the scene that indicated the death was anything but natural. In a case like that, they aren't going to do an autopsy."

"What were the details of his death? How'd he die?"

"Respiratory arrest."

"Did he choke on anything?"

"He aspirated vomitus."

It felt like my feet were glued to the floor. Like the world had kept on spinning and left me behind. "Fucking shit. He was murdered."

A guy walking up the steps to the kitchen turned and looked at me, and I realized my voice had carried.

"Did they check for signs of a gag?"

"I think you need to tell me what's going on."

"Something I overheard. Something these guys said indicated that they'd been with this guy when he vomited, and he'd choked."

Ralston was quite for a moment.

"What about his mouth?" I said. "Did they find evidence of a gag? Duct tape residue?"

"You're not listening. If they'd found anything like that, they would've performed an autopsy."

"What about needle marks on his arms or marks left by a stun gun? How long was it before they found his body? Would evidence like that be difficult to find after a while, especially if they weren't looking for it?"

"I'm not liking this," he said.

"Oh, come on."

"It all depends, but sure, the longer he's exposed to the environment, the more likely decomposition or lividity will skew the findings."

"Lividity. What's that?"

"Over time, gravity causes blood to settle on the underside of the body, forming dark areas, except for blanching at pressure points. Albert was found on his stomach on the bed with his head, arms, and a portion of his upper torso draped over the edge, so there was a good bit of lividity in those areas that could have masked something like a needle prick."

"So it's a dead end?"

"I think it's time you told me what you're doing." When I didn't say anything, he said, "You're at Washington, right?"

"Yeah."

"Which barn?"

"Sixteen."

"I'm coming over."

"I'm working right now."

"When then?"

"I get off at eleven. I'll meet you in the barn office."

"Do you think you can stay out of trouble until then?"

"Probably."

"And I want your father there, too," Ralston said, then hung up.

Stingray got stuck with Ace, which was fine by me, and as the morning drew to a close, I only saw Reece one other time. Tyson never did show up, and I was acutely aware of the fact that Trudy had done everything in her power to avoid me.

Chapter 19

By eleven-thirty, the day had warmed up to a pleasant eighty-three degrees, and everyone had taken off to eat lunch or take a nap or do laundry. It was Jay's week, and he hadn't looked too happy about it as he'd slung the black trash bag over his shoulder and stalked out into the sunlight.

I headed to Kessler's office. When I noticed he was on the phone, I paused in the doorway, and Runt lifted his head off his paws and wagged his stump of a tail. The security monitor was dark, and I thought about last night and wondered for the hundredth time how much of our encounter had been caught on film. Runt jumped to his feet and trotted over as a fax machine on top of the file cabinets whirred to life. I squatted down and scratched him behind his ears.

Kessler crossed the room with the phone still tucked against his ear, held out a menu from a Chinese restaurant, and mimed that I should call in an order. He handed me his cell phone, then pointed to number seventy-one, Hunan spicy chicken. I ordered the same thing, and when I learned that they delivered to the track, I told them to bring it to barn sixteen.

I laid the phone on a dog-eared condition book, then sat in the chair alongside the desk. Runt planted his paws on my knees and nudged my hand. I patted his head and rubbed his ears, and as I waited for Kessler to get off the phone, I leaned back in the chair and stretched. When I straightened, a heavy green book caught my eye.

I reached over and picked up Kessler's copy of *Guide to Pharmaceuticals and Biologicals* and flipped to page 379. I thought back to the note printed on the piece of scrap paper McCormick had used to mark the page. GIVE 4 CC PTX IM 12 TO 20 HRS. BEFORE POST, 6 CC IF NECESSARY, COMBINED WITH LSX. CC and IM, of course, meant the drug would be injected directly into the muscle. I scanned 378 and 9 and decided that PTX stood for either Pentoxifylline, Pentoxil, or Pentoxifylline, all of which appeared to improve circulation. Nothing exciting in that. I flipped to the L's and, by process of elimination, deciphered that LSX stood for Lasix, a diuretic commonly used at the track. It was given to bleeders, horses whose lungs bled when they raced, and it was common knowledge that it masked other drugs.

Kessler had hung up, and he looked over my shoulder.

I flipped back to 378 and ran my finger down the PTX possibilities. "Are these drugs legal?"

"I don't think so. Why?"

"McCormick combines them with Lasix. Improving circulation would speed them up, right?"

"That would be my guess." Kessler was looking at me like he'd all but given up on expecting me to stay in line.

I glanced at the menu. "They're busy. The food won't be here for forty-five minutes to an hour."

He nodded, then sat down behind his desk. "What did you want to tell me?"

I wedged the book between two binders and settled back in my chair. "I know who all the players are, except one."

Kessler leaned forward in his chair, and I described how I'd pretty much spooked Tyson and Green and the reaction it had triggered.

"Reece? I can't believe it."

"Well, believe it. The timing was enough to convince me."

"Oh, but wait a minute. I'd forgotten. Reece is Tyson's uncle, so I guess it isn't so hard to believe that they'd be in it together. But it still doesn't get us anywhere because there's no proof."

"Maybe we won't need it. Not if one of them goes to the cops."

Kessler leaned back in his chair and shook his head. "What if they decide to come after you, instead? Did you think about that?"

"He hasn't so far," Ralston said from the doorway. "No reason to think he'll start now."

Kessler rocked his chair forward onto all fours, I spun around, and Runt bounded toward the door with his hackles raised.

Detective James Ralston totally ignored the fat little dog as he stepped into the room. "What happened to your face?"

I touched my cheek as I stood. "Nothing important."

He stared impassively, waiting, and I knew him well enough to know that he didn't take no for an answer. I glanced at Kessler, then said, "I've missed a couple mornings work since I started here, so this black guy's convinced I'm getting special treatment because I'm white, and he wanted me to know how much it pissed him off."

"Marcus," Kessler said, then frowned. "Why didn't you tell me?"

I shrugged. "No point in it, really, because he's right. I am getting special treatment, he's just working with the wrong premise."

Ralston glanced around the room, and when his gaze held briefly on the monitor and VCR, I thought he'd probably noticed the surveillance cameras in the eaves. He looked from Kessler to me and said, "So, he's not connected to your...activities?"

"It's unlikely." I introduced them, and as they shook hands, I noted the chemistry between the two men.

I'd come to think of Kessler as an open, honest man who didn't necessarily give much thought to the atrocities human beings were capable of. Ralston, on the other hand, appeared to evaluate everyone he met with an air of cautious suspicion, no doubt a byproduct of years of police work, and it wasn't lost on Kessler. He sat down and looked at both of us, and I guessed he was wondering how we knew each other.

Detective Ralston leaned a hip against the desk and crossed his arms. He was wearing a lightweight sports coat over a striped Oxford and jeans, and he needed a shave. "Okay, Steve. You mentioned race-fixing on the phone, and you're convinced Daniel Albert was murdered, so tell me what you've gotten mixed up with this time," he said as he withdrew a small spiral bound notepad and pen from his jacket pocket.

I stayed on my feet because I felt too wired to sit. Kessler and I took turns outlining what had happened so far. He described the attempts at pressuring him into running his horses to order, then I told Ralston about the attack on Abby's porch and my confrontation with Randy Tyson two days later. I described the exchange of envelopes between Tyson and the pharmacist, Nathan Green, then Kessler told him how he'd found me after Speedwell had been drugged.

Ralston slowly turned his head and looked at me. He was unnaturally still, as if he were preparing to hear something he knew he wasn't going to like. I could feel heat creeping up my neck as I considered how best to tell him without sounding melodramatic. The room was suddenly quiet. I could hear the dog's slow breathing as he lay stretched out on the floor. There simply wasn't a way to describe what had happened without being humiliated by it. I cleared my throat and told him about that night, and only when I'd finished did I realize how fast I'd run through it.

"So." I cleared my throat. "That pretty much sums up what's happened since I started at the track fourteen days ago."

"You should have reported the attack in your room. Laurel PD would have canvassed the area. It sounds like there's enough people roaming around here at night," Ralston said, and I thought of Trudy, "that someone might have heard or seen something useful. A vehicle description, for one. Even a plate number."

Ralston pushed his sunglasses farther up his nose. "But Mr. Kessler's right. Without the surveillance tape and syringe and fingerprints, you don't have proof of anything. Hearsay and circumstantial, if that. Nothing any prosecutor will look at."

The guy from the Chinese restaurant rapped on the door-jamb, then walked around to the side of the desk. Runt, who'd grudgingly sprawled on the concrete when his menacing behavior had gone unnoticed, pranced around the delivery guy, eyeing the white paper bags with anticipation.

Kessler cleared a space on his desk, paid for the food, then left it sitting untouched on the blotter. The spicy aroma filled the small room and started my mouth watering.

Ralston shifted his weight on the desk. "I'm in class the next three days, but when I get back, I'll find out what Laurel's got, then I'll see what I can stir up." He looked at me. "You think you can stay out of trouble that long, Steve?"

"I think I can manage that."

He jotted down Kessler's phone number, slipped the notepad into his jacket pocket, then handed Kessler his card. He crossed his arms over his chest and looked at me for a long moment. "Interesting therapy, wouldn't you say?"

I thought about the psychologist's business card that he'd given me the last time I'd seen him. That I'd thrown in the trash. "You know how the saying goes," I said. "When you fall off the horse…"

"This isn't any damned horse. And if your suspicions about Albert are correct, and I'm not saying they are, then you're doubly foolish." When I didn't say anything, he continued. "As far as undermining the group goes, your tactics weren't that bad. It's a technique we use at times. But it can blow up in your face. You're smart enough to know that. Why aren't you smart enough to stay out of it?"

"He's young," Kessler said. "He thinks he's invincible."

Ralston leveled his gaze on me. "Not after the last time, he doesn't."

Kessler looked from Ralston to me, and I was beginning to feel like a damned specimen in an experiment. "What 'last time'?"

Ralston jerked his head in my direction. "Ask him."

I looked at both of them in turn.

"Go back to Foxdale, Steve," Ralston said. "Or get a job somewhere else." He turned to Kessler. "If you care about him, you'll get him out of here."

"I've tried."

"Try harder." With that, Detective Ralston left.

I plopped down in the chair alongside the desk, stretched out my legs, and glanced at the crisp white bags from the Chinese restaurant. I'd been starving earlier, but I had absolutely no desire to eat now. Kessler fiddled with a pencil.

After a long moment of silence, I said, "What?"

"He's right, you know?"

Another pause. "You want me to quit?" I said.

Kessler leaned back in his chair. "I've been thinking about asking you to stay on permanently, if you're interested, but…"

I said nothing.

"I agree with the detective. You need to get away from here until they're arrested."

"But why? They'd be crazy to try anything, now. We know their names, and with Hurp's men so obviously handling the surveillance, it would be insane."

"You're right. I doubt they'll try to dope any of the horses at this point, but as far as they're concerned, you're the reason it's all coming apart. They've already proven that they're damned ruthless, so it's not inconceivable that they'd go after you."

Kessler rocked his chair back onto all fours, then he opened the bags, handed me a soda, and separated out the cartons. When he popped open his Hunan chicken, the aroma wafted across the room, and I was suddenly hungry again.

We ate our meals out of the cardboard boxes, using flimsy plastic forks. Runt couldn't make up his mind whom to watch first, so he alternated between both of us with his head moving on a swivel, watching every bite we took, and I figured he was practically wrung out with anticipation by the time I scooped out my last chunk of chicken. I dropped it back into the box, dumped my leftover rice on top, and held it low to the ground. He trotted over and stuffed his head between the flaps.

"What if I go home at night? They won't know where to find me, and during the day, it's safe enough around here. Plus, I'd like to see how it plays out. Did you notice Tyson didn't come in today?"

Kessler shook his head.

"Maybe he's spooked." Runt snuffled as he pressed his snout deeper into the box. I pulled it off his head and looked inside. He'd licked it clean. "Did you catch what Ralston said about Albert?"

"They don't think he was murdered."

"Nope. It was recorded as natural because nothing looked out of place, and they don't do autopsies when it's a natural death like that."

"Like I told you."

"Yeah." I rubbed my forehead. "But I don't like coincidences, and Albert and Reece living in the same motel is just too coincidental for me."

"No, it isn't. Think about it. Lots of people who work on the backside can't afford anything but cheap, and the Briarwood's cheaper than most of the apartments in town."

Runt nudged my thigh.

"What?"

The dog wagged his tail, a movement that started at the tip of his tail and traveled up his spine until his entire body wriggled. I smoothed my hand over his head and ruffled his ears.

"What did Detective Ralston mean about the 'last time'?" Kessler said.

He sat quietly, waiting for me to answer, and the room suddenly felt airless. Beyond the doorway, the barn seemed unnaturally still. I had a feeling that we were approaching a turning point in our relationship. He fully expected me to explain. A matter of trust. What he didn't realize was that telling him had nothing to do with trust and everything to do with embarrassment and humiliation.

I cleared my throat and stared directly ahead, at the cluttered bookshelves and the back wall hung with racing photographs that defined a long career filled with success.

"It started in February, with a horse theft at Foxdale," I said and told him the rest of it. I told him how I'd watched someone executed before me. How I'd killed a man myself, in self-defense. How sometimes, at night, it still made me sick.

When I finished, I swallowed against the taste of bile at the back of my throat. The food I'd just eaten sat in my gut like a brick. Kessler remained silent, and I couldn't bring myself to look at him for a very long time. When I did, I was nearly overwhelmed by the look of compassion in his eyes.

I stood up, and Runt heaved himself into a sitting position. "I'm going home," I said. "See you in the morning." I turned toward the door.

"Wait." Kessler came around the desk. "I'm sorry."

I shrugged. "Nothing to be sorry about."

"I meant what I said about a permanent job."

I thought about Abby. "I'll think about it."

I walked slowly down the shedrow. The fans were set to low, and except for the distant sound of a truck's hydraulics straining as it loaded one of the large green bins full of straw and manure, ready to be hauled away and replaced with an empty one, the backside was deserted. Most of the horses stood dozing in their stalls with their heads lowered and a hind leg cocked.

I didn't want Tyson and his crew thinking that anything had changed, so I left my gear at the track and drove home. After two weeks spent sleeping in stalls or in my roach-infested room, the loft looked like the Ritz. I cranked open the windows, left the screen door open, and lay on the bed. As I stared at the ridge beam high above me, I wondered what would happen next. Would one of them rat out the others, or would they band together? And if they did, what would they do then? I closed my eyes and felt my breathing slow. My body felt weighted to the mattress as I slipped into a deep, dreamless sleep.

Chapter 20

A thin breeze, smelling strongly of honeysuckle, drifted across my skin. I rolled over and opened my eyes. A band of sunlight touched the edge of the south-facing windows and cut horizontally across the kitchen countertop, turning the white Formica to gold. I checked my watch and saw that I'd slept for almost five hours.

I used the bathroom, then I peered at my reflection in the mirror. My hair was longer than I liked, and I desperately needed a shave, but the bruise on my cheek wasn't as bad as I'd expected, partly because, after two weeks working outside, I was no longer pale. Tomorrow, it would look worse.

I opened the cabinet beneath the sink before I remembered that my razor and shampoo and soap, and even the ibuprofen I kept in the kitchen, were at the track.

Well, that was brilliant, Cline.

I drove past the guard post and parked along the perimeter fence. Both sides of barn sixteen were quiet. Neither McCormick nor Reece had a runner that day, but across the alley, barn seventeen was wired. The Jamaicans had their radio cranked up, and judging by the whooping and hollering and backslapping that was going on, they'd had a winner.

All of Kessler's horses had poked their heads over their stall guards and were watching the activity with interest. Ruskie in particular seemed intent on the action, like he understood its significance. I paused alongside him, and even though he knew I was there, he didn't acknowledge my presence.

I smoothed my hand down his sleek neck. "That's okay, boy. One day, not too long from now, everyone will know you're the best there is."

He dipped his head toward me, then stared across the alley once again.

I patted his neck, then walked past him, certain that he would have shifted his position to look around me if I'd been foolish enough to block his view for too long.

The office door stood open, and a long rectangular block of light spilled down the loam and sawdust path toward me. As I approached, the light winked as a large man darkened the doorway, and for a brief second, I thought Marcus was coming out of the office. Then he stepped into the short aisle where the gray dusky light caught the side of his face, and I realized I didn't know him.

"What were you doing to that horse?"

"Nothing." I glanced beyond him at the monitor on the bookshelf and could see the top of his head in the image caught by the security camera. "Where's Phil? He still sick?"

The guy shrugged. "What's your name?"

"Steve Cline. I work for Mr. Kessler."

"You do, huh?"

"Yeah. I do."

He checked my badge, then flipped open a cell phone, and I followed him into the office as he leaned over the desk and peered at a notepad. He punched in a number with thick fingers the size of sausages. I listened as he spoke to Kessler and checked that I was legit, then I asked if I could talk to him. He shrugged again but handed over the phone without comment.

"Don't worry," I said into the phone. "I'm sticking with the program. I just needed to get some of my gear."

"Good. You had me worried there for a second. Listen, on your way out, check on CT. She didn't clean up her evening feed."

"Okay."

"If her tub's empty, pull it out of her stall, okay? Call me if she hasn't cleaned up."

"All right."

I disconnected, and as I held out the phone, Hurp walked into the office, carrying an extra large pizza box and a six-pack of Coke. He narrowed his eyes when he caught sight of me. "You here every night?"

I didn't feel like telling him different, so I said, "Like always."

A knowing smile spread across his lips, and the look in his eyes made me feel dirty. "Guess I'd be doing the same thing if I wasn't married." He turned to his man. "Here, Grabinowski. Didn't know if you had a chance to eat."

"Thanks, boss."

Hurp looked at me. "You can have some, too."

"Thanks," I said and tried to keep the surprise I felt out of my voice.

As I left the room, Hurp thanked Grabinowski for coming in on such short notice.

I observed CT as I walked down the shedrow. She was bright and attentive, curious about her surroundings. She nuzzled my arm when I reached over to unclip the stall guard. Before I unlatched the last snap, I saw Hurp step out of the office, then head out. The guy was plain weird.

I stood quietly inside CT's stall and watched her breathe. There was no evidence of discharge from her nostrils, her breathing wasn't labored, and her respiration rate was within range. I glanced at the stall floor as I ducked under her neck and moved to the corner of the stall. Her droppings looked normal, and the bedding hadn't been disturbed like it would have been if she'd been pawing. I checked her feed tub. She'd finished her dinner, so I unclipped the tub and lowered it to the ground outside the stall, then I stepped to her side. I ran my hand down her face and smoothed my fingers under her cheekbones until I found her pulse, then I watched the seconds count down on my watch. Her heart rate was normal, and even though I didn't have a thermometer, I was fairly certain her temperature was normal, as well. I lifted her upper lip and pressed my thumb down on her gums. Her color was good, and when I released the pressure, the blanched area colored quickly.

The standing bandages Trudy had wrapped around the mare's front legs looked smooth and professional, and CT had left them alone, so they probably weren't bothering her. I squatted down and cupped my hand over her left coronary band, where the hoof wall blends into the hair on her leg. Her hoof felt cool to the touch. I reached across and checked her right hoof. She was fine.

Leaving the mare felt odd, knowing that she'd be racing the following day. I latched the stall guard and looked down the shedrow. Grabinowski had his knee planted on Kessler's chair as he faced the back wall, and from the way his head was bobbing around, I figured he was on the phone.

A dozen cockroaches scattered when I switched on the light in my room. I grabbed my stuff and headed out.

I'd been looking forward to spending the night in the loft until I actually opened the door and stepped into the quiet emptiness.

I picked up the phone and punched in Rachel's number. When she picked up and said "hello," I couldn't face the prospect of hearing the bitterness creep into her voice when she realized who was on the other end, so I hung up. I closed my eyes and pictured her as she'd hovered beneath the water's surface with her hair moving in the current like a mermaid's. Her face had looked pale in the blue light as tiny bubbles broke free from her lips and rose to the surface when she smiled. I remembered how the water lapped against her breasts as she lay on the steps, and I pictured the expression on her face, a mixture of provocation and shyness, as she looked at me through half closed eyes and spread her thighs.

◇◇◇

I woke shortly after midnight and couldn't go back to sleep, which wasn't surprising. I jacked up a Nickelback CD, popped open a can of Coke, and finished off a bag of pretzels, then

I wandered around the loft. I was restless and bored, and I considered going to the track. Just check the barn and come home. In and out. What were the odds of my running into the dopers? I probably had a better chance of running into Trudy. I smiled. The girl did not sleep. But then, that was my real reason, wasn't it?

But I'd made a promise.

I thought about taking a swim but knew I'd just think about Rachel. Instead, I went back into the kitchen, dumped a can of spaghetti into a saucepan, and heated it on the stove. I grabbed another Coke and a bottle of ketchup, cleared a space at the island counter, and sat down. The stuff tasted like slop, but it was cheap.

I slid a stack of magazines and catalogues down the counter and idly flipped through them. When I picked up an old issue of *Equus* that my boss had given me, an envelope dropped onto the counter.

I stared at it, and when the realization of who'd penned the letter sunk in, my breath caught in my throat.

When I picked it up, my hand was shaking. I looked at the postmark. April twenty-fifth. At first, I thought it was the same letter Marty had rescued from my trash after I'd tossed it there unopened, but that had been delivered in early March. This letter had been mailed shortly after I'd gotten out of the hospital, and it must have been mixed in with the magazines during one of my halfhearted efforts to tidy up the place. I turned it over in my hand and stared at the flap while the spaghetti congealed on my plate.

I was still sitting there half an hour later when I finally got up the courage to read it. I swallowed as I slipped my knife under the edge of the flap, then carefully peeled it away from the envelope. As I reached in and pulled out his letter, my fingers trembled.

When I finally stood up, I felt hollow inside.

I folded the letter, creasing the folds exactly as my father had done, slid it back into the envelope, and folded it in half. I put it in my back pocket and just stood there as an emptiness seeped into my soul, and I felt weary with the weight of it.

I couldn't stay there alone for another minute.

"Fuck it."

I jumped in the Chevy and flew down 95, pushing the engine until the fluttering valves reached a crescendo, and the steering wheel shook in my hands. As I drove through the gate, I glanced at the guard through the scratched Plexiglas. His arms were crossed, and his chin was resting on his chest. The old guy had fallen asleep. I checked the time. Two-forty-five. Kessler and Abby and everyone else would be in the barn in an hour, give or take, and I didn't see where one hour would make any goddamn difference.

I entered the barn down by the feed room, and before I'd gone two paces, I knew something was wrong. The horses should have been resting. Instead, most of them had their heads over their stall guards, and they were tense. I stood still and listened for the sound of a horse cast in its stall or in pain, and as I watched them, it registered that they were peering down the aisle toward CT's stall with their ears flicking back and forth.

Somewhere deeper in the barn, a horse snorted, a high-pitched exhalation through its nose. An alert to the rest of the herd that signaled danger.

I sprinted down the aisle and skidded to a halt outside CT's empty doorway. She jerked her head up and rolled her eyes, and the whites around her irises shone in the dark like twin crescent moons.

"Whoa, CT. It's okay, girl."

The mare swung her head in a long sideways arc, a movement not unlike a person beckoning to someone with his hand, then she lowered her nose to the stall floor and snorted. When I saw what she was worried about, the blood ran cold in my veins.

A woman's sandal lay upside down in the straw, and just beyond it, a pale foot with delicate toes pointed toward the ceiling. I leaned over the stall guard.

Trudy was sprawled on her back with an arm flung over her head and her left leg twisted beneath her body. Her shirt was jammed up around her throat, exposing her breasts and the unnatural curve of her spine as she lay tangled in the straw. Her shorts were peeled down to her thighs, except on the left, where the elastic had caught on her hip.

I scrabbled under the stall guard, crouched beside her, and pressed my fingertips along her carotid artery. I couldn't find a pulse.

"Come on, damn it!"

I grabbed her wrist and lowered my face to her lips, hoping to feel her breath on my cheek. Nothing. I couldn't remember the last time that I'd prayed, but I prayed as I ran into Kessler's office and called 911. When I hung up, I flicked on the barn lights and raced back to the stall.

CPR. What the fuck were the steps? Airway. Clear the airway, first. I knelt in the straw, placed my right hand on her forehead, and slipped my left hand under her neck so that I could tilt her chin up and straighten her airway. As I pressed upward, something shifted beneath my fingers at the base of her skull. Bone grating against bone. I jumped back and stared at her in stunned silence.

The harsh glare from the overhead light blanched her pale skin, and she looked tiny and frail and deflated as she lay sprawled on the honey-colored straw. Her facial muscles were slack, and her lips were parted as if she were a young child, deeply asleep.

"Oh, Trudy."

I rubbed my face.

The mare pawed the ground behind me, and her hoof grazed my hip. I stood up, and a wave of clammy dizziness washed over me as I ducked under the stall guard. I braced my hands on my knees and waited for it to pass. After a minute or two, I unlocked the tack room, grabbed a shank, and paused in CT's doorway. I didn't want to look at Trudy, but I did anyway, like a rubbernecker slowing down to gawk at a mangled wreck on the side of the road.

As I reached out to unlatch the stall guard, I saw that her eyelids weren't completely closed, and beneath her pale lashes, her corneas already looked dull. I swallowed and worked to slow my breathing.

I put CT in one of Mr. Reece's empty stalls and headed back to Kessler's side of the barn as a lone siren off to the southwest cut through the night air. The pitch changed as the cruiser turned off 198, half a mile away, and accelerated down Brown Bridge Road, heading for the back gate. Thirty seconds later, the scrub land beyond the chain-link fence was washed in red and blue as the cruiser sped past with its engine whining at full throttle.

At the gate, the siren died down to nothing, and in a moment, I heard gravel popping under the tires as the driver threaded his way through the barns. Headlights swept across barn seventeen, and a white Chevy Lumina, with a shield on the door and a stripe running down the side, glided to a stop at the mouth of the alley. Alternating bursts of light streaked dizzily up and down the length of both barns, and the queasiness in my gut increased a notch. I met him in the alley.

"You have someone down?"

Someone down? I guessed you could call it that.

I led him to CT's stall, and after he looked around the doorframe and saw Trudy, he told me to stand outside as he keyed his mike.

Several minutes later, he found me where I leaned against the wall by Abby's garden. He started in on the questions. When he asked me if I'd seen anyone else in or near the barn, I thought about Hurp's man and realized it was the first time I'd thought about him since finding Trudy. I spun around, intending to go into the office, and the cop braced his hand on my chest.

"You can't go in there, sir."

I waved my arm toward the doorway. "But there's a security monitor set up in the office, and whoever killed Trudy might be on tape."

"The detectives will check it, sir."

I glanced toward the road as a second cruiser pulled next to the first, and the throb of a heavy diesel engine echoed and bounced off the walls and rumbled beneath my feet as a medic truck inched its way around the corner. At the other end of the barn, a fire engine drove down the perimeter road and rolled to a stop just short of the alley. The air was unnaturally still and filled with noise and voices and flashing light, and the space between the two long barns seemed to shrink as if someone had clamped an invisible lid over the alley.

"I need to use the phone."

"You'll have to wait, sir."

If he said 'sir' one more time, I thought I'd lose it.

"But I have to tell my father…" I paused. Referring to Kessler as my father had been automatic and unexpected. I said more calmly, "I need to let the trainer know what's going on."

"I'm sure he'll be told, sir."

I shifted my weight from one foot to the other. "Can I use a pay phone? It's just the other side of barn seventeen."

"I'm afraid you'll have to stay here, sir."

"But you don't understand," I said. "All this activity's spooking the horses. He needs to know."

A sergeant joined us as two paramedics, a man and a woman, lugged gear that they wouldn't need into the barn.

I turned to the sergeant. "I need to make a phone call."

"You'll have a chance, later. Right now, I have to ask you a few questions." His voice and demeanor were neutral, but beneath the surface, I sensed a level of confidence bordering on arrogance.

I looked past him into the shedrow, and as I watched the paramedics step into the stall, I believed, without doubt, that the dopers had been coming for me but had run into Trudy, instead. I was certain of it, and that knowledge made me physically sick. For a brief second, I imagined that I was the one dead on the floor. I pictured Kessler hearing the news, then I thought of Rachel. She'd been right all along. I should have stayed the hell out of it.

"Sir!"

I blotted out the image of Trudy lying in the straw, that seemed to be permanently seared into my retinas, and focused on the cop. He'd been talking, and I hadn't heard a word.

"What?"

"Come with me." He led me to his patrol car as the other officer popped the trunk of his car and grabbed a roll of yellow crime scene tape. He strung it between the barns as the sergeant started in on the exact same questions that I'd already answered. When he finished, he switched off his lightbar and powered down the windows, then he patted me down. He took my knife and had me sit in the front seat, which was a damned sight better than the back.

They left me alone for what seemed like a long time. I braced my elbows on my knees, slipped my fingers through my hair, and rested my forehead on my palms. The muscles in my arms and legs were tight with the flood of adrenaline that still coursed through my veins, and my stomach felt like it had dropped into another dimension, as if I'd just rocketed over the highest apex on a monster roller coaster ride.

Eventually, I sat up and leaned my head against the headrest. My neck felt tense and weak at the same time. The sky had lightened to a charcoal gray. I checked the time, four-thirty, then I looked through the driver's side window. A middle-aged man, wearing a suit and tie, stood in the shedrow, talking to the sergeant who'd interviewed me. They both glanced in my direction. As I turned away, a light flashed in CT's stall, and I realized they were taking pictures. I gazed through the bug-splattered windshield and felt that I was still being watched. I turned my head to the right.

A crowd had gathered along the barricade, and Dennis Hurp stood among them with his hands in his pockets and his gaze on me.

I flung the door open and started toward him. Someone yelled, and a cop who'd been standing near the mouth of the alley jogged across the hard-packed ground and intercepted me.

I skidded to a halt and yelled over his shoulder, "What happened to your man, Hurp? Why wasn't he in the barn?"

The sergeant hurried over, and they unceremoniously put me back in the cruiser and shut the door. He nodded to someone in the shedrow, then he climbed behind the wheel and started up the engine. As he shifted into reverse, I looked toward the barn as they brought Trudy out of the stall.

I hunched forward and closed my eyes, and when the cop asked me if I was going to puke, I shook my head.

When we arrived at the station, he left me in an interview room, told me a detective would be along eventually, then he clicked the door shut.

Chapter 21

Around seven-forty-five, I heard movement in the room next door, then nothing for the next half hour. The interview room wasn't much different from the one at the police barracks on Reisterstown Road where Ralston worked. A table, three chairs, a foot-square window in the door. I folded my arms on the table and rested my head and didn't realize that I'd fallen asleep until the door creaked inward on its hinges.

The man I'd seen in the shedrow, with a suit and tie, dumped a briefcase on the table and shook my hand.

"Bill McAffee, Investigative Services Division."

"Steve Cline."

He held out a paper bag. "Danish and coffee?"

"Sure."

While I peeled off the lid and stirred in a packet of sugar, McAffee popped open the briefcase and laid a notepad and tape recorder on the table. He looked like an ordinary guy, medium build and wiry and totally unimposing, and if I'd seen him on the street, I never would have guessed he was a cop. He was in his fifties, with wavy brown hair and a thick mustache that looked out of place in a paramilitary organization. He peered over his gold-rimmed bifocals with pale, watery eyes. "Do you have any objections to my recording this interview?"

I shook my head and swallowed some coffee. "Did you review the surveillance tape in the barn office?" I said.

"We'll get to that." He switched on the recorder, stated the specifics of the meeting, asked me to consent to the recording verbally, then he started in on the questions in earnest. He wrote down everything from my social security number to my mother's maiden name, and when he got to my father, I told him about Kessler, as well, then I explained why he'd hired me and briefly described my routine at the track. I bit into the Danish, and the sweetness turned my stomach. I set it back on the waxed paper and pushed it away.

McAffee watched me for a moment. "Something wrong with the food?"

"No." I crossed my arms over my chest and looked around the room, and when he didn't say anything, I started to tell him what I'd learned about Green, Reece, and Tyson, but he cut me off. He opened the door and signaled to someone, and a big black man entered the room. McAffee introduced him as he pulled a chair up to the table.

"I'd like to ask you some questions about last night, but first, I'm going to read you your rights."

I jerked my head up and saw that he was holding a sheet of paper in his hand. "Am I under arrest?"

"You're a suspect." He read the familiar text, even though I'm sure he knew it backward and forward. When he finished, he laid the paper on the table in front of me and said, "Do you understand your rights, and are you willing to make a statement?"

I nodded.

"Please respond verbally."

"Yes, I'm willing to make a statement."

McAffee had me sign and date the form, then he slid it across the table, and the black man signed it.

McAffee settled into the chair across from me. "When was the last time you saw Ms. Wood alive?"

I swallowed, and the sticky sweetness soured in my throat. "Around ten-thirty yesterday morning. She was bathing one of her horses in the alley."

"So, Wednesday morning was the last time you saw her?"

"Yes."

"You didn't see her in the barn last night or early this morning?"

"No, I didn't."

"You're sure?"

"Of course I'm sure."

He flipped through his notepad. "She was found in a stall where a horse named Contrail is housed. Is that correct?"

"Yes."

"And you were seen going into Contrail's stall around nine o'clock last night, is that right?"

I shrugged. "Closer to eight-forty-five, but I only spent a couple minutes in there before I went home."

"Then why didn't Mr. Grabinowski see you leave since he was watching the surveillance monitor in the barn office?"

"He was on the phone with his back to the door. Check the surveillance tape. It'll show me leaving. What happened to him, anyway? Why wasn't he in the barn when I came back this morning?"

"Didn't you see him go home?"

"No. I told you. I wasn't there."

"You claim you left the stall after five minutes, but wasn't it your routine to remain in the horse's stall all night?"

"Yes, but Mr. Kessler didn't want me doing that anymore."

"Why not?"

I explained that the dopers were getting nervous, and that Kessler feared retaliation and no longer wanted me in the barn at night.

"So why go in the horse's stall in the first place?"

"Mr. Kessler asked me to look in on the mare because she didn't clean up her afternoon feed. Check with him."

"When you went home, did you see anyone? Talk to anyone?"

"No."

"You didn't stop for gas anywhere, or shop for groceries?"

I shook my head.

"Please respond verbally."

I glanced at the cassette tape spinning soundlessly around the spool. "No, I didn't see or talk to anyone."

"What about neighbors? Any chance they would have seen you come home or leave in the morning?"

"No. The only neighbors I have are the people I rent my apartment from, and they're away on vacation."

"So what you're saying is that you don't have an alibi?"

"Check the goddamn tape, and you'll see."

"You said you came back to the barn at two-forty-five this morning?"

"That's right."

The black man shifted in his chair and spoke for the first time since entering the room. "But you stated earlier that Mr. Kessler didn't want you in the barn in the middle of the night, so why'd you come back?"

I thought about my father's letter and how I couldn't have stayed in the loft for another minute with nothing to do and said, "I couldn't sleep."

He raised his eyebrows. "You couldn't sleep?"

"Yeah. I was used to being up all night, and I got bored and figured going in early wouldn't be so bad."

McAffee said, "Why weren't you on the log at the gate?"

I rubbed my face. "The guard was asleep when I drove through."

"And he didn't wake up? I find that hard to believe." When I didn't respond, he said, "How well did you know Ms. Wood?"

I thought about what we had done and how little I really knew about her and didn't know how to respond. I cleared my throat. "Trudy was a private person. I didn't know her very well."

"But you knew her well enough to have sex with her?"

I didn't say anything for a moment. "Who told you that?"

"Several people."

I became aware that I'd been bouncing my legs. I stopped and sat up straighter and tried to relax the muscles in my back.

"Was it consensual?"

"Yes."

"Then why did she hit you?"

"She didn't," I said with more heat than I'd intended. I described my encounter with Marcus. "Ask Jay Foiley. He was there."

He wrote down Jay's name. "When you saw Ms. Wood last night, did you expect more of the same?"

"I didn't expect anything because I didn't see her."

McAffee leaned back in his chair. "It's understandable. A woman like that comes on to you the way she did, wearing next to nothing, you expect her to put out. What did she do, get all hot and heavy with you, then change her mind?"

"I told you. I didn't see her last night."

"This morning, then."

"No."

"Did you know that the trainer's daughter," he glanced at his notebook, "Abigail Kessler, and Ms. Wood had a bet going to see who you'd hook up with first?"

"No," I said and felt sick. "I didn't."

McAffee raised his eyebrows and looked up from his notes. "And isn't Ms. Kessler your sister?"

"Half-sister, but she doesn't know." I told him that I'd only learned that Kessler was my father three weeks ago and explained our reasoning for not telling Abby.

"So, Ms. Wood had intercourse with you first, and she wins the bet. It's understandable that the next night, you'd think you were going to pick up where you left off, only she no longer needs to go along with the program."

"There wasn't a second night," I said slowly.

"She lets you feel her up, a little skin on skin, then she changes her mind, and you figure she doesn't really mean no, right? Not after the last time."

I glanced at the black man, then looked back at McAffee. "I didn't do it."

"Do what?"

"Kill her," I said through clenched teeth.

"You're a strong young man, used to handling those hot-blooded racehorses. How much do they weigh?"

"What?"

"The horses. How much do they weigh?"

I shrugged and folded my arms across my chest. "I don't know. Around a thousand pounds."

"Really?" McAffee leaned forward in his chair. "How much do you think Ms. Wood weighs, Steve?"

I rubbed my hands over my face and cleared my throat. "A hundred pounds."

"Maybe," he said. "Soaking wet."

I glanced at him, then looked at the table, and an image of Trudy standing naked in the stall with her shorts stretched between her ankles flashed in my mind. I shifted in my seat. A fluorescent tube in a ceiling fixture buzzed over the hum of the ventilation system. I could feel the cooled air sliding across the back of my neck, yet my skin felt hot.

"It would be easy to overestimate the force you'd need to restrain her when she resisted. Isn't that what happened, Steve? An accident?"

I unclenched my teeth. "I never saw her after morning stables, Wednesday."

"Do you have any scratches?"

"What?"

"Marks on your body consistent with being scratched."

I pictured Trudy, fighting for her life in a dark stall in the middle of a lonely night, with no one there to help her, and a cold hatred seeped into my chest. "No," I said. "I told you. I didn't hurt her."

McAffee glanced at the wall behind my back. "Calm down, Steve."

"I *am* calm."

"Will you take off your shirt so I can check?"

"Sure," I said. "Anything to get you off my back."

I stood up and yanked off my tee shirt, and McAffee examined my hands and arms, then asked me to turn around.

I faced the wall behind my chair. It was fitted with what I assumed was one-way glass, and I wondered if anyone was watching from the next room. Despite my best effort, heat crept up my neck and flushed my face.

"All right."

I pulled on my shirt and sat down. "I didn't hurt Trudy," I said, and my voice sounded hoarse.

"You had a sexual relationship with the victim. You were the last person seen going into the stall where she was found dead with her clothes half off. No one saw you come out. No one saw you leave the track. No one saw you return, as you state. You don't have an alibi. Except for you and the security guard, no one else was around the barn all night long. What would you think?"

I stared at the table for a long moment. Somewhere in another room, a phone rang. I uncrossed my arms and hooked my thumbs in my pockets. I looked at the red light glowing on the recorder, at McAffee's briefcase and the form that I'd signed lying on the table. I looked at the Danish I'd pushed off to the side and the coffee I'd long since forgotten. When I noticed the concentric ripples moving across the coffee's surface, I quit bouncing my leg.

McAffee drew in a long breath. "If you confess, the judge will take that into consideration."

I crossed my arms over my chest and thought it ironic, hearing my own words thrown back at me. "I don't understand. What about the surveillance tape? It'll back up my statement. You'll see that I left and came back when I said I did, and it would have picked up Trudy, too, and whoever came into the barn while she was there and killed her."

"How many people know about the cameras?"

I shrugged. "I don't know. Dennis Hurp's people. The dopers. Probably half the staff know they're there."

"And you?"

"Yeah, and me."

"That's interesting, don't you think? Because you would have known to dispose of the tape after you killed Ms. Wood."

I sat forward and felt myself go numb. "It's missing?"

"It sure is. Where'd you put it, Steve?"

"I didn't do it," I said.

"Do what? Kill Ms. Wood or get rid of the tape?"

"I can't believe this." I ran my hands through my hair. "Did Grabinowski ever get his fat ass out of his chair and look in on the horses? He would have seen that I wasn't there if he did." When McAffee didn't respond, I said, "He sure as shit can't swear I was in the barn all night, since he wasn't even around when I came back. And why wasn't he? Maybe *he* killed Trudy and took off. Have you talked to him, yet? Asked him if he has any scratches?" I lifted my head and looked at him. "Did you?"

When he didn't respond, I said, "Trudy and I had sex, but that doesn't mean I killed her."

McAffee rooted through his briefcase and pulled out a form. "I'd like you to submit to a saliva swab for DNA testing. If you're innocent, you don't have anything to worry about."

"I don't have a problem with that, as a matter of fact, I welcome it. The sooner you quit wasting your time with me, the sooner you'll be looking for the killers. And I mean killers. And if I were you, I'd start with David Reece, Randy Tyson, and Nathan Green. I'd be very interested to know where *they* were last night."

McAffee hadn't wanted to hear it earlier, but I told him what I'd learned in the past two weeks, anyway. Even though he seemed unimpressed, at least he wrote down their names.

"It wasn't inconceivable that they'd come back," I said. "In fact, we expected it." One of the ballasts in the fluorescent lighting above my head was malfunctioning, and the resultant buzz grated on my nerves. "Maybe Trudy ran into them."

"All you have is a hunch," he said.

"Same as you," I said. "Only I know I'm innocent."

McAffee laid a consent form for the DNA test on the table, and after I'd signed it, he asked if I'd agree to a consent search of my room at the track and my apartment. When I said yes, they took me with them, looked through every inch of my belongings, and when they were done, they left me alone in the interview room. Again.

An hour later, the door opened, and a police officer stood just inside the room while a technician swabbed my mouth. I asked them when I could leave, but neither one knew. They closed the door on their way out, and I sat down and rested my chin in my hand. The fluorescent tube hummed and flickered, and the tiny room felt airless. I shut my eyes and waited.

Around four o'clock, McAffee and the other detective came into the room. This time, they didn't bother with a Danish and coffee but reminded me of my rights and asked if I was still willing to provide a statement.

I felt like I was going to throw up. "Am I under arrest?"

"No."

They started in on their questions, and I cradled my arm across my stomach and bounced my legs and didn't give a shit whether or not I looked guilty. As I listened to them, it gradually occurred to me that their focus had shifted slightly, as if they were gathering information but were no longer bent on hanging Trudy's death around my neck.

By five-thirty, I realized I was having trouble staying focused. I stood up.

McAffee paused in mid-sentence.

"Detective," I said, "am I under arrest?"

He stared at me for a long moment, then said, "Not yet."

"You're wasting your time. I didn't kill Trudy, and the DNA test will bear that out. Since the tape's missing, and Grabinowski was away from the barn, anyone could have been in there last night. You need to find out who." I glanced at my watch. "I've been here for almost thirteen hours, and right now, I'm tired, and I'm hungry, and I'm going home."

I walked past them and put my hand on the doorknob. I fully expected them to stop me as I tightened my grip against a tremor that shook my hands.

"Stay available," McAffee said to my back. "Understand?"

I nodded.

"If I have a hard time finding you when I need you, I'll figure out something to hold you on, believe me."

I opened the door and walked out of the room, feeling numb and strung up at the same time.

Chapter 22

I paused at the end of the hall and looked through the one-way glass in the door that opens into the lobby. A lone man sat in one of the chairs with his elbows on his knees and his head bowed. When I recognized him, all of the emotions that I'd managed to bottle up and smother under a layer of cold reasoning rose to the surface and threatened to loosen any semblance of control I'd managed to latch onto.

I swallowed and blinked to focus my eyes, and when I opened the door, Kessler stood and turned toward me.

He paused, then stepped forward and put his arm around my shoulders. "You okay?"

I nodded because I didn't trust my voice. This man, who'd been a complete stranger as little as three weeks ago, meant more to me than I could possibly imagine.

Kessler led me toward the exit. "Where do you want to go?"

"Home. I need to take a shower and change, then I want to go back to the track."

"Why?"

If I didn't go now, and face what had happened head on, the odds were good that I never would. "Because I need to."

Kessler ushered me through the double doors, and I paused on the sidewalk and squinted against the sun that warmed my skin and shone brightly in a cloudless sky. The air was so clean and still, the sounds of birds and sporadic voices and traffic noise carried clear and true, and I was momentarily startled to see that life had proceeded uninterrupted and uncaring after the horror of last night.

I climbed into Kessler's Lincoln LS, and he worked his way over to US 1, then turned right onto Talbott. The roads were congested with people getting on with their lives. Most of them would never hear about Trudy's death. Her life would be condensed to a single paragraph in the newspaper, read over breakfast, then forgotten.

Kessler glanced at me once or twice during the drive, and when he pulled into the parking lot behind the foaling barn and switched off the engine, I sat there without moving. I didn't have the energy to get out. The old man who took care of my landlord's horses came out of the barn, and when he saw me in the passenger's seat, he nodded, then went back inside.

"They think I killed Trudy," I said, and my voice sounded like it belonged to someone else.

"That's ridiculous."

"I know, but it looks bad."

He powered down the windows, and I told him what happened.

"I'll call your detective friend," Kessler said.

"Won't do any good. He's in class, remember?"

"Sure it will. He'll talk to these guys." Kessler shifted in his seat and slipped his wallet out of his back pocket. "And if they question you again, for God's sake, don't answer them unless you have a lawyer with you." He rooted around in his wallet, pulled out a business card, and handed it to me. "The guy who owns Speedwell's a lawyer. He's a good man. I'll call him and explain what's going on. He'll probably want to meet with you, but even if he doesn't, you call him the minute they try to question you, all right?"

I'd always thought that calling a lawyer made you look guilty.

"Don't be stupid, Steve," Kessler said as if he knew what I was thinking. "I'll handle his fee, too, if that's what you're worried about."

I hooked my fingers around the door handle. "Thanks."

"Do you want me to wait for you or come back when you're ready to go?"

I thought about the bottle of Gordon's vodka and knew that I'd start drinking as soon as I was alone, until I stopped thinking and feeling. I'd done it before, avoiding everyone and everything that mattered, and right now, if I was going to figure out who killed Trudy, I needed to keep my mind clear. "I won't be long," I said and climbed out.

I jammed the shower's dial to its hottest setting and stood under the spray until my skin turned red, then I soaped up and rinsed off and stayed in the shower until the hot water began to cool.

Kessler insisted that we get something to eat, so we stopped at Denny's. I ordered a grilled cheese and fries, even though I was fairly certain I wouldn't be able to eat, and after the waitress brought our drinks, I asked Kessler what had happened with Hurp's man.

"The guy got sick. Hurp told him he could go home around two, and that he'd be there in a few minutes, but he had car trouble and didn't make it to the barn until almost three-thirty."

"Well, that's just great." I dropped my straw in my Coke, balled up the paper wrapper, and flicked it on the table. "Really good coverage, wouldn't you say? Why didn't he just take a cab?"

"I asked that very question. He said he thought he'd get the car going in a minute or two, and before he knew it, an hour had passed before he actually got it running."

The service was fast, and I ended up eating everything on my plate. Neither one of us said much, which was fine by me.

Kessler asked if I wanted anything else to eat, and when I said no, he leaned back in his chair and swirled the ice in his glass. "I had to tell Abby."

I lifted my head. "How much?"

"What you've been doing for me." He looked up from his drink. "And the rest of it."

I rubbed my face. "You were right. It was a mistake not to tell her from the start."

"True, but she'll come around."

"How upset is she?"

"She's embarrassed more than anything. I think she was starting to like you," he paused, "in a romantic context, and now she feels like she's made a fool of herself."

I thought about her bet with Trudy and thought she was feeling something else, as well.

Kessler idled the Lincoln down the alley between barns sixteen and seventeen, and my gaze was drawn to CT's stall out of morbid curiosity. Both the upper and lower sections of the Dutch door, normally latched open in nice weather, were bolted shut and crisscrossed with yellow police tape.

"Is CT still in Reece's stall?"

"No. As soon as we found him, I moved Ace over to a friend's barn and put CT in Ace's stall."

"Must have been a hell of a shock, coming in this morning."

Kessler glanced at me, then looked back at the barn. "It was horrible. They were wheeling Trudy out of the shedrow when we arrived, and for a second," he cleared his throat, "I thought it was you they were taking out."

I swiveled in my seat, and for the first time that day, I really looked at him. In fact, it was the first time since I'd found Trudy that I actually took the time to think about someone besides myself. The lines around his eyes had deepened, and his shoulders were stooped as if all his strength had drained out of his body like tap water. He looked like he'd aged ten years.

"I'm sorry," I said.

He shook his head. "Not your fault."

"Did Reece and Tyson come in today?"

"I saw both of them first thing this morning. After that, I can't say."

"Did anyone talk to them?"

"Not that I know of."

I opened the door, and as I climbed out, I noticed someone standing in the doorway to Kessler's office. Jay. I nodded to him, and he moved his head a fraction in acknowledgment before he stepped back into the room.

Kessler walked around the hood of the Lincoln and said, "I'm rotating the crew in the afternoons so that someone's in the barn at all times, except when Hurp's people are here, of course."

Hurp. I was beginning to have a problem with him.

"I should have done it a long time ago."

"Yeah, but like you said, you didn't know who to trust." I stepped into the shedrow. "Can I borrow Jay for an hour?"

"What for?"

"I need to talk to a couple people, and I'd like to take him along…" I wanted to say, *for impact*, but changed my mind and said, "as a witness."

Kessler frowned. "What people?"

"Tyson, Reece, and Green."

He shook his head. "Now that the police are involved, you need to stay out of it, Steve."

"Like they're gonna figure it out? Come on. I'll bet they haven't even interviewed them yet, they're so busy looking at me. We'll only spend a minute or two with each one, just to check their reactions. See if they're weirded out. Jay'll make sure I don't get into trouble."

Kessler thought about it for a moment, and I wondered if he suspected I'd do it whether I had his permission or not. "Okay, but be careful."

I walked into the office and closed the door. "How do you feel about what happened to Trudy?" I said.

Jay scraped his chair back and stood up, and my scalp tingled. His pecs stretched the tank top he was wearing, and even though it was comfortable in the office, his heavily muscled arms were filmed with a sheen of perspiration. The guy was built like a goddamned tank.

"What you need done?"

"I'm going to talk to some people who may know what happened to her, and I'd like you to come with me. Give them something to think about."

Jay straightened his arms and shook them, like he was ridding them of tension, then he smoothed a thick hand across his shaved head and down the back of his neck and came the closest to smiling as I'd ever seen.

"You know which room Tyson's in?" I asked.

"Tyson." Jay rolled the word around his mouth like he was trying to taste it. "Sure. He in your building. First floor. Room nine."

"Let's go."

I rapped on Tyson's door for the third time, and we finally heard movement, then a groan. Jay and I looked at each other, and I put my hand on the doorknob and opened the door.

Tyson was sprawled on his cot, and my first thought was that he was sick until I noticed the empty Budweiser cans lying on the floor and smelled the alcoholic fumes that drifted toward the open door. I stepped across the room, leaned over him, and said his name. He mumbled something incoherent, and his breath just about knocked me over. When I put my hand on his shoulder and shook him, he opened his eyes and flapped his arm at me, then went back to sleep.

"Ain't gonna scare a guy who tanked out like that, man."

I shook him again, and he tried to roll over. I straightened and asked Jay to close the door. As I stood over Tyson, I thought back to the night when they'd come into my room with their damn stun gun, and I heard Randy's voice in my head, boasting that he could beat the information out of me. I closed my eyes and pictured Trudy as she lay in the straw with her shirt jammed around her throat, and I remembered how the overhead light had blanched her skin and highlighted the tangle of hair between her legs so that it looked like a cloud of spun gold. I remembered her half-closed eyes that stared at nothing, and a ringing filled my ears.

Jay cleared this throat. "Ain't gonna be a fair fight, you work him over now."

I looked down at my hands and saw they were clenched into fists. "And what happened to Trudy was fair?"

"No. But you do him now, you as bad as him."

I turned my back to Tyson and tried to push the images from my mind and concentrate on the room, instead.

Tyson was a true racetracker. He'd done everything possible to make the ten-by-ten space a home. He'd covered the floor with a carpet remnant and papered the walls with posters of rock groups and cars and girls. Clothes hung in the far corner above a stack of plastic storage containers, and except for the empties lying on the floor, the room was surprisingly neat.

I moved to the foot of the bed and squatted in front of a mini refrigerator Tyson had wedged into the corner. I opened the door. A half-gallon of milk and a quart of orange juice rattled in the lower door rack. The milk was unopened and the orange juice was half-empty. The upper rack held a carton of eggs. I pried up the lid and found four brown eggs and a twisted baggie with what looked like oregano stuffed into one corner. I opened the bag and sniffed. Marijuana. About two ounces. I put it back and checked the box of hamburger patties. It hadn't been opened, so I left it untouched. A small microwave sat on top of the fridge and, on top of that, a combination grill and electric burner. I opened the microwave. Nothing in there. The grill's grease tray was full and smelled rancid in the heat. I searched the rest of the room and found nothing of interest.

We drove to Green's pharmacy, and I went inside despite the fact that his car wasn't in the lot. The woman behind the counter thought he was on vacation, so we went to his house. I pulled the Chevy into his driveway, right up to the garage door, and Jay disappeared around the corner to check the windows while I stepped onto the front porch.

I leaned on the doorbell for a full minute, then listened. If Green was home, he wasn't moving around.

I strolled down to the end of the driveway and peered in his mailbox. It was empty, and so was the box for the *Washington Post*. I straightened as Jay hopped the fence and walked around to the front yard. He shrugged when he saw me, and we climbed back into the pickup. Three girls on bikes pedaled down the sidewalk with streamers swirling from their handlebars and trading cards, held in place by clothespins, clicking among the spokes like out of control metronomes. A summer afternoon in the suburbs. As I backed onto the street and shifted into drive, one of Green's neighbors made a show of watching us as he stepped off his front porch and walked down the sidewalk.

Jay noticed him, too. "Guy don't look too happy, seein' us in his hood."

"He'll get over it."

I bumped the Chevy into the Briarwood Motel's pothole-ridden lot, backed into the mouth of the gravel alley that circled the long rectangular block of rooms, and cut the engine. We climbed out and walked down the sidewalk without speaking. Reece's Chrysler was parked outside his unit, and he'd drawn his curtains against the afternoon sun that slanted across US 1 and bounced off the cinder-block walls and radiated from the asphalt in waves of heat and glare. Sometime in the distant past, his door had been painted red, but years of sun and rain and neglect had faded the varnish to a putrid pink network of veins where the color remained embedded in the grain, reminding me of an old man's hands lined with dirt.

I cocked my head and listened at his door but heard nothing except the constant traffic noise and the hum of the air-conditioner unit below the window. I rapped on his door and waited. I jiggled the doorknob.

"Let's check the back," I said, then paused. I slipped my hand into my shirt and wiped my fingerprints off the knob.

Jay raised his eyebrows.

"Let's just say that, after today, I'm not eager to be questioned by the police."

We walked behind the building. It appeared that each unit had a two-foot-square window placed high up near the eaves. When we stopped under the fourth one, Jay and I looked at each other. He shrugged, then braced his legs and latched his hands together like he was getting ready to hoist me onto a horse's back. I flatted my hands on the wall and put my foot in his hands, and he boosted me off the ground. I grabbed the window ledge and peered through the glass. The window was positioned over the john in a cramped bathroom. The floral plastic curtains that hung in the window were parted in the middle, giving me a six-inch opening to work with. The door leading from the bathroom was wide open, revealing a slice of Reece's bedroom.

I craned my neck and saw the edge of a bed, a night stand, and a bureau. A bag of Lay's potato chips, a box of crackers, a jar of peanut butter, and a six-pack of 7-Up sat on the part of the bureau that was visible. The bed had been made, but the spread was rumpled, and a newspaper lay open on the pillow as if someone had just been reading it. The light above the night stand was switched on, and an empty drinking glass and an open bottle of prescription medicine sat next to the clock radio. There was no sign of Reece. For all I knew, he could have been sprawled in a recliner, watching television.

I decided to tap on the glass. Reece wouldn't have any trouble ignoring a knock on his door, but I doubted he'd be as inclined to overlook someone at his bathroom window. As I raised my hand, the shadow cut the glare bouncing off the glass, and what I saw on the bedroom floor at the foot of the bed tightened my chest and made the hair on the back of my neck stand on end.

Reece was lying face down with his nose buried in the cheap carpet. His right hand was visible at shoulder height, and it looked like he was trying to claw his way across the floor, except he wasn't moving, and I had a sinking feeling he wasn't going to any time soon. The tendons in his neck stood out like ropy cords, but what chilled the blood in my veins was how his mouth was wrenched open like he was screaming.

Chapter 23

"Shit." I started to lose my balance. Jay lowered his hands and caught hold of my arm before I landed on my ass.

"What, man?"

"He's on the floor, and I think he's dead. Come on." I spun around, ran to my truck, and the Chevy's tires kicked up a spray of gravel as Jay drew his right leg into the truck and slammed the door.

I hung a right, pulled into a gas station a block down the road, and slid to a stop next to a pay phone. I'd planned on calling the hotel manager, but the phone book was missing, so I dialed 911 instead, told them they had a man down in unit four of the Briarwood Motel, and hung up.

When I pulled back onto the road, my hands were shaking.

"What you wanna do now?" Jay said.

I glanced at my watch. It was seven-forty-five on a hot Thursday evening toward the end of July and quite possibly the last day of David Reece's life. "Go back. There's nothing left to do."

Jay detoured to the restroom while I headed to the office to tell Kessler what we'd found. I paused in the doorway. The ever-present piles of paperwork cluttered his desk but sat untouched as he stared into space. He raised his head when he sensed me at the door, and I told him that Reece, in all probability, was dead.

"My God." Kessler braced his elbows on the desk and leaned forward. "Do you think he was murdered?"

"Maybe." I blocked out the image of his contorted face and concentrated on what I'd seen on the night stand. A prescription bottle and an empty water glass. "He might have committed suicide, though."

"Who?"

Kessler ducked his head so he could see around me, and I pivoted slowly to face Abby.

She stood in the threshold with her arms crossed under her breasts. Her eyes were cold and hard, and I didn't fully understand the extent of her animosity. Although I'd anticipated that she would feel threatened by my arrival in her life, I was unprepared for the degree of hate evident in her eyes and manner.

When neither one of us answered, she jabbed her nose with the back of her hand and sniffed. "Who'd you help kill this time, Cline?" she said, emphasizing my name in a way that made it clear she wanted no part of me in her life.

"What?"

"You heard me. One wasn't good enough, you had to try for two?"

"Abby," Kessler snapped. "Steve didn't—"

I raised my hand and cut him off. "I'm sorry, Abby. I'm sorry about Trudy, and I'm sorry about deceiving you. That was a mistake." I paused. "It was my mistake. Your father wanted to tell you, but I was afraid Jeff would find out."

"Oh, let me guess. Because I'm a woman, right? Heaven knows, we can't keep a secret. My boyfriend just looks at me, and I swoon all over him and tell him anything he wants to know."

"Back then, I didn't know how tough you are."

She narrowed her eyes. "Trudy's dead because of you."

I swallowed.

Abby's eyes filled with tears as she stepped closer and dropped her arms to her sides. I glanced down and saw that she'd clenched her hands. "This never would have happened if you hadn't come here." She inhaled sharply, and a drop of water fluttered in her nostril. "I hate you."

When I didn't say anything, she clutched her arms around her waist, looked up at the ceiling, and blinked back tears that I knew angered her. "So, who else is dead?"

"Mr. Reece, I think."

She brought her gaze down from the ceiling, looked at me hard, then shook her head. "Why don't you go home before someone else gets killed?"

"I'm sorry," I said, and my voice cracked.

Abby spun around and strode down the aisle, and I heard Kessler's chair creak behind me as he stood. "I'll go talk to her."

"No," I said, "don't. Nothing you say will make her feel differently. Any change she makes has got to come from her."

Kessler walked around and stood by my shoulder, and we both looked down the long shedrow. Abby paused, then leaned against the doorway to one of the horse's stalls. Her hair hung down her back and shimmered in the evening sun that drew deep shadows behind the waist-high wall and bathed the stall fronts in orange.

"She's wrong, you know?"

"Is she?"

Kessler glanced at me. "It's not your fault, Steve."

I wanted to believe him.

Jay strode into the barn and hesitated when he saw us. "You want me in, now, Mr. K?"

Kessler nodded. "Thanks, Jay. Until the security man comes in."

Kessler halfheartedly tidied his desk, then said he was going home. I watched him heft his briefcase off the desk and walk slowly into the alley, then I sat on a bale of straw that someone had left in the aisle but shouldn't have, propped my elbows on my knees, and hung my head. The truth of the matter was, the only way I'd gotten through the day so far was by clinging to the thought that Trudy had gone to the barn for the sole purpose of checking her horses. The reality was something else altogether. She was dead because of me, and that knowledge filled me with an emptiness that seeped into my pores like a cloud through gauze. It hollowed out my gut and tightened around my chest and spread through my limbs until they felt weighted and useless.

I closed my eyes and felt the sinking sun burn into my scalp and press against my shoulders. The horse behind me stamped a hoof and rattled the brass fittings on his halter when he shook his neck to dislodge a fly. A radio switched on in barn seventeen, and distant voices drifted in the warm air, but otherwise, the backside was quiet.

Abby cried out, and I flinched. I jerked my head up in time to see her thump her palm on the wooden Dutch door and yell at a horse to get up, and that meant only one thing. One of them was colicking, and she was trying to keep it from rolling in the stall, because horses with a buildup of abdominal gas were notorious for twisting a gut when they thrashed around on the ground.

She turned her head toward me and yelled, "Steve—" but I was already on the move.

I grabbed a shank from the tack room and joined her outside Icedancer's stall. The mare stretched out and nosed her gut where patches of sweat darkened her brown hair to black. I clipped the lead on Dancer's halter as Abby went to get a thermometer. We took her vitals, which weren't all that bad.

"Get her walking," Abby said, "and I'll call Charles."

While she talked to Kessler's vet, I led Dancer around the shedrow until Abby told me to put her back so we could see if she'd improved. After I latched the stall guard, we stood in the doorway and waited.

Abby glanced at me, then went back to watching the mare. "I'm sorry about what I said earlier. I didn't mean it." She smoothed her fingers under her eyes. "Who do you think killed Trudy?"

"I don't know, but I'm going to find out."

She leaned against the doorjamb, hooked her right leg behind the left, and rested her head on the wood. After a minute, she said, "You see, Steve. It wasn't really your fault, at all."

Her voice sounded tiny and frail as if she'd spoken from a great distance. She swiped the back of her hand under her eyes, and I realized she was crying.

"We were doing something stupid." She sniffed and swallowed, and for a second, I thought she was going to choke. "God! I can't believe we were so stupid. And it got her killed." Abby dragged her hand under her nose.

"It wasn't your fault, Abby."

Dancer pawed the ground and began to circle her stall.

"Oh-oh. Steve, get the Banamine out of the fridge, will you?"

"Okay."

"The syringes are in there, too, in a baggie."

I walked into the feed room and opened the door to an ancient refrigerator that, at one time back in the eighties, had been a putrid avocado color but was now an even more disgusting blend of ingrained dirt and worn enamel. Glass bottles and vials of medicine and vitamin supplements rattled in the door rack. I selected a half-empty bottle of Banamine, then scanned the top shelf. It was stuffed with plastic containers of carrot pulp, cans of soda, and someone's half-eaten tuna sandwich.

I squatted and rooted through the lower shelf. I shifted a pizza box and found the Ziploc bag full of syringes and needles. As I pulled the bag out, the box settled back into place, and I glanced at the strip of paper glued to the edge that showed who'd ordered the pizza. *Hurp* was printed in faded dot matrix along with the date and time. I lifted the box out of the fridge and glanced at my watch. He'd ordered it on July 16th, Wednesday night.

The same night Grabinowski had gone home sick.

The night Trudy was murdered.

A tingle crept up my spine and settled at the base of my skull. What if it hadn't been the pizza that made Grabinowski sick, but something put *on* the pizza?

Hurp knew the system inside and out, and his job put him in easy contact with all kinds of people who were not above altering the outcome of a race. He knew what our barn routine was like, where the surveillance cameras were, who'd most likely be in the barn at night. And if he wanted to get to a horse, or catch someone alone in the barn, he'd know how to get rid of his own man.

I thought back to the night on Abby's porch, to the man who'd had his arm clenched around her neck. Hurp was the right build. I closed my eyes and tried to remember his voice and the shape of his head.

"Scrounging for leftovers?"

My grip tightened on the box at the sound of Hurp's voice.

Chapter 24

He stared down at me over the refrigerator door, and something predatory and primordial fluttered across his pupils and spread outward until the little room felt dank and foul.

He stepped toward me, then froze when Abby called my name.

I straightened, took a step backward, and casually dropped the pizza box in the trash, then I gathered together the Banamine and the bag of syringes. As I closed the refrigerator door, I hoped like hell that he couldn't see my hands shaking. He hadn't moved, and his face looked bloodless, as if the skin and muscle were stretched over chiseled granite.

The room was small, with no space for maneuvering. I gestured for him to back up, and it would have seemed odd if he didn't.

He glanced at the trash can, then backed into the aisle. I reached into the room, flipped the lock, and closed the door, then I joined Abby outside Dancer's stall.

"You find another rat in there? You look spooked."

"A very big rat," I said softly, and Abby cocked her head and frowned at me, and when I said nothing further, she got busy with the injection. I tried to slow my breathing as I watched her draw the clear liquid into the syringe. She tapped the air up into the hub and squeezed the plunger until a drop of the anesthetic formed at the needle's tip.

At one end of the barn, Jay sat behind Kessler's desk with his feet propped on the blotter and his fingers laced behind his neck. He gazed down the shedrow at Abby and me, and even from that distance, the guy was imposing. His dorsi muscles, just below his armpits, were so developed, they looked like wings, and his biceps were wider than his shaved head. I turned slowly and met Hurp's gaze.

He was still standing in the short aisle by the feed room door, and as I watched, he glanced past me toward Jay, then he stepped out of view as he headed toward McCormick's end of the barn.

At eight o'clock, Hurp's man, Grabinowski, strolled into the barn. I caught Jay on his way out and asked him to follow me into the feed room.

"I need a favor," I said as I pulled the pizza box out of the trash and opened the lid. Three slices of pepperoni and mushroom lay cemented to the cardboard. While I snagged a plastic bag off the work table and pried a slice of pizza out of the box, I explained what I thought had happened the night Trudy was killed.

I dropped one slice into the bag and handed it to Jay. "For backup," I said. "I'm taking this box in for testing. If it gets…lost, make sure Detective McAffee gets that one, okay?"

"Sure, man. When you headin' out?"

"Soon as Dancer's in the clear."

I went back to the office and asked Grabinowski if anyone had stopped by the barn after I left the night he got sick, and when he said no, I said, "How often does Mr. Hurp bring his employees food?"

"First time I ever known him to do it."

"How long have you worked for him."

Grabinowski shrugged. "Six years, five months."

When Dancer improved, Abby got us both something to eat from Burger King. I ate a couple of fries but couldn't stomach anything else. I checked my watch. Eleven o'clock. The mare had been quiet for almost three hours.

"Think she'll be okay?" I said.

Abby was in the stall, sitting sideways on a bale of straw with her legs drawn up to her chin and her arms wrapped around her shins. She nodded, and a portion of her thick hair slid forward onto her shoulder.

"Did you call your father?"

She shook her head. "He's exhausted. I didn't want to bother him with this, not now that she's doing so well."

I looked at the mare. She was eating her hay and seemed perfectly content.

Abby yawned. "I'm going home. I might come in later and check on her."

"It's not safe, Abby. Call Grabinowski and have him check while you've got him on the phone."

She tilted her head, rested her cheek on her knee, and looked at me.

"Promise."

She closed her eyes. "Oh, okay. I promise. I won't come in until morning."

"Until your dad does," I said.

She nodded and flicked me a glance that seemed to say, he's your dad, too.

"Can I borrow your cell phone until tomorrow morning?" I said. "If you don't like what you hear when you talk to Hurp's man, call me, and I'll come in and check on her."

"Okay." She stood and stretched, then smoothed her hand down Dancer's neck. "She's never been sick a day in her life. Do you think she's upset," Abby hesitated, "because of Trudy?"

"Maybe. Or all the commotion around here this morning could have upset her."

Abby pressed her forehead against Dancer's neck and just stood there. The mare stopped chewing. She tensed her muscles ever so slightly and flicked her ears back and forth. When Abby straightened and turned around, her eyes were moist. She ducked under the stall guard, pulled her phone out of her fanny pack, and when she held it out to me, she noticed the pizza box in my hand.

"Dumpster diving?"

I took her phone, then glanced at the box. "No. Reeling in a fish," I said and hoped I wouldn't be the one who got caught.

She shook her head, and when I told her I was going to walk her to her car, I thought she'd protest, but she didn't.

I watched Abby's little black Taurus bump down the access road, and after a minute, I heard the engine whine as she pulled away from the guard's post and headed toward 198.

I walked past the stalls and stepped quietly into the alley. I hung close to the exterior wall, keeping to the shadows, and checked the access road when I reached the corner. It was deserted, with nothing suspicious or out of place. The area where I'd parked was poorly lit, but empty. No vehicles were parked next to mine, and the grassy border was clear for a hundred yards in both directions. I glanced over my shoulder, then looked back at the truck, and when I was satisfied, I slipped my keys out of my pocket and crossed the road.

I reached the Chevy unaccosted. I tossed the pizza box on the bench seat as I slid behind the wheel, then I fitted the key into the ignition. The passenger's door flew open, and Dennis Hurp leveled a shotgun into the cab.

I turned the key as he scrambled onto the seat and jammed the twin barrels into my ribs. He clicked the door shut, then switched the gun to his right hand and settled sideways in the seat. "Let's go for a ride."

"What do you want?" I said, and my voice sounded strained.

"I never wanted to hurt anyone, but you've given me no other choice."

"What about Daniel Albert?"

"His heart gave out. Not my fault."

"I thought he suffocated."

"Heart, lungs. Same thing."

"But you helped him."

"No," he said, but I could tell by the tone of his voice that he'd had a part in it.

"And Trudy? What about her?"

He jabbed my side. The cylindrical metal felt thin and hard and cold through my shirt. "Let's go."

I shifted the Chevy into drive, pulled off the shoulder, and drove toward the exit. In the distance, a security light shone down on the guard shack and pooled on the ground. The old man was in there, leaning in his chair with his back to us. As we approached, he lifted his hand and scratched his neck. I didn't think he was armed, but if I signaled to him, he might still be able to help me.

I rested my elbow on the doorframe, then slowly lowered my forearm out the door.

"Forget it," Hurp said. "Make a left."

I hesitated, and he said, "Try anything, and he dies, too."

I turned as instructed, before we reached the exit, and followed the road that loops back toward the track. We passed the rows of barns, dark and quiet this time of night, and headed toward the utility buildings where the tractors and mowers and harrows are stored.

Hurp pointed to a long shed with a mercury-vapor lamp high up near the peak. "Drive around behind that building."

I turned the wheel, and the Chevy dropped off the asphalt, and loose sand and dirt sucked at the tires and increased the drag tenfold. I inched the truck around the corner, and the headlights swept across the two-story-high piles of sand and clay and loam that are kept on hand and added to the track surface as needed.

"Turn in there." Hurp pointed to a track between the mountainous piles, and as I pulled through the gap, I thought it was a godawful place to die.

Chapter 25

My palms were slick with sweat, and the steering wheel wrenched and bucked in my hands as the Chevy's tires thumped across the rutted ground. As I straightened the wheel, the headlights glinted off a wall of vines that covered the chain-link fence that separates the backside from the rest of the world.

I let the pickup coast to a stop. The engine idled roughly, but the piles of earth sucked the sound from the air. Beyond the fence lay Brown Bridge Road, then a stretch of barren scrub land.

"Cut the engine."

I turned the key, and the old 350 dieseled as the cylinders shut down. The resultant quiet settled into the cab.

Hurp twisted his hand in my shirt and dragged me across the seat as he climbed out. I scrambled through the opening and barely got my feet on the ground before he had the shotgun pressed against my sternum.

"You scared?" he said.

"No, Hurp." I gritted my teeth. "I'm just fucking fine."

"Killing you was never my goal, but I got to admit, I was tempted the night I ran a little reconnaissance, and you and that fox took a dip in the pool."

My skin felt clammy in the humid air.

Hurp pushed me toward the fence. "Doing both of them," he said to my back, "at least you'll die happy."

The footing was rough, and my knees felt like liquid.

"A little to the right," he said, "move the vines aside, and you'll see a gap in the fence."

Hurp checked that no one was on the road, then he pushed me through the opening in the fence and followed on my heels. As we crossed to the other side, he jabbed the shotgun between my shoulder blades, and my shirt stuck to the sweat that trickled down my back. Even in the dark, I could see that a path had been beaten down in the tall grass beyond the shoulder. I followed it for about ten yards, until Randy Tyson stepped out from behind a clump of twisted saplings. He turned and walked into a clearing where a four-door sedan sat low to the ground, its nose pointed toward the road. Randy walked around to the back bumper, pivoted, and as he watched me approach, he popped the trunk. The light in the lid shone on his face, and his eyes glimmered with a sick mixture of trepidation and thrill.

I froze.

Hurp shoved me around to the back bumper. I glanced at the car, then looked in the trunk, at a collection of old newspapers and oil jugs, at a bundle of road flares and a coil of rope, and fear squeezed my chest and burned in my veins. I turned my head toward Randy as he reached into the trunk and picked up the rope.

"Your uncle's dead. Did you know that?" I said and glimpsed movement behind my head a fraction too late. Hurp had swung the stock around, and he slammed it against the back of my skull.

The impact lit up my brain and tipped me forward. He scooped my feet off the ground, and as he folded my legs into the trunk, Randy must have flung the bundle of rope because it slapped the side of my face and slithered over my hand.

I kept my eyes closed and stayed perfectly still, hoping Hurp wouldn't bother tying me if he thought I was unconscious, and with all the swirling going on in my head, I wasn't quite sure I *was* conscious.

"What did you do?" Randy screamed as the lid slammed shut. I opened my eyes, but the world had turned to black. I could feel my breath eddy over my fingers but couldn't see my hand in front of my face.

Randy said something I couldn't make out over the roar of blood between my ears, and Hurp yelled at him to shut the hell up.

The Buick rocked when one of them climbed into the driver's seat, then the engine turned over, but we just sat there. I was lying on my right side, essentially forced into a fetal position in a goddamned trunk while part of me was falling off a cliff thanks to the spinning going on in my head. I rolled over as far as I could, because I was afraid I was going to vomit, and blinked the sweat out of my eyes. I clenched the rope in my hands and tried to catch my breath.

Don't panic. Think! I swallowed the bile that coated the back of my throat and forced myself to think of options, to develop a plan. I thought of everything I'd seen in the trunk, and an idea, tenuous as it was, crystallized in my mind.

I wriggled around to get my knife, and when I jammed my hand in my jeans pocket, I felt Abby's phone. I flipped it open and dialed 911. Even though the engine was running, when the dispatcher answered, I whispered as I identified myself and told her what had happened.

"We're on Brown Bridge Road," I said as the Buick rocked, and the passenger's door closed. The car suddenly shot forward, and I was thrown against the trunk wall. Abby's cell phone slipped from my hand and skittered away into darkness.

The phone's top must have flipped down, because the light went out, and it wasn't until that moment that I realized how much I'd relied on it. I swallowed, and fear clamped around my chest like a vice. The grass was coated with dew, and the Buick's rear end fishtailed as the driver gunned it toward the road. He hit the asphalt running hard and wrenched the steering wheel to the left. The back tires squealed, and my head rammed into the side wall. I heard Hurp yelling over the whine of the engine and figured Randy was driving. Hurp had probably planned it that way so he could have control of the gun.

As the car settled into a cruise, I found the phone near the trunk latch, flipped it open, and hit REDIAL.

The same dispatcher answered.

"We're on Brown Bridge Road," I said. "Right across from the racetrack, heading south toward 198 in a light-colored Buick LS four-door. New." I rattled off the plate number and told her to hurry.

"We have units headed that way now, sir."

"Hurry, please," I said again and hated the desperation that quivered in my voice.

She told me not to hang up.

I smoothed my hand over the thick felt that lined the trunk and tried to orient myself. My head was pointing toward the driver's side, and I was facing the back bumper. I pushed the rope into the corner near the taillight, then I felt around until I found the newspapers and oil jugs. I jammed them alongside the side wall, then I pulled the felt lining away from the corner of the trunk and found the wires that fed into the taillight. As I fiddled with the housing, I realized that the car had slowed.

"We're stopping," I said into the phone, then I held my breath and listened. A car drove past in front of us. Not fast, then Randy turned left. "We've turned left, possibly onto 198," I said, and if I was wrong, they were going to be looking for us in the wrong place.

I yanked the light housing out of its socket, and the bulb lit up the inside of the trunk like a spotlight. "I just took out the driver's side taillight," I said.

"Can you estimate your speed, sir?"

"It's hard to tell." I listened to the sound of the tires on the pavement. "Forty-five, fifty. The road's smooth. Moderate traffic."

"Single or double lane?"

I listened. "Double, I think. I'm going to put the phone down for a minute."

"Make sure you don't lose the connection, sir. We're triangulating your location, now."

I grabbed the coil of rope and shifted until my feet were deeper into the trunk, then I yanked out the wires that operate the latch remotely. That would slow Hurp down a little.

I unwound the rope until I found an end, then I tried to push it through the metal loop that's welded to the floor where the latch mechanism catches. It wouldn't go. The rope was too thick for the narrow gap. As I rolled farther onto my back and pulled my knife out of my jeans, I caught a sound up ahead. The distinctive Doppler effect of a lot of vehicles speeding past from opposing directions, yet somewhere among the whine of engines and hum of tires on asphalt, there was a dead zone where the sound was absorbed by something massive and solid. Like a bridge.

I grabbed the phone. "We're crossing a bridge over a highway," I said. "Hurry up, damn it. They're going to kill me when they get to wherever they're going."

The dispatcher reassured me that they'd find the car, but I knew the chance of them finding me alive diminished with each passing mile.

I closed my eyes, and the dispatcher's voice faded as I pictured Rachel in my mind, and a hollow ache filled my chest and burned in my throat. I thought about Kessler and Abby. I thought about Marty, holding down my job at Foxdale and hating every minute of it. Then an image of Trudy, lying on the stall floor, flashed behind my eyes. As I thought of her death, I saw the hazy Baltimore skyline before me, and I was back on that grassy hillside, standing under the canopy with Rachel's warm hand pressed in mine as I stared down at the white roses draped across the dark mahogany casket.

"Sir?"

"Huh?"

"What do you hear, now?"

I listened. "Not much. No traffic," I said, and that bothered me a lot. Earlier, I'd heard Randy and Hurp's muffled voices, but they were quiet now, and that bothered me, too.

"Your speed?"

"Forty-five. Fifty. Like before."

I set the phone down and wedged the blade of my knife into the rope and pushed it through the gap, then I pulled the frayed end until a foot's length had passed through the slot. As I cut the excess rope and tossed it aside, the car slowed and turned right. I picked up the phone, and the car came to a stop. I wiped the sweat from my eyes and listened. A car off in the distance sped past, and that was it. I pressed the phone to my lips and whispered that we'd turned right and were stopped, and it took all the self-control I possessed not to scream it into the phone.

Randy cut the wheel to the left and inched the Buick forward, then he turned the wheel in the other direction as the car sat motionless, and it was so quiet, I could hear the rubber dragging over grit on the road. He backed up, and cut the wheel again, and I realized he was turning around.

I looped the longer end of the rope through one of the gaps in the lid's underside and tied it to the short end that stuck out of the latch. Another delay that Hurp would have to work through, and I had a feeling that, in a very short time, every second would count.

Randy turned left, I assumed, onto the road we'd just been on.

I told the dispatcher, and almost immediately, Randy made another left. "We've turned left, again," I said. "You need to hurry. We're on a dirt road, and he's going slow." I took the phone away from my ear. I could hear the muffled swoosh of the Buick's tires on dirt and an occasional stone popping out from beneath the tread. And nothing else.

"He's turning left, again, and he didn't stop or change speed much. Wherever we are, it's fucking isolated. I don't think I have much time left."

She started to say something, but I ignored her. I grabbed the newspaper and flares, scrunched around so that I was facing forward and found what I was looking for. A short nylon strap dangled in each upper corner of the trunk. Their ends were attached to the back seat. I knew from experience, after a night of party-hopping with a bunch of high school buddies in a car that didn't have enough seats, that the straps would release the backrest. I'd be able to fold it forward onto the seat and get out. I shoved the oil bottles in the corner and bunched the newspapers on top of them, then I used my knife and slit through the paper on all the flares but one. I pressed them into the newspaper, then I squeezed around and cut the wires to the taillight. The sudden dark tightened a knot in my stomach.

I faced the front as Randy turned right onto another road.

I picked up the phone and whispered, "Where are you guys? I'm running out of time here."

"We're narrowing down your location now, sir."

"It's real quiet," I said, again, thinking that that fact alone should tell them where we were. "He turned right, and now he's turning to the left, and I hear lots of insects and tree frogs. We must be in some kind of park."

"We think we know where you are, sir."

"Well, hurry up, because—" The car coasted to a stop, and a vibration shuddered beneath my knees as the gearshift was shoved into park. The engine cut off.

I slipped the phone into my pocket and picked up the flare that I'd kept separate.

Both car doors clicked open, and the sounds were cannon blasts in the night air. Boots scrunched on the ground as Randy and Hurp stepped out. I pulled the cap off the flare and turned it in my fingers as they shut the doors. I listened to their footsteps as they walked toward the back bumper and prayed that I was right about Randy being the driver. If I wasn't, and Hurp was on the driver's side of the car, I'd pop out directly in his line of fire.

"What the fuck?" Randy said, and I imagined that he'd pressed the trunk's remote.

I pulled the strap, and the latch in the backrest released.

As Randy slotted the key into the trunk lid, I pushed the cushion forward a fraction of an inch to make sure I was going to be able to get out.

The lock released. "Hey?" Randy yanked on the lid and the car rocked on its springs. "What the hell?"

"Open it!" Hurp yelled.

The car rocked forward again and again as Randy jerked up on the trunk. I struck the cap and lit the flare, then I jammed it into the scrunched up papers. They ignited and flared up like a bonfire.

I pushed the backrest down, flopped onto the seat, and got my hand on the door latch as the trunk lid sprung upward. It took Randy and Hurp a second to process what they were seeing, and in that second, I got the door open.

Hurp yelled as my boot touched the asphalt, and as I twisted around the open door and lunged toward the front of the car, I saw Hurp move forward on the other side.

He didn't wait to clear the car but racked a round into the chamber. I drew level with the closed driver's door and had already started to dive forward when he pulled the trigger and loosened a blast of shot that took out both front windows and part of the windshield in a shower of glass and lead. A shock wave of sound slammed into my right ear as my hands hit the road. I caught my balance and pushed off like a runner out of the blocks.

Before me lay an empty stretch of road with guardrails on both sides, and I realized we were on a narrow bridge. If I kept running straight, Hurp would mow me down for sure. I cut to the left and hesitated when I reached the guardrail. As I looked down into a pitch black void, he pulled the trigger.

The impact pitched me over the rail.

I landed in water, flat on my back, and went under the surface into a world of muffled noise and dark until I hit bottom. As I started to rise, I pushed off with my feet and broke through the surface.

I shook the water from my face and looked toward the sky as I floated under the bridge. I spun around and saw that I'd be in the clear in seconds. Right where Hurp would expect to see me. Yet, if I hid under the bridge, there was nothing to stop him from hustling down the bank and finishing me off. My feet hit rock, and as I scrambled into shallow water and put weight on my right hand, pain cut through my shoulder, and my arm buckled. I got to my knees and cradled my arm, and that's when I noticed the orange glow that lit up the trees nearest the bridge.

A faint roar was audible over the sound of water lapping against the shore. Hurp's car. It had gone up fast.

The water swirled around me, threatening my balance, and I was running out of time. I had multiple choices. Upstream, downstream, climb up a bank and risk walking straight into Hurp, or stay where I was. Upstream was out of the question, and I wasn't sure my shoulder would handle swimming downstream, either.

I pulled Abby's cell phone out of my back pocket, and water flowed down my hand. I hit REDIAL anyway, but the phone was dead. I stuffed it back into my jeans and scanned the area.

I was kneeling in a pocket of darkness, but on either side, beyond the bridge's shadow, light glinted off the moving water, and the trees and vegetation glowed orange.

An explosion shuddered the span above my head, and I watched a chunk of twisted metal spin down from the bridge and clatter onto a boulder near the riverbank, followed by a piece of burning cushion that landed on the water's surface like a feather. As I straightened, movement caught my eye.

Hurp was coming down the steep slope to my left, and he had a flashlight.

"Shit." I cradled my arm and let the current push me forward until I bumped into a large boulder. I scrunched behind it, pulled my knife out of my jeans, and opened the blade.

I waited.

I pressed my left hand against the boulder. The surface was slippery. My right hand shook, and I wondered if I'd even be able to use my arm. The rounded stones and rocks underfoot were treacherous and as slick as ice. The black water swirled past and lapped against the bank. And I waited.

The flashlight's beam skimmed the water to my right and bounced off rocks along the riverbank. Hurp's head moved into view above the boulder as he waded upstream. He took two steps before he saw me.

I lunged at him as he swung the gun around.

Life or death was a matter of time and space, and I didn't have enough of either. There was no way I was going to get close enough for the knife to be of any use before he shot me, so I dropped it and grabbed the gun with both hands. Hurp squeezed the trigger.

Hot gases and flame and a load of shot exploded from the muzzle a foot from my right ear.

We struggled for control of the gun, slipping and sliding on the uneven footing with the river swirling around our knees, and my right arm was giving out. He screamed at me as he shoved me backward, but I couldn't hear his words.

My right ankle twisted on the rocky bottom, and I went down.

The black water caved in on top of me, and Hurp shoved me deeper until my shoulders dug into the rocks. He put his full weight on the gun as it stretched across my chest. My right hand dropped off the barrel, useless. I squirmed and kicked, but the water dragged on my limbs, and I felt as if I were moving in slow motion. I couldn't shift him.

The roar in my head grew louder, and my lungs burned as strength drained from my muscles. The world had turned black, except for white dots that flitted in front of my eyes.

My left hand lost its grip, and Hurp bumped the shotgun over my collarbone and jammed it against my throat.

The noise in my head sounded like a freight train.

I pictured Trudy fighting for her life, and Daniel Albert. An old man, helpless against three men. I stretched my left arm straight out to my side, felt the river bottom until my fingers brushed against a rock. I grasped it in my hand and slammed it into the side of Hurp's head.

He toppled over, and I burst through the surface and gasped as I rolled onto my knees. Hurp was still up, on his hands and knees, and I didn't know where the damn gun was. I gulped a lungful of air and clambered to my feet.

I smashed the rock into the back of his head, and he pitched forward and went under. I braced my hands on my thighs and took another breath as Hurp's body bobbed in the current and began a slow drift down river.

I thought about Trudy and almost left him like that. But I couldn't do it. I stumbled after him, latched onto his shirt collar with my left hand, and pulled him toward the riverbank. I dragged him across some rocks until his head and shoulders were out of the water, then I dropped to my knees, and the trembling in my right arm spread until my entire body was shaking.

I sank back on my heels and cradled my right arm and the water rose to my waist and drained the warmth from my body.

I didn't notice the lights moving along the riverbank, not until they shone in my face.

Above them, bursts of red and blue painted the trees alongside the bridge, and I felt dizzy with relief.

Chapter 26

They let me out of the hospital Saturday afternoon, and Kessler and Abby picked me up at the front door.

I settled into the Lincoln's soft leather seat and closed my eyes, breathed in that wonderful earthy aroma that cleansed my senses of the lingering antiseptic odor that coated my sinuses and clung to the back of my throat. No one spoke as Kessler steered his golden car into the bright sunlight of a gorgeous July day.

Hurp was in the same hospital in a coma.

He wouldn't be talking anytime soon, but they couldn't shut Randy up. The cops had picked him up somewhere in the Patuxent Research Refuge, a mile from the bridge.

McAffee had interviewed me twice in the hospital but I'd learned more from the papers and the little Ralston had been willing to share.

Hurp had been the mastermind behind an extremely lucrative race-fixing scheme, and with his extensive knowledge of security practices and a well-established network of less than desirable track personnel, he'd had no trouble finding or persuading people to join him. And as Kessler already knew firsthand, Hurp wasn't above applying pressure to get what he wanted.

Green was Hurp's ace-in-the-hole. He'd provided insulin, of all things, to slow the target horses. Apparently, an excess or deficit of the hormone wreaks all kinds of havoc with a healthy animal, and because it's a naturally occurring substance, no drug screen would have picked it up. Green also supplied the drug that had messed me up and killed Daniel Albert by slowing his breathing to the point of suffocation, as well as the laxative that had sent Grabinowski home sick.

In a way, Randy's statement to the police was a study in irony. Hurp had caught him doping a horse two years ago, and instead of prosecuting him, he'd recruited him. As it turned out, Randy's involvement eventually drew Reece into the scheme. The night the three of them met at Green's house, they'd decided to break away from Hurp and cover their tracks. All three of them were afraid of him, and when Randy learned of his uncle's death, he was convinced that Hurp had murdered Reece to keep him quiet, a point no one felt compelled to clarify as long as his ignorance kept him talking.

In actuality, Reece's death had been ruled a suicide, presumably because of what had happened in the barn Wednesday night…to Trudy.

I swallowed and kept my eyes closed against the warm sunlight that slanted through the windshield and warmed my skin. She'd interrupted Hurp and Randy when they thought they were sneaking up on me, and according to Randy, she'd been smart enough to put it together but not clever enough to hide the fact that she had.

"Steve?" Kessler's voice.

"Hmm?"

"You okay?"

I nodded. "Just sore." In truth, most of my body ached, and my shoulder throbbed and burned every time I moved my arm. They'd dug two pellets out of my arm, and I'd lost some hearing in my right ear, but I'd been lucky. Luckier than Daniel Albert, and a damn sight luckier than Trudy.

"They find Green yet?" I said.

"Nope. While Hurp and Randy were making their plans to nab you, Green was closing out all his accounts and taking off for parts unknown."

"He's thrown away his career to win a couple races."

Kessler shook his head. "I'll bet he's made thousands doing this. Only problem is, he'll lose it if he hasn't already. Gamblers always do. He'll show up at some other track, I suppose. For him, giving up gambling would be like stopping the sun from rising."

I looked out the window as we passed the Briarwood Motel and thought about the two lives that had ended there.

"Did Detective McAffee tell you they're going to revisit Daniel Albert's death because of Tyson's statement?" Kessler said.

"Yeah."

He pulled off US 1 into a shopping center and took my prescriptions in to be filled. More bills. I wondered what this hospital stay would cost me.

Abby shifted in the back seat and cleared her throat. "Steve?"

"Hmm."

"I'm glad you're okay."

"Thanks."

"You know, I was kind of disappointed when I found out that you're my brother."

I smiled. "So I heard."

"From who?"

I decided to try it on for size and said, "Dad."

She kicked the back of my seat. "You call him that, he'll have a heart attack, he's so damn sure you'll never get around to feeling that comfortable."

I didn't say anything, and after a moment, she settled back in her seat. "You almost getting killed made me realize something."

"What's that?"

"I feel guilty about what happened to Trudy, and I probably always will, but after what Hurp did to you, seeing how evil he is, I guess I'm willing to put most of it on him."

"Good, but put all of it on him because that's where it belongs."

"You remember that, too, Steve."

◇◇◇

Wednesday afternoon, I went to the races. I left the sling in the truck, walked through the grandstand, and met Kessler as the horses headed onto the track. Jay was there, and Gordi. Abby and Jeff were leaning on the fence by the track, their heads close together.

"Let's watch the race upstairs, all right?" Kessler said.

"Sure."

Mr. McCormick pushed through the double doors as we opened them to go inside. He wore the same gray suit that he'd worn in the winner's circle on my first day at the track. He nodded to Kessler, totally ignored me, and strode down the aisle toward the track.

I'd disliked him so much, it had been easy to believe he was involved.

We rode the elevator to the fifth floor, and Kessler led the way to a private room with comfortable chairs and a table pushed against a side wall. The far wall was sheer glass with a handrail at waist height. We crossed the carpet and looked down at the track. The horses were warming up under a crystalline blue sky, moving fluidly across the dirt track as if gravity didn't concern them.

I spotted Ruskie almost immediately, with his chestnut coat on fire under the hot sun.

"How will he do?" I said.

"They don't have a chance." Kessler smoothed both hands through his hair, then turned toward me, and I felt his gaze on my face.

"I meant what I said before, about a permanent job."

I glanced at him, then looked down at the track. "Abby needs it more than I do, you know?"

"She won't mind."

"Let me think about it, okay?"

Kessler nodded. "Oh, that woman you connected me with looked at Ace yesterday afternoon, and she's going to buy him."

"Great."

"She seemed competent enough. If he settles down a little, they'll be a good match."

I casually crossed my arms so that I could support my shoulder and hoped it wasn't obvious. "It was fun, wasn't it," I said, "at the beginning?"

"Yeah, it was."

And then it all went to hell. Yesterday, we'd buried Trudy, we being most of Kessler's crew and absolutely no one else. Apparently, she had no family. Only some friends at the track. And her horses.

I glanced at Kessler, then watched the horses circle at the gate. "Did you hear, they found her necklace in Hurp's apartment? The one with the cross."

He shook his head. Kept his gaze on the track.

The starter's assistants loaded the last two horses, and the gates sprung open. I heard Kessler groan before I realized what had happened. Ruskie had stumbled coming out of the gate. He threw his head up and caught his balance and lunged forward in a choppy, uneven stride. By the time he'd gone three strides, he'd regained his action, but the field had seven lengths on him.

Kessler rubbed his face. "Well, that's it."

"Maybe not," I said. "Look."

The big chestnut colt stretched his neck and lengthened his stride. He ran for all he was worth, as if he had broken his bond with the earth, and nothing could hold him back. Kessler and I stood motionless in that quiet distant room high above the track as he closed the gap, then passed the leaders as if they were standing still. When he entered the stretch, he was out front. All alone.

Garcia rode him under the wire in a hand ride, and we heard the cheering from where we stood, five stories up with the heavy concrete flooring beneath our feet and the thick wall of glass before us.

Kessler silently watched his colt slow to a canter, then loop around and head toward the winner's circle with Garcia standing in the stirrups and slapping the chestnut's neck with each stride.

He let his hand drop from the rail, and as he turned toward me, there were tears in his eyes.

He blinked them away.

I didn't know what to say, so I said nothing.

He cleared his throat. "What will you do next?"

"Go back to Foxdale," I said.

He nodded, then let his gaze drift back to the track.

"But I'll be back from time to time, if that's okay, Dad?"

He jerked his head up and looked me in the eyes.

I glanced down at the track as Abby and Gordi took Ruskie into the winner's circle, then I turned back and held out my hand.

My father took my hand in his, but instead of shaking it, he pulled me into his arms and hugged me.

The sun warmed my back, and a weak breeze trickled through my hair as I stared at the blue-gray haze that choked the Baltimore skyline and blurred the edges of the buildings until it was difficult to see where steel and sky met.

I pulled the envelope out of my back pocket, unfolded the single sheet of paper that had grown stiff after my swim in the river, and read my father's letter. The ink had smeared, but his words were burned into my mind.

April 24

Dear Stephen,

When I saw you lying in that hospital bed last week, I'm sure you thought I was angry with you, but the truth is, I was disgusted with myself. You see, I blamed you for something that was not your fault, but as the realization of just how close I'd come to losing you sank in, I saw, for the first time, what a horrible mistake I have made.

It's ironic really. I've always considered myself to be exceptionally confident. Some would even say arrogant, and yet, I can't bring myself to pick up the phone and call my own son, I'm so sure you want nothing to do with me. I know you're bitter, and you have every right to be.

In some ways, we are more alike than different. We are both stubborn, and unfortunately, I let my pride get in the way of good judgment. I was wrong. I am deeply sorry for the way I have treated you, and I ask for your forgiveness with all my heart.

I'd like to see you. Please call me, Stephen. I miss you.

Love,

Your father

I swallowed, and a single tear glinted in the sunlight as it tumbled through the humid air and splashed on the white paper that trembled in my hand. The blue ink bled into the surrounding fibers, and my throat burned.

I folded his letter and stared down at the cold, hard slab of granite that marked his grave. I thought of him spending the last two months of his life convinced that I despised him, and a sadness so intense and thorough gripped my heart and spread into my soul.

I closed my eyes against the tears that slipped down my cheeks and whispered, "I'm so sorry, Father."

I felt weightless, standing there in the hot sunlight with the grass beneath my feet and the leaves rustling in the trees behind me, and disconnected, as if the rest of the world had dissolved away to nothing.

Farther down the hill, a car door clicked shut. I tucked the letter back in my jeans and walked to where Rachel had parked her Camry. She wrapped her arms tightly around my waist, and I closed my eyes and buried my face in her hair, and we stood like that for a long time.

When I finally straightened, she asked me if I was ready, and I nodded. She drove south on 95 with the windows up and the air-conditioner on high, and as she pulled into Foxdale's long gravel drive, I spotted Marty by the gate to the outdoor arena.

He looked up at the sound of the tires crunching over gravel, and when he saw me sitting in the passenger's seat, a wide grin spread across his face.